**Praise for *New York Times* bestselling author
RaeAnne Thayne**

"RaeAnne Thayne is quickly becoming one of my
favorite authors… Once you start reading, you
aren't going to be able to stop."

—*Fresh Fiction*

"Thayne's beautiful, honest storytelling goes
straight to the heart."

—*RT Book Reviews*

"This quirky, funny, warmhearted romance will
draw readers in and keep them enthralled to the
last romantic page."

—*Library Journal* on *Christmas in Snowflake Canyon*

**Praise for *USA TODAY* bestselling author
Patricia Davids**

"Patricia Davids pens a captivating tale…
The Color of Courage is well researched, with a
heartwarming conclusion."

—*RT Book Reviews*

"With its even pacing, *A Matter of the Heart* is a
touching and wonderful story that's not to be
missed."

—*RT Book Reviews*

RaeAnne Thayne finds inspiration in the beautiful northern Utah mountains, where the *New York Times* and *USA TODAY* bestselling author lives with her husband and three children. Her books have won numerous honors, including RITA® Award nominations from Romance Writers of America and a Career Achievement Award from *RT Book Reviews*. RaeAnne loves to hear from readers and can be contacted through her website, raeannethayne.com.

After thirty-five years as a nurse, *USA TODAY* bestselling author **Patricia Davids** hung up her stethoscope to become a full-time writer. She enjoys spending her free time visiting her grandchildren, doing some long-overdue yard work and traveling to research her story locations. She resides in Wichita, Kansas. Pat always enjoys hearing from her readers. You can visit her online at patriciadavids.com.

New York Times Bestselling Author

RAEANNE THAYNE

THE VALENTINE TWO-STEP

◆ **HARLEQUIN®** BESTSELLING AUTHOR COLLECTION

ISBN-13: 978-1-335-46820-8

The Valentine Two-Step

Copyright © 2018 by Harlequin Books S.A.

The publisher acknowledges the copyright holders of the individual works as follows:

The Valentine Two-Step
Copyright © 2002 by RaeAnne Thayne

The Color of Courage
Copyright © 2007 by Patricia MacDonald

Recycling programs for this product may not exist in your area.

This edition published by arrangement with Harlequin Books S.A.

For questions and comments about the quality of this book, please contact us at CustomerService@Harlequin.com.

Printed in U.S.A.

CONTENTS

Also by RaeAnne Thayne

HQN Books

Haven Point

Harlequin Special Edition

The Cowboys of Cold Creek

Visit the Author Profile page
at Harlequin.com for more titles.

THE VALENTINE TWO-STEP

RaeAnne Thayne

To Lyndsey Thomas, for saving my life
and my sanity more times than I can count!
Special thanks to Dr. Ronald Hamm, DVM,
animal healer extraordinaire,
for sharing so generously of his expertise.

Prologue

"It's absolutely perfect." Dylan Webster held her hands out imploringly to her best friend, Lucy Harte. "Don't you see? It's the only way!"

Lucy frowned in that serious way of hers, her gray eyes troubled. In the dim, dusty light inside their secret place—a hollowed-out hideaway behind the stacked hay bales of the Diamond Harte barn loft—her forehead looked all wrinkly. Kind of like a shar-pei puppy Dylan had seen once at her mom's office back in California.

"I don't know…" she began.

"Come on, Luce. You said it yourself. We should have been sisters, not just best friends. We were born on exactly the same day, we both love horses and despise long division and we both want to be vets like my mom when we grow up, right?"

"Well, yes, but…"

"If my mom married your dad, we really *would* be sisters. It would be like having a sleepover all the time. I could ride the school bus with you and everything, and I just know my mom would let me have my own horse if we lived out here on the ranch."

Lucy nibbled her lip. "But, Dylan…"

"You want a mom of your own as much as I want a dad, don't you? Even though you have your aunt Cassie to look after you, it's not the same. You know it's not."

It was exactly the right button to push, and she knew it. Before her very eyes, Lucy sighed, and her expression went all dreamy. Dylan felt a little pinch of guilt at using her best friend's most cherished dream to her own advantage, but she worked hard to ignore it.

Her plan would never work if she couldn't convince Lucy how brilliant it was. Both of them had to be one-hundred-percent behind it. "We'd be sisters, Luce," she said. "Sisters for real. Wouldn't it be awesome?"

"Sisters." Lucy burrowed deeper into the hay, her gray eyes closed as if, like Dylan, she was imagining family vacations and noisy Christmas mornings and never again having to miss a daddy-daughter party at school. Or in Lucy's case, a mother-daughter party.

"It *would* be awesome." That shar-pei look suddenly came back to her forehead, and she sat up. "But, Dylan, why would they ever get married? I don't think they even like each other very much."

"Who?"

"My dad and your mom."

Doubt came galloping back like one of Lucy's dad's horses after a stray dogie. Lucy was absolutely right. They *didn't* like each other much. Just the other day, she heard her mom tell SueAnn that Matt Harte was a stubborn old man in a younger man's body.

"But what a body it is," her mom's assistant at the clinic had replied, with a rumbly laugh like grown-ups make when they're talking about sexy stuff. "Matt Harte and his brother have always been the most gorgeous men in town."

Her mom had laughed, too, and she'd even turned a little bit pink, like a strawberry shake. "Shame on you. You're a happily married woman, Sue."

"Married doesn't mean dead. Or crazy, for that matter."

Her mom had scrunched up her face. "Even if he is… attractive…in a macho kind of way, a great body doesn't make up for having the personality of an ornery bull."

Dylan winced, remembering. Okay, so Lucy's dad and her mom hadn't exactly gotten along since the Websters moved to Star Valley. Still, her mom thought he was good-looking and had a great body. That had to count for something.

Dylan gave Lucy what she hoped was a reassuring smile. "They just haven't had a chance to get to know each other."

Lucy looked doubtful. "My dad told Aunt Cassie just last week he wouldn't let that city quack near any of his livestock. I think he meant your mom."

Dylan narrowed her eyes. "My mom's not a quack."

"I know she's not. I think your mom's just about the greatest vet around. I'm only telling you what he said."

"We just have to change his mind. We have to figure out some way to push them together. Once they get to know each other, they'll have to see that they belong together."

"I'm not so sure."

Dylan blew out a breath that made her auburn bangs flutter. Lucy was the best friend anybody could ask for—the best friend she'd ever had. These last three months since they'd moved here had been so great. Staying overnight at the ranch, riding Lucy's horses, trading secrets and dreams here behind the hay bales.

They were beyond best, best, best friends, and Dylan loved her to death, but sometimes Lucy worried too much. Like about spelling tests and missing the bus and letting her desk get too messy.

She just had to convince her the idea would work. It would be so totally cool if they could pull this off. She wanted a dad in the worst way, and she figured Matt Harte—with his big hands and slow smile and kind eyes—would be absolutely perfect. Having Lucy for a sister would be like the biggest bonus she could think of.

Dylan would just have to try harder.

"It's going to work. Trust me. I know it's going to work." She grabbed Lucy's hand and squeezed it tightly. "Before you know it, we'll be walking down the aisle wearing flowers in our hair and me and my mom will be living here all the time. See, I have this plan…."

Chapter 1

"They did *what?*"

Ellie Webster and the big, gruff rancher seated beside her spoke in unison. She spared a glance at Matt Harte and saw he looked like he'd just been smacked upside the head with a two-by-four.

"Oh, dear. I was afraid of this." Sarah McKenzie gave a tiny, apologetic smile to both of them.

With her long blond hair and soft, wary brown eyes, her daughter's teacher always made Ellie think of a skittish palomino colt, ready to lunge away at the first provocation. Now, though, she was effectively hobbled into place behind her big wooden schoolteacher's desk. "You're telling me you both *didn't* agree to serve on the committee for the Valentine's Day carnival?"

"Hell no." Matt Harte looked completely horrified by the very idea of volunteering for a Valentine's Day carnival committee—as astonished as Ellie imagined he'd be if Ms. McKenzie had just asked him to stick one of her perfectly sharpened number-two pencils in his eye.

"I've never even heard of the Valentine's Day carnival until just now," Ellie offered.

"Well, this does present a problem." Ms. McKenzie folded her hands together on top of what looked like a grade book, slim and black and ominous.

Ellie had always hated those grade books.

Despite the fact that she couldn't imagine any two people being more different, Ellie had a brief, unpleasant image of her own fourth-grade teacher. Prissy mouth, hair scraped back into a tight bun. Complete intolerance for a scared little girl who hid her bewildered loneliness behind defiant anger.

She pushed the unwelcome image aside.

"The girls told me you both would cochair the committee," the teacher said. "They were most insistent that you wanted to do it."

"You've got to be joking. They said we *wanted* to do it? I don't know where the he—heck Lucy could have come up with such a harebrained idea." Matt Harte sent one brief, disparaging glare in Ellie's direction, and she stiffened. She could just imagine what he was thinking. *If my perfect little Lucy has a harebrained idea in her perfect little head, it must have come from you and your flighty daughter, with your wacky California ways.*

He had made it perfectly clear he couldn't understand the instant bond their two daughters had formed when she and Dylan moved here at the beginning of the school year three months earlier. He had also made no secret of the fact that he didn't trust her or her veterinary methods anywhere near his stock.

The really depressing thing was, Harte's attitude seemed to be the rule, not the exception, among the local ranching community. After three months, she was no closer to breaking into their tight circle than she'd been that very first day.

"It does seem odd," Ms. McKenzie said, and Ellie chided herself for letting her mind wander.

Right now she needed to concentrate on Dylan and this latest scrape her daughter had found herself in. Not on the past or on the big, ugly pile of bills that needed to be paid, regardless of whether or not she had any patients.

"I thought it was rather out of character for both of you," the quiet, pretty teacher went on. "That's why I called you both and asked you to come in this evening, so we all could try to get to the bottom of this."

"Why would they lie about it?" Ellie asked. "I don't understand why on earth the girls would say we volunteered for something I've never even heard of before now."

The teacher shifted toward her and shrugged her shoulders inside her lacy white blouse. She made the motion look so delicate and airy that Ellie felt about as feminine as a teamster in her work jeans and flannel shirt.

"I have no idea," she said. "I was hoping you could shed some light on it."

"You sure it was our girls who signed up?"

Ms. McKenzie turned to the rancher with a small smile. "Absolutely positive. I don't think I could possibly mix that pair up with any of my other students."

"Well, there's obviously been a mistake," Matt said gruffly.

Ms. McKenzie was silent for a few moments, then she sighed. "That's what I was afraid you would say. Still, the fact remains that I need two parents to cochair the committee, and your daughters obviously want you to do it. Would the two of you at least consider it?"

The rancher snorted. "You've got the wrong guy."

"I don't think so," the teacher answered gently, as if chiding a wayward student, and Ellie wondered how she could appear to be so completely immune to the potent impact of Matt Harte.

Even with that aggravated frown over this latest scheme their daughters had cooked up, he radiated raw male appeal, with rugged, hard-hewn features, piercing blue eyes and broad shoulders. Ellie couldn't even sit next to him without feeling the power in those leashed muscles.

But Sarah McKenzie appeared oblivious to it. She treated him with the same patience and kindness she showed the fourth graders in her class.

"I think you'd both do a wonderful job," the teacher continued. "Since this is my first year at the school, I haven't been to the carnival myself but I understand attendance has substantially dropped off the last two years. I'm sure I don't have to tell you what a problem this is."

"No," the rancher said solemnly, and Ellie fought the urge to raise her hand and ask somebody to explain the gravity of the situation to her. It certainly didn't seem like a big deal to her that some of the good people of Salt River decided to celebrate Valentine's Day somewhere other than the elementary school gymnasium. Come to think of it, so far most of the people she'd met in Salt River didn't seem the types to celebrate Valentine's Day at all.

"This is a really important fund-raiser," Ms. McKenzie said. "All the money goes to the school library, which is desperately in need of new books. We need to do something to generate more interest in the carnival, infuse it with fresh ideas. New blood, if you will. I think the two of you are just the ones to do that."

There was silence for a moment, then the rancher sat forward, that frown still marring his handsome features. "I'm sorry, Miz McKenzie. I'd like to help you out, honest. I'm all in favor of getting more books for the library and I'd be happy to give you a sizable donation if that will help at all. But I'm way out of my league here. I wouldn't know the first thing about putting together something like that."

"I'm afraid this sort of thing isn't exactly my strong point, either," Ellie admitted, which was a bit like saying the nearby Teton Mountain Range had a couple of pretty little hills.

"Whatever their reasons, it seemed very important to your daughters that you help." She shifted toward Matt again. "Mr. Harte, has Lucy ever asked you to volunteer for anything in school before? Reading time, lunch duty, anything?"

The rancher's frown deepened. "No," he finally answered the teacher. "Not that I can think of."

"All of her previous teachers describe Lucy as a shy mouse of a girl who spoke in whispers and broke into tears if they called on her. I have to tell you, that is not the same girl I've come to know this year."

"No?"

"Since Dylan's arrival, Lucy participates much more in class. She is a sweet little girl with a wonderfully creative mind."

"That's good, right?"

"Very good. But despite the improvements, Lucy still seems to prefer staying in the background. She rarely ventures an opinion of her own. I think it would be wonderful for her to help plan the carnival under your supervision. It might even provide her with some of the confidence she still seems to be lacking."

"I'm a very busy man, Miz McKenzie—"

"I understand that. And I know Dr. Webster is also very busy trying to establish her practice here in Star Valley."

You don't know the half of it, Ellie thought grimly.

"But I think it would help both girls. Dylan, as well," the teacher said, shifting toward her. "I've spoken with you before with some of my concerns about your daughter. She's a very bright girl and a natural leader among the other children, but she hasn't shown much enthusiasm for anything in the classroom until now."

The teacher paused, her hands still folded serenely on her desk, and gave them both a steady look that had Ellie squirming just like she'd been caught chewing gum in class. "It's obvious neither of you wants to do this. I certainly understand your sentiments. But I have to tell you, I would recommend you put your own misgivings aside and think instead about your daughters and what they want."

Oh, she was good. *Pour on the parental guilt, sister. Gets 'em every time.*

Out of the corner of her gaze Ellie could see Harte fighting through the same internal struggle.

How could she possibly do this? The last thing on earth she wanted was to be saddled with the responsibility for planning a Valentine's Day carnival. Valentine's Day, for heaven's sake. A time for sweethearts and romance, hearts and flowers. Things she had absolutely no experience with.

Beyond that, right now she was so busy trying to salvage her floundering practice that she had no time for anything but falling into her bed at the end of the day.

Still, Dylan wanted her to do this. For whatever reasons, this was important to her daughter. Ellie had already uprooted her from the only life she'd known to bring her here, to an alien world of wide-open spaces and steep, imposing mountains.

If being involved in this stupid carnival would make Dylan happy, didn't she owe it to her to try?

And maybe, just maybe, a selfish little voice whispered, *this might just be the ticket to help you pile drive your way into the closed circle that is the Star Valley community.*

If she could show the other parents she was willing to volunteer to help out the school, they might begin to accept her into their ranks. Lord knows, she had to do something or she would end up being the proud owner of the only veterinary practice in Wyoming without a single patient to its name.

"I suppose I'm game," she said, before she could talk herself out of it. "What about you, Harte?"

"It's a Valentine's Day carnival. What the hell do I know about Valentine's Day?"

She snickered at his baffled tone. She couldn't help herself. The man just rubbed her wrong. He had gone out of his way to antagonize her since she arrived in

town. Not only had he taken his own business else-
where, but she knew he'd convinced several other ranchers to do the same. It hurt her pride both professionally
and personally that he made no secret of his disdain for
some of her more unconventional methods.

"You mean nobody's sent you one of those cute little
pink cards lately? With that sweet disposition of yours,
I'd have thought you would have women crawling out
of the woodwork to send you valentines."

She regretted the snippy comment as soon as she
said it. Whatever her views about him, she should at
least try to be civil.

Still, she felt herself bristle when he glowered at her,
which seemed to be his favorite expression. It was a
shame, really. The man could be drop-dead gorgeous
when he wasn't looking like he just planted his butt on
a cactus. How such a sweet little girl like Lucy could
have such a sour apple of a father was beyond her.

Before he could answer in kind, the schoolteacher
stepped in to keep the peace with the same quiet diplo-
macy she probably used to break up schoolyard brawls.
"There's no reason you have to make a decision today.
It's only mid-November, so we still have plenty of time
before Valentine's Day. Why don't both of you take a
few days to think it over, and I'll talk to you about it
next week."

Ms. McKenzie rose from behind her desk. "Thank
you both for coming in at such short notice," she said,
in clear dismissal. "I'll be in touch with you next week."

Left with no alternative, Ellie rose, as well, and
shrugged into her coat. Beside her, Lucy's father did
the same.

"Sorry about the mix-up," he said, reaching out to

shake hands with Ms. McKenzie. Ellie observed with curiosity that for the first time the other woman looked uncomfortable, even nervous. Again she thought of that skittish colt ready to bolt. There was an awkward pause while he stood there with his hand out, then with a quick, jerky movement, the teacher gripped his hand before abruptly dropping it.

"I'll be in touch," she said again.

What was that all about? Matt wondered as he followed the city vet out of the brightly decorated classroom into the hall. Why did Miz McKenzie act like he'd up and slapped her when all he wanted to do was shake her hand? Come to think of it, she'd behaved the same way when he came in a month earlier for parent-teacher conferences.

She and Ellie Webster ought to just form a club, since it was obvious the lady vet wasn't crazy about him, either. Matt Harte Haters of America.

He didn't have time to dwell on it before they reached the outside door of the school. The vet gave him a funny look when he opened the door for her, but she said nothing, just moved past him. Before he could stop himself, he caught a whiff of her hair as her coat brushed his arm. It smelled clean and fresh, kind of like that heavenly lemon cream pie they served over at the diner.

He had absolutely no business sniffing the city vet's hair, Matt reminded himself harshly. Or noticing the way those freckles trailed across that little nose of hers like the Big Dipper or how the fluorescent lights inside the school had turned that sweet-smelling hair a fiery red, like an August sunset after an afternoon of thunderstorms.

He pushed the unwanted thoughts away and followed Ellie Webster out into the frigid night. An icy wind slapped at them, and he hunched his shoulders inside his lined denim coat.

It was much colder than normal for mid-November. The sky hung heavy and ugly overhead, and the twilight had that expectant hush it took on right before a big storm. Looked like they were in for a nasty one. He dug already cold fingers into his pockets.

When he drove into town earlier, the weatherman on the radio had said to expect at least a foot of snow. Just what he needed. With that Arctic Express chugging down out of Canada, they were sure to have below-zero temperatures tonight. Add to that the windchill and he'd be up the whole damn night just trying to keep his cattle alive.

The city vet seemed to read his mind. "By the looks of that storm, I imagine we'll both have a busy night."

"You, too?"

"I do still have a few patients."

He'd never paid much mind to what a vet did when the weather was nasty. Or what a vet did any other time, for that matter. They showed up at his place, did what he needed them to do, then moved on to their next appointment.

He tried to imagine her muscling an ornery cow into a pen and came up completely blank. Hell, she looked hardly big enough to wrestle a day-old calf. He'd had the same thought the first day he met her, back in August when she rode into town with her little girl and all that attitude.

She barely came up to his chin, and her wrists were delicate and bony, like a kitten that had been too long without food. Why would a scrawny city girl from California want to come out to the wilds of Wyoming and wrestle cattle? He couldn't even begin to guess.

There were only two vehicles in the school parking lot, the brand spankin' new dually crew cab he drove off the lot last week and her battered old Ford truck. He knew it was hers by the magnetized sign on the side reading Salt River Veterinary Clinic.

Miz McKenzie must have walked, since the little house she rented from Bob Jimenez was just a couple blocks from the school. Maybe he ought to offer her a ride home. It was too damn cold to be walking very far tonight.

Before he could turn around and go back into the school to make the offer, he saw Ellie Webster pull her keys out of her pocket and fight to open her truck door for several seconds without success.

"Can I help you there, ma'am?" he finally asked.

She grunted as she worked the key. "The lock seems to be stuck...."

Wasn't that just like a city girl to go to all the trouble to lock the door of a rusty old pickup nobody would want to steal anyway? "You know, most of us around here don't lock our vehicles. Not much need."

She gave him a scorcher of a look. "And most of you think karaoke is a girl you went to high school with."

His mouth twitched, but he refused to let himself smile. Instead, he yanked off a glove and stuck his bare thumb over the lock.

In the pale lavender twilight, she watched him with a confused frown. "What are you doing?"

"Just trying to warm up your lock. I imagine it's frozen and that's why you can't get the key to turn. I guess you don't have much trouble with that kind of thing in California, do you?"

"Not much, no. I guess it's another exciting feature unique to Wyoming. Like jackalopes and perpetual road construction."

"When we've had a cold wet rain like we did this afternoon, moisture can get down in the lock. After the sun goes down, it doesn't take long to freeze."

"I'll remember that."

"There. That ought to do it." He pulled his hand away and took the key from her, then shoved it into the lock. The mechanism slid apart now like a knife through soft wax, and he couldn't resist pulling the door open for her with an exaggerated flourish.

She gave him a disgruntled look then climbed into her pickup. "Thank you."

"You're welcome." He shoved his hand into his lined pocket, grateful for the cozy warmth. "Next time you might want to think twice before you lock your door so it doesn't happen again. Nobody's going to steal anything around here."

She didn't look like she appreciated his advice. "You do things your way, I'll do things mine, Harte."

She turned the key, and the truck started with a smooth purr that defied its dilapidated exterior. "If you decide you're man enough to help me with this stupid carnival, I suppose we'll have to start organizing it soon."

His attention snagged on the first part of her sentence. "If I'm man enough?" he growled.

She grinned at him, her silvery-green eyes sparkling, and he fought hard to ignore the kick of awareness in his stomach. "Do you think you've got the guts to go through with this?"

"It's not a matter of guts," he snapped. "It's a matter of having the time to waste putting together some silly carnival."

"If you say so."

"I'm a very busy man, Dr. Webster."

It was apparently exactly the wrong thing to say. Her grin slid away, and she stiffened like a coil of frozen rope, slicing him to pieces with a glare. "And I have nothing better to do than sit around cutting out pink and white hearts to decorate the school gymnasium with, right? That's what you think, isn't it? Lord knows, I don't have much of a practice thanks to you and all the other stubborn old men around here."

He set his jaw. He wasn't going to get into this with her standing out here in the school parking lot while the windchill dipped down into single digits. "That's not what I meant," he muttered.

"I know exactly what you meant. I know just what you think of me, Mr. Harte."

He sincerely doubted it. Did she know he thought about her a lot more than he damn well knew he ought to and that he couldn't get her green eyes or her sassy little mouth out of his mind?

"Our daughters want us to do this," she said. "I don't know what little scheme they're cooking up—and to tell you the truth, I'm not sure I want to know—but it seems to be important to Dylan, and that's enough for me. Let me know what you decide."

She closed the door, barely missing his fingers, then shoved the truck into gear and spun out of the parking lot, leaving him in a cloud of exhaust.

Chapter 2

Matt drove his pickup under the arch proclaiming Diamond Harte Ranch—Choice Simmentals and Quarter Horses with a carved version of the brand that had belonged to the Harte family for four generations.

He paused for just a moment like he always did to savor the view before him. The rolling, sage-covered hills, the neat row of fence line stretching out as far as the eye could see, the barns and outbuildings with their vivid red paint contrasting so boldly with the snow.

And standing guard over it all at the end of the long gravel drive was the weathered log and stone house his grandfather had built—with the sprawling addition he had helped his father construct the year he turned twelve.

Home.

He loved it fiercely, from the birthing sheds to the maze of pens to the row of Douglas fir lining the drive.

He knew every single inch of its twenty thousand acres, as well as the names and bloodlines of each of the three dozen cutting horses on the ranch and the medical history of all six hundred of the ranch's cattle.

Maybe he loved it too much. Reverend Whitaker's sermon last week had been a fiery diatribe on the sin of excess pride, the warning in Proverbs about how pride goeth before destruction.

Matt had squirmed in the hard pew for a minute, then decided the Lord would forgive him for it, especially if He could look down through the clouds and see the Diamond Harte like Matt saw it. As close to heaven as any place else on earth.

Besides, didn't the Bible also say the sleep of a laboring man was sweet? His father's favorite scripture had been in Genesis, something about how a man should eat bread only by the sweat of his face.

Well, he'd worked plenty hard for the Diamond Harte. He'd poured every last ounce of his sweat into the ranch since he was twenty-two years old, into taking the legacy his parents had left their three children so suddenly and prematurely and building it into the powerful ranch it had become.

He had given up everything for the ranch. All his time and energy. The college degree in ag economy he was sixteen credits away from earning when his parents had died in that rollover accident. Even his wife, who had hated the ranch with a passion and had begged him to leave every day of their miserable marriage.

Melanie. The woman he had loved with a quicksilver passion that had turned just as quickly to bitter, ferocious hate. His wife, who had cheated on him and lied to him and eventually left him when Lucy wasn't even three months old.

She'd been a city girl, too, fascinated by silly, romantic dreams of the West. The reality of living on a ranch wasn't romantic at all, as Melanie had discovered all too soon. It was hard work and merciless weather. Cattle that didn't always smell so great, a cash flow that was never dependable. Flies in the summer and snowstorms in the winter that could trap you for days.

Melanie had never even made an effort to belong. She had been lost. He could see that now. Bitterly unhappy and desperate for something she could never find.

She thought he should have sold the ranch, pocketed the five or six million it was probably worth and taken her somewhere a whole lot more glitzy than Salt River, Wyoming. And when he refused to give in to her constant pleading, she had made his life hell.

What was this thing he had for women who didn't belong out here? He thought of his fascination with the California vet. It wasn't attraction. He refused to call it attraction. She was just different from what he was used to, that's all. Annoying, opinionated, argumentative. That's the only reason his pulse rate jumped whenever she was around.

A particularly strong gust of wind blew out of the canyon suddenly, rattling the pickup. He sent a quick look at the digital clock on the sleek dashboard, grateful for the distraction from thoughts of a woman he had no business thinking about.

Almost six. Cassie would have dinner on soon, and then he would get to spend the rest of the night trying to keep his stock warm. He eased his foot off the brake and quickly drove the rest of the way to the house, parking in his usual spot next to his sister's Cherokee.

Inside, the big house was toasty, welcoming. His stomach growled and his mouth watered at the delectable smells coming from the kitchen—mashed potatoes and Cassie's amazing meat loaf, if he wasn't mistaken. He hung his hat on the row of pegs by the door, then made his way to the kitchen. He found his baby sister stirring gravy in a pan on the wide professional stove she'd insisted he install last year.

She looked up at his entrance and gave him a quick smile. "Dinner's almost ready."

"Smells good." He stood watching her for a moment, familiar guilt curling in his gut. She ought to be in her own house, making dinner for her own husband and a whole kitchen full of rug rats, instead of wasting her life away taking care of him and Lucy.

If it hadn't been for the disastrous choices he made with Melanie, that's exactly where she would have been.

It wasn't a new thought. He'd had plenty of chances in the last ten years to wish things could be different, to regret that he had become so blasted dependent on everything Cassie did for them after Melanie ran off.

She ought to go to college—or at least to cooking school somewhere, since she loved it so much. But every time they talked about it, about her plans for the future, she insisted she was exactly where she wanted to be, doing exactly what she wanted to be doing.

How could he convince her otherwise when he still wasn't completely sure he could handle things on his own? He didn't know how he could do a proper job of raising Lucy by himself and handle the demands of the ranch at the same time.

Maybe if Jesse was around more, things might be different. He could have given his younger brother some of the responsibilities of the ranch, leaving more time to take care of things on the home front. But Jess had never been content on the Diamond Harte. He had other dreams, of catching the bad guys and saving the world, and Matt couldn't begrudge him those.

"Where's Lucy?" he asked.

"Up in her room fretting, I imagine. She's been a basket case waiting for you to get back from the school. She broke two glasses while she was setting the table, and spent more time looking out the window for your truck than she did on her math homework."

"She ought to be nervous," he growled, grateful for the renewed aggravation that was strong enough to push the guilt aside.

Cassie glanced up at his tone. "Uh-oh. That bad? What did she do?"

"You wouldn't believe it if I told you," he muttered and headed toward the stairs. "Give me five minutes to talk to her, and then we'll be down."

He knocked swiftly on her door and heard a muffled, "Come in." Inside, he found his daughter sitting on her bed, gnawing her bottom lip so hard it looked like she had chewed away every last drop of blood.

Through that curtain of long, dark hair, he saw that her eyes were wide and nervous. As they damn well ought to be after the little stunt she pulled. He let her stew in it for a minute.

"Hey, squirt."

"Hi," she whispered. With hands that trembled just a little, she picked up Sigmund, the chubby calico cat she'd raised from a kitten, and plopped him in her lap.

"So I just got back from talking with Miz McKenzie."

Lucy peered at him between the cat's ears. She cleared her throat. "Um, what did she say?"

"I think you know exactly what she said, don't you?"

She nodded, the big gray eyes she'd inherited from her mother wide with apprehension. As usual, he hoped to heaven that was the only thing Melanie had passed on to their daughter.

"You want to tell me what this is all about?"

She appeared to think it over, then shook her head swiftly. He bit his cheek to keep a rueful grin from creeping out at that particular piece of honesty. "Tough. Tell me anyway."

"I don't know."

"Come on, Luce. What were you thinking, to sign me up for this Valentine's carnival without at least talking to me first?"

"It was Dylan's idea," Lucy mumbled.

Big surprise there. Dylan Webster was a miniature version of her wacky mother. "Why?"

"She thought you'd be good at it, since you're so important around here and can get people to do whatever you want. At least that's what her mom says."

He could picture Ellie Webster saying exactly that, with her pert little nose turned up in the air.

"And," Lucy added, the tension easing from her shoulders a little as she stroked the purring cat, "we both thought it would be fun. You know, planning the carnival and stuff. You and me and Dylan and her mom, doing it all together. A bonding thing."

A bonding thing? The last thing he needed to do was *bond* with Ellie Webster, under any circumstances.

"What do you know about bonding? Don't tell me that's something they teach you in school."

Lucy shrugged. "Dylan says we're in our formative preteen years and need positive parental influence now more than ever. She thought this would be a good opportunity for us to develop some leadership skills."

Great. Now Ellie Webster's kid had his daughter spouting psychobabble. He blew out a breath. "What about you?"

She blinked at him. "Me?"

"You're pretty knowledgeable about Dylan's views, but what about your own? Why did you go along with it?"

Lucy suddenly seemed extremely interested in a little spot on the cat's fur. "I don't know," she mumbled.

"Come on. You can do better than that."

She chewed her lip again, then looked at the cat. "We never do anything together."

He rocked back on his heels, baffled by her. "What are you talking about? We do plenty of things together. Just last Saturday you spent the whole day with me in Idaho Falls."

She rolled her eyes. "Shopping for a new truck. Big whoop. I thought it would be fun to do something completely different together. Something that doesn't have to do with the ranch or with cattle or horses." She paused, then added in a quiet voice, "Something just for me."

Ah, more guilt. Just what he needed. The kid wasn't even ten years old and she was already an expert at it. He sighed. Did females come out of the box with some built-in guilt mechanism they could turn off and on at will?

The hell of it was, she was absolutely right, and he knew it. He didn't spend nearly enough time with her. He tried, he really did, but between the horses and the cattle, his time seemed to be in as short supply as sunshine in January.

His baby girl was growing up. He could see it every day. Used to be a day spent with him would be enough for her no matter what they did together. Even if it was only shopping for a new truck. Now she wanted more, and he wasn't sure he knew how to provide it.

"Wouldn't it have been easier to tell me all this *before* you signed me up? Then we could have at least talked it over without me getting such a shock like this."

She fidgeted with Sigmund, who finally must have grown tired of being messed with. He let out an offended mewl of protest and rolled away from her, then leaped from the bed gracefully and stalked out the door.

Lucy watched until his tail disappeared down the end of the hall before she answered him in that same low, ashamed voice. "Dylan said you'd both say no if we asked. We thought it might be harder for you to back out if Ms. McKenzie thought you'd already agreed to it."

"That wasn't very fair, to me or to Dr. Webster, was it?" He tried to come up with an analogy that might make sense to her. "How would you like it if I signed you up to show one of the horses in the 4-H competition without talking to you first?"

She shuddered, as he knew she would. Her shyness made her uncomfortable being the center of attention, so she had always avoided the limelight, even when she was little. In that respect, Miz McKenzie was right— Dylan Webster had been good for her and had brought her out of her shell, at least a little.

"I wouldn't like it at all."

"And I don't like what you did any better. I ought to just back out of this whole crazy thing right now."

"Oh, Dad, you *can't!*" she wailed. "You'll ruin *everything.*"

He studied her distress for several seconds, then sighed. He loved his daughter fiercely. She was the biggest joy in his life, more important than a hundred ranches. If she felt like she came in second to the Diamond Harte, he obviously wasn't trying hard enough.

Lucy finally broke the silence. "Are you really, really, really mad at me?" she asked in a small voice.

"Maybe just one really." He gave her a lopsided smile. "But don't worry. I'll get you back. You'll be sorry you ever heard of this carnival by the time I get through with you."

Her eyes went wide again, this time with excitement. "Does that mean you'll do it?"

"I guess. I think we're both going to be sorry."

But he couldn't have too many regrets, at least not right now. Not when his daughter jumped from her bed with a squeal and threw her arms tightly around his waist.

"Oh, thank you, Daddy. Thank you, thank you, thank you. You're the best."

For that moment, at least, he felt like it.

"No way is Matthew Harte going to go through with it. Mark my words, if you agree to do this, you're going to be stuck planning the whole carnival by yourself."

In the middle of sorting through the day's allotment of depressing mail, Ellie grimaced at SueAnn Clayton, her assistant. She had really come to hate that phrase. *Mark my words, you're not cut out to be a large animal vet. Mark my words, you're going to regret leaving California. Mark my words, you won't last six months in Wyoming.*

Just once, she wished everybody would keep their words—and unsolicited advice—to themselves.

In this case, though, she was very much afraid SueAnn was right. There was about as much likelihood of Matt Harte helping her plan the carnival as there was that he'd be the next one walking through the door with a couple of his prize cutting horses for her to treat.

She sighed and set the stack of bills on SueAnn's desk. "If he chickens out, I'll find somebody else to help me." She grinned at her friend. "You, for instance."

SueAnn made a rude noise. "Forget it. I chaired the Halloween Howl committee three years in a row and was PTA president twice. I've more than done my share for Salt River Elementary."

"Come on, SueAnn," she teased. "Are you forgetting who pays your salary?"

The other woman rolled her eyes. "You pay me to take your phone calls, to send out your bill reminders and to hold down the occasional unlucky animal while you give him a shot. Last I checked, planning a Valentine's Day carnival is nowhere in my job description."

"We could always change your job description. How about while we're at it, we'll include mucking out the stalls?"

"You're not going to blackmail me. That's what you pay Dylan the big bucks for. Speaking of the little rascal, how did you punish her, anyway? Ground her to her room for the rest of the month?"

That's what she should have done. It was no less than Dylan deserved for lying to her teacher. But she'd chosen a more fitting punishment. "She's grounded from playing with Lucy after school for the rest of the week *and* she has to finish reading all of *Little Women* and

I'm going to make sure she does a lot of the work of this carnival, since it was her great idea."

"The carnival she ought to be okay with, but which is she going to hate more, reading the book or not playing with her other half?"

"Doesn't matter. She has to face the music."

SueAnn laughed, and Ellie smiled back. What would she have done without the other woman to keep her grounded and sane these last few months? She shuddered just thinking about it.

She winced whenever she remembered how tempted she'd been to fire her that first week. SueAnn was competent enough—eerily so, sometimes—but she also didn't have the first clue how to mind her own business. Ellie had really struggled with it at first. Coming from California where avoiding eye contact when at all possible could sometimes be a matter of survival, dealing with a terminal busybody for an assistant had been wearing.

She was thirty-two years old and wasn't used to being mothered. Even when she'd *had* a mother, she hadn't had much practice at it. And she had been completely baffled by how to handle SueAnn, who made it a point to have her favorite grind of coffee waiting every morning, who tried to set her up with every single guy in town between the ages of eighteen and sixty, and who brought in Tupperware containers several times a week brimming with homemade soups and casseroles and mouthwatering desserts.

Now that she'd had a little practice, she couldn't believe she had been so fortunate to find not only the best assistant she could ask for but also a wonderful friend.

"What's on the agenda this morning?" Ellie asked.

"You're not going to believe this, but you actually have two patients waiting."

"What, are we going for some kind of record?"

SueAnn snickered and held two charts out with a flourish. "In exam room one, we have Sasha, Mary Lou McGilvery's husky."

"What's wrong with her?"

"Him. Sasha, oddly enough, is a him. He's scratching like crazy, and Mary Lou is afraid he has fleas."

"Highly doubtful around here, especially this time of year. It's too cold."

"That's what I tried to tell her. She's convinced that you need to take a look at him, though."

Dogs weren't exactly her specialty, since she was a large animal veterinarian, but she knew enough about them to deal with a skin condition. She nodded to SueAnn. "And patient number two?"

Her assistant cleared her throat ominously. "Cleo."

"Cleo?"

"Jeb Thacker's Nubian goat. She has a bit of a personality disorder."

"What does that mean?"

"Well, let's put it this way. Ben used to say that if she'd been human, she'd have been sent to death row a long time ago."

Ellie grinned, picturing the old codger who had sold her the practice saying exactly that. Ben Nichols was a real character. They had formed an instant friendship the first time they met at a conference several years ago. It was that same bond that had prompted him to make all her dreams come true by offering her his practice at a bargain basement price when he decided to retire, to her shock and delight. He and his wife were now thoroughly enjoying retirement in Arizona.

"What's Cleo in for?"

"Jeb didn't know, precisely. The poor man 'bout had a panic attack right there when I tried to get him to specify on the paperwork. Blushed brighter than one of his tomatoes and said he thought it was some kind of female trouble."

A homicidal goat with female trouble. And here she thought she was in for another slow morning. "Where's Jeb?"

"He had to go into Afton to the hardware store. Said he'd be back later to pick her up."

"In that case, let's take care of the dog first since Mary Lou's waiting," she decided. She could save the worst for last.

It only took a few moments for her to diagnose that Sasha had a bad case of psoriasis. She gave Mary Lou a bottle of medicated shampoo she thought would do the trick, ordered her to wash his bedding frequently and scheduled a checkup in six months.

That done, she put on her coat and braved the cold, walking to the pens behind the clinic to deal with the cantankerous goat. Cleo looked docile enough. The brown-and-white goat was standing in one of the smaller pens gnawing the top rail on the fence.

Ellie stood near the fence and spoke softly to her for a moment, trying to earn the animal's trust. Cleo turned and gave her what Ellie could swear was a look of sheer disdain out of big, long-fringed brown eyes, then turned back to the rail.

Slowly, cautiously, she entered the pen and approached the goat, still crooning softly to her. When she was still several feet away, she stopped for a cursory look. Although she would need to do a physical exam to be certain, she thought she could see the problem—one of Cleo's udders looked engorged and red. She probably had mastitis.

Since Cleo wasn't paying her any mind, Ellie inched closer. "You're a sweet girl, aren't you?" she murmured. "Everybody's wrong about you." She reached a hand to touch the animal, but before her hand could connect, Cleo whirled like a bronco with a burr under her saddle. Ellie didn't have time to move away before the goat butted her in the stomach with enough force to knock her on her rear end, right into a puddle of what she fervently hoped was water.

With a ma-aaa of amusement, the goat turned back to the fence rail.

"Didn't anybody warn you about Cleo?" a deep male voice asked.

Just what she needed, a witness to her humiliation. From her ignominious position on the ground, she took a moment to force air into her lungs. When she could breathe again, she glanced toward the direction of the voice. Her gaze landed first on a pair of well-worn boots just outside the fence, then traveled up a mile-long length of blue jeans to a tooled silver buckle with the swirled insignia of the NCHA—National Cutting Horse Association.

She knew that buckle.

She'd seen it a day earlier on none other than the lean hips of her nemesis. Sure enough. Matt Harte stood there just on the other side of the pen—broad shoulders, blue eyes, wavy dark hair and all.

She closed her eyes tightly, wishing the mud would open up underneath her and suck her down. Of all the people in the world who might have been here to watch her get knocked to her butt, why did it have to be him?

Chapter 3

Matt let himself into the pen, careful to keep a safe distance between his own rear end and Jeb Thacker's notoriously lousy-tempered goat, who had retreated to the other side of the pen.

"Here, let me help you." He reached a hand down to the city vet, still sprawled in the mud.

"I can do it," she muttered. Instead of taking his hand, she climbed gingerly to her feet by herself, then surreptitiously rubbed a hand against her seat.

Matt cleared his throat. "You okay?"

"I've had better mornings, but I'll live."

"You hit the ground pretty hard. You sure nothing's busted?"

"I don't think so. Just bruised. Especially my pride," she said wryly. She paused for a minute, then smiled reluctantly. "I imagine it looked pretty funny watching me get tackled by a goat."

She must not take herself too seriously if she could laugh about what had just happened. He found himself liking her for it. He gazed at her, at the way her red hair had slipped from its braid thingy and the little smudge of dirt on her cheek. Her eyes sparkled with laughter, and she was just about the prettiest thing he'd seen in a long time.

When he said nothing, a blush spread over her cheeks and she reached a hand to tuck her stray hair back. "Did you need something, Mr. Harte?"

He was staring at her, he realized, like some hayseed who'd never seen a pretty girl before. He flushed, astounded at himself, at this completely unexpected surge of attraction. "You might as well call me Matt, especially since it looks like we'll be working on this stupid school thing together."

Her big green eyes that always made him think of new aspen leaves just uncurling in springtime widened even more. "You're going to do it?"

"I said so, didn't I?" he muttered.

She grinned. "And you sound so enthusiastic about it."

"You want enthusiasm, you'll have to find somebody else to help you."

"What made you change your mind?"

He didn't know how to answer that, and besides, it wasn't any of her business. He said he'd do it, didn't he? What more did she need? But somehow the sharp retort he started to make changed into something else.

"Miz McKenzie's right," he finally said. "Lucy's done better in school this year than she ever has. She never would have wanted to organize something like this last year. I don't want to ruin the improvement she's made. Besides, she usually doesn't ask for much. It's a small price to pay if it's going to make her happy."

Ellie Webster cocked her head and looked at him like she'd just encountered a kind of animal she'd never seen before.

"What?" he asked, annoyed at himself for feeling so defensive.

"Nothing. You're just full of surprises, Mr. Harte."

"Matt," he muttered. "I said you should call me Matt."

"Matt." She smiled suddenly, the most genuine smile she'd ever given him. He stared at it, at her, feeling like he'd just spent a few hours out in the hard sun without his hat.

"Is that why you stopped?" she asked. "To tell me you decided to help with the carnival?"

He shrugged and ordered his heartbeat to behave itself. "I had to drop by the post office next door anyway. I thought maybe if you had a second this morning, we could get a cup of coffee over at the diner and come up with a game plan. At least figure out where to start."

Again, she looked surprised, but she nodded. "That's a good idea. But if you're just looking for coffee, SueAnn makes the best cup this side of the Rockies. We can talk in my office."

"That would be fine. I've already had breakfast. You, ah, need to get cleaned up or anything?"

She glanced down at her muddy jeans, then at the goat with a grimace. "Can you wait ten minutes? Since I'm already muddy, I might as well take a look at Cleo now."

He thought of the million-and-one things he had to do at the ranch after he ran to the parts store in Idaho

Falls—the buyers he had coming in later in the after-noon, the three horses waiting for the farrier, the inevi-table paperwork always confronting him.

He should just take a rain check, but for some rea-son that completely baffled him, he nodded. "Sure, I can wait." His next question surprised him even more. "Need me to give you a hand?"

She smiled again, that sweet, friendly smile. "That would be great. I'm afraid Cleo isn't too crazy about her visit to the vet."

The next fifteen minutes were a real education. With his help, Ellie miraculously finessed the ornery goat into holding still long enough for an exam. She murmured soft words—nonsense, really—while her hands moved gently and carefully over the now docile goat.

"Okay, you can let go now," she finally said. He obeyed, and the goat ambled away from them.

"What's the verdict?" he asked.

She looked up from scribbling some notes on a chart. "Just as I suspected. Mastitis. She has a plugged milk duct. I'll run a culture to be sure, but I think a round of antibiotics ought to take care of her."

"Just like a cow, huh?"

"Just like. Same plumbing involved."

"Cleo's a hell of a lot uglier than any of my ladies."

She grinned at him again. "Beauty's in the eye of the beholder, Harte. I imagine Jeb Thacker wouldn't agree. Anyway, thanks for your help."

She led the way inside the small building where she worked. While she went in the back to change her clothes, he shot the breeze with SueAnn, who went to high school with him and whose husband ran the local nursery in town.

In a surprisingly short time, Ellie returned wearing a pair of surgical scrubs. He figured she probably was supposed to look cool and professional in the scrubs, but instead they made her look not much older than one of Lucy's friends on her way to a sleepover, especially with her auburn hair pulled back in that ponytail.

"Sorry to keep you waiting," she said, sounding a little out of breath.

"No problem."

SueAnn hopped up and poured a cup of coffee for Ellie. "Here you go, sugar."

"Thanks. We'll be in my office if you need me."

"Take your time."

Matt didn't miss the not-so-subtle wink SueAnn sent the vet or the quick frown Ellie volleyed back. Before he could analyze the currents going on here, she walked into a cluttered office with books and papers everywhere. Dominating one wall was a window framing a beautiful view of the Salt River mountain range that gave the town its name. On the other was a big print of a horse—a Tennessee walker, if he wasn't mistaken—running across a field of wildflowers, all grace and power and beauty.

"Thanks again for helping me with Cleo," Ellie said as soon as he was seated.

"No problem. It was interesting to see you working on her."

She raised an eyebrow. "Interesting in what way?"

He shrugged. "I kept waiting for you to pull out the needles or whatever it is you use for that stuff you do."

"That stuff I do?"

There were suddenly as many icicles in her voice as

he had hanging from his barn. "You know, that acupuncture stuff. You don't do that all the time, then?"

Whatever friendliness might have been in her expression faded away, and she became guarded once more. "Just when the situation calls for it."

"And this one didn't?"

Her smile was paper-thin. "See that diploma on the wall? I'm a board-certified vet with several years' experience in traditional veterinary medicine. The acupuncture stuff, as you call it, was just extra training to supplement my regular skills. I only use it as an alternative when some of the more orthodox treatments have failed or aren't appropriate."

"And when would that be?"

"A lecture on veterinary acupuncture is not the reason you stopped by, Mr. Harte."

"I'm curious about what you do."

She hesitated for a moment before answering. "Animals I treat most often are horses with performance problems, like short stepping or mysterious lameness. I've treated moon blindness successfully and also older horses with degenerative conditions like arthritis or joint disease. You'd be surprised at how effective acupuncture can be."

He didn't doubt that. He didn't want to sound too skeptical, not when they were going to have to work together for the next few months, but he thought the whole thing was a bunch of hooey. Her California crowd might buy all this New Age crap, but folks in Wyoming looked at things like this a little differently.

For a minute, he thought about keeping his mouth shut and changing the subject, but she and her kid had been good for his daughter. He didn't want to see her practice go under, since Lucy would just about wither away if Dylan moved.

He cleared his throat. "Don't take this the wrong way, Dr. Webster, but it seems to me you might be better off focusing on those more traditional things you were talking about and leave the rest of that, er, stuff back in California."

She pursed her lips together tightly. "Thank you for the advice," she said, in a tone that left him in no doubt of her real feelings. And they probably didn't include gratitude.

He should have stopped right there, but something made him push the issue harder. "Look, it's no secret around town that you've lost a lot of customers in the last few months to Steve Nichols, Ben's nephew. Hell, I've been using him myself. A lot of people don't understand why Ben sold his practice to you in the first place instead of to Steve. Anyway, I'm pretty sure you could lure some of those folks back if you didn't focus so much on the acupuncture side of things in your ads and all."

"I don't tell you how to run your ranch," she said quietly, folding her hands tightly on the desk. "So please don't tell me how to operate my practice."

He sat back in the chair, aware he sounded like an idiot. Bossy and arrogant, just like Cassie always accused him of being. "Sorry," he muttered. "It's none of my business what you do. Just thought you should know that out here we tend to prefer the things we know, the way we've always done things, the way they've been done for generations. Especially when it comes to our stock."

"Tell me about it."

"Sorry if I offended you."

She shrugged. "You're only saying to my face what I'm sure everyone else has been saying behind my back. I appreciate your frankness. Now can we talk about the carnival?"

"Uh, sure." Who would have dreamed twenty-four hours ago that he would consider a Valentine's Day carnival a safe topic of conversation?

"So I was thinking about calling it A Fair to Remember," she said. "What do you think?"

He scratched his cheek, not quite sure where she was going with this.

"From the movie. You know, Deborah Kerr, Cary Grant. Empire State Building. The one Meg Ryan bawled about in *Sleepless in Seattle*."

At his continued blank look, she shrugged. "Never mind. We can talk about it later. We have ten weeks to work out all the details."

Ten weeks working closely with Ellie Webster, with her green eyes and her wisecracks and her shampoo that smelled like lemon pie. He knew damn well the idea shouldn't appeal to him so much.

Chapter 4

"So we're agreed then," Ellie said fifteen minutes later. "Given our mutual lack of experience, we need to delegate as much as humanly possible. Our first step is to set up committees for booths, decorations, refreshments and publicity. Once we get some other willing victims, er, parents on board, we can go from there."

Matt scratched the back of his neck. "I guess. You know as much about this as I do. I just hope we can pull this off without making complete fools of ourselves. Or having the whole thing go down in history as the worst carnival ever."

He looked so completely uncomfortable at the task ahead of them that Ellie had to smile. He must love Lucy very much to be willing to put himself through it despite his obvious misgivings. Not many men she knew would be willing to take on such a project for their ten-year-old daughters, and she felt herself softening toward him even more.

"I can talk to Sarah this afternoon if you'd like and tell her we've both agreed to do it," she said.

"I'd appreciate that. I've got to run over to Idaho Falls to pick up a part for the loader, and it might be late before I get back in." He unkinked his considerable length from the low chair and rose, fingering his hat.

He was so tall she had to crane her neck to look into those startling blue eyes. Just how did the man manage to make her little office shrink to about the size of a rabbit hutch by his presence? The awareness simmering through her didn't help matters one bit.

"Sure you're not too busy to talk to Miz McKenzie?" he asked.

"I should be able to carve out a few moments," she murmured dryly. Her appointment schedule for the rest of the day was woefully empty, as she was fairly certain he must realize.

Sure enough, he looked even more ill at ease. After a moment, he cleared his throat. "Think about what I said before, would you? About folks around here being more comfortable with what they know. Your business might pick up if you keep that in mind. You never know."

Any soft feelings she might have been harboring toward him fluttered away like migrating birds. Before she could snap at him again to mind his own business, he shoved his hat on his head and walked out of her office with that long, ground-swallowing stride.

She might be annoyed with him, but that couldn't keep her from wandering out of her office to the reception area to watch through the window as he climbed into a shiny new pickup that probably cost as much as her entire practice.

He drove out of the parking lot with deliberate care, as she was sure he did everything.

She had a sudden wild desire to know if he would kiss a woman that way. Thoroughly. Studiously. Carefully exploring every single inch of her lips with that hard mouth until he memorized each curve, each hollow. Until her knees turned to jelly and her body ached with need....

"Dreamy, isn't he?"

Ellie whirled and found SueAnn watching her, mouth twitching with amusement. She swallowed hard and fought the urge to press a hand to her suddenly trembling stomach. "I don't know what you're talking about," she lied.

SueAnn just laughed. "Right. Whatever you say. You want me to pick that tongue off the floor for you?"

She snapped said tongue firmly back into her mouth. "Don't you have some work to do?"

"Oh, watching you go weak in the knees is much more fun."

"Sorry to ruin your entertainment, but one of us *does* have some work waiting. If you need me, I'll be in my office."

"No problem. Looks like we'll see plenty of Matt Harte between now and Valentine's Day."

That's exactly what she was afraid of. She sighed and headed for her office. She had only been at her desk for a few moments when the cowbell on the door jangled suddenly. From her vantage point, she couldn't see who came in, but she could watch SueAnn's ready smile slide away and her expression chill by several degrees.

Curious as to who might have earned such a frosty glare from the woman who invented congeniality, Ellie rose and walked to the door of her office for a better look.

Steve Nichols, her main competition in town and the nephew of the vet who had sold her the practice, was just closing the door behind him.

She should have known. SueAnn had a good word to say about everybody in town except for Ben's nephew. When it came to Steve, she was as intractable as Jeb Thacker's goat.

Ellie couldn't understand her animosity. From the day she arrived, Steve had gone out of his way to make her feel welcome in Salt River—treating her as a friend and respected colleague, not as a business rival who had bought his uncle's practice out from under him.

"Steve." She greeted him warmly to compensate for SueAnn's noticeable lack of enthusiasm.

His mouth twisted into a smile underneath his bushy blond mustache, then he gestured toward the parking lot. "Was that Matt Harte I just saw driving out of here?"

For no earthly reason she could figure out, she felt a blush soak her cheeks. "Er, yes."

"Is there a problem with one of his animals? Anything I should know about?"

"Oh, no. Nothing like that." She would have left it at that, but Steve continued to study her expectantly. Finally, she had to say something. "Our girls are in the same class and we're working on a school project together," she finally said. "We were just discussing some of the details."

"Really? What kind of project?"

She didn't understand this strange reluctance to divulge any information—maybe she was just embarrassed—but couldn't bring herself to answer.

"They're cochairs for the annual Valentine's Day carnival." SueAnn finally broke the silence, her voice clipped and her expression still cool.

His mouth sagged open, then a laugh gurgled out. "You've got to be kidding me. Matt Harte planning a school carnival? That's the most ridiculous thing I've ever heard. Next thing I know, you're going to tell me he's opening up a beauty salon in town."

Steve's reaction matched her own when she had first heard about the carnival, so why did she feel so annoyed at him for it? And so protective of a bossy, arrogant rancher who couldn't seem to keep his nose out of her business?

"He's doing it for his daughter," she said with a coolness to match SueAnn's. "What's so ridiculous about that?"

"It just doesn't seem like his thing. Matt's not exactly the PTA type, you know what I mean?"

She didn't want to get into this with him, so she abruptly changed the subject. "Was there something you needed, Steve?"

He shrugged, letting the matter drop. "Do I need a reason to stop by and visit my favorite vet?"

Behind him, SueAnn made a rude noise that she quickly camouflaged behind a cough. Ellie didn't need to phone a psychic hot line to read her mind. She was fairly sure SueAnn thought Steve's favorite vet looked back at him in the mirror each morning.

The other woman opened her mouth to say something snide along those lines, Ellie imagined. She quickly gave her a warning glare. To her relief, after a moment SueAnn clamped her lips tightly shut.

"You don't need a reason to visit, Steve. You know that." Ellie spoke quickly to head off any more trouble. "You're always welcome here. But surely you wouldn't have dropped by during the middle of your busy time of day just to chat, right?"

He sent her that boyishly charming smile of his. "You caught me. Actually, I did have an ulterior motive for dropping by. I'm in a bit of a bind. I ran out of brucellosis vaccine this morning and I'm scheduled to inoculate the herd at Paul Blanchard's ranch in an hour."

Paul Blanchard! He was another of her regular clients, one of the few who had stayed with the clinic after she took over from Ben. Ellie's heart sank. Another deserter. They were dropping like flies.

SueAnn sent her a speaking glance, but before she could answer, Steve went on. "I've ordered a rush job on more but it won't be here until tomorrow. You wouldn't happen to have a few doses to tide me over until the shipment arrives, would you?"

"You want me to loan you some of my brucellosis vaccine for Paul Blanchard's stock?"

Steve seemed completely oblivious to the sheer audacity of asking a favor for an account he had just appropriated. He gave her a pleading smile. "If it's not too much of a bother. You won't need any before tomorrow, will you?"

She might have, if she had been the one treating Blanchard cattle. As it was, it looked as if she would have vaccine to spare. She ground her teeth in frustration. Her first instinct was to say no, absolutely not. He could find his own damn vaccine. But in her heart she knew it wasn't really Steve's fault her practice was struggling.

She also couldn't blame him for setting up his own competing clinic after Ben unexpectedly sold this one to her. If their roles had been reversed and she'd been the one left out in the cold by a relative, she would have done exactly the same thing. And probably wouldn't have treated the usurper with nearly the kindness Steve had shown her.

She forced a smile. "I'll go check my supply."

Trying hard not to mutter to herself, she pushed through the swinging doors that separated the front office and waiting room from the treatment area.

The refrigerator in the back was well-stocked, and she found a case immediately. For one moment, she debated telling him she couldn't find any but she knew that was petty and small-minded so she picked it up and shouldered her way through the swinging doors again.

Steve wasn't where she left him by the front desk, and she lifted a curious eyebrow at SueAnn, who scowled and jerked her head toward Ellie's office. Steve was sitting behind her desk, browsing through her planner where she meticulously recorded appointments and scheduled treatments.

With great effort, she swallowed her irritation. "Here you go," she said loudly. His gaze flew to hers, and he didn't seem at all embarrassed to be caught nosing around in her office.

"Thanks, Ellie. I really appreciate this." His mustache twitched again with his smile.

"Glad to help," she lied, and was immediately ashamed of herself for the ugly knot of resentment curdling in her stomach. "Read anything interesting in there?" she asked pointedly.

"Sorry. Professional curiosity. You don't mind, do you? I'm intrigued by the improvement you've noted here in that thoroughbred of Jack Martin's. I thought nothing would cure her. She's a beauty of a horse, and it would have been a real shame to have to put her down, but I thought she would always be lame."

"She's responded well to a combination of treatments. Jack and I are both pleased."

"So are things picking up?"

Not with you stealing my clients one by one, she thought. "Actually, it's been a pretty busy day."

"Have you given any more thought to my offer?"

She blew out a breath. She absolutely did not want to go into this with him today. "I have. The answer is still no, Steve. Just like it's been for the last month."

He rose from the chair and walked around to the other side of the desk. "Come on, Ellie. Think about it. If we combined our practices, we could each save tens of thousands a year on overhead. And pooling our workload would ease the burden on each of us."

What burden? She would kill for a little workload to complain about. Ellie sighed. His offer made common sense and, heaven knows, would help boost her meager income, but it also held about as much appeal to her as being knocked on her rear end by a hundred goats.

She didn't want to be partners, not with Steve or with anyone else. She wanted to stand on her own, to make her own decisions and be responsible for the consequences.

She had spent her entire adult life working for others, from volunteering in clinics while she was still in high school to the last seven years working for an equine vet in Monterey.

She was tired of it, of having to play by others' rules. Constantly having someone else tell her what animals she could treat and how she should treat them had been draining the life out of her, stealing all her satisfaction and joy in the career she loved.

It went deeper than that, though. If she were honest, her ferocious need for independence had probably been rooted in her childhood, watching her mother drink herself to an early grave because of a man and then being shuttled here and there in the foster care system.

She learned early she would never be able to please the endless parade of busybody social workers and foster parents who marched through her life. She couldn't please them, and she couldn't depend on them. Too often, the moment she began to care for a family, she was capriciously yanked out and sent to another one. Eventually, she learned not to care, to carefully construct a hard shell around her heart. The only one she could truly count on was herself.

This was her chance. Hers and Dylan's. The opportunity to build the life she had dreamed of since those early days cleaning cages.

She wasn't ready to give up that dream, patients or none.

Besides that, she had SueAnn to consider. With the animosity between the two, she and Steve would never be able to work together, and she didn't want to lose her as a friend or as an assistant.

"I'm not going to change my mind, Steve," she finally said. "It's a good offer and I appreciate it, really I do, but I'm just not interested right now."

If Dylan had given her that same look, Ellie would have called it a pout. After only a moment of sulking, Steve's expression became amiable again. "I'll keep working on you. Eventually I'll wear you down, just watch."

He picked up the case of vaccine and headed for the door. "Thanks again for the loan. I'll drop my shipment off tomorrow, if that's all right with you."

"That would be fine," she said.

At the door he paused and looked at her with a grin. "And have fun working with Matt Harte. The man can be tough as a sow's snout, but he's a damn hard worker. He's single-handedly built the Diamond Harte into a force to be reckoned with around here. I'm not sure that will help when it comes to planning a school carnival, but it ought to make things interesting."

Interesting. She had a feeling the word would be a vast understatement.

He was hiding out, no denying it.

Like a desperado trying frantically to stay two steps ahead of a hangin' party and a noose with his name on it.

A week after visiting Ellie at her clinic, Matt sat trapped in his office at the ranch house, trying to concentrate on the whir and click of the computer in front of him instead of the soft murmur of women's voices coming from the kitchen at the end of the hall.

As usual, he had a hundred and one better things to occupy his time than sit here gazing at a blasted screen, but he didn't dare leave the sanctuary of his office.

She was out there.

Ellie Webster. The city vet who had sneaked her way

into his dreams for a week, with that fiery hair and her silvery-green eyes and that determined little chin.

He thought she was only driving out to the Diamond Harte to drop her kid off for a sleepover with Lucy. She was supposed to be here ten minutes, tops, and wouldn't even have to know he was in here.

Things didn't go according to plan. He had a feeling they rarely would, where Ellie Webster was concerned. Instead of driving away like she should have done, she had apparently plopped down on one of the straight-backed kitchen chairs, and now he could hear her and Cassie talking and laughing like they'd been best friends for life.

They'd been at it for the last half hour, and he'd just about had enough.

He wasn't getting a damn thing done. Every time he tried to focus on getting the hang of the new livestock-tracking software, her voice would creep under the door like a sultry, devious wisp of smoke, and his concentration would be shot all to hell and back.

Why did it bug him so much to have her invading his space with that low laugh of hers? He felt itchy and bothered having her here, like a mustang with a tail full of cockleburs.

It wasn't right. He would have to get a handle on this awareness if he was going to be able to work on the school thing with her for the next few months. As to how, he didn't have the first idea. It had been a long time since he'd been so tangled up over a woman.

Maybe he should ask her out.

The idea scared him worse than kicking a mountain lion. He wasn't much of a lady's man. Maybe he used to be when he was younger—he'd enjoyed his share of buckle bunnies when he rodeoed in college, he wouldn't deny it—but things had changed after Melanie.

He had tried to date a few times after he was finally granted a divorce in absentia after her desertion, but every attempt left him feeling restless and awkward.

After a while he just quit trying, figuring it was better to wake up lonely in his own bed than in a stranger's.

He wasn't lonely, he corrected the thought quickly. He had Lucy and Jess and Cassidy and the ranch hands. He sure as hell didn't need another woman messing things up.

He cleared his throat. The action made him realize how thirsty he was. Parched, like he'd been riding through a desert for days.

The kitchen had water. Plenty of it, cold, pure mountain spring water right out of the tap. He could walk right in there and pour himself a big glass and nobody could do a damn thing about it.

Except then he'd have to face *her*.

He heaved a sigh and turned to the computer until the next wisp of laughter curled under the door.

That was it. He was going in. He shoved back from the desk and headed toward the door. He lived here, dammit. A man ought to be able to walk into his own kitchen for a drink if it suited him. She had no right to come into his house and tangle him up like this.

No right whatsoever.

Chapter 5

As soon as he walked into the big, warm kitchen, he regretted it.

He felt like the big, bad wolf walking in on a coop full of chickens. All four of them—Ellie, Cass and both of the girls—looked up, their cutoff laughter hanging in the air along with the sweet, intoxicating smell of chocolate chip cookies baking in the oven.

"Sorry. Didn't mean to interrupt," he muttered. "I, uh, just needed a drink of water and then I'll get out of your way."

"You didn't interrupt," Cassie said. "Sit down. The cookies will be done in a minute, and I know how much you love eating them right out of the oven."

Information his baby sister didn't need to be sharing with the whole damn world, thank you very much. Made him sound like a seven-year-old boy snitching goodies after school. "I've got things to do," he muttered.

"They can wait five minutes, can't they?"

His jaw worked as he tried to come up with a decent-sounding excuse to escape without seeming rude. How was a man supposed to think straight when he had four females watching him so expectantly?

Finally, he muttered a curse under his breath and pulled out a chair. "Just five minutes, though."

Like a tractor with a couple bad cylinders, the conversation limped along for a moment, and he squirmed on the hard chair, wishing he were absolutely anywhere but here. He was just about to jump up and rush back to the relative safety of his office—excuse or none—when Lucy ambushed him.

She touched his arm with green-painted fingernails—now where did she get those? he wondered—and gazed at him out of those big gray eyes. "Daddy, Dylan and her mom aren't going anywhere for Thanksgiving dinner since they don't have any family around here. Isn't that sad?"

Keeping his gaze firmly averted from Ellie's, he made a noncommittal sound.

"Do you think they might be able to come here and share our family's dinner?"

Despite his best efforts, his gaze slid toward Ellie just in time to catch her mouth drop and her eyes go wide—with what, he couldn't say for sure, but it sure looked like she was as horrified as he was by the very idea.

"I don't know, honey—" he began.

"That's a great idea," Cassie said at the same time. "There's always room at the table for a few more, and plenty of food."

"Oh, no. That's okay," Ellie said quickly. "We'll be fine, won't we, Dylan?"

Dylan put on a pleading expression. "Come on,

Mom. It would be so cool. Lucy's aunt Cassie is a great cook. I bet she never burns the stuffing like you do."

Ellie made a face at her daughter, and Matt had to fight a chuckle. And he thought *Cass and Lucy* were bad at spilling family secrets.

"Be that as it may," Ellie said, her cheeks tinged slightly pink, "I'm sure the Hartes have a lovely family dinner planned. They don't need to be saddled with two more."

"It's no problem," Cassie said. "We'd love to have you come. Wouldn't we, Matt?"

He cleared his throat. Again, he couldn't seem to make his brain work fast enough to come up with an excuse. "Uh, sure."

Ellie raised an eyebrow at his less-than-enthusiastic response. He obviously didn't want to invite her for Thanksgiving any more than she wanted to accept.

"Good. It's settled," Cassie said, oblivious to their objections. "It's usually really casual. Just family—Matt, Lucy, our brother Jess and whichever of the ranch hands stick around for the holidays. We eat around two but you're welcome to come out any time before then, especially if you're into watching football with the guys."

What she knew about football would fit into a saltshaker. Ellie sighed heavily. And what she knew about big rowdy Thanksgiving family dinners wouldn't even fit on a grain of salt.

It looked like she was going to be stuck with both things. So much for her good intentions about having as little as possible to do with the man who somehow managed to jumble up her insides every time she was around him.

What choice did she have, though? She didn't want

to hurt his daughter or sister's feelings by refusing the invitation. Lucy was a dear, sweet and quiet and polite. Exactly Dylan's opposite! It was a wonder they were friends, but somehow the two of them meshed perfectly. They brought out the best in each other.

To her surprise, she and Cassie had also immediately hit it off. Unlike Matt, his sister was bubbly and friendly and went out of her way to make her feel welcomed.

She would sound churlish and rude if she refused to share their holiday simply because the alpha male in the family made her as edgy as a hen on a hot griddle and sent her hormones whirling around like a Texas dust storm.

"Can I bring something?" she finally asked, trying to accept the invitation as gracefully as she could manage.

"Do you have a specialty?" Cassie asked.

Did macaroni and cheese count as a specialty? She doubted it. "No. I'm afraid not."

"Sure you do, Mom." Dylan spoke up. "What about that pie you make sometimes?"

She made pecan pie exactly twice, but Dylan had never forgotten it. Hope apparently springs eternal in a nine-year-old's heart that someday she would bake it again. "I don't know if I'd call that a specialty."

"Why don't you bring it anyway?" Cassie suggested. "Or if you'd rather make something else, that would be fine."

I'd rather just stay home and have our usual quiet dinner for two, she thought. But one look at Dylan revealed her daughter was ecstatic about the invitation. Her eyes shone, and her funny little face had the same kind of expectancy it usually wore just before walking downstairs on Christmas morning.

She looked so excited that Ellie instantly was awash in guilt for all the years they had done just that—stayed home alone with their precooked turkey and instant mashed potatoes instead of accepting other invitations from friends and colleagues.

Why had she never realized her daughter had been missing a big, noisy celebration? Dylan was usually so vocal about what she wanted and thought she needed. Why had she never said anything about this?

"Whatever you want to bring is fine," Cassie assured her. "Really, though, you don't have to bring anything but yourselves. Like I said, there's always plenty of food."

"I'll bring the pecan pie," she said, hoping her reluctance didn't filter into her voice.

"Great. I usually make a pumpkin and maybe an apple so we'll have several to choose from. Knowing my brothers, I doubt any of them will last long."

She looked at Matt out of the corner of her eyes and found him watching her. What was he thinking? That she was an interloper who had suddenly barged her way in to yet another facet of his life when he had plainly made it clear she wasn't welcome? She couldn't tell by the unreadable expression in those startling blue eyes.

The timer suddenly went off on the oven.

"That would be the cookies." Cassie jumped up and opened the oven door, releasing even more of the heavenly aroma.

A smell so evocative of hearth and home that Ellie's heart broke a little for all the homemade cookies she never had time to bake for her daughter. She had shed her last tear a long time ago for all the missing cookies in her own childhood.

Cassie quickly transferred at least half a dozen of the warm, gooey treats onto a plate for Matt, then poured him a glass of milk from the industrial-size refrigerator.

She set both in front of him, and he quickly grabbed them and stood up. Ellie smiled a little at the blatant relief evident in every line of his big, rangy body.

"Thanks," he mumbled to his sister. "I'll let you ladies get back to whatever you were talking about before I interrupted you."

The girls' giggles at being called ladies trailed after him as Matt made his escape from the kitchen.

"Wow, Mom. You look really great," Dylan said for about the fifth time as they made their way up the walk to the sprawling Diamond Harte ranch house.

Ellie fought her self-consciousness. Matt's sister said Thanksgiving dinner would be casual, but she didn't think her usual winter attire of jeans and denim work shirts was quite appropriate.

Instead, she had worn her slim wool skirt over soft black leather boots and a matching dove-gray sweater— one of her few dressy outfits that only saw the light of day when she went to professional meetings. Was she hideously overdressed? She hoped not. She was nervous enough about this as it was without adding unsuitable clothes to the mix.

She shouldn't be this nervous. It was only dinner, nothing to twist her stomach into knots over or turn her mouth as dry as a riverbed in August.

She cleared her throat, angry with herself, at the knowledge that only part of her edginess had to do with sharing a meal with Matt Harte and his blue eyes and powerful shoulders.

That might be the main reason, but the rest had more to do with the holiday itself. She had too many less-than-pleasant memories of other years, other holidays. Always being the outsider, the one who didn't belong. Of spending the day trying to fit in during someone else's family celebration in foster home after foster home.

This wasn't the same. She had a family now—Dylan. All she could ever want or need. Her funny, imaginative, spunky little daughter who filled her heart with constant joy. She was now a confident, self-assured woman, content with life and her place in it.

So why did she feel like an awkward, gawky child again, standing here on the doorstep, hoping this time the people inside would like her?

Dylan, heedless of her mother's nerves, rushed up the remaining steps and buzzed hard on the doorbell, and Ellie forced herself to focus on something other than her own angst.

She looked around her, admiring the view. In the lightly falling snow, the ranch was beautiful. Matt kept a clean, well-ordered operation, she could say that for him. The outbuildings all wore fresh paint, the fences were all in good repair, the animals looked well cared for.

Some outfits looked as cluttered as garbage dumps, with great hulking piles of rusty machinery set about like other people displayed decorative plates or thimble collections. Here on the Diamond Harte, though, she couldn't see so much as a spare part lying around.

It looked like a home, deeply loved and nurtured.

What must it have been like to grow up in such a place? To feel warm dirt and sharp blades of grass under your bare feet in the summertime and jump into big piles of raked leaves in the fall and sled down that gently sloping hill behind the barn in winter?

To know without question that you belonged just here, with people who loved you?

She pushed the thoughts away, angry at herself for dredging up things she had resolved long ago. It was only the holiday that brought everything back. That made her once more feel small and unwanted.

To her relief, the door opened before she could feel any sorrier for herself, sending out a blast of warmth and a jumble of delectable smells, as well as a small figure who launched herself at Dylan with a shriek of excitement.

"You're here! Finally!"

"We're early, aren't we?" Ellie asked anxiously. "Didn't your aunt say you were eating at two? It's only half past one."

"I don't know what time it is. I've just been *dying* for you to get here. Dylan, you have *got* to come up to my room. Uncle Jess bought me the new 'N Sync CD and it's so totally awesome."

Before Ellie could say anything else, both girls rushed up the stairs, leaving her standing in the two-story entry alone, holding her pecan pie and feeling extremely foolish.

Okay. Now what did she do? She'd been in the huge, rambling ranch house a few times before to pick up Lucy or drop off Dylan for some activity or other, but she had always entered through the back door leading straight into the kitchen. She had no idea how to get there from the front door, and it seemed extremely rude to go wandering through a strange house on her own.

She could always go back and ring the doorbell

again, she supposed. But that would probably lead to awkward questions about why her daughter was already upstairs while she lingered by the door as if ready to bolt any moment.

She was still standing there, paralyzed by indecision, when she heard loud male groans at something from a room down the hall, then the game shifted to a commercial—somebody hawking razor blades.

"You want another beer?" she heard Matt's deep voice ask someone else—his brother, she presumed, or perhaps one of the ranch hands. The deep timbre of it sent those knots in her stomach unraveling to quiver like plucked fiddle strings.

Seconds later—before she could come up with a decent place to hide—he walked out in the hall wearing tan jeans and a forest-green fisherman's sweater. She was still ordering her heart to start beating again when he turned and caught sight of her standing there like an idiot.

"Doc!" he exclaimed.

"Hi," she mumbled.

"Why are you just standing out here? Come in."

She thought about explaining how the girls had abandoned her for their favorite boy band, then decided she would sound even more ridiculous if she tried. She held up the pie instead. "Where's the best place for this?"

"Probably in the kitchen. I was just heading there myself, I can show you the way. Here. Let me take your coat first."

She tensed as he came up behind her and pulled her coat from her shoulders while she transferred the pie from hand to hand. Despite her best efforts, she was intensely aware of him, his heat and strength and the leathery smell of his aftershave.

After he hung her coat in a small closet off the entry, he took off down the hall. She followed him, trying fiercely not to notice the snug fit of his jeans or those impossibly broad shoulders under the weave of his sweater. Something was different about him today. It took her a moment to figure out what. He wasn't wearing the black Stetson that seemed so much a part of him, nor was his hair flattened from it.

The dark waves looked soft and thick. They would probably be like silk under her fingers, she thought. The impulse to reach out and see for herself was so strong, she even lifted a hand a few inches from her side, then dropped it quickly in mortification.

It was much safer to look around her. This part of the house was one she hadn't seen before, but it had the same warmth of the rest of the house, with family pictures grouped together on one wall and a huge log cabin quilt in dark greens and blues hanging on the other.

As they neared the kitchen, the smells of roasting turkey and vegetables grew stronger, and her stomach gave a loud, long rumble. She pressed a hand to it, hoping no one else could hear but her.

When she looked up, though, she found Matt giving her a lopsided grin, and she flushed.

"Oh, Ellie! You made it!" Matt's sister looked pretty and flustered as she stirred something on the stove with one hand while she pulled a pan of golden dinner rolls out of the oven with the other. "When it started to snow, I was afraid you'd decide not to make the drive."

"It's not bad out there. A few flurries, that's all. Just enough to make everything look like a magic fairyland."

"Wait until you've lived here for a few years. You won't describe the snow quite so romantically. Oh, is that your famous pie? Does it need to go in the refrigerator?"

"No. I don't think so."

"Good. I'm not sure I could find room for it." Cassie blew out a breath and tucked a stray strand of hair behind her ear just as the timers on the stove and microwave went off at the same time. The frazzled look in her eyes started to border on panic.

"Uh, anything I can do to help?" Matt asked suddenly.

His sister sent him a grateful look. "Actually, there is. Can you finish chopping the raw vegetables to go with that dip you like? Oh, rats," she exclaimed suddenly. "I forgot to bring up the cranberry sauce from the storeroom. Ellie, would you mind stirring this gravy for me? I think most of the lumps are out of it—just make sure it doesn't burn on the bottom."

"Uh, sure."

She set her pie on the only bare patch of countertop she could find and took the wooden spoon from Cassie, who rushed from the room, leaving her and Matt alone.

He immediately went to work on the vegetables. The cutting surface was on a work island in the middle of the kitchen with only a few feet separating it from the stove, forcing them to stand side by side but facing opposite directions.

Again she felt that sizzle of awareness but she sternly tried to suppress it. They lapsed into an awkward silence while they did their appointed jobs.

"Everything smells divine," she finally said.

He seized on the topic. "Yeah, Cassidy's a great cook.

I've always thought she should have her own restaurant."

"I didn't know Cassie was short for Cassidy." She paused, remembering something SueAnn had told her about the middle brother, the Salt River chief of police. "Let me get this straight, you have a brother named Jesse James and a sister named Cassidy?"

His low, rueful laugh sent the hairs on the back of her neck prickling. "Our dad was what I guess you'd call a history buff. One of his ancestors, Matt Warner, was a member of Butch Cassidy's Wild Bunch, and Dad grew up hearing stories about him handed down throughout the years. Dad was always fascinated by outlaws and lawmen of the Old West. The romanticism and the adventure and the history of it, I guess."

"So you're named after this scofflaw of an ancestor?"

"Yeah." His voice sounded rueful again. "Matthew Warner Harte. When the others came along, I guess he just decided to stick with the same theme."

A Wild West outlaw. Why didn't it surprise her that he had that blood churning through his veins? "And how did your mother handle having her own little wild bunch?"

His shrug brushed his shoulder into hers, and the subtle movement sent a shiver rippling down her spine. "My parents adored each other," he answered. "Mom probably wouldn't have complained even if Dad wanted to name us Larry, Moe and Curly."

He sent her another lopsided grin, and she was helpless to prevent herself from returning it. They gazed at each other for a moment, side by side across shoulders, both smiling. Suddenly everything seemed louder, more intense—the slurp and burble of the gravy in the pan, the chink of the knife hitting the cutting board, the slow whir of the ceiling fan overhead.

His gaze dropped to her mouth for an instant, just enough for heat to flare there as if he'd touched her, then his eyes flashed to hers once more before he turned abruptly, guiltily, back to the vegetables.

Now *that* was interesting.

She was still trying to come up with something to say in the midst of the sudden tension—not to mention trying to remind her lungs what they were there for—when their daughters burst into the kitchen in mid-giggle.

They both stopped short in the doorway when they saw their parents working side-by-side. Ellie opened her mouth to greet them but shut it again when two pairs of eyes shifted rapidly between her and Matt, then widened.

The girls looked at each other with small, secretive smiles that sent the fear of God into her. They were definitely up to something. And she was very much afraid she was beginning to suspect what it might be.

Chapter 6

"So tell us what brings a pretty California beach girl like yourself to our desolate Wyoming wilderness."

Matt sat forward so he could hear Ellie's answer across the table. If *he* had asked that question, he grumped to himself, she probably would have snapped at him to mind his own business. But it didn't seem to bother her at all that his brother wanted to nose around through her past.

Instead, she smiled at Jesse, seated to her left. "I'm afraid there weren't too many beaches around Bakersfield."

"Bakersfield? Is that where you're from?" Cassie asked.

If he hadn't been watching her so intently, Matt would have missed the way her smile slid away and the barest shadow of old pain flickered in her green eyes for just a moment before she shifted her gaze to the full plate in front of her. "Until I was seven. After that, I moved around a lot."

What happened when she was seven? he wondered. And why did she phrase it that way? *I moved around a lot,* not *My family moved around a lot?*

Before he could ask, Jesse spoke. "Even if you're not a beach girl, you're still the best-looking thing to share our Thanksgiving dinner since I can remember."

She laughed, rolling her eyes a little at the compliment, while Matt battled a powerful urge to casually reach over and shove his brother's face into his mashed potatoes.

He didn't want to admit it bugged the hell out of him the way Jesse flirted with her all through dinner, hanging on her every word and making sure her glass was always full.

Ellie didn't seem to mind. She teased him right back, smiling and laughing at him like she'd never done with Matt.

Not that he cared. He was just worried about her getting a broken heart, that's all. Maybe somebody ought to warn her about Jesse. His little brother wasn't a bad sort. Not really. In fact, for being such a wild, out-of-control son of a gun after their parents died, Jess turned out pretty okay.

Matt would be the first one to admit the kid did a fine job protecting the good people of Salt River as the chief of police, a whole hell of a lot better than the last chief, who'd spent more time lining his own pockets than he did fighting crime.

But Jess still had a well-earned reputation with the ladies as a love 'em and leave 'em type. He rarely dated a woman longer than a few weeks, and when he did, she was usually the kind of girl their mother would have described as "faster than she ought to be."

'Course, it was none of his business if Ellie Webster wanted to make a fool of herself over a charmer like Jesse James Harte, he reminded himself.

"So what brought you out here?" the charmer in question asked her again.

"My mom always wanted to move to the mountains and be a cowgirl," Ellie's daughter offered, helping herself to more candied yams.

A delicate pink tinged the doc's cheeks. "Thanks for sharing that, sweetheart."

"What?" Dylan asked, all innocence. "That's what you said, isn't it?"

She laughed ruefully. "You're right. I did. The truth is, I've always wanted to live and work in the Rockies. I met Ben Nichols when I was giving a lecture a few years ago. Afterward, when he told me about Star Valley and his practice here, I told him how much I envied him and casually mentioned I had always dreamed of living out here. I never imagined he would offer to sell his practice to me when he retired."

So that explained what brought her to Wyoming. What interested him was why a tiny little thing like her would choose such a physically demanding job as a large-animal vet in the first place. If she wanted to be a vet, she would have been better off with little things like dogs and cats instead of having to muscle a half-ton of steer into a chute.

He didn't think she'd appreciate the question, so he asked another one. "Where were you working before?"

She shifted her gaze across the table to him as if

she'd forgotten he was sitting there. "I worked at a clinic in the Monterey area. That's on the central coast of California—so I guess you were right, Jesse. Technically I suppose you could call me a beach girl, although I rarely had a chance to see it."

"I've heard that's a beautiful area," Cassie said.

"It is. Pebble Beach is just south of it, and Carmel-by-the-Sea."

"How many cattle operations did you find in the middle of all those golf courses and tourist traps?" he asked abruptly, earning a curious look from Cassie.

"Not many, although there are a few farther inland. My clients were mostly horses—thoroughbreds and jumpers and pleasure horses."

The conversation turned then to the physical differences between working horses and riding horses and then, with much prompting by Dylan, onto the best choice for a pleasure horse for a nine-year-old girl. Matt contented himself listening to the conversation and watching Ellie interact with his family.

Even after three years of marriage, Melanie had never fit in half as well. He felt vaguely guilty for the thought, but it was nothing less than the truth. She and Cassie had fought like cats and dogs from the beginning, and Jess had despised her.

So much for his grand plan to give his younger siblings more of a stable home environment by bringing home a wife.

He should have known from the first night he brought her home after their whirlwind courtship and marriage at the national stock show in Denver that he had made a disastrous mistake. She spent the entire evening bickering with Cassie and completely ignoring Jess.

But by then it was too late, they were already married. It took him three more years of the situation going from bad to worse for him to admit to himself how very stupid he had been.

He wouldn't make that mistake again.

He hated thinking about it, about what a fool he had been, so he yanked his mind off the topic. "Everything tastes great, as usual," he said instead to Cassie.

She grinned suddenly. "Remember that first year after Mom and Daddy died when you tried to cook Thanksgiving dinner?"

Jess turned his attention long enough from Ellie to shudder and add his own jab. "I remember it. My stomach still hasn't forgiven me. The turkey was tougher than roasted armadillo."

"And the yams could have been used to tar the barn roof."

He rolled his eyes as the girls giggled. Jess and Cassie teased him mercilessly about that dinner. Usually it didn't bother him—but then again, usually he didn't have Ellie Webster sitting across from him listening to the conversation with that intrigued look in her green eyes.

"Give me a break," he muttered. "I did my best. You're lucky you got anything but cold cereal and frozen pizza."

He'd been twenty-two when their parents died in a rollover on a slippery mountain road. That first year had been the toughest time of his life. Grieving for his parents and their sudden death, trying to comfort Cassie, who had been a lost and frightened thirteen-year-old, doing his damnedest to keep Jess out of juvenile detention.

Trying to keep the ranch and the family together when he didn't know what the hell he was doing.

It had been a rough few years, but they had survived and were closer for it.

"At least we had to only go through Matt's attempts to poison us for a while." Jess grinned. "Then Cassie decided to save us all and learned to cook."

"I had no choice," she retorted. "It was a matter of survival. I figured one of us had to learn unless we wanted to die of food poisoning or starve to death. Matt was too busy with the ranch and you were too busy raising hell. That left me."

Jesse immediately bristled, gearing up for a sharp retort, and Matt gave a resigned sigh. Cassie always knew how to punch his buttons. Jesse's wild, hard-drinking days after their parents died were still a sore point with him, but that never stopped Cass from rubbing his nose in it.

Before he could step in to head trouble off, Ellie did it for him. "Well, you learned to cook very well," she assured Cassie, with an anxious look toward Jess's glare. "You'll have to give me the recipe for your stuffing. I tend to over-cook it. Is that sausage I taste in there?"

She prattled on in a way that seemed completely unlike her, and it was only after she had successfully turned the conversation completely away from any trouble spots that he realized she had stepped in to play peacemaker as smoothly as if she'd been doing it all her life.

Had she done it on purpose? He wondered again about her background. She hadn't mentioned brothers or sisters, but that didn't mean she had none. What had happened when she was seven, the year after which she said she'd moved around so much?

He wanted badly to know, just as he was discovering he wanted to know everything about her.

"Come on, Ellie. It's our turn to watch football."

She looked at the dishes scattered across the table. "I can help clean up...."

"No way. The men get to do it—it's tradition. That's why I try to make the kitchen extra messy for them." She smiled sweetly at her brothers. "I think I used just about every single dish in the house."

Matt and Jesse groaned in unison. Unmoved, Cassie stood up. "Have fun, boys."

With guilt tweaking her, Ellie let Matt's sister drag her from the dining room, Dylan and Lucy following behind.

Cassie led her into a huge great room dominated by a towering river-rock fireplace. A big-screen TV and a pair of couches took up one corner, and a pool table and a couple of video games jostled for space in the other. As large as the room was, though, it was comfortable. Lived in, with warm-toned furniture and shelves full of books.

The girls immediately rushed to the pool table, and Cassidy plopped down on one of the plump, tweedy couches. "Boy, it feels good to sit down. I had to get up at four to put the turkey in, and I haven't stopped since."

"I'm sorry if I made extra work for you."

"Are you kidding? I didn't do anything I wouldn't have done anyway, and it's wonderful to have somebody else with a Y chromosome at the table besides Lucy!"

Cassie picked up the remote. "So which game do you want to watch? We have blue against red—" she flipped the channel "—or black against silver."

"I'm not crazy about football," she confessed.

The other woman sent her a conspiratorial grin. "Me, neither. I hate it, actually. When you spend your whole life around macho men, you don't really need to waste your time watching them on TV. Let's see if we can find something better until the boys come in and start growling at us to change it back."

She flipped the remote, making funny comments about every station she passed until stumbling on an old Alfred Hitchcock film with Jimmy Stewart.

"Here we go. *Rear Window.* This is what I call real entertainment. Could Grace Kelly dress or what?"

Ellie settled on the couch, the seductive warmth from the fireplace combining with the turkey put her into a pleasant haze.

She couldn't remember enjoying a meal more. The food had been delicious. And with the exception of the strange tension between her and Matt, the company had been great, too.

Their banter and teasing and memories of other holidays had been a revelation. This was what a family was all about, and if she closed her eyes, she could almost pretend she was a part of it.

One strange thing, though. For all their reminiscing, they hadn't brought up Lucy's mother one single time. It was almost as if the woman had never existed. Come to think of it, nobody had ever mentioned the mystery woman to Ellie.

"What happened to Lucy's mother?"

She didn't realize she had asked the blunt question out loud until Cassidy's relaxed smile froze, and she shot a quick glance at her niece. Ellie winced, appalled at herself. When would she ever learn to think before she opened her big mouth? At least neither of the girls was paying any attention to them, Ellie saw with relief.

"I'm so sorry," she said quickly. "That was terribly rude of me. It just slipped out. It's none of my business, really. You don't have to answer."

"No. It's just a…a raw subject." She looked at her niece again, and Ellie thought she saw guilt flicker in her blue eyes, then she flashed a bitter smile. She lowered her voice so the girls couldn't hear. "Melanie ran off with my…with one of our ranch hands. Lucy wasn't even three months old."

Ellie's jaw dropped. She tried to picture Matt in the role of abandoned husband and couldn't. Her heart twisted with sympathy when she imagined him taking care of a newborn on his own—late-night feedings, teething and all.

What kind of woman could simply abandon her own child like that? She thought of those first few months after Dylan was born, when she had been on her own and so very frightened about what the future might hold for the two of them.

Despite her fear, she had been completely in awe of the precious gift she'd been handed. Some nights she would lie awake in that grimy two-room apartment, just staring at Dylan's tiny, squishy features, listening to her breathe and wondering what she had done to deserve such a miracle.

She couldn't even comprehend a woman who would walk away from something so amazing.

Or from a man like Matt Harte.

"I'm so sorry," she said, knowing the words were terribly inadequate.

Cassidy shrugged and looked toward the girls. From

the raw emotion exposed on her features like a winter-bare tree branch, Ellie had the odd suspicion there was more to the story than losing a sister-in-law.

"It was a long time ago," Cassie said quietly. "Anyway, Matt's much better off without her. He'd be the first to tell you that. Melanie hated it here. She hated the ranch, she hated Wyoming, she hated being a mother. I was amazed she stuck around as long as she did."

Why on earth would he marry a woman who hated ranch life? Ellie wondered. For a man like Matt who so obviously belonged here—on this land he loved so much—it must have been a bitter rejection seeing it scorned by the woman he married.

She must have been very beautiful for him to marry her in the first place and bring her here. Ellie didn't even want to think about why the thought depressed her so much.

Cassie quickly turned the conversation to the Hitchcock movie, but even after Ellie tried to shift her attention to the television, her mind refused to leave thoughts of Matt and the wife who had deserted him with a tiny daughter.

As much as she hated bringing up such an obviously painful topic, she had to admit she was grateful for the insight it provided into a man she was discovering she wanted to understand.

No wonder he sometimes seemed so gruff, so cold. Had he always been that way or had his wife's desertion hardened him? Had he once been like Jesse, all charm and flirtatiousness? She couldn't imagine it. Good grief, the man was devastating enough with his habitual scowl!

After a moment, Cassie turned the tables. "What

about Dylan's father?" she asked suddenly. "Is he still in the picture?"

"He was never *in* the picture. Not really," Ellie answered calmly. After so many years the scab over her heart had completely healed. "Our relationship ended when Kurt saw that plus sign on the pregnancy test."

He had been so furious at her for being stupid enough to get pregnant, as if it were entirely her fault the protection they used had failed. He could lose his job over this, he had hissed at her, that handsome, intelligent face dark with anger. Professors who impregnated their star students tended to be passed over when tenures were being tossed around. Didn't she understand what this could do to him?

It had always been about him. Always. She had only come to understand that immutable fact through the filter of time and experience. In the midst of their relationship, she had been so amazed that someone of Kurt's charisma—not to mention professional standing—would deign to take her under his wing, first as a mentor and adviser, then as a friend, then as a lover during her final year of undergraduate work.

She might have seen him more clearly had she not been seduced by the one thing she had needed so desperately those days—approbation. He had told her she had talent, that she would be a brilliant, dedicated doctor of veterinary medicine one day.

No one else had believed in her. She had fought so hard every step of the way, and he was the only one who seemed to think she could do it. She had lapped up his carefully doled-out praise like a puppy starving for attention.

She thought she had loved him passionately and had

given him everything she had, while to him she had been one more in a long string of silly, awestruck students.

It was a hard lesson, but her hurt and betrayal had lasted only until Dylan was born. As she held her child in her arms—hers alone—she realized she didn't care anymore what had led her to that moment; she was only amazed at the unconditional love she felt for her baby.

"So you raised Dylan completely on your own while you were finishing vet school?" Cassie asked.

She nodded. "I took her to class half the time because I couldn't find a sitter, but somehow we did it."

Cassie shook her head in sympathetic disgust. "Men are pigs, aren't they?" she muttered, just as Jesse entered the great room.

He plopped next to Ellie on the couch, scowling at his sister. "Hey, I resent that. Especially since it just took two of us the better part of an hour to clean up the mess *you* made in the kitchen."

"I meant that figuratively," she retorted. "When it comes to knowing what a woman needs and wants out of a relationship, most of you have about as much sense as a bucket of spit."

"Don't listen to her, Doc. My baby sister has always been far too cynical for her own good."

Jesse grabbed Ellie's hand, and for one horrified second she thought he was going to bring it to his lips. To her vast relief, he just squeezed it, looking deep into her eyes. "Not all men are pigs. I, for one, always give a woman exactly what she wants. And what she needs."

His knowing smile fell just a few inches short of a leer, and she felt hot color crawl across her cheekbones at finding herself on the receiving end of it, especially from a man as dangerously attractive as Jesse James Harte.

Before she could come up with a reply, his little sister gave an inelegant snort. "See? What did I tell you? A bucket of spit."

Ellie smiled, charmed beyond words by both of them and their easy acceptance of her. Before she could answer, she felt the heat of someone's gaze on her. She turned around and found Matt standing in the doorway, arms crossed and shoulder propped against the jamb as he watched his brother's flirting with an unreadable look in those vivid blue eyes.

The heated blush Jesse had sparked spread even higher, until she thought her face must look as bright as the autumn leaves in his sister's centerpiece.

What was it about that single look that sent her nerves lurching and tumbling to her stomach, that affected her a thousand times more intensely than Jesse's teasing?

His daughter spotted him at almost the same time she did. "Daddy, come play with us," she demanded from the pool table.

He shifted his gaze from Ellie to the girls, his mouth twisting into a soft smile that did funny, twirly things to her insides. "I will in a bit, Lucy Goose. I have to go out and check on Mystic first, okay?"

"Mystic?" Ellie's question came out as a squeak that nobody but her seemed to notice.

"One of our mares," Matt answered.

"Mystic Mountain Moon," Lucy said. "That's her full name."

"She's pregnant with her first foal and she's tried to lose it a couple times," Matt said.

"She's a real beauty." Cassie joined in. "Moon Ranger

out of Mystic Diamond Lil. One heck of a great cutting horse. Matt tried her out in a few local rodeos last summer, and she blew everybody away."

"Her foal's going to be a winner, too," Matt said. "If she can hang on to it for a few more months, anyway."

He paused and looked at Ellie again. "You, uh, wouldn't want to come out and check on her with me, would you?"

She stared at him, astonished at the awkward invitation, an offer she sensed surprised him as much as it had her. She opened her mouth to answer just as he shook his head. "I guess you're not really dressed to go mucking around in the barn. Forget it."

"No," she said quickly. "These boots are sturdier than they look. I would love to." She suddenly discovered she wanted fiercely to go with him, to see more of the Diamond Harte and his beauty of a mare.

"Let me just grab my coat." She jumped up before he could rescind the invitation. Whatever impulse had prompted him to ask her to accompany him, she sensed he was offering her more than just a visit to his barn. He was inviting her into this part of his life, lowering at least some of the walls between them.

She wasn't about to blow it.

"Okay then." He cast his eyes around the room for a moment as if trying to figure out what to do next, then his gaze stopped on his daughter, pool cue in her hand.

"We shouldn't be long," he said. "I promise I'll be back in just a little while to whup both of your behinds."

The girls barely heard him, Ellie saw, too busy sharing another one of those conspiratorial looks that were really beginning to make her nervous. "You two take your time, Dad," Lucy said in an exaggerated voice. "Really, we can use all the practice we can get."

He looked vaguely startled by her insistence, then gave her another one of those soft smiles before turning to Ellie. "I'll go get your coat."

A few moments later, he returned wearing that black Stetson and a heavy ranch jacket and holding out her coat. He helped her into it and then led the way into the snow that still fluttered down halfheartedly.

Though it was still technically afternoon, she had discovered night came early this time of year in Wyoming. The sun had already begun to sink behind the Salt River mountains, and the dying light was the same color as lilac blossoms in the spring.

Her chest ached at the loveliness of it, at the play of light on the skiff of snow and the rosy glow of his outbuildings in the twilight. There was a quiet reverence here as night descended on the mountains. As if no one else existed but the two of them and the snow and the night.

He seemed as reluctant as she to break the hushed beauty of the scene. They walked in silence toward the huge red barn a few hundred yards from the house. When he finally spoke, it was in a low voice to match the magic of the evening. "Mystic likes to be outside, even as cold as it's been. I'll check to see if she's still in the pasture before we go inside the barn. You can wait here if you want."

"No. I'll come with you," she said in that same hushed voice.

They crunched through snow to the other side, with Matt just a few steps ahead of her. She was looking at her feet so she didn't fall in the slick snow when he growled a harsh oath.

She jerked her gaze up. "What is it? What's wrong?"

He pointed to the pasture. For a moment, she couldn't figure out what had upset him, then her gaze sharpened and she saw it.

Bright red bloodstains speckled the snow in a vivid, ugly trail leading to the barn.

Chapter 7

Dread clutched at her stomach. "Do you think it was a coyote?"

"I doubt it," he said tersely. "Not this close to the house and not in the middle of the day. They tend to stay away from the horses, anyway."

"What, then?"

"Mystic, I'd guess. She's probably lost the foal. Damn."

If the mare was hemorrhaging already, it was probably too late to save the foal, and Matt obviously knew it as well as she did. He jumped the fence easily and followed the trail of blood. Without a moment's hesitation, she hiked her skirt above her knees and climbed over the snow-slicked rails as well, then quickly caught up with him.

With that frown and his jaw set, he looked hard and dangerous, like the Wild West outlaw he was named after.

"I'm sorry," she offered softly.

He blew out a breath. "It happens. Probably nothing we can do at this point. I had high hopes for Mystic's foal, though. The sire is one hell of a cutter, just like—"

Before he could finish the sentence, they heard a high, distressed whinny from inside the barn, and both picked up their pace to a run. He beat her inside, but she followed just a few seconds later. She had a quick impression of a clean, well-lit stall, then her attention immediately shifted to the misty-gray quarter horse pacing restlessly in the small space.

A quick visual check told her the blood they saw in the snow was from a large cut on the horse's belly, probably from kicking at herself in an attempt to rid her body of what she thought was bothering her—the foal.

It relieved her mind some, but not much. "She hasn't lost it yet," she said.

Matt looked distracted as he ran his hands over the horse. "She's going to, though, isn't she?"

"Probably. I'm sorry," she said again. She had seen the signs before. The sweat soaking the withers, the distress, the bared teeth as pain racked the mare.

All her professional instincts screamed at her to do something, not just stand here helplessly. To soothe, to heal. But Mystic wasn't hers to care for, and her owner didn't trust Ellie or her methods.

Still, she had to try. "Will you let me examine her?"

She held her breath as he studied her from across the stall, praying he would consent. The reluctance in his eyes shouldn't have hurt her. He had made no secret of his opinions. But she still had to dig her fingers into the wood rail at the deep, slicing pain.

He blew out a breath. "I don't know...."

"I'm a good vet, Matt. Please. Just let me look at her. I won't do anything against your wishes."

His hard, masculine face tense and worried, he studied Ellie for several seconds until Mystic broke away from him with another long, frantic whinny.

"Okay," Matt said finally. "Do what you can for her."

"My bag's in the pickup. It will just take me a minute to get it."

Her heart pounding, she ran as fast as she dared out of the barn and across the snow toward the house, cursing the constricting skirt as she went. This was exactly why she preferred to stick to jeans and work shirts. Of course she had to choose today, of all days, to go outside her comfort zone just for vanity's sake.

She slipped on a hidden patch of ice under the bare, spreading branches of a huge elm, and her legs almost went out from under her. At the last minute, she steadied herself on the trunk of the tree and paused for just an instant to catch her breath before hurrying on, anxious for the frightened little mare.

She hated seeing any animal in distress, always had. That was her first concern and the thought uppermost in her head. At the same time, on a smaller, purely selfish level that shamed her to admit it to herself, part of her wanted Matt to see firsthand that she knew what she was doing, that she would try anything in her power to save that foal.

At last she reached her truck, fumbled with the handle, then fought the urge to bang her head against it several times. Locked. Rats! And her keys were in her purse, inside the house.

With another oath at herself for not learning her lesson the night he had to thaw out her locks, she hurried up the porch steps and through the front door. She was rifling for her purse on the hall table, conscious that with every second of delay the foal's chances grew ever more dim, when Cassie walked out of the family room.

Matt's sister stopped short, frowning. "What is it? Is something wrong?"

"Mystic," Ellie answered grimly. "She's losing the foal. I'm just after my bag in the truck. Naturally, it's locked."

"Oh, no. What a relief that you're here, though! Can you save it?"

As she usually did before treating an animal, Ellie felt the heavy weight of responsibility settle on her shoulders. "I don't know. I'm going to try. Listen, we might be a while. Is Dylan okay in here without me?"

"Sure. She and Lucy have ganged up on Jess at the pool table. They haven't even noticed you've been gone. Is there anything I can do to help?"

Pray your stubborn brother will let me do more than look. Ellie kept the thought to herself and shook her head. "Just don't let Dylan eat too much pie."

She rushed out the door and down the steps to her truck and quickly unlocked it. Her leather backpack was behind the seat and, on impulse, she also picked up the bag with her sensors and acupuncture needles, then ran to the horse barn.

Matt had taken off his hat and ranch coat, she saw when her eyes once more adjusted to the dim light inside the barn, and he was doing his best to soothe the increasingly frantic animal.

The worry shadowing his eyes warmed her, even in the midst of her own tension. Matt Harte obviously cared deeply for the horse—all of his horses, judging by the modern, clean facilities he stabled them in—and her opinion of him went up another notch.

"Sorry it took so long." She immediately went to the sink to scrub. "Anything new happen while I was gone?"

"No. She's just as upset as she was before."

She snapped on a sterile pair of latex gloves and was pleased he had the sense to open the stall for her so she could keep them clean.

"What do you need me to do?" he asked, his voice pitched low to avoid upsetting the horse more than she already was.

"Can you hold her head for me?"

He nodded and obeyed, then scrutinized her closely as she approached the animal slowly, murmuring nonsense words as she went. Mystic, though still frantic at the tumult churning her insides, calmed enough to let Ellie examine her.

What she found heartened her. Although she could feel contractions rock the horse's belly, the foal hadn't begun to move through the birth canal. She pressed her stethoscope to the mare's side and heard the foal's heart beating loud and strong, if a little too fast.

"Can you tell what's going on?" Matt asked in that same low, soothing voice he used for the mare.

She spared a quick glance toward him. "My best guess is maybe she got into some mold or something and it's making her body try to flush itself of the fetus."

He clamped his teeth together, resignation in his eyes. "Can you give her something to ease the pain, then? Just until she delivers?"

"I could." She drew in a deep breath, her nerves kicking. "Or I can calm her down and try to save the foal."

He frowned. "How? I've been around horses all my life, certainly long enough to know there's not a damn thing you can do once a mare decides a foal has to go."

"Not with traditional Western medicine, you're right. But I've treated similar situations before, Matt. And saved several foals. I can't make any guarantees but I'd like to try."

His jaw tightened. "With your needles? No way."

She wanted to smack him for his old-school stubbornness. "I took an oath as a veterinarian. That I'll first do no harm, just like every other kind of medical doctor. I take it very seriously. It won't hurt her, I promise. And it might help save the foal's life where nothing else will."

Objections swamped his throat like spring runoff. He liked Ellie well enough as a person—too much, if he were completely honest with himself about it—but he wasn't too sure about her as a vet.

Her heart seemed to be in the right place, but the idea of her turning one of his horses into a pincushion didn't appeal to him whatsoever.

"If she's going to lose the foal anyway, what can it hurt to try?" she asked.

Across Mystic's withers, he gazed at Ellie and realized for the first time that she still wore the soft, pretty skirt she'd had on at dinner and those fancy leather boots. The boots were covered in who-knew-what, and a six-inch-wide bloodstain slashed across her skirt where she must have brushed up against Mystic's belly during the exam.

Ellie didn't seem to care a bit about her clothes, though. All her attention was focused on his mare. She genuinely thought she could save the foal—he could see the conviction blazing out of those sparkly green eyes—and that was the only thing that mattered to her right now.

Her confidence had him wavering. Like she said, what could it hurt to let her try?

A week ago he wouldn't have allowed it under any circumstances, would have still been convinced the whole acupuncture thing was a bunch of hooey. But he'd done a little reading up on the Internet lately and discovered the practice wasn't nearly as weird as he thought. Even the American Veterinary Association considered acupuncture an accepted method of care.

Mystic suddenly jerked hard against the bit and threw her head back, eyes wild with pain.

"Please, Matt. Just let me try."

What other choice did he have? The foal was going to die, and there was a chance Mystic would, too. He blew out a breath. "Be careful," he said gruffly. "She's a damn fine mare, and I don't want her hurt."

He watched carefully while she ran her hands over the animal one more time, then placed her finger at certain points, speaking quietly to both of them as she went.

"According to traditional Chinese veterinary acupuncture, each animal's body—and yours, too—has a network of meridians, with acupoints along that meridian that communicate with a specific organ," she said softly as she worked. "When a particular organ is out of balance, the related acupoints may become tender or show some other abnormality. That's what I'm looking for."

Mystic had a dozen or so needles in various places

when Ellie inserted one more and gave it a little twist. Mystic jumped and shuddered.

He was just about to call the whole blasted thing off and tell Ellie to get away from his horse when the mare's straining, panting sides suddenly went completely still.

After a moment, the horse blew out a snorting breath then pulled away from him. With the needles in her flesh still quivering like porcupine quills, she calmly ambled to her water trough and indulged in a long drink of water.

He stared after her, dumbfounded at how quickly she transformed from panic-stricken to tranquil. What the hell just happened here?

Ellie didn't seem nearly as astonished. She followed the horse and began removing the needles one by one, discarding them in a special plastic container she pulled out of her bag. When they were all collected, she cleaned and dressed the self-inflicted wounds on Mystic's belly, then ran her hands over the horse one last time before joining Matt on the other side of the stall.

"Is that it?" he asked, unable to keep the shock out of his voice.

Her mouth twisted into a smile. "What did you expect?"

"I don't know." He shook his head in amazement. "I've got to tell you, Doc, that was just about the damnedest thing I've ever seen."

Despite the circumstances, her low laugh sent heat flashing to his gut. "I had the same reaction the first time I saw an animal treated with acupuncture. Some animals respond so instantly it seems nothing short of a miracle. Not all do, but the first horse I saw responded exactly like Mystic just did."

"Was she another pregnant mare?"

"No. It was a racehorse that had suddenly gone lame. For the life of me, I couldn't figure out what was wrong. I tried everything I could think of to help him and nothing worked. He just got worse and worse. Finally, as a last-ditch effort before putting him down, the owners decided against my advice to call in another vet who practiced acupuncture.

"I thought they were completely nuts, but I decided to watch. One minute the vet was sticking in the needles, the next he opened the door and Galaxy took off into the pasture like a yearling, with no sign whatsoever of the lameness that had nearly ended his life. I called up and registered for the training course the next day."

Her face glowed when she talked about her work. Somehow it seemed to light up from the inside. She looked so pretty and passionate it was all he could do to keep from reaching across the few feet that separated them and drawing her into his arms.

"How does it work?" he asked, trying to distract himself from that soft smile and those sparkling eyes and the need suddenly pulsing through him.

"The Chinese believe health and energy are like a stream flowing downhill—if something blocks that flow, upsetting the body's natural balance, energy can dam up behind the blockage, causing illness and pain. The needles help guide the energy a different way, restoring the balance and allowing healing to begin."

"And you buy all that?"

She sent him a sidelong look, smiling a little at his skeptical voice. "It worked for Mystic, didn't it?"

He couldn't argue with that. The mare was happily munching grain from her feed bag.

"I'm not a zealot, Matt. I don't use acupuncture as a treatment in every situation. Sometimes traditional Western medicine without question is the best course of action. But sometimes a situation calls for something different. Something more."

"But doesn't it conflict with what you know of regular medicine? All that talk about energy and flow?"

"Sometimes. It was hard at first for me to reconcile the two. But I've since learned it's a balance. Like life."

She smiled again. "I can't explain it. I just know acupuncture has been practiced for six thousand years—on people as well as animals—and sometimes it works beautifully. One of my instructors used to say that if the only tool in your toolbox is a hammer, the whole world looks like a nail. I want to have as many tools in my toolbox as I possibly can."

"You love being a vet, don't you?"

She nodded. "It's all I've ever wanted."

"Why?" He was surprised to find he genuinely wanted to know. "What made you become one?"

She said nothing for several moments, her face pensive as she worked out an answer. He didn't mind, strangely content just watching her and listening to the low, soothing sounds of the barn.

Finally she broke the comfortable silence between them. "I wanted to help animals and I discovered I was good at it. Animals are uncomplicated. They give their love freely and without conditions. I was drawn to that."

Who in her life had put conditions on loving her? Dylan's father? He longed to ask but reminded himself it was none of his business.

"Did you overrun your house with pets when you were a kid?" he asked instead.

Her laugh sounded oddly hollow. "No. My mother never wanted the bother or the mess."

She was quiet for a moment, gazing at Mystic, who was resting quietly in the stall. He had the feeling Ellie was miles away, somewhere he couldn't even guess at.

"I take that back," she said slowly. "I had a dog once when I was ten. Sparky. A mongrel. Well, he wasn't really mine, he belonged to a kid at one of the…"

She looked at him suddenly, as if she'd forgotten he was there.

"At one of the foster homes I lived in," she continued stubbornly, her cheeks tinted a dusky rose. "But that didn't stop me from pretending he was mine."

Her defiant declaration broke his heart and helped a lot of things about her finally make sense. "You lived in many foster homes?"

"One is too many. And yeah, I did."

She was quiet again, and he thought for a moment she was done with the subject. And then she spoke in a quiet, unemotional voice that somehow affected him far more than tears or regrets would have.

"My dad was a long-haul trucker who took a load of artichokes to Florida when I was five and decided to stay. Without bothering to leave a forwarding address, of course. My mother was devastated. She couldn't even make a decision about what shampoo to use without a man in her life, so she climbed into a bottle and never climbed back out. I stayed with her for about a year and then child-protective services stepped in." She paused. "And you can stop looking at me like that."

"Like what?"

"Like you're feeling sorry for the poor little foster

girl playing make-believe with some other kid's dog." She lifted her chin. "I did just fine."

He didn't like this fragile tenderness twisting around inside him like a morning glory vine making itself at home where it wasn't wanted. Did not like it one single bit.

"I never said otherwise," he said gruffly.

"You didn't have to say a word. I can see what you're thinking clear as day in those big baby blues of yours. I've seen pity plenty of times—that's why I generally keep my mouth shut about my childhood. But I did just fine," she said again, more vehemently this time. "I've got a beautiful daughter, a job I love fiercely and now I get to live in one of the most beautiful places on earth. Not bad for a white-trash foster kid. I turned out okay."

"Which one of us are you trying to convince?"

Her glare would have melted plastic. "Neither. I know exactly where I've been and where I'm going. I'm very happy with my life and I really don't care what you think about me, Harte."

"Good. Then it won't bother you when I tell you I think about you all the time. Or that I'm overwhelmed that you'd be willing to wade through blood and muck in your best clothes to save one of my horses. Or—" he finished quietly "—when I tell you that I think you're just about the prettiest thing I've ever seen standing in my barn."

Somewhere in the middle of his speech her jaw sagged open and she stared at him, wide-eyed.

"Close your mouth, Doc," he murmured wryly.

She snapped it shut with a pop that echoed in the barn, and he gave a resigned sigh, knowing exactly what he was going to do.

He had a minute to think that this was about the stupidest thing he'd ever done, then his lips found hers and he stopped thinking, lost in the slick, warm welcome of her mouth.

For a moment after his mouth captured hers, Ellie could only stand motionless and stare at him, his face a breath away and those long, thick eyelashes shielding his glittering eyes from her view.

Matt Harte was kissing her! She wouldn't have been more shocked if all the horses in the stable had suddenly reared up and started singing Broadway show tunes as one.

And what a kiss it was. His mouth was hot and spicy, flavored with cinnamon and nutmeg. Pumpkin-pie sweet. He must have snuck a taste in the kitchen when he was cleaning up.

That was the last coherent thought she had before he slowly slid his mouth over hers, carefully, thoroughly, as if he didn't want to miss a single square inch.

Ellie completely forgot how to breathe. Liquid heat surged to her stomach, pooled there, then rushed through the rest of her body on a raging, storm-swollen river of desire.

Completely focused on his mouth and the incredible things the man knew what to do with it, she wasn't aware of her hands sliding to his chest until her fingers curled into the soft fabric of his sweater. Through the thick cotton, steel-hard muscles rippled and bunched beneath her hands, and she splayed them, fascinated by the leashed power there.

He groaned and pulled her more tightly against him, and his mouth shifted from leisurely exploring hers to conquering it, to searing his taste and touch on her senses.

His tongue dipped inside, and she welcomed it as his lean, muscular body pressed her against the stall. His heat warmed her, wrapped around and through her from the outside in, and she leaned against him.

How long had it been since she'd been held by a man like this, had hard male arms wrapped around her, snugging her against a broad male chest? Since she'd been made to feel small and feminine and *wanted?*

It shocked her that she couldn't remember, that every other kiss seemed to have faded into some distant corner of her mind, leaving only Matt Harte and his mouth and his hands.

Even if she *had* been able to recall any other kisses, she had a feeling they would pale into nothingness anyway compared to this. She certainly would have remembered something that made her feel as if she were riding a horse on a steep mountain trail with only air between her and heaven, as if the slightest false step would send her tumbling over the edge.

She'd been right.

The thought whispered through her dazed and jumbled mind, and she sighed. She had wondered that day in her office how Matt would go about kissing a woman and now she knew—slowly, carefully, completely absorbed in what he was doing, as if the fate of the entire world hinged on him kissing her exactly right.

Until she didn't have a thought left in her head except *more*.

She had no idea how long they stood there locked together. Time slowed to a crawl, then speeded up again in a whirling, mad rush.

She would have stayed there all night, lost in the amazing wonder of his mouth and his hands and his strength amid the rustle of hay and the low murmuring of horses—if she had her way, they would have stayed there until Christmas.

But just as she twisted her arms around the strong, tanned column of his neck to pull him even closer, her subconscious registered a sound that didn't belong. Girls' voices and high-pitched laughter outside the barn, then the rusty-hinged squeak of a door opening.

For one second they froze, still tightly entwined together, then Matt jerked away from her, his breathing ragged and harsh, just as both of their daughters rounded the corner of a stall bundled up like Eskimos against the cold.

"Hi." The girls chirped the word together.

Ellie thought she must have made some sound but she was too busy trying to grab hold of her wildly scrambled thoughts to know what it might have been.

"We came out to see if you might need any help," Lucy said.

Ellie darted a quick look at Matt and saw that he looked every bit as stunned as she felt, as if he'd just run smack up against one of those wood supports holding the roof in place.

"Is something wrong?" Dylan's brows furrowed as she studied them closely. "Did…did something happen to the foal?"

She'd forgotten all about Mystic. What kind of a veterinarian was she to completely abandon her duties while she tangled mouths with a man like Matt Harte? She jerked her gaze to the stall and was relieved to find the pregnant mare sleeping, her sides moving slowly and steadily with each breath. In a quick visual check, Ellie could see no outward sign of her earlier distress.

She rubbed her hands down her skirt—filthy beyond redemption, she feared—and forced a smile through the clutter of emotions tumbling through her. "I think she's going to be okay."

"And her foal, too?" Lucy asked, features creased with worry.

"And her foal, too."

Matt cleared his throat, looking at the girls and not at her. "Yeah, the crisis seems to be over, thanks to Doc Webster here."

"She's amazing, isn't she, Dad?" Lucy said. Awe that Ellie knew perfectly well she didn't deserve in his daughter's voice and shining in her soft powder-gray eyes.

Finally Matt met her gaze, and Ellie would have given a week's salary to know what he was thinking. The blasted man could hide his emotions better than a dog burying a soup bone. His features looked carved in granite, all blunt angles and rough planes.

After a few moments of that unnerving scrutiny, he turned to his daughter. "I'm beginning to think so," he murmured.

Nonplussed by the undercurrents of meaning in his voice, Ellie couldn't come up with an answer. She flashed him a quick look, and he returned it impassively.

"Are you sure you don't need our help?" Dylan asked.

She wavered for a moment, suddenly desperate for the buffer they provided between her and Matt. But it was cowardly to use them that way, and she knew it.

"No," she murmured. "I'd just like to stick around a little longer out here and make sure everything's all right. Both of you should go on back to the house where you can stay warm."

"Save us a piece of pie," Matt commanded.

Lucy grinned at her father. "Which kind? I think there are about ten different pies in there."

He appeared to give the matter serious thought, then smiled at her. "How about one of each?"

"Sure." She snickered. "And then I'll bring in a wheelbarrow to cart you around in since you'll be too full to move."

"Deal. Go on, then. It's chilly out here."

Dylan sent her mother another long, searching look, and Ellie pasted on what she hoped was a reassuring smile for her daughter. "It was sweet of you both to come out and check on Mystic, but what she really needs now is quiet and rest."

"Okay."

"But—" Lucy began, then her voice faltered as Dylan sent her a meaningful look.

"Come on. Let's go back inside," she said, in that funny voice she'd using lately. She grabbed Lucy's arm and urged her toward the door, leaving Ellie alone with Matt and the memory of the kiss that had left her feeling as if the whole world had just gone crazy.

Dylan clutched her glee to her chest only until they were outside the barn and she had carefully shut the door behind them, then she grabbed Lucy's coat, nearly toppling her into the snow. She pulled her into a tight hug and hopped them both around in wild circles. "Did you see that? Did you see it?"

"What? Mystic? She looked fine, like nothing had happened. Your mom is really something."

She gave Lucy a little shake. "No, silly! Didn't you see them? My mom and your dad?"

"Well, yeah. We just talked to them two seconds ago." Lucy looked at her as if her brain had slid out.

"Don't you get it, Lucy? This is huge. It's working! I know it's working! I think he kissed her!"

"Eww." Lucy's mouth twisted in disgust like Dylan had just made her eat an earwig.

"Come on, Luce. Grow up. They have to get mushy! It's part of the plan."

Her mouth dropped open like she'd never even considered the possibility. For a moment she stared at Dylan, then snapped her jaws shut. "How do you know? What makes you think they were kissing? They seemed just like normal."

Dylan thought of her mother's pink cheeks and the way Lucy's dad kept sneaking looks at Ellie when he didn't think any of them were watching him. "I don't know. I just think they were."

She wanted to yell and jump up and down and twirl around in circles with her arms wide until she got too dizzy and had to stop. A funny, sparkling excitement filled her chest, and she almost couldn't breathe around it. She was going to have a father, just like everybody else!

"I can't believe it. Our brilliant plan is working! Your dad likes her. I told you he would. He just needed the chance to get to know her."

She pulled Lucy toward her for another hug. "If your dad likes my mom enough to kiss her, it won't be long before he likes her enough to marry her. We're going to be sisters, Luce. I just know we are."

Lucy still couldn't seem to get over the kissing. Her face still looked all squishy and funny. "Now what?"

"I guess we keep doing what we're doing. Trying everything we can think of to push them together. Why mess with it when everything seems to be working out just like we planned?"

As soon as the girls left the barn, Ellie wished fiercely that she could slither out behind them. Or hide away among the hay bales. Or crawl into the nearest stall and bury her head in her hands.

Anything so she wouldn't have to face the tight-lipped man in front of her. Or so she wouldn't have to face herself and the weakness for soft-spoken, hard-eyed cowboys that had apparently been lurking inside her all this time without her knowledge.

And why was he glowering, anyway, like the whole bloody thing was her fault? He was the one who kissed *her.* She was an innocent victim, just standing here minding her own business.

And lusting over him, like she'd been doing for weeks.

The thought made her cringe inwardly. So she was attracted to him. So what? Who wouldn't be? The man was gorgeous. Big and masculine and gorgeous.

Anyway, it wasn't like she had begged him to kiss her. No, he'd done that all on his own. One minute they had been talking, the next thing she knew he pulled her into his arms without any advance warning and covered her mouth with his.

She shivered, remembering. The man kissed like he meant it. Her knees started to feel all wobbly again, but she sternly ordered them to behave. She had better things to do then go weak-kneed over a gruff, distrustful rancher who seemed content to remain mired in a rut of tradition.

Still, he *had* unbent enough to let her treat Mystic, despite his obvious misgivings. He deserved points for that, at least. Of course, then he had completely distracted her with a fiery kiss that washed all thoughts of her patient out of her head.

But no more. She took a deep breath. She had a job to do here. The mare wasn't out of the woods yet, and she needed to make sure Mystic didn't lose her foal. To do it, she needed to focus only on the horse and not on her owner.

"I'd better take another look at Mystic to make sure the contractions have completely stopped."

"You think she still might be in danger?"

"Like I told the girls, it's too early to say. We'll have to wait and see."

With a great deal of effort, she turned her back on him and focused on the horse again. Somehow she managed to put thoughts of that kiss out of her head enough to concentrate on what she was doing.

She was working so hard at it, centering all her energy on the horse, that she didn't hear Matt come up behind her until she turned to pick her stethoscope out of her bag and bumped into hard, immovable man.

She backed up until she butted against the horse and clutched her chest. "Oh. You startled me."

A muscle worked in his jaw. "Look, Doc. I owe you an apology. I had no business doing that."

She deliberately misconstrued his meaning. "Startling me? Don't worry about it. Just make a little more noise next time."

"No," he snapped impatiently. "You know that's not

what I mean. I'm talking about before. About what happened before the girls came in."

Heat soaked her cheekbones. "You don't have to worry about that, either."

He pressed doggedly forward. "I shouldn't have kissed you. It was crazy. Completely crazy. I, uh, don't know what came over me."

Uncontrollable lust? She seriously doubted it. Still, it wasn't very flattering for him to look as astounded at his own actions as a pup did when he found out his new best friend was a porcupine.

"You shouldn't have," she said as curtly, hoping he would let the whole thing drop.

Out of the corner of her gaze, she watched that muscle twitch along his jaw again, but the blasted man plodded forward stubbornly. "I apologize," he repeated. "It won't happen again."

"Good. Then let's get back to business."

"I just don't want what happened here to affect our working relationship."

"We don't have a working relationship, Matt. Not really. We're running a school carnival together, but that will be over in a few months. Then we can go back to ignoring each other."

"I'd like us to. Have a working relationship, I mean. And not just with the stupid Valentine's carnival, either." He paused. "The thing is, I was impressed by what you did for Mystic. Hell, who wouldn't have been impressed? It was amazing."

Okay, she could forgive him for calling their kiss crazy, she decided, as warmth rushed through her at the praise.

He rubbed a hand along Mystic's withers, avoiding

her gaze. "If you're interested, I'd like to contract with you to treat the rest of my horses."

She stared at him, stunned by the offer. "All of them?"

"Yeah. We generally have anywhere from twenty to thirty, depending on the time of the year. The ranch hands usually have at least a couple each in their remudas, and I usually pay for their care, too."

She was flabbergasted and couldn't seem to think straight. How could the man kiss her one minute, then calmly talk business the next while her hormones still lurched and bucked? It wasn't fair. She could barely keep a thought in her head, even ten minutes later. How was she supposed to have a coherent conversation about this?

"What about Steve?" she finally asked.

"Nichols is a competent vet." He paused, as if trying to figure out just the right words. "He's competent, but not passionate. Not like Ben. Or like you.

"Don't get me wrong," he added. "Steve does a good job with the cattle. But to be honest, I'm looking for a little more when it comes to my horses. I can't expect somebody to spend thirty thousand and up for a competition-quality cutter that's not completely healthy."

He smiled suddenly, and she felt as if she'd just been thrown off one of those champion cutters of his. "I'd like to have a veterinarian on staff who's not content with only one tool in her toolbox. What do you think?"

She blew out a breath, trying to process the twists and turns the day had taken. The chance to be the Diamond Harte's veterinarian was an opportunity she'd never even dared dream about. She couldn't pass it up, even if it meant working even more closely with Matt.

"Only your horses?" she asked warily. "Not the cattle?"

He shrugged. "Like I said, Steve seems to be handling that end of things all right."

Steve. She gave an inward wince. What would he think when she took the lucrative Diamond Harte contract from him? It would probably sting his pride, at the very least.

On the other hand, he had no qualms about doing the same thing to her countless times since she arrived in Star Valley. If she was going to run her own practice, she needed to start thinking like a businesswoman. They were friends but they were also competitors.

"Do we have a deal?" Matt asked.

How could she pass it up? This is what she wanted to do, why she'd traveled fifteen hundred miles and uprooted her daughter and risked everything she had. For chances like this. She nodded. "Sure. Sounds great. When do you want me to start?"

"Maybe you could come out sometime after the holiday weekend and get acquainted with the herd and their medical histories."

"Okay. Monday would work for me."

"We can work out the details then." He paused for a moment, then cleared his throat. "And, uh, if you're at all concerned about what happened here today, I swear it won't happen again. I was completely out of line—a line I won't be crossing again. You have my word on that."

She nodded and turned to Mystic, not wanting to dwell on all the reasons his declaration made her feel this pang of loss in her stomach.

Chapter 8

Hours later, Matt sat in his favorite leather wing chair in the darkened great room of the Diamond Harte, listening to the tired creaking of the old log walls and the crackle and hiss of the fire while he watched fat snowflakes drift lazily down outside the wide, uncurtained windows.

He loved this time of the night, when the house was quiet and he could finally have a moment to himself to think, without the phone ringing or Lucy asking for help with her math homework or Cassie hounding him about something or other.

Ellie Webster would probably call what he was doing something crazy and far-out, like meditating. He wouldn't go that far. His brain just seemed to work better when he didn't have a thousand things begging for attention.

When the weather was warm, he liked to sit on the

wide front porch, breathing the evening air and watching the stars come out one by one—either that or take one of the horses for a late-night ride along the trails that wound through the thousands of acres of Forest Service land above the ranch.

Most of his problems—both with the ranch and in his personal life—had been solved on the porch, on the back of a horse or in this very chair by the fire.

And he had plenty of problems to occupy his mind tonight.

Ellie and her daughter had gone home hours ago, but he swore if he breathed deeply enough he could still smell that sweet, citrusy scent of her—like lemons and sunshine—clinging subtly to his skin.

She had tasted the same way. Like a summer morning, all fresh and sweet and intoxicating. He thought of how she had felt in his arms, of the way her mouth had softened under his and the way her body melted into him like sherbet spilled on a hot sidewalk.

He only meant to kiss her for an instant. Just a brief experiment to satisfy his curiosity, to determine if the reality of kissing her could come anywhere close to his subconscious yearnings.

So much for good intentions.

He might have been content with only a taste—as tantalizing as it had been—but then she murmured his name when he kissed her.

He didn't think she was even aware of it, but he had heard it clearly. Just that hushed whisper against his mouth had sent need exploding through his system like a match set to a keg of gunpowder, and he had been lost.

What the hell had he been thinking? He wasn't the kind of guy to go around stealing kisses from women, especially prickly city vets who made it abundantly clear they weren't interested.

He'd been just as shocked as she was when he pulled her into his arms. And even more shocked when she responded to him, when she'd kissed him back and leaned into him for more.

He sipped at his drink and gazed out the window again. What was it about Ellie Webster that turned him inside out? She was beautiful, sure, with that fiery hair and those startling green eyes rimmed with silver.

It was more than that, though. He thought of the way she had talked so calmly and without emotion about her childhood, about being abandoned by both her parents and then spending the rest of her youth in foster homes.

She was a survivor.

He thought of his own childhood, of his dad teaching him to rope and his mom welcoming him home with a kiss on his cheek after school every day and bickering with Jess and Cassie over who got the biggest cookie.

Ellie had missed all that, and his chest ached when he thought of it and when he realized how she'd still managed to make a comfortable, happy life for her and her daughter.

Despite his earlier misconceptions, he was discovering that he actually liked her.

It had been a long time since he had genuinely liked a woman who wasn't related to him. Ellie was different, and that scared the hell out of him.

But any way he looked at it, kissing her had still been a damn fool thing to do.

He must be temporarily insane. A rational man would have run like the devil himself was riding his heels after being twisted into knots like that by a woman he shouldn't want and couldn't have.

But what did he do instead? Contract with her to take care of his horses, guaranteeing he'd see plenty of her in the coming weeks, even if it hadn't been for the stupid Valentine's carnival their girls had roped them into.

It was bound to be awkward. Wondering if she was thinking about their kiss, trying to put the blasted thing out of his own mind. He was a grown man, though, wasn't he? He could handle a little awkwardness, especially if it would benefit his horses.

And it would definitely do that. He'd meant it when he told her he'd never seen anything like what she'd done to Mystic. He never would have believed it if he hadn't seen it for himself. *Something* had happened in that barn while she was working on the horse. He wasn't the sort of man who believed in magic—in his own humble opinion, magic came from sweat and hard work—but what she had done with Mystic had been nothing short of miraculous.

Maybe that was one of the reasons for this confounded attraction he had for her—her wholehearted dedication to her job, to the animals she worked with. He respected it. If not for that, he probably wouldn't have decided to go with his gut and offer her the contract to care for all of his horses.

He had given up plenty of things for the good of the ranch in the years since his folks died. It shouldn't be that hard to put aside this strange attraction for a smart-mouthed little redhead with big green eyes and a stubborn streak a mile wide.

Especially since he knew nothing could ever come of it anyway.

The room suddenly seemed colder, somehow. Darker. Lonely.

Just the fire burning itself out, he told himself. He jumped up to throw another log onto it, then stood for a moment to watch the flames curl and seethe around it. It was an intoxicating thing, a fire on a snowy night. Almost as intoxicating as Ellie Webster's mouth.

Disgusted with himself for harping on a subject better left behind, he sighed heavily.

"Uh-oh. That sounded ominous."

He turned toward his sister's voice. She stood in the doorway, still dressed in her jeans and sweater. "You're up late," she said.

He shrugged. "Just enjoying the night. What about you? I thought you turned in hours ago."

"Forgot I left a load of towels in the washing machine this morning. I just came down to throw them in the dryer."

"I can do that for you. Go on to bed."

"I already did it. I was just on my way back upstairs."

She stood half in, half out of the room, her fingers drumming softly on the door frame. He sensed an odd restlessness in her tonight. Like a mare sniffing out greener pastures somewhere in the big wide world.

In another woman he might have called it melancholy, but Cassie had always been the calm one. The levelheaded one. The soft April rain to Jesse's wild, raging thunderstorm.

Tonight she practically radiated nervous energy, and it made him uneasy—made him want to stay out of her way until she worked out whatever was bothering her.

He couldn't do that, though. He loved her too much, owed her too much. If something was bugging her, he had an obligation to ferret it out then try to fix it.

"Why don't you come in and keep me company?" he invited.

"I don't want to bother you."

"No bother. Seems like we're always so busy I hardly ever get a chance to talk to you anymore."

She studied him for a moment, then moved into the room and took a seat on the couch, curling her long legs under her. "What were you thinking about when I came in that put that cranky look on your face?"

It wasn't tough for him to remember, since that stolen kiss in the barn with Ellie Webster had taken center stage in his brain for the last six hours. For one crazy moment, he debated telling Cassie about it. But he couldn't quite picture himself chatting about his love life—or lack thereof—with his little sister.

"Nothing important," he lied, and forced his features into a smile. Knowing how bullheaded she could be about some things—a lot like a certain redhead he didn't want to think about—he decided he'd better distract her. "What did Wade Lowry want when he called earlier?"

Cassie picked at the nubby fabric of the couch. "He wanted me to go cross-country skiing with him tomorrow into Yellowstone."

Could that be what had her so edgy? "Sounds like fun. What time are you leaving?"

He didn't miss the way her mouth pressed into a tight line or the way she avoided his gaze. "I'm not. I told him we had family plans tomorrow."

He frowned. "What plans? I don't know of any plans."

In the flickering light of the fire, he watched heat crawl up her cheekbones. "I thought I'd help you work with Gypsy Rose tomorrow," she mumbled. "Didn't you say you were going to start training her in the morning? You'll need another pair of hands."

And he could have used any one of the ranch hands, like he usually did. No, there was more to this than a desire to help him out with the horses.

"What's wrong with Lowry? He's not a bad guy. Goes to church, serves on the library board, is good with kids. The other ladies seem to like him well enough. And he seems to make a pretty good living with that guest ranch of his. He charges an arm and leg to the tourists who come to stay there, anyway. You could do a whole lot worse."

She made a face, like she used to do when Jess yanked on her hair. "Nothing's wrong with him. I just didn't feel like going with him tomorrow. Since when was it a crime to want to help your family?"

"It's not. But it's also not a crime to get out and do something fun for a change."

"I do plenty of fun things."

"Like what?"

"Cooking dinner today. That was fun. And going out on roundup with you. I love that. And taking care of Lucy. What greater joy could I find? My whole life is fun."

Every one of the things she mentioned had been for someone else. His hands curved around his glass as tension and guilt curled through him, just like they always did when it came to his baby sister and the sacrifices he had let her make. She needed more than cooking and cleaning for him and for Lucy.

"You can't give everything to us, Cass," he said quietly. "Save some part for yourself."

She sniffed. "I don't know what you're talking about."

She did, and they both knew it. They'd had this very conversation many times before. Just like always, he was left frustrated, knowing nothing he said would make her budge.

He opted for silence instead, and they sat quietly, listening to the fire and the night and the echo of words unsaid.

She was the first to break the silence. "Do you ever wonder if they're still together?" she said after several moments.

He peered at her over the rim of his glass. "If who are together?"

She made a frustrated sound. "Who do you think? Melanie and Slater."

His wife and her fiancé, who had run off together the week before Cassie's wedding. A whole host of emotions knifed through him. Betrayal. Guilt. Most of all sharp heartache for the sweet, deliriously happy girl his little sister had been before Melanie and that bastard Slater had shattered her life.

They rarely talked about that summer. About how they had both been shell-shocked for months, just going about the constant, grinding struggle to take care of the ranch and a tiny, helpless Lucy.

About how that love-struck young woman on the edge of a whole world full of possibilities had withdrawn from life, burying herself on the ranch to take care of her family.

"I don't waste energy thinking about it," he lied. "You shouldn't, either."

He didn't mean to make it sound like an order, but

it must have. Cassie flashed him an angry glare. "You can't control everything, big brother, as much as you might like to. I'll think about them if I want to think about them, and there's not a damn thing you can do about it."

"Aw, Cass. Why torture yourself? It'll be ten years this summer."

She stared stonily ahead. "*Get over it.* Is that what you mean?"

Was it? Had he gotten over Melanie? Whatever love he might have once thought he felt for her had shriveled into something bitter and ugly long before she left him. But he wasn't sure he could honestly say her desertion hadn't affected him, hadn't destroyed something vital and profound inside of him.

Maybe that was why he was so appalled to find himself kissing a city girl like Ellie Webster and for craving the taste of her mouth again so powerfully he couldn't think around it.

He looked at his sister, at her pretty blue eyes and the brown hair she kept ruthlessly short now and the hands that were always busy cooking and cleaning in her brother's house. He wanted so much more for her.

"You've got to let go, Cassie. You can't spend the rest of your life poking and prodding at the part of you that son of a bitch hurt. If you keep messing at it, it will never be able to heal. Not completely."

"I don't poke and prod," she snapped. "I hardly even think about Slater anymore. But I'm not like you, Matt. I'm sorry, but I can't just shove away my feelings and act like they never existed."

He drew in a breath at the sharp jab, and Cassie immediately lifted a hand to her mouth, her eyes horrified.

"Oh, Matt. I'm sorry. I shouldn't have said that. I should never have brought them up. Let's just drop it, okay?"

"Which brings us back to Wade Lowry. You need to go out more, Cass, meet more people. Give some other lucky guy a chance to steal you away from us."

She snorted. "Oh, you're a fine one to talk. When was the last time you went out on a date?"

She had him there. What would his sister say if she knew he'd stolen a kiss from the vet earlier in the barn? And that his body still churned and ached with need for her hours later? He took a sip of his drink, willing Ellie out of his mind once more.

Cassie suddenly sent him a sly look. "You know who would be really great for you? Ellie Webster."

He sputtered and coughed on his drink. "What?"

"Seriously. She's pretty, she's smart, she's funny. I really like her."

So did he, entirely too much.

"I think the two of you would be perfect together," Cassie said.

He refused to let his baser self think about exactly how perfect they might be together at least in one area of a relationship, judging by the way she had melted into his arms.

"Thanks for the romantic advice," he said gruffly, "but I think I'll stick to what I know. The ranch and the stock and Lucy. I don't have time for anything else."

She was quiet for a moment, then she grabbed his hand. "We're a sorry pair, aren't we? You're the one who told me not to put my life on hold. If I go skiing with Wade Lowry tomorrow, will you at least think about taking Ellie out somewhere? Maybe to dinner in Jackson or something?"

"Sure," he answered. "If you'll go skiing with Wade and promise to have a good time, I'll think about taking Doc Webster to dinner."

But thinking about it was absolutely the only thing he would do about it.

"So I'm off. I'll see you in the morning."

Ellie glanced up from her computer and found SueAnn in the doorway bundled into her coat and hat with that big, slouchy bag that was roomy enough to hide a heifer slung over her shoulder.

She blinked, trying to force her eyes to focus. "Is it six already?"

"Quarter past. Aren't you supposed to be heading out to the Diamond Harte pretty soon?"

"The carnival committee meeting doesn't start until seven. I should still have a little more time before I have to leave. I'm taking advantage of the quiet without Dylan to try to finish as much as I can of this journal article."

"She's with Lucy again?"

"Where else?"

Dylan had begged to ride the school bus home with her friend again. And since Ellie knew she would be able to pick her up when she went out to the ranch later in the evening, she gave in.

"I've got to turn this in by the end of the week if I want to have it considered for the next issue, and I'm way behind."

"I imagine you haven't had much time these last few weeks for much of anything but your patients, have you?"

Ellie knew her grin could have lit up the whole town of Salt River. "Isn't it something?"

"Amazing. We haven't had a spare second around here since Thanksgiving."

Christmas was only a few weeks away. The towns scattered throughout Star Valley gleamed and glittered. Everybody seemed to get into the spirit of the holiday—just about every ranch had some kind of decorations, from stars of Bethlehem on barn roofs to crèches in hay sheds to fir wreaths gracing barbed-wire fences. The other night she had even seen a tractor decorated with flashing lights.

With her heavy workload, Ellie hadn't had much time to enjoy it. She hadn't even gone Christmas shopping for Dylan. If she didn't hurry, there would be nothing left in any of the stores.

Still, she couldn't regret the last-minute rush. For the first time since she and Dylan had moved to Wyoming, she was beginning to feel like she had a chance at succeeding here, at making a life for the two of them.

Word had spread quickly after Thanksgiving about how she had saved Mystic's unborn foal and how Matt Harte had hired her to treat the rest of his champion horses.

She wasn't exactly sure how everyone had learned about it. She hadn't said a word to anyone, and Matt certainly didn't seem the type to blab his business all over town. But somehow the news had leaked out.

The Monday after the holiday, she'd barely been in the office ten minutes before her phone started ringing with other horse owners interested in knowing more about her methods and scheduling appointments for their animals.

She couldn't exactly say business was booming, but she was more busy than she ever expected to be a month ago. Ellie couldn't believe how rewarding she was finding it. It was everything she had always dreamed of—doing exactly what she loved.

"So how are the carnival plans going?"

She jerked her attention to SueAnn. "Good. We've got a really great crew working with us now. Barb Smith, Sandy Nielson, Terry McKay and Marni Clawson."

"That *is* a good committee. They'll take care of all the dirty work for you. And how's our favorite sexy rancher?"

She frowned at SueAnn's sly grin. "If you're talking about Matt Harte, I wouldn't know," she said brusquely. "I haven't seen much of him."

She wasn't disappointed, she told herself. Honestly, she wasn't. "He missed the last meeting, and every time I've gone out to treat his horses, he's had one of his ranch hands help me."

She'd only caught fleeting glimpses of him out at the Diamond Harte. If she didn't know better, she'd think he was avoiding her after their heated kiss in the barn. But he didn't strike her as the kind of man to run away from a little awkwardness.

"Well, you'll see him tonight. He can't very well miss a meeting when it's at his own house."

Ellie didn't even want to think about this wary anticipation curling through her at the thought.

After SueAnn left, Ellie tried to concentrate once more, but the words on the computer screen in front of her blurred together.

It was all SueAnn's fault for bringing up Matt. Ellie had tried for two weeks to keep him out of her mind, but the blasted man just kept popping in at all hours.

She couldn't seem to stop thinking about his smile or his blue eyes or the way he teased Lucy and Dylan.

Boy, she had it bad. One kiss and she completely lost all perspective. It had become increasingly difficult to remember all the reasons that kiss was a lousy idea and why it would never happen again.

She blew out a breath. No sense wasting her time sitting here when she wasn't accomplishing anything. She might as well head out early to the ranch. Maybe she could have a few minutes to talk to Matt and work this crazy longing out of her system.

After putting on her coat and locking up the clinic, she walked to her beat-up old truck, relishing the cold, invigorating air. With the winter solstice just around the corner, night came early to this corner of the world. Already, dozens of stars peppered the night sky like spangles on blue velvet. She paused for a moment, hands curled into her pockets against the cold and her breath puffing out in clouds as she craned her neck at the vast, glittering expanse above her.

The moon was full, pearly and bright. It glowed on the snowy landscape, turning everything pale.

She loved it here. The quiet pace, the wild mountains, the decent, hardworking people. Moving here had been just what she and Dylan had needed.

Humming off-key to the Garth Brooks Christmas CD SueAnn had been playing before she left, Ellie reached her truck. She didn't bother fishing for her keys, confident she'd left it unlocked. It had taken a while to break herself of the habit of locking the battered truck, but now she felt just like one of the locals.

Next thing she knew, she'd be calling everyone darlin' and wearing pearl-button shirts.

Laughing at herself, she swung open the door, then froze, her hand on the cracked vinyl of the handle.

Something was different. Very, very wrong.

Through the moonlight and the dim glow from the overhead dome, she saw something odd on the passenger seat, something that didn't quite belong here.

It took her a moment to realize what it was—the carcass of a cat, head lolled back in a death grimace and legs stiff with rigor mortis.

Icy cold knifed through her, and her pulse sounded loud and scattered in her ears. As if that wasn't horrifying enough to find in the cab of her truck, she could see a note stuck to the poor animal's side—fastened firmly into place with one of her acupuncture needles.

Her hands trembled like leaves in a hard wind as she reached for the slip of white paper and pulled it carefully away, needle and all, so she could hold it up to the dome light.

It was printed on plain computer paper and contained only five words in block capital letters, but they were enough to snatch away her breath and send shock and fear coiling through her stomach.

WE DON'T WANT YOU HERE.

Chapter 9

If somebody told him a month ago he would be hosting a gaggle of women chattering about decorations and refreshments and publicity, he probably would have decked them.

Matt sat in the corner of his dining room, afraid his eyes were going to glaze over any minute now. The only streamers he even wanted to *think* about were on the end of a fly rod.

The things he did for his kid! He only hoped when she was stretching her wings in rebellious teenagedom and thinking her dad was the most uncool person on the planet, she would look back on this whole carnival thing and appreciate the depth of his sacrifice for her.

At the far end of the big table, Ellie reached for her water glass, sipped at it quickly, then set it down hard enough that water sloshed over the top and splattered the legal pad in front of her.

For a moment, she didn't react, just stared at the spreading water stain. Finally he cleared his throat and handed down one of the napkins Cassie had set out to go with her walnut brownies before she took off to see a movie in town.

Ellie jolted when Terry McKay passed her the napkin. Her gaze flew up and collided with his. Heat soaked her cheeks, then she quickly turned her attention to sopping up the spill.

The only consolation Matt could find in the whole evening was that she seemed to feel just as out of place as he did, at least judging by her jumpy, distracted mood.

He supposed it was pretty petty of him to feel such glee at her obvious discomfort. But he liked knowing he wasn't the only one who didn't want to be stuck here.

Only half-listening to the conversation—centering on the crucial question of whether to sell tickets at the door or at each booth—he finally allowed himself the guilty pleasure of really looking at Ellie for the first time all evening.

She looked bright and pretty with her hair in some kind of a twisty style and a subtle shade of lipstick defining her mouth.

That mouth. Full and lush and enticing. He hadn't been able to stop thinking about it for two frustrating weeks. The way it had softened under his. The way those lips had opened for him, welcoming him into the hot, slick depths of her mouth. The way her tongue had ventured out tentatively to greet his.

Today it had been worse, much worse, knowing she

would be coming to the ranch for this meeting. His concentration had been shot all to hell. In the middle of stringing a fence line, he'd let go of the barbed wire and ended up taking a nasty gash out of his cheek.

Tonight wasn't much better. He couldn't concentrate on the meeting for the life of him. All he could think about was how she had felt in his arms. With an inward, resigned sigh, he tried to turn his attention to the conversation.

"I hope I have this kid before the carnival so I can help," Marni Clawson, wife of one of his high school buddies, was saying. "I would really hate to miss it."

"How much longer?" Sandy Nielson asked her with that goggly-eyed look women get when the talk centers on babies.

Marni smiled softly. "Three weeks. I'll tell you, I'm ready right now. I just want to get this over with. Speaking of which, you're all going to have to excuse me for a minute. These days my bladder's about the size of a teaspoon. I think I need to pee about every half hour."

Information he didn't need to know, thanks very much. All the women except Ellie laughed in sympathy. As heat crawled over his face, Matt felt as out of place as the town drunk in the middle of a church picnic.

Marni must have spotted his discomfort. She gave him an apologetic look. "Sorry, Matt."

"No problem," he said gruffly, praying the night would end soon.

As Marni slid back her chair, it squeaked loudly along the wood floor. Ellie jumped as if the sound had been a gunshot. She clutched the napkin in her hand so tightly her knuckles whitened.

He straightened in his chair, his gaze sharpening.

What the hell? He could see that what he had mistaken for simple restlessness was something more. Something edgier, darker.

She looked frightened.

Sensing his scrutiny again, she lifted her eyes from the papers in front of her. They stared at each other across the table for several seconds, his gaze probing and hers rimmed with more vulnerability than he'd ever seen there, then her lashes fluttered down and she veiled her green eyes from his view once more.

What happened? Who hurt you?

He almost blurted out the questions, then reined in the words. Not now, not here. He would wait until everyone else left, then force her to tell him what was going on.

He spent the rest of the evening tense and worried, amazed and more disconcerted than he wanted to admit at the powerful need coursing through him to protect her. To take care of her.

He didn't like the feeling. Not one bit. It reminded him painfully of all the emotions Melanie had stirred up in him the first time he met her, when they'd bumped into each other at a dingy little diner.

She'd had a black eye and had been running scared from a nasty boyfriend who had followed her to Denver from L.A. She'd needed rescuing and for some reason decided the hick cowboy from Wyoming was just the man to save her.

Matt flinched when he thought about how eagerly he'd stepped forward to do it, sucked under by a beautiful woman with a hard-luck story and helplessness in her eyes.

He didn't know if there really had been a nasty boyfriend at all or if it had been another of her lies. But Melanie had needed rescuing anyway, from herself more than anything.

Unfortunately, he'd failed, and his marriage had failed, too.

He pushed the thought away and focused on Ellie and that stark fear in her eyes.

Finally, when he wasn't sure he could stand the tension another moment, the meeting began to wrap up, and one by one the committee members walked into the cold, clear night, leaving him and Ellie alone in the dining room.

She rose and began clearing the napkins and glasses from the table with quick, jerky movements. "We've made a lot of headway tonight, don't you agree? I don't think we should have to meet again until February, right before the carnival."

She continued chattering about the meeting until he finally reached out and grabbed her arm. "Doc, stop."

She froze, and her gaze flashed to his once more. The raw emotions there made him swear.

"What's going on?"

She looked at the table, but not before he saw her mouth wobble, then she compressed it into a tight, uncompromising line. "I don't know what you're talking about."

"Come on, Ellie. Something's wrong. I can see it in your eyes."

"It's nothing. I'm just tired, that's all. It's been a hectic couple of weeks." She pasted on a smile that fell miles short of being genuine. "Thank you, by the way. I don't know how you did it, but you've single-handedly managed to convince people to give me a chance around here. I appreciate it, more than I can tell you."

"I didn't do anything other than let a few people know I'm now using you to treat my horses."

"You obviously have enough influence to make people think that what's okay for the Diamond Harte is okay for them."

He was arrogant enough to know what she said was true. That's why he'd tried to spread the word, whenever he had the chance, that he had contracted for Ellie's veterinary services, so business would pick up for her. It sounded like it had worked.

She picked up the dishes and headed for the kitchen with them, and he followed a moment after her.

"Shall I wash these?" she asked.

"No. I'll throw them in the dishwasher in a while."

"Okay. In that case, I'd better grab Dylan and head home." She looked about as thrilled by the idea as a calf on its way to be castrated.

"You could stay." His offer seemed to shock her as much as it did him. On reflection, though, he warmed to the idea. He didn't like thinking about her going home to her empty house, especially not when she was so obviously upset about something.

"It's late and bound to be icy out there," he said gruffly. "We have plenty of room—you and Dylan could both stay the night in one of the guest rooms and go home in the morning."

How could he have known that the idea of walking into her dark, empty house had been filling her with dread all night? What if she found another charming little warning there, as well? It would be so much worse with Dylan along when she discovered it.

Matt couldn't possibly know what was going on. He was picking up on her nervousness, on the anxiety she knew she had been unable to conceal.

For a moment she was tempted to confide in him. He knew the valley and its inhabitants far better than she did. Maybe he would know who might be capable of delivering such a macabre message.

It would be such a relief to share the burden with someone else, especially someone solid and reassuring like Matt, to let those strong shoulders take the weight of her worry....

She reined in the thought. She wasn't her mother. She wasn't the kind of woman to fall apart at the first hint of crisis, to act helpless and weak so that everyone else would have to take care of her. This was her problem, and she would deal with it.

"I appreciate the offer," she said abruptly, "but we'll be fine. My truck has four-wheel drive."

"Are you sure?"

"Positive."

He sighed heavily. "You are one stubborn woman. Did anybody ever tell you that?"

"A few times." She forced a smile.

"More than a few, I'd bet," he grumbled under his breath. "Since you're not going to budge, I guess we'd better round up Dylan so you two can hit the road."

He led the way up the stairs, then rapped softly on the door of Lucy's bedroom. Ellie couldn't hear any sound from inside. After a moment, Matt swung open the door. They found both girls tucked under a quilt at opposite ends of Lucy's ruffly pink bed, with their eyes closed and their breathing slow and even, apparently sound asleep.

It was oddly intimate standing shoulder-to-shoulder in the doorway watching over their respective children. She'd never done this with a man before and she found it enormously disconcerting.

She could feel the heat emanating from him and smell the leathery scent of his aftershave, and it made her more nervous than a hundred threatening letters.

"Do you think they're faking it?" Matt whispered.

"I wouldn't put it past them," she whispered back, trying to ignore the way his low voice set her stomach quivering. "I think they'd try anything for an extra sleepover."

She stepped forward, grateful for even that foot of space between them. "Dylan?" she called softly. "Come on, bug. Time to go home."

Neither girl so much as twitched an eyelid.

"At least let Dylan stay the night," Matt murmured. "It seems like a pretty dirty trick to wake the kid out of a good sleep just to drag her out in the cold."

"She's always sleeping over. I swear, she spends more time here than she does in her own bed."

"We don't mind. She's good for Lucy. I've got to run into town in the morning, and it would be no big deal for me to drop her back home on the way."

If she hadn't been so nervous about Dylan stumbling onto another grisly discovery like the one she had found in the truck earlier, she would have argued with him. She was dreading the idea of going home alone, but at least this way she wouldn't have to worry about Dylan, too.

"Are you sure?"

"Don't worry about it, Doc. She'll be fine."

With one more suspicious look to see if any fingers twitched or eyelids peeked open, Ellie backed out of the room and joined him in the hall.

"I can't shake the feeling that we're being conned," she said.

"So what? If this is an act, they're pretty good at it and deserve a reward. Wouldn't hurt them to have a sleepover."

"So you want to encourage your daughter's fraudulence?"

He smiled. "I'm just glad to see her doing normal kid things for a change. Lucy's always been too serious for her own good. Dylan's done wonders for her. She's a great kid."

She smiled, genuinely this time. "What mother doesn't want to hear that her child is great? I think she's pretty cool, too."

Their gazes locked, and suddenly his eyes kindled with something deeper that she didn't dare analyze. She dropped her gaze and felt her cheeks heat as she vividly remembered those stolen moments in his horse barn.

"I should be going," she said, her voice hoarse.

"I'll walk you out."

"That's not necessary," she began.

"I know. But I'm going to do it anyway."

How did a woman go up against a man who was about as intractable as the Salt River Range? With a sigh, she followed him down the stairs and to the great room for her coat.

"Here. Let me carry that for you," he said gruffly, and pointed to her bulky leather backpack that held everything from her planner to basic medical supplies.

She opened her mouth to argue that she carried it around by herself all the time, but she closed it at the defiant look on his face, like he was daring her to say something about it.

"Thank you," she murmured instead, handing it to him. She had to admit she found it kind of sweet, actually. Like when Joey Spiloza offered to carry her books home from school in the first grade.

She hadn't let him, of course, completely panicked at the idea of anyone at school knowing what a trash heap she lived in. Or worse, what if her mom wandered out to the sagging porch in her bathrobe, bleary-eyed and stinking like gin?

She pushed the memory away and walked into the cold, clear Wyoming night with Matt. He was silent and seemed distracted as they crunched through the snow, even after his little brindle Australian shepherd sidled up to him for some attention.

At her truck, he opened the door and she climbed inside.

"Well, thanks for everything," she said. "I guess I'll see you tomorrow when you drop off Dylan."

"Right. Be careful on the roads." He stood at the open truck door studying her out of those blue eyes that seemed to glow in the moonlight. His shoulders leaned forward slightly, and for one crazy moment, she thought he would kiss her again.

At the last moment, he jerked back. "Oh. Don't forget your bag."

She stopped breathing completely when he reached across her to set the backpack on the passenger side, and his arm brushed the curve of her breast. He probably didn't realize it since she was swaddled in a thick winter coat, but she did, in every single cell. To her horror, she could feel her hormones immediately snap to attention and her nipple bud to life.

Even leaning back until her spine pressed against the seat wasn't enough to escape him or the first physical contact between them since that heated kiss on Thanksgiving.

She could vaguely hear the crackling of paper under the backpack as he set it down on the seat. "Sorry. I set it on something." He shoved the pack toward the other door, leaning into her even more. "Is it important?"

She blinked, feeling slightly feverish. "What?"

"Whatever I tossed this onto. Here. Let me see."

She looked down and saw what he was reaching for, that damned note with the needle still stuck through it.

"What's this?"

"It's nothing." She made a futile grab for it, but he held it out of her reach and up to the dome light. When he lowered the note, his expression burned with anger.

"Where did you find this?"

"I told you, it's nothing."

"Dammit, Doc. Where did this come from?"

She took one more look at his face, then blew out a breath. Somehow she didn't think he was going to rest until he bullied the truth out of her. "Someone left it in my truck. I found it when I left the office before driving out here tonight. It was, um, impaled in the carcass of a cat."

His expression darkened even more, and he let out a long string of swearwords. "Who would do such a thing?"

"Obviously not the Salt River Welcome Wagon."

"Did you call Jess to report it?"

She shook her head. "It's just a stupid prank, Matt. I didn't see the need to call in the police."

"This is more than a prank. Anybody who would leave this for you to find must have a sick and twisted mind. I'll call Jesse and have him come out to the ranch to get the details from you. There's no question now of you going home. You'll stay the night."

She bristled at his high-handedness. "That's not necessary. I appreciate your concern but I'm fine. Honestly. I was a little shaky before but now I'm just mad. I'll call the police in the morning and deal with it then."

"Doc, I'm not letting you go home alone tonight. Not after this. A person sick enough to torment you with something as warped as this could be capable of anything. Think about what's best for Dylan if you won't think about yourself."

He picked up her backpack as if the matter were settled, and Ellie pursed her lips. She had two choices, as she saw it. She could start the truck and make a run for it or she could follow him inside the house.

After his brother arrived, she would have backup. He'd have a tough time keeping her there against her will with a cop on the premises, even if the cop happened to be his brother.

Inside, he took off her coat and settled her into a chair as if she were too fragile to take care of herself.

"Tell me what happened. Could you tell if your truck had been broken into?"

She flinched. In the city this never would have happened. This is what she deserved for trying so hard to fit in. "No," she mumbled. "I left it unlocked."

"And you saw the dead cat when you opened the door?"

She nodded. "It was a little hard to miss there on the passenger's seat, with the note pinned between the third and forth ribs on the left side."

Storm clouds gathered on his features again, making him look hard and mad and dangerous. "Where's the cat now?"

"I took it inside the clinic. I'll autopsy it in the morning to try to figure out cause of death. From an initial exam, it looked like it was a feral cat that died of natural causes, but I'll know more tomorrow after I've had a chance to take a closer look."

He took a moment to digest the information, then frowned again. "Who would do this? Do you have any enemies?"

"Believe me, I've racked my brain all evening trying to figure it out. I honestly don't know."

"You been in any fights lately?"

"Yeah," she said dryly. "Didn't you hear? I went four rounds with Stone Cold Steve Austin in the produce aisle of the supermarket just last week."

"Seriously. Can't you think of anyone who might have done this?"

She shrugged. "I've had a few little disagreements with ranchers over treatment of their animals. It's part of the territory. Just business as usual for a vet."

"What kind of disagreements?"

"Well, for one thing, you'd be amazed at some of the conditions people think are perfectly okay for their animals. I'd like to see some of them try to stay healthy when they're living knee-deep in manure. And then they think it's their vet's fault if their animals don't thrive."

"How heated did these little disagreements get?"

"Not hot enough for something like this."

"Well, I still think you better come up with a few names for Jess to check out. Some of these old-timers are set in their ways and don't like an outsider coming in and telling them how to take care of their animals."

Outsider. The word stung like vinegar poured on a cut. How long would it take before she was no longer considered a foreigner in Star Valley? Would that day ever come?

She didn't bother to point out the obvious to Matt—that, for the most part, he still had the exact same attitude. Before she could come up with a nonconfrontational answer, they heard a car door slam.

"That will be Jess," Matt said, a few seconds before his brother burst into the kitchen.

"It's about damn time," Matt snapped. "Where have you been?"

The police chief snorted. "Give me a break. You couldn't have called more than ten minutes ago. What do you want from me? The department's Bronco only goes up to a hundred twenty."

Before Matt could growl out a rejoinder, Ellie rose, stepping forward in an instinctive effort to keep the peace between the brothers. "Thank you for coming out, Jesse, although it's really not necessary. I told your brother we could have done this in the morning."

Jesse immediately shifted his attention to her. To her complete shock, he reached both arms out and folded her into a comforting hug as if they'd been friends for years. "I'm so sorry you had to go through something like this. How are you holding up, sweetheart?"

She stepped away, flustered and touched at once, in time to catch Matt glare at his brother and Jesse return it with a raised eyebrow and a look she could only call speculative.

"Fine," she said quickly. "As I tried repeatedly to tell your brother, I'm really okay. He won't listen to me."

"Matt's a hardheaded son of a gun. Always has been." Jesse grinned at her, then removed his hat and coat and hung them on the rack by the door before making a detour to the fridge.

"I'm starving. Been on since noon. Anything I can eat while Ellie gives her statement?" he asked his older brother.

Matt scowled. "This is serious. Feed your face on your own time."

Jesse ignored him and pulled out a plastic-wrap-covered plate. "Here we go. Cassie's incredible fried chicken. The woman's an angel."

He set the plate on the table, straddled a chair, then nodded to Ellie. "Okay. I'm ready. Why don't you tell me what's been going on? Start at the beginning."

Her mind felt as scattered as dandelion fluff on a windy day, and for a moment she gazed at the two brothers as she tried to collect her thoughts. That didn't help at all. The two of them together in such close proximity were nothing short of breathtaking.

She'd never considered herself a particularly giddy kind of female, but any woman who said her pulse didn't beat a little harder around the Harte brothers—with their dark good looks and those dangerous eyes—would have to be lying.

Matt was definitely the more solemn of the two. There was a hardness about him his younger brother lacked. Jess certainly smiled more often, but she thought she had seen old pain flash a few times in his eyes, like at the dinner table the other day when the talk had turned to their parents.

"Anytime here, Doc."

She pursed her lips at Matt's impatience, but quickly filled the police chief in on what had happened, only pausing a few times to glare at his brother for interrupting.

"I still think it's a prank, nothing more," she finished. "Just a really ghoulish one."

"Hmm. I don't know." Jesse wiped his mouth with a napkin. "The only thing I can do at this point is check out these names you've given me and maybe something will shake out. In the meantime—"

The radio clipped to his belt suddenly squawked static. With an oath, Jesse pulled it out and pressed a button. Then Ellie heard a disembodied voice advising of a rollover accident on U.S. 89 with multiple injuries.

Jesse rose with surprising speed from the chair. "Shoot. I've got to run out to that. We're shorthanded, and the only other officer on patrol is J. B. Nesmith. He won't be able to handle this one on his own. Sorry, Ellie. I was going to tell you to be extra cautious at home and at the clinic. I'll try to have my officers keep an eye on both places whenever they can while the investigation is ongoing."

He shrugged into his coat and shoved on his hat. "Promise you'll call right away if anything else unusual happens. Anything at all." He gave her another quick hug, then rushed out, snagging a leftover brownie as he went.

Chapter 10

The subtle tension simmering between her and Matt had eased somewhat while Jesse was there. After he walked out of the kitchen and left them alone once more, her nerves started humming again like power lines in the wind.

She blew out a quick breath and picked up her backpack from the table. "I think I'll just head home now, too."

Matt's frown creased the weathered corners of his mouth. "I thought we agreed it would be best for you to stay here tonight."

"*We* didn't agree on anything." She stared him down. "You made a proclamation and expected me to simply abide by your word."

He gave her a disgusted look. "I swear, you are the stubbornest damn woman I have ever met."

"That's why you like me so much." She smiled sweetly.

For one sizzling moment he studied her, a strange, glittery light in his eyes. "Oh, is that why?" he finally murmured.

Heat skimmed through her, and she gripped her bag more tightly. She found it completely unfair that he could disarm her with a look, that he could make her insides go all soft and gooey without even trying.

"Please stay, Doc. Just for tonight. You know, if you went home I'd spend the whole night worrying about you, and I've got a horse to train in the morning. You wouldn't want me to make some dumb mistake and ruin her just because I didn't get any sleep, would you?"

"Nice try, cowboy."

He flashed a quick smile that sent her heartbeat into overdrive. "Humor me. It would make me feel a whole lot better knowing you're not at that house by yourself after what happened tonight."

She gave a disgruntled sigh. How could she continue to argue with him when he was being so sweet and protective?

On the other hand, she thoroughly despised this insidious need curling through her to crawl right into his arms and let him take all her worry and stress onto those wide, powerful shoulders.

She could take care of herself. Hadn't she spent most of her life proving it? She wasn't her mother. She didn't need a man to make her feel whole, to smooth the jagged edges of her life.

She could do that all by herself.

"Come on." He rose and headed for the door. "I'll show you to one of the guest rooms."

She looked at the stubborn set of his jaw and sighed. Like water on sandstone, he wasn't going to give up until he totally wore her down. Either that or he would probably insist on following her home and inspecting every single inch of her house for imaginary bogeymen before he could be satisfied it was safe.

The idea of him invading her home—her personal space—with all that masculine intensity was far more disturbing to her peace of mind than spending the night in his guest room.

"This isn't necessary," she grumbled.

"It is for me." He didn't bother to turn around.

She huffed out a disgruntled breath. She would spend this one night in his guest room and then she was going to do her best to stay as far away from Matt Harte as she possibly could, given the facts that Salt River had only five thousand residents, that she was contracted to treat his animals and that they had to plan a carnival together.

He was as dangerous to her heart as his outlaw namesake to an unprotected pile of gold.

The blasted woman wouldn't leave him alone.

Matt jerked the chute up with much more force than necessary. No matter how much he tried to stay away from her, to thrust her from his mind, she somehow managed to work herself right into his thoughts anyway. He couldn't shake her loose to save his life.

Ever since the week before when she had stayed at the ranch, his mind had been filled with the scent of her and the way she had looked in the morning at the kitchen table eating breakfast and laughing with Cassie and the girls. Fresh and clean and so pretty he had stood in the doorway staring at her for what felt like hours.

She haunted his thoughts all day long—and the nights were worse. Try as he might, he couldn't stop thinking about the taste of her mouth and the way she had melted in his arms.

This, though. This was getting ridiculous. He damn well ought to be able to find a little peace from the woman while he was in the middle of checking the pre-natal conditions of his pregnant cows.

But here was Steve Nichols bringing her up while he had one hand inside a bawling heifer. "You hear what happened to Ellie last week?" he asked over his shoulder.

Matt scowled at her name and at the reminder of the grisly offering left in her truck. "Yeah. I heard."

Nichols's blond mustache twitched with his frown. "Your brother have any leads?"

"Not yet. Ellie thinks it's just a prank."

The vet looked at him. "But you don't?"

He shrugged. "I think whoever is capable of doing something like that is one sick son of a bitch."

But a canny one, Matt acknowledged. One who knew how to lay low. Nothing out of the ordinary had happened in the week since she'd found the dead cat in her truck—a stray that, she learned during an autopsy, had indeed died of a natural cause, feline leukemia.

To be cautious, Ellie had installed an extra lock at her house and had hired Junior Zabrinzki's security company to check on the clinic during the night. So far, everything had been quiet, although she still claimed that she sometimes had the eerie feeling someone was watching over her shoulder.

He didn't know any of this firsthand. He'd only seen Ellie once since she had stayed at the ranch, the day before, when she'd come out to treat some of his horses. Despite his best efforts to pry information out of her, somehow the contrary woman managed to steer every single conversation back to his animals.

Good thing his little brother was the chief of police. If he hadn't forced Jesse to give him regular progress reports on the investigation, he would have been a whole lot more annoyed at Ellie.

Progress was far too optimistic a word, though, from the reports he'd been getting. Jess was still as stumped by the threat as he'd been that first night, and Matt was getting pretty impatient about it.

"You talk to a lot of ranchers around here," he said suddenly to Nichols. "You have any ideas who might be angry enough at Ellie to threaten her like that?"

Steve shook his head, regret in his eyes. "I wish I did, but I'm as baffled as anybody else. I know she's had a rough time of it with some of the old-timers. Ellie's not exactly afraid to speak her mind when she sees things she doesn't like and, I have to admit, some of her ideas are a little out there. But I really thought things had been better for her in the last month or so."

He had to give Nichols credit for not showing any sign that he minded Ellie's presence in Star Valley. He wasn't sure he would have been so gracious in the same circumstances if a rival suddenly moved in to his business turf.

"I'd sure like to find out who it is, though," Steve said, his voice tight and his movements jerky. "It kills me to think about her finding something as sick as that.

Of being so frightened. Ellie's a good vet and a wonderful person. She didn't deserve that."

Matt sent the other man a swift look, surprised by his vehemence. Maybe it was just professional respect, but somehow he didn't think so. Nichols acted more like a man with a personal stake in her business.

Did the two of them have a thing going? The thought left a taste in his mouth about as pleasant as rotten crab apples, and he had a sudden, savage urge to pound something.

But what business was it of his if she was seeing Steve? He had no claim on her, none at all. They were friends, nothing more. And not even very good friends at that.

Did she kiss Nichols with the same fiery passion she'd shown him? he wondered, then instantly regretted it.

"The investigation is still open," he said tersely. "Sooner or later Jess will get to the bottom of it."

"I hope so. I really hope so."

They turned to the cows and were running the last heifer through the chute when Hector Aguella hurried into the pens, his dark, weathered face taut with worry. "Boss, I think we got a problem."

"What's up?"

"Some of the horses, they're acting real strange. Like they got into some bad feed or something. I don't know. They're all shaking and got ugly stuff coming out their noses."

"How many?"

"Six, maybe. You better take a look."

"I'll come with you," Nichols said.

The noonday sun glared off the snow as he and Steve

headed toward the horse pasture. When they were close enough to see what was happening, Matt growled an oath.

Even from here, it was obvious the horses were sick. They stood in listless little groups, noses running and tremors shaking their bodies.

"Call Doc Webster and get her out here fast," he ordered Hector, breaking into a run. "And send Jim and Monte over to help me separate the healthy animals from the sick ones. If this is some kind of epidemic, I don't want to lose the whole damn herd."

"Do you want me to examine them?" Nichols called after him.

He hesitated for only a moment. Technically, the horses were Ellie's territory, but it seemed idiotic to refuse the other vet's offer of help when it could be an hour or more before she arrived at the ranch. "Yeah. Thanks."

With the help of the ranch hands, they quickly moved the animals who weren't showing any sign of sickness to a different pasture, then Steve began taking temperatures and doing quick physical exams.

"What do you think they've got?" Matt asked after the vet had looked at the last sick horse.

Steve scratched his head where thinning hair met scalp. "I've never seen anything like this. It looks like some kind of staph infection. They've all got the same big, oozing abscess."

"What kind?"

"I don't know. Whatever it is, it's hit them all the same. They've all got fevers, runny noses and chills. We'll have to run a culture to find out for sure. Whatever it is, it's damn scary if it can cause these symptoms to come on so fast. You said they were fine yesterday, right?"

"Yeah. I didn't notice anything unusual. So you're thinking a bacterial infection? Not something they ate?"

"That's what it looks like. I'm concerned about the abscess."

"How could something like that have hit them all at the same time?"

"I don't know." Steve paused. "When I was in vet school I heard about a herd getting something similar to this. Same symptoms, anyway."

"What was the cause there?"

"If I remember right, it was traced to unsanitary syringes used for vaccinations. Ellie hasn't given them any shots lately, has she?"

"She was out yesterday, but all she did was that acupuncture stuff on some of the mares to ease some of their pregnancy discomfort." He stopped, an ugly suspicion taking root.

Yesterday. Ellie had been here yesterday with her needles. Could she have done something that caused the animals to become deathly ill? Could she have used bad needles or something?

He couldn't believe it—didn't *want* to believe it. But it was one hell of a coincidence. He pushed the thought away. Now wasn't the time for accusations and blame. Not when his horses needed treatment. "So what can we do?"

"Push high dosages of penicillin and wait and see. That's about all we can do for the time being."

"You got any antibiotics with you?"

"Not much but enough, I think. It's in my truck over by the chutes. Let's hope it's the right one. I'll run a culture as soon as I can so we'll know better what we're dealing with."

He was only gone a few moments when Ellie's rattletrap of a pickup pulled up, and she emerged from it flushed and breathless.

"What's happening? Hector said you've got an emergency but he didn't say what. Is it Mystic? Is she threatening to lose the foal again?"

Before he could answer, her gaze landed on the horses, still shuddering with chills, and all color leached from her face. "Holy cow. What happened to them?"

"You tell me," Matt growled.

She sent him a startled look. "I...I can't know that without a thorough examination. How long have they been like this?"

Faster than a wildfire consuming dry brush, anger scorched through him—at her and at himself. He should have known better, dammit, than to let a pretty face convince him to go against his own judgment.

He should never have let her touch his stock with her wacky California ideas. He wouldn't have, except she had somehow beguiled him with her soft eyes and her stubborn chin and her hair that smelled like spring.

And now his horses were going to pay the price for his gullibility.

"What did you do to them?" He bit the words out.

She paled at the fury in his voice and stepped back half a pace. "What do you mean?"

"They were fine yesterday until you came out messing around with your New Age Chinese bull. What did you do?"

"Nothing I haven't done before. Just what you hired me to do, treat your horses."

She narrowed her green eyes at him suddenly. "Wait a minute. Are you blaming me for this? You think *I* caused whatever is making them sick?"

"Nichols says he thinks it's some kind of virulent bacterial infection. Maybe even—"

She interrupted him. "What does Steve have to do with this?"

"We were giving prenatal exams to the cows," he said impatiently. "He was with me when Hector came to tell us about the horses."

"And he thinks *I* infected these horses?"

"He said he's seen a similar case caused by infected syringes. The only needles these animals have seen in a month have been yours, Doc. You and your acupuncture baloney."

He refused to let himself be affected by the way her face paled and her eyes suddenly looked haunted. "You...you can't believe that's what caused this."

"You have any other ideas? Because from where I'm sitting, you're the most logical source."

She looked bewildered and lost and hurt, and he had to turn away to keep from reaching for her, to fold her into his arms and tell her everything would be okay.

"You can leave now," he said harshly, angry at himself for the impulse. "Steve is handling things from now on."

He had to hand it to her. She didn't back down, just tilted that chin of hers, all ready to take another one on the jaw. "We have a contract for another two months."

"Consider it void. You'll get your money, every penny of it, but I don't want you touching my horses again."

He drew a deep breath, trying to contain the fury

prowling through him like a caged beast. It wasn't just the horses. He could deal with her making a mistake, especially since the tiny corner of his brain that could still think rationally was convinced she would never willfully hurt his animals.

But he had trusted her. Had let himself begin to care for her. He had given her a chance despite his instincts to the contrary, and she had violated that trust by passing on a potentially deadly illness to six of his animals.

He refused to look at her, knowing he would weaken when he saw the hurt in her eyes. He was a fool when it came to women. An absolute idiot. First Melanie with her needy eyes and her lying tongue and now Ellie with her sweet-faced innocence.

She had suckered him into completely forgetting his responsibilities—that the ranch came first, not pretty red-haired veterinarians. He was thirty-six years old and he damn well should have known better.

"That's your decision, of course," she said quietly after a moment, her voice as thin and brittle as old glass. "I certainly understand. You have to do what you think is right for your animals. Goodbye, Matt."

She walked out of the barn, her shoulders stiffen with dignity. He watched her go for only a moment, then turned to his horses.

What was she doing?

Hours later, Ellie navigated the winding road to the Diamond Harte while the wipers struggled to keep the windshield clear of the thick, wet snow sloshing steadily down.

She should be home in bed on a snowy night like tonight, curled into herself and weeping for the loss of a reputation she had spent five months trying to establish in Salt River. A reputation that had crumbled like dry leaves in one miserable afternoon.

That's what she wanted to be doing, wallowing in a good, old-fashioned pity party. Instead, here she was at nearly midnight, her stomach a ball of nerves and the steering wheel slipping through her sweat-slicked hands.

Matt would be furious if he found her sneaking onto the Diamond Harte in the middle of the night. The way he had spoken to her earlier, she wouldn't be surprised if he called his brother to haul her off to jail.

But despite his order to stay away, she knew she needed to do this. Cassie had tried to reassure her that the horses' conditions had improved when Ellie called earlier in the evening, but it wasn't good enough. She would never be able to sleep until she could be sure the animals would pull through.

She couldn't believe this was happening, that in a single afternoon her whole world could shatter apart like a rickety fence in a strong wind.

Matt's horses had only been the first to fall ill. By mid-afternoon, she'd received calls from the three other ranches she'd visited the day before reporting that all the horses she had seen in the last forty-eight hours had come down with the same mysterious symptoms.

She'd done her best for the afflicted animals, treating them with high dosages of penicillin while she struggled exhaustively to convince the ranchers to continue allowing her to treat their stock.

And to convince herself this couldn't be her fault.

The evidence was mounting, though. And damning. It did indeed look like staph infection, centered near the entry marks where she had treated each horse with acupuncture the day before.

How could this be happening? She was so careful. Washing her hands twice as long as recommended, using only sterile needles from a reputable supplier.

Maybe she'd gotten a bad batch somehow, but she couldn't imagine how that was possible. Each needle came wrapped in a sterile package and was used only once.

The same questions had been racing themselves around and around in her head until she was dizzy from them, but she was no closer to figuring out how such a nightmare could have occurred.

Hard to believe the day before she'd felt on top of the world, had finally begun to think she had actually found a place she could belong here in Salt River.

All her dreams of making a stable, safe, fulfilling life for Dylan and for herself were falling apart. When this was over, she was very much afraid she would be lucky to find a job selling dog food, let alone continue practicing veterinary medicine anywhere in western Wyoming.

Every time she thought about the future, all she could focus on was this sick, greasy fear that she would have to sell the practice at a huge loss and go back to California and face all the smug people who would be so ready with I-told-you-so's.

She would have to leave the people she had come to care about here. SueAnn. Sarah McKenzie. Cassie Harte.

Matt.

Her chest hurt whenever she thought about him, about the way he had looked at her earlier in the day.

With contempt and repugnance, like she was something messy and disgusting stuck to the heel of his boot.

He shouldn't have had the power to wound her so deeply with only a look, and it scared her to death that he could. How had she come to care for him—for his opinion of her—so much?

He should mean nothing more to her than the rest of her clients. Only another rancher paying her to keep his horses healthy, that's all. So why couldn't she convince her heart?

The pickup's old tires slid suddenly on a patch of black ice hidden beneath the few inches of snow covering the road, and panic skittered through her for the few seconds it took the truck to find traction again. When it did, she blew out a breath and pushed away thoughts of Matt Harte and his chilling contempt for her. She needed to concentrate on the road, not on the disaster her life had turned into.

At the ranch, she pulled to the back of the horse barn, grateful it was far enough from the house that she could sneak in undetected. She climbed out of the truck on bones that felt brittle and achy and crunched through the ankle-deep snow to the door.

Inside, the horse barn was dark except for a low light burning near the far end where, she supposed, the sick mares were being kept. She made her way down the long row of stalls and was about halfway there when a broad-shouldered figure stepped out of the darkness and into the small circle of light.

Chapter 11

Matt.

Her heart stuttered in her chest, and for a moment she forgot to breathe, caught between a wild urge to turn around and run for the door in disgrace and a stubborn determination to stand her ground.

His little brindle-colored cow dog gave one sharp bark, then jumped up to greet her, tail wagging cheerfully. Ellie reached down and gave her a little pat, grateful at least somebody was happy to see her.

"Zoe, heel," he ordered.

With a sympathetic look in her brown eyes, the dog obeyed, slinking back to curl up at his feet once more.

"What are you doing here?" he asked.

Maybe it was wishful thinking on her part, but she could almost believe he sounded more resigned than angry to find her sneaking into his barn. At least he didn't sound quite ready to call the cops on her. That gave her enough courage to creep a few steps closer to that welcoming circle of light.

Behind him, she caught sight of a canvas cot and a rumpled sleeping bag. Matt had surrendered the comfort of his warm bed to stay the night in a musty old barn where he could be near his ailing horses.

The hard, painful casing around her heart began to crack a little, and she pressed a hand to her chest, inexplicably moved by this further evidence of what a good, caring man he was.

"Doc?" he prompted. "What are you doing here?"

She drew in a shaky breath. "I know you told me to stay away, but I couldn't. I…I just wanted to check on them."

"Cass said you called. Didn't you believe her when she told you the antibiotics seemed to be working?"

Heat crawled up her cheeks despite the chill of the barn. "I did. I just had to see for myself. I'm sorry. I know I have no right to be here. Not anymore. I won't touch them, I swear. Just look."

His jaw flexed but he didn't say anything and she took that as tacit permission. Turning her back on him, she slowly walked the way she had come, down the long line of stalls, giving each animal a visual exam.

As Cassie had reported, the infection seemed to have run its course. At least their symptoms seemed to have improved. Relief gushed over her, and she had to swallow hard against the choking tears that threatened.

"Delilah seems to have been hit the worst," Matt said just behind her, so close his breath rippled across her cheek. "She's still running a fever but it's dropped quite a bit from earlier."

Trying fiercely to ignore the prickles of awareness as he invaded her space, she followed the direction of his gaze to the dappled gray. "What are you putting on that abscess on her flank?"

He told her and she nodded. "Good. That should take care of it."

"Now that you mention it, it's probably time for another application." He picked up a small container of salve from the top rail of the fence and entered the stall.

Speaking softly to the horse, he rubbed the mixture onto the painful-looking sore, and Ellie watched, feeling useless. She hated this, being sidelined into the role of observer instead of being able to *do* something. It went against her nature to simply stand here and watch.

He finished quickly and crossed to the sink to wash his hands. An awkward silence descended between them, broken only by the soft rustling of hay. Matt was the first to break it. "How are all the other horses faring?" he asked.

"You know about the others?" Why did she feel this deep, ugly shame when she knew in her heart none of this could be her fault?

He nodded. "Nichols told me. Three other ranches, a dozen horses in all including my six."

She had to fight the urge to press her hand against her roiling stomach at the stark statistics. "Just call me Typhoid Mary."

To her surprise, instead of the disdain she expected to see, his eyes darkened with sympathy. "So how are they?" he asked.

"I lost one." Her voice strained as she tried to sound brisk and unaffected. "One of Bob Meyers's quarter horses. She was old and sickly anyway from an upper respiratory illness and just wasn't strong enough to fight off the infection, even after antibiotics."

Despite her best efforts, she could feel her chin wobble a little and she tightened her lips together to make it stop.

The blasted man never did as she expected. Instead of showing her scorn, he reached a hand out to give her shoulder a comforting squeeze, making her chin quiver even more.

"I'm sorry," he murmured.

She let herself lean into his strength for just a moment then subtly eased away. "I don't know what happened, Matt. I am so careful. Obsessively so. I always double scrub. Maybe I got a bad shipment of needles or something. I just don't know."

"It's eating you up inside, isn't it?"

"I became a vet to heal. And look what I've done!"

His fingers brushed her shoulder again. "You can't beat yourself up about it for the rest of your life."

He was silent for a moment, then sent her a sidelong glance. "I said some pretty nasty things to you earlier. Treated you a lot worse than you deserved. I'm sorry for that."

His brusquely worded apology fired straight to her heart. "You were worried about your horses."

"I was, but I still shouldn't have lashed out at you like that. I apologize."

"You have nothing to be sorry about. You had every right to be upset—I would have been if they were my horses. I understand completely that you want to bring Steve back on-board. He seems to have handled the situation exactly right."

He shrugged. "Well, they all seem to be doing okay

now. Mystic was the one I was most worried about, but she was eating fine tonight, and neither she or her foal seem to be suffering any ill effects."

Something in what he said briefly caught her attention, like a wrong note in a piano concerto. Before she could isolate it, he continued. "As for the others, I think we're out of the danger zone."

"But you decided to stay the night out here anyway."

He shrugged. It might have been a trick of the low lighting, but she could swear she saw color climbing up his cheeks. "It seemed like a good idea, just to be on the safe side."

"Well, I'm sorry I woke you."

"You didn't. I was just reading."

She looked over his shoulder and saw a well-worn copy of Owen Wister's *The Virginian* lying spine up on the army-green blanket covering the cot. "Apparently your father was not the only one interested in the Old West."

A wry smile touched his lips. "It's a classic, what can I say? The father of all Westerns."

She could drown in that smile, the way it creased at the edges of his mouth and softened his eyes and made him look years younger. She could stay here forever, just gazing at it....

"Wait a minute." The jarring note from before pounded louder in her head. "Wait a minute. Did you say Mystic was sick, too?"

He nodded and pointed to the stall behind them. Dust motes floated on the air, tiny gold flakes in the low light. Through them she could see the little mare asleep in the stall.

The implications exploded through her, and she

rushed to the stall for a better look. "I didn't treat her yesterday!" she exclaimed. "Don't you remember? I was going to. She was on my schedule. But I ran out of time and planned to come back later when I could spend more time with her."

"What does that have to do with anything?"

"Don't you get it? If Mystic came down with the same thing the others had, it can't be because of me, because of any staph infection I might have introduced through unsanitary needles, like Steve implied. I didn't even touch her yesterday!"

He frowned. "You did a few weeks ago."

"So why didn't she show symptoms of illness much earlier than yesterday, when all the other horses became sick?"

"Maybe it was some delayed reaction on her part. Just took it longer to hit her."

"No. That doesn't make sense. I've been through at least two boxes of needles since then. They couldn't have all been bad, or every single one of my patients would have the same illness. Don't you see? Something else caused this, not me!"

She wasn't thinking, caught up only in the exhilaration—this vast, consuming relief to realize she hadn't unknowingly released some deadly plague on her patients. If her brain had been functioning like it should have been, she certainly would never have thrown her arms around Matt in jubilation.

She only hugged him for a moment. As soon as reality intruded—when she felt the soft caress of his chamois shirt against her cheek and smelled the clean, male scent of him—she froze, mortified at her impulsiveness. Awareness began as a flutter in her stomach, a hitch in her breathing.

"Sorry," she mumbled and pulled away.

He stood awkwardly, arms still stiff at his sides, then moved to rest his elbows on the top rail of Mystic's stall to keep from reaching for her again. "We've still got twelve sick animals here, then. Any ideas why?"

"No. Nothing." She frowned. "Steve's right, it has all the signs of a bacterial infection, but it's like no other I've ever seen before. And how could it spread from your ranch to the rest that have been hit, unless by something I did? I seem to be the only common link."

"Maybe you tracked something on your boots somehow."

"I don't know of anything that could be this virulent in that kind of trace amount. And what about the abscesses?"

He had no more answers than she did, so he remained silent. After a long moment, she sighed. "The grim reality is, we might never know. I'll get some blood work done and send the rest of the needles from the same box to the lab and see what turns up. Who knows. We might get lucky and they can identify something we haven't even thought about. Something that's not even related to me."

"I hope so," he said gruffly.

He wasn't sure when the anger that had driven him all afternoon had begun to mellow, but eventually his common sense had won out. Even if she had spread the infection, he had no doubt it was accidental, something beyond her control.

She was a good vet who cared about her patients. She would never knowingly cause them harm.

"I really hope for your sake everything turns up clean," he said quietly.

She flashed him another one of those watery smiles that hid a wealth of emotions. This had to be killing her. It would be tough on any vet, but especially for one as passionate and dedicated as Ellie.

"Thanks." After a moment, she let out a deep breath. "It's late. I should go so you can get back to your book."

She didn't look very thrilled at the idea. Truth be told, she didn't look at all eager to walk out into the mucky snow. She looked lonely.

"Where's Dylan tonight?" he asked.

"At SueAnn's. I was afraid I'd get called out in the middle of the night to one of the other ranches and would have to leave her home alone. I really hate doing that, so Sue offered to take her for the night."

"You have no reason to rush off, then?"

She blinked. "No. Why?"

"You could stay. Keep me company."

Where the hell did that come from? He wanted to swallow the words as soon as they left his mouth, but it was too late now. She was already looking at him, as astounded as if he'd just offered to give her a make-over or something.

"You…you really want my company after today?"

The doubt in her voice just about did him in. He was such a pushover for a woman in distress. She only had to look at him out of those big, wounded eyes and he was lost, consumed with the need to take care of her—to relieve that tension from her shoulders, to tease a laugh or two out of her, to make her forget her troubles for a moment.

"Yeah," he said gruffly. "Come on. Sit down."

Still looking as wary as if she had just crawled in to a wolverine's den, she unzipped her coat and shrugged out of it. Underneath, she wore a daisy-yellow turtleneck covered by a fluffy navy polar fleece vest.

She looked young and fresh and sweet, and he suddenly realized what a disastrous error in judgment he had just committed. Why hadn't he shoved her out the door when he had the chance?

His control around her was shaky at the best of times. Here, alone in a dimly lit barn with only the soft murmur of animals and rustling of hay surrounding them, he hoped like hell he would be able to keep his hands off her.

She perched on the edge of his cot while he rounded up the old slat-backed wooden chair that probably dated back to his grandfather's day. He finally found it near the sink under a pile of old cattle magazines and carried it to the circle of light near the cot.

She was leafing through *The Virginian,* he saw after he sat down. Her smile was slow, almost shy. "I read this in high school English class. I remember how it made me want to cry. I think that's when I first decided I wanted to move to Wyoming. I'll have to see if the library in town has a copy I could read again."

"You can borrow that one when I'm finished if you want."

This time her smile came more quickly. "Thanks."

"It was one of my dad's favorites. He loved them all. Louis L'Amour, Zane Grey, Max Brand. All the good ones. During roundup when we were kids, he always kept a book tucked in his saddlebags to read to us by the glow of the campfire. We ate it up."

"You miss him, don't you?"

He thought of the gaping hole his parents' deaths had left in his life. "Yeah," he finally said. "We didn't always get along but he was a good man. Always willing to do anything for anyone. I'd be happy if I could die with people thinking I was half the man he was."

"Why didn't you get along?"

Zoe shoved her nose against his knee, and he gave her an obligatory pat, trying to form his answer. "Mom always said we were so much alike we brought out the worst in each other. I don't know. I thought he should have done more with the ranch. Expanded the operation, bid on more grazing rights so we could take on a bigger herd. I thought he didn't have any ambition. Took me a long time to realize he might not have seemed ambitious to his cocky eighteen-year-old son, but only because he didn't have to be. He didn't see the need to strive for more when he already had everything he wanted from life."

"Do you?"

His hand stilled on Zoe's ruff. "What?"

"Have everything you want?"

He used to think so. A month ago he would have said yes without hesitating. He had the ranch and Lucy and his family, and it should have been enough for him. Lately, though, he'd been restless for more. Hungry. He prowled around the house at night, edgy inside his skin.

A month ago he had kissed her just a few feet from here.

He pushed the memory away. That had nothing to do with it. Absolutely nothing.

"I'd like somebody to invent a horse that never needs shoes. But other than that, yeah. I guess I'm content."

It wasn't really a lie. Right now, at least, he was more relaxed than he'd been in a long time. He refused to dwell on exactly why that might be the case and whether it had anything to do with Ellie.

"I'd still like to expand the operation a little more, especially the cutting horse side of it. I guess you could say that's where my heart is, in training the horses. The cattle are the lifeblood for the ranch but for me, nothing compares to turning a green-broke horse into a savvy, competition-quality cutter."

He paused, waiting for her to respond. When she didn't, he peered through the dim light and realized he'd been baring his soul to the horses. Ellie was asleep, her head propped against the rough plank wall and her sable-tipped lashes fanned out over her cheeks.

He watched her sleep for several moments, struck again by how beautiful she was. In sleep, she couldn't hang on to that tough, take-it-on-the-chin facade she tried to show the world. Instead, she looked small and fragile, all luminous skin and delicate bones.

For just a moment, he had a wild, fierce wish that things could be different. That he was free to slide beside her on the cot and press his mouth to that fluttering pulse at the base of her neck. That he could waken her with slow, languid kisses then spend the rest of the night making love to her in the hushed secrecy of the barn.

As tempting as the idea was—and it had him shifting in the hard slat chair as blood surged to his groin— he knew it was impossible. In the first place, she likely wouldn't be too thrilled to wake up and find him slobbering all over her.

In the second, even if she didn't push him away, even if by some miracle she opened her arms to him, welcomed him with her mouth and her hands and her body, what the hell good would it do? It wouldn't change anything.

Now that she was asleep, he could admit to himself that she was the cause of this restlessness prowling inside his skin. But even if he were free to kiss her again, it couldn't change the indisputable fact that he had nothing to give her but a few heated moments of pleasure.

For a woman like Ellie, that would never be enough. He knew it instinctively, just as he suddenly feared making love with her once would only whet his hunger, leave him starving for more. Like a little kid who was only allowed one quick lick of a delectable ice-cream cone.

She was soft and gutsy and spirited, and if he wasn't damn careful, he could lose his heart to her. The thought scared him worse than being in the rodeo ring with a dozen angry bulls.

He'd been in that position once. He had loved Melanie in the beginning—or thought he did, anyway—and it had nearly destroyed him.

Here in the silent barn, he could see his ex-wife as clearly as if she were sitting beside him. Dark, curling hair, haunted gray eyes, features delicate as a porcelain doll.

She had been so unhappy from the very beginning. Nothing he did had been enough for her. If he brought her roses, she wanted orchids. If he took her to dinner, she would make some small, wistful comment about how much she enjoyed quiet evenings at home.

Everything had always been hot or cold with her. Either she was on fire for him and couldn't get enough or she wouldn't let him touch her, would screech at him to keep his rough, working hands to himself.

In retrospect, he could see all the signs of manic depression, but he'd been too young and too damn stubborn to admit then that she needed professional help. It had taken him years to realize he couldn't have saved her, that her unhappiness had been as much a part of her as her gray eyes.

When he couldn't fill the empty spot inside her, when he finally gave up trying, she had turned to other men, throwing her many conquests in his face at every opportunity. The first one had eaten him up inside, and he'd gone to the Renegade to beat the hell out of the unlucky cowhand. By the fourth or fifth affair, he told himself he didn't care.

He could still remember his cold fury when he found out she was pregnant, the bitter, hateful words they had flung at each other like sharp heavy stones.

At first he'd been afraid Lucy had been the product of one of her other relationships. The first time he held her, though, it had ceased to matter. He'd completely lost his heart to the chubby little girl with the big gray eyes, and he would have fought to the death if someone tried to take her from him.

But now, as Lucy grew into her looks, it became obvious she was a Harte through and through, from that dimple in her chin to her high cheekbones to her Cupid's bow of a mouth. She looked exactly like pictures of his mother at that age.

Something snapped inside Melanie after Lucy was born. It might have been postpartum depression, he didn't know, but everything she did had taken on a desperate edge. She'd spent every night haunting the Renegade in town, looking for trouble, trying to find some way out of Salt River, Wyoming. She'd found both in Zack Slater.

He blew out a breath. Why was he even thinking about this, about her? Maybe because Melanie was the reason he could never let another woman inside him. Why he would always be quick to fury and start throwing blame around, like he'd done with Ellie earlier that day.

He was afraid the wounds Melanie had carved in his soul would always make doubt and suspicion lurk just below the surface.

Ellie didn't deserve that. She deserved a man who could give her everything, especially the safe, secure home she'd never had as a kid. A man who could love her completely with a heart still whole and unscarred.

Whoa. Where did love fit in the picture? He didn't love her. No way. He was attracted to her and he admired certain qualities about her. Her resilience, her stubborn determination to succeed in the face of overwhelming adversity, her passion for her work. The same qualities that most irritated him, he admitted ruefully.

And he was fiercely attracted to her, no doubt about that.

But love? No way.

He shifted, trying to find a more comfortable spot on the unforgiving wood chair. He didn't want to think about this. He couldn't give her what she deserved so he had to settle for giving her nothing.

He knew it, had known it since he met her. So why did the realization make him so damned miserable?

He pushed away the thoughts. They weren't doing him any good. Instead, he turned his mind to the puzzle of the sick horses. What was the connection between them?

Ellie.

He wished he could be as convinced as she appeared to be that she had nothing to do with the sick horses. But what other link could there be? Like she'd said, the ranches that had been hit were miles apart and didn't appear to share anything else in common but their veterinarian.

Or at least they *had* shared Ellie. He had a feeling she would have a hard time keeping any clients unless she could prove without a doubt she wasn't to blame for the epidemic.

He would contract with her again to treat his horses. He had to. She would be devastated if she lost the practice. That and her kid were everything to her.

If someone wanted to destroy her practice, they had hit on the perfect method—shattering her reputation.

The thought had him sitting up straighter as he remembered the grisly message left in her truck. Someone out there didn't want her in Star Valley. If he was twisted enough to leave a dead cat in her truck, wouldn't he be capable of anything? Even something as sick and warped as harming a dozen innocent animals in order to implicate Ellie? To force her to leave by driving away her patients?

No. He couldn't believe it. Who would do such a thing? And how would anyone possibly manage it? Some of the animals might have been pastured near enough to roads or in distant enough corrals for someone to slip them something—maybe give them a shot without anyone noticing—but sneaking onto the Diamond Harte would be damn near impossible.

Still, it wouldn't hurt to mention the theory to Jess. If there was a connection between the sick horses and the warning note, his little brother would find it.

Ellie made a little sound in her sleep, drawing his attention again. She'd be a whole lot more comfortable under the blanket with her head on his pillow instead of sitting up like that.

Of course, then he'd be forced to find another place to sleep for the night.

He sighed and rose to his feet, then gently eased her to the cot, knowing he didn't have a choice. She didn't stir at all when he drew the heavy blanket over her shoulders and tucked it under her chin.

He returned to the hard wooden chair, leaned his head against the rough plank wall and watched her sleep for a long time.

Chapter 12

Ellie wasn't sure what awakened her. One moment she was dreaming of lying beside Matt Harte on a white-sand beach somewhere while a trade wind rustled the leaves on the palm trees around her and water lapped against the shore, and the next her senses were filled with the musty-sweet smell of hay and the soft, furtive rustling of the horses in their stalls.

She blinked for a moment, stuck in that hazy world between sleep and consciousness, and tried to remember why she wearing her clothes and curled up on a hard cot in someone's barn. Her back was stiff, her neck ached from sleeping in an odd position and she felt rumpled and uncomfortable in her Ropers and jeans.

She sat up, running a hand through tangled hair. As she did, her gaze landed on Matt across the dim, dusty barn, and the events of the night before came rushing back like the tide.

This was *his* barn. She was curled up in *his* makeshift bed.

Ellie winced and hit the light on her watch. Four a.m. She must have been sleeping for hours. The last time she remembered checking her watch had been midnight, when Matt had been talking about his horses.

Embarrassed guilt flooded through her. Not only had she been rude enough to drift off in the middle of their conversation, but she had fallen asleep in the man's bed, forcing him to sleep in that torturous hard-backed chair.

He couldn't possibly be comfortable, with his neck twisted and his head propped against the wall like that. But he was definitely asleep. His eyes didn't so much as flutter, and his chest moved evenly with each slow, deep breath.

She watched for a moment, hypnotized by the cotton rippling over his hard chest with the soft rise and fall of his breathing, then her gaze climbed higher, over the tanned column of his neck to roam across the rugged planes and angles of his face. The strong blade of a nose, the full, sensuous lips, the spike of his dark eyelashes.

He was sinfully gorgeous and completely one in his surroundings, like something out of a Charles Russell painting.

Had he watched *her* this way after she drifted off? The thought unnerved her, made her insides feel hot and liquid, but wasn't enough to compel her to turn away. Even though it was probably an invasion of his privacy, watching him like this was a temptation she couldn't resist.

In sleep, Matt lost the hard edges that made him

seem so tough and formidable. He looked younger, more relaxed, as if only in sleep was he free to shake the mantle of responsibility that had settled on his strong, capable shoulders so young.

What must it have been like for him after his parents died? She tried to imagine and couldn't. He had been twenty-two and suddenly responsible for a huge ranch and two troublesome, grieving younger siblings.

No wonder he seemed so remote and detached sometimes. He had grown up and become an adult at a time when many other young men were still having fraternity parties and taking trips to Fort Lauderdale for spring break. Instead of raising hell, Matt had raised his younger brother and sister.

And yet he had another side. She thought of the teasing grin he reserved for his daughter, the soft, soothing voice he used to calm a fractious horse, the woofs of a contented cow dog being stroked by his gentle hands.

He was so different from the perceptions she had formed about him that first day in Ms. McKenzie's classroom. Before then, even. She had thought him narrow-minded and humorless. Stuffy and set in his ways. But in the weeks since, she'd come to appreciate the many layers beneath that tough exterior. Hardworking rancher, devoted family man. Honest and well-respected member of the community. He was all those things and more.

It wouldn't take much for her to fall headlong in love with him.

The thought bulleted into her brain and completely staggered her. She paled, reaching for the edge of the cot to steady herself as a grim realization settled in her heart.

She was already more than halfway there.

She shivered, suddenly chilled to the bone despite the blanket he must have thrown across her knees.

How had she let things go so far? After her disastrous relationship with Kurt, she had been so diligent. So fiercely careful not to let anyone into her heart.

She didn't need anyone else—she and Dylan managed just fine, dammit.

Emotions like love were messy and complicated. They made a woman needy and vulnerable and stupid. Like her mother had been, like she had been with Kurt.

Besides, she had enough on her plate right now, trying to keep the practice alive and food in her daughter's mouth. She didn't have room in her life for a man, especially one like Matt Harte who would demand everything and more from her. He wasn't the kind of man who would be content to stay put in a neat little compartment of her life until she had time for him. He would want it all.

She could try to convince herself until she was blue in the face but it wouldn't change the fact that he had somehow managed to sneak into her heart when she wasn't looking.

Was it possible to be only a little in love with someone? If so, maybe she could stop things right now before she sunk completely over her head. It would be hard but not impossible to rebuild the protective walls around her heart, especially if she kept her distance for a while.

She could do it. She had to try. The alternative was just too awful to contemplate.

She would start by leaving this cozy little corner of the barn and going back to her own house where she belonged. Soundlessly, she pushed away the blanket and planted her boots on the ground, wincing a little as stiff muscles complained at being treated so callously. If she was this sore, she imagined Matt would be much worse when he awoke.

She thought about waking him up so he could take the cot and even went so far as to reach a hand out to shake him from his slumber, then yanked it back. No. Better to sneak out and avoid any more awkwardness between them.

She shrugged into her coat and headed for the door. As she passed Mystic's stall, the little mare nickered softly in greeting, and Ellie stopped, jerking her head around to see if Matt woke up. He was still propped against the wall like one of those old-time wooden dime-store Indians, and she let her breath out in relief.

It wouldn't hurt to take a look at the horse while she was here, she decided. She could do it quietly enough that it didn't disturb Matt. Straw whispered underfoot as she made her way to the little mare's stall. The door squeaked when she opened it, but Matt slept on.

"You're a pretty girl, aren't you?" She pitched her voice low, running her hands over the horse's abdomen to feel for the foal's position. "Yes, you are. And you'll be a wonderful mama in just a few more months. The time will go so fast and before you know it your little one will be dancing circles around you and tumbling into trouble."

The mare made a noise that sounded remarkably like a resigned sigh, and Ellie laughed softly again. "Don't start complaining now. It's your own fault. You should have thought about what you might be in for when you cuddled up to that big handsome stud who got you this way. You had your fun and now you have to pay the piper."

Mystic blew out a disgusted puff of air through her nose and lipped at her shoulder, and Ellie nodded in agreement. "I know. Men. But what's a girl to do? They look at you out of those gorgeous blue eyes and it's all you can do to remember to breathe, let alone keep your heart out of harm's way."

"You carry on heart-to-heart chats with all your patients?"

She jerked her head up at the rough, amused voice behind her and found Matt leaning his forearms on the top rail of the stall, his hair mussed a little from sleep and a day's growth stubbling his cheeks.

As predictable as the sunrise, she forgot to breathe again. "Hi," she said after a moment, her voice high and strained.

"Going somewhere?" He gestured to her coat.

"Home. I've stayed long enough. I only wanted to check Mystic one more time before I go. I hope that's okay."

He didn't answer, just continued watching her out of solemn blue eyes, and her stomach started a long, slow tremble.

"I'm sorry I took your bed. I didn't mean to. I must have just drifted off. Yesterday was a pretty rough day all around, and I guess all that stress took its toll on me." She was babbling but couldn't seem to help herself. "Anyway, you should have booted me out and sent me home. You must be one big bundle of aches right now."

"I ache," he finally said, his low voice vibrating in the cool predawn air. "I definitely ache."

She was suddenly positive he wasn't talking about a

stiff neck. The trembling in her stomach rippled to her knees, to her shoulders, to her fingers. She shoved her hands into the deep pockets of the fleece vest, praying he wouldn't notice, but she couldn't do anything about the rest except take a shaky breath and hope her knees would wait to collapse until she made it out of the barn.

"Well, I, um, I should be going," she mumbled.

Nerves scrambling, she patted Mystic one last time, then walked out of the stall. She managed to avoid looking at him until she had carefully closed the door behind her.

When she did—when she finally lifted her gaze to his—she was stunned by the raw hunger blazing in his eyes.

She must have made some sound—his name, maybe—and then he ate up the distance between them in two huge strides, and she was in his arms.

His mouth descended to hers, hot and hungry and needy.

He devoured her, like he'd just spent days in the saddle crossing the Forty-Mile Desert and she was a long, cool drink of water on the other side. His hands yanked her against him, held her fast.

Not that she was complaining. She was too busy kissing him back, meeting him nip for nip, taste for taste.

Somewhere in a dim and dusty corner of her mind, her subconscious warned her this was a lousy idea. If her grand plan was to stay away from him until she had her unruly emotions under control, she could probably do a better job than this.

She didn't care. Not now, when her senses spun with the taste and scent and feel of this man she was coming to care for entirely too much.

With a groan, he framed her face with his work-rough hands and pressed her back against the wood stall as he had the first time he'd kissed her. She felt his arousal press against her hip, and her body responded instantly, leaning in to him, desperate to be closer.

She almost cried out in protest when he slid his mouth away, but the sound swelling in her throat shifted to something different, something earthy and aroused, when his lips trailed across the curve of her cheekbone to nip at her ear. His ragged breathing sent liquid heat bubbling through her.

"I think about you all the time," he growled softly into her ear, and her heart gave a couple of good, hard kicks in her chest.

"No matter what I'm doing, you're there with me. I hate it," he went on in that same disgruntled tone. "Why won't you get out of my head?"

"Sorry." Her voice was breathless, aroused. "I'll try harder."

His low, strained laugh vibrated along her nerve endings. "You do that, Doc. You do that."

He dipped his head and captured her mouth again in another of those mind-bending kisses. She wasn't aware they had moved from Mystic's stall until the edge of the cot pressed behind her knees, and then he lowered her onto it, the hard length of him burning into her everywhere their bodies touched.

"I hope this thing holds both of us," he murmured against her mouth, and she laughed softly, a quick mental picture flitting through her mind of them tumbling to the ground.

Before she could answer, his mouth swept over hers, his tongue slipping inside her parted lips. She lost track of time, lost in the wonder of Matt, of being in his arms again. She wanted to hold him close and never let go, to cradle that dark head against her breast, to share a thousand moments like this with him.

She wanted him.

The knowledge terrified her. She wanted Matt Harte the way she'd never wanted anyone—never *allowed* herself to want anyone.

She was supposed to be so independent. So strong and self-sufficient. How could she know she had this powerful need inside her to be held like this, to feel fragile and feminine and *cherished?*

There it was, though, scaring the hell out of her.

But not scaring her enough to make her pull away. She needed more. She needed to feel his skin under her fingertips. He must have untucked his shirt before he fell asleep, and she found it an easy matter to slip her hands underneath, to glide across the smooth, hot skin of his back, loving the play of hard muscle bunching under her hands.

She was so enthralled with his steely strength that she was only vaguely aware of his busy, clever fingers unzipping her fleece vest until he caressed the curve of one breast through the knit of her shirt. Desire flooded through her, and she felt as if she were swimming through some wildly colorful coral reef without nearly enough air in her lungs.

She went completely under when his fingers slipped beneath her shirt and began to slowly trace the skin just below her bra. For once, she was impatient with his careful, measured movements. *All right, already,* she wanted to shout, suddenly sure she would die if he didn't put those hands on her.

Finally, when she didn't know if she could stand the sensual torture another instant, she felt his hands working the front clasp of her bra, then the raw shock of his fingers skimming over her breasts.

She closed her eyes against the overwhelming sensations pouring through her one after another.

"You are so beautiful," he murmured, his voice rough with desire. "The first time I saw you, you made me think of a sunset on a stormy August evening, all fire and color and glory."

To a woman who had spent her whole life feeling like an ugly, scrawny red-haired duckling, his words caressed her more intimately than his fingers. No one had ever called her beautiful before, and she had no defenses against his soft words.

This time she kissed him, lost to everything but this man, this hard, gorgeous cowboy. She arched against his fingers, begging for more of those slow, sensuous touches. He pulled away from her mouth, but before she could protest he slid down her body, pushing her shirt aside so his mouth could close over one taut nipple.

A wild yearning clawed to life inside her, and she closed her eyes and clasped him to her, her fingers tangled in his silky dark hair. He shoved one of his muscled legs between her thighs, and the hard pressure was unbearably arousing. While his mouth teased and tasted her, she arched against him, desperate for more.

He slid a hand between their bodies, working the snaps of her jeans, and her breath caught in her throat as she waited for him to touch her, to caress her *there*. Just before he reached the last snap of her jeans, though, he froze, his breathing ragged.

He pressed his forehead to hers and groaned softly. "Stop. Dammit. We have to stop."

She didn't want to listen to him, lost to everything

but this wild, urgent need pouring through her. With her hands still tangled in his hair, it was an easy matter to angle his mouth so she could kiss him again in another of those long, drugging kisses.

He cooperated for a moment, his tongue dancing with hers, then he groaned again. "Ellie, I mean it. We have to stop."

"Why?"

He pulled away from her, and she shivered as cold air rushed to fill the space he had been in, to dance across her exposed skin with icy fingers.

Matt raked a hand through his hair. "A hundred reasons. Hell, a thousand. The most urgent one being I don't have any protection."

Her mind still felt fuzzy, and for a moment she didn't know what he was talking about. "You...you don't?"

"Sorry," he said wryly. "It's not something I generally stock in my barn." She flushed, suddenly jerked to reality, to the grim fact that she was less than a scruple away from making love to Matt Harte on a hard canvas cot. In his barn, no less, with a dozen horses as witnesses, where any of his ranch hands could stumble upon them any minute.

Dear heavens. What had she been *thinking?*

She hadn't been. She had been so desperately hungry for him that she hadn't been thinking at all, had completely ignored the warning voice yelling in her head.

What had she done? This was absolutely *not* the right way to go about yanking him out of her heart. She was supposed to be grabbing hold of a branch to keep herself from falling any further in love with him, doing her best to hoist herself to safe ground, to sanity. She wasn't supposed to gleefully fling herself over the edge like this.

She was too late.

The realization shuddered through her. She had been so stupid to think she could stop things in mid-step. She was already in love with him.

"I have to go. I really have to go." She stood up and frantically began putting her clothes in order, snapping and tucking and zipping.

He saw her fingers tremble as she tried to set to rights what his hands had undone, and he had to shove his fingers into his pockets to keep from reaching for her again.

She was mortified.

He could see it in her eyes, even though she wouldn't look directly at him, just around and over him as if he didn't exist, as if he weren't standing here in front of her, frustrated and aroused.

He didn't know what to say to make it right, to ease her awkwardness. There was probably nothing he *could* say.

All he knew was that he still wanted her, that his blood pulsed thick and heavy through his veins just looking at her, all tousled and sexy from his hands and his mouth.

As awkward as things were, he had to stop it. He had no choice. They would make love—he suddenly knew that without a doubt—but this wasn't the right time, the right place. She deserved better than a quick tussle in a dusty old horse barn. She deserved flowers and candles and romance, things he suddenly wanted fiercely to give her.

She jerked on her coat and started for the door, but he reached a hand out to stop her. "Ellie—"

"I hope everything turns out all right with your horses," she said quickly. "As soon as I hear from the lab on the test results, I'll let you know."

He sighed. He was still hard enough to split bricks,

and she was going on about test results. A vast, terrifying tenderness welled inside him. As much as it scared him, he knew he couldn't walk away from it. And he couldn't let her walk away, either.

She was in his system and had been since she'd first blown into town. Trying to ignore it had only heightened his attraction for her, made him more hungry than ever. It was the mystery of her, he told himself. The fact that she was off-limits. Like that kid he was thinking about before who had been denied a scrumptious ice-cream cone, suddenly that was the only thing he could think about.

Maybe giving in to it, spending more time with her, might help work her out of his system so he could have things back the way they were before she whirled into his life.

"Are you busy tonight?"

In the process of slipping on her boots, she blinked at him suspiciously. "What?"

"Have dinner with me. I know this great place in Jackson Hole that's not usually too overrun with tourists this time of year. I'm sure I could arrange it with Cassidy to watch the girls. Or we could take them with us, if you'd rather."

"Dinner?"

"Yeah. Or we could go to a movie, if that appeals to you more. If you don't want to go to the show in town, there are a couple of theaters in Jackson or we could drive over to Idaho Falls. I'm sure we could find something we'd both enjoy."

She narrowed her gaze suspiciously. "Are you asking me out on a date, Harte?"

"I think so. At least that's the way things used to be done. I'm a little rusty at the whole dating thing."

"Why?" she asked, her voice blunt.

He shrugged. "I just haven't done it in a while. But don't worry, I'm sure it will all come back to me."

She gave him an impatient glare. "No. I meant, why are you asking me out?"

"The usual reasons people go out on a date." He cleared his throat and looked away. "I'm, uh, attracted to you. I guess you probably figured that out. And I'm not a real good judge of these things, but I think you'd be lying if you said you were immune to me. I think we should get to know each other, since it's pretty clear where we're heading with this thing between us."

Everything about her seemed to freeze. Even the vein pulsing in her neck seemed to stop. "To bed? Is that where you think we're heading?"

He shifted, suddenly feeling as if he were walking barefoot across a pasture full of cow pies. "Uh, it sure looked that way five minutes ago."

"Yeah? Well, that was five minutes ago. Things change." She started toward the door again.

He plodded valiantly forward. "So you're saying no to dinner?"

"Right. No to dinner or to a movie or to any friendly little roll in the hay."

By the time she reached the door, his temper had flared, and he stalked after her. "What the hell did I do that's got you acting like a wet hen all of a sudden? All I did was ask you out on a date, for crying out loud."

She stopped at the door, her back to him, then she turned slowly, green eyes shadowed. "You're right. I'm sorry, Matt. You didn't do anything. This is just a bad idea for me right now. Yes, I'm attracted to you, but I don't want to be."

"Yeah, well, join the club," he growled. "I'm not too thrilled about it, either."

"Exactly my point. Neither of us wants this. I can't be interested in any relationship with you right now beyond vet and client, and now we don't even have that."

"I already told you last night I was sorry for the way I jumped down your throat yesterday. I'd still like to keep you on as my equine vet."

"Despite everything that's happened?"

"Yeah. Despite all of it. Mistakes happen. Whatever you did to the horses, it wasn't intentional. Consider yourself rehired."

She went stiff all over again, and he knew he'd screwed up. Before he could figure out how—let alone do anything to make it right—she drew in a deep breath and shielded her eyes from his view with her lashes, studying the tips of her Ropers. "You don't get it, do you?"

"What?"

"Never mind." Her voice sounded sad suddenly. Like she'd just lost something precious. "I think you'd be better off with Steve as your vet. You don't have time to constantly stand over my shoulder to make sure I don't mess up again. And I don't think I could work that way."

"What about the rest of it? About what happened a few minutes ago?"

She swung open the door and stood framed in the pearly predawn light. "I'm sure if we try really hard, we can both forget that ever happened."

Without another look at him, she walked out into the cold.

Chapter 13

"I don't understand," Dylan moaned into the phone. "Why isn't this working?"

"Maybe they just don't like each other as much as we thought they would." Lucy sounded as discouraged as Dylan, her voice wobbling like she wanted to cry.

Dylan lay on her bed and stared out the window at the black night, thoughts whizzing around in her head like angry bees. It was two days after Christmas, and she should have been happy. She didn't have to go back to school for another week, she got the new CD player and cross-country skis she'd been hinting about for Christmas, and she and Lucy were going to be having a mini New Year's Eve sleepover at the ranch in just a few days.

But the one thing she wanted more than anything else—having a dad and a sister and living happily ever after on the Diamond Harte—seemed as distant as those stars out there.

Things were not going right. Her mom and Mr. Harte didn't seem any closer to falling in love than they had when she and Lucy first came up with the plan.

In fact, they didn't seem to be getting along at all. Every time she brought up his name, her mom's face went all squishy and funny like she just stepped on a bug.

Right before Christmas she asked her mom to drive her out to the ranch so she could take Lucy her present. It had all been carefully arranged for a time when Lucy's dad would be at the ranch house, but then her mom ruined everything. She wouldn't go into the house, just said she'd rather stay out in the truck while Dylan dropped her gift off. She wouldn't even go in to say hello.

She knew her mom was really worried about work ever since a bunch of animals got sick, and Dylan felt a little selfish worrying about herself and what she wanted when her mom had so much big stuff on her mind.

But she just wanted her to be happy. She and Lucy's dad were perfect for each other. Even though he was old, he was super nice and treated his animals well and he always gave Lucy a big, squeezy hug whenever he saw her.

Why couldn't her mom just cooperate and fall in love with him?

"Dylan? Are you still there?"

She cleared the lump out of her throat so Lucy wouldn't hear how upset she was. How small and jealous those squeezy hugs always made her feel. "Yeah. I'm still here. I was just thinking."

"Do you have any ideas?"

She sighed. "I know they like each other. We just have to make them admit it to each other."

"How?"

"I think we're going to have to do something drastic."

"Like what?" Lucy sounded nervous.

"I read a book once about a girl whose parents were in the middle of a big divorce. She was all mad at them and ran away from home and while they were out looking for her, her mom and dad realized they still loved each other and didn't want to get a divorce after all. It was really mushy and kind of stupid, but maybe we could try that."

Lucy was quiet for a moment. "I don't *want* to run away, do you?" she finally asked. "It's almost January and it's cold outside. We'll freeze to death."

"We could just pretend to run away and hide out somewhere on the ranch or something. Or we don't even have to pretend to run away. We could just pretend we got lost. They'd still have to look for us."

"It doesn't seem very nice to trick them like that. Wouldn't they be awfully mad when they figured it out?"

"I'm doing the best I can," Dylan snapped. "I don't see you coming up with any great ideas." Frustration sharpened her voice, made her sound mean. "I'm starting to think maybe you don't want this to work. Maybe you don't really want to be sisters as much as I do."

Lucy's gasp sounded loud and outraged in her ear. For a minute, Dylan thought she was going to cry. "That's not fair," Lucy said in a low, hurt voice. "I've worked just as hard as you to push them together. It's not my fault nothing has worked."

The hot ball of emotions in her stomach expanded to include shame. "You're right. I'm really sorry, Luce.

I'm just worried. I heard Mom on the phone to SueAnn tonight, and she sounded really depressed. I'm afraid if we don't come up with something fast to bring them together, we're going to end up having to move back to California."

"Your mom's having a tough time, isn't she?" Lucy asked quietly.

"Yeah," Dylan said, her voice glum. "I think things are really bad at work. Nobody wants her to treat their animals after what happened to your dad's horses and the others."

Lucy was quiet for a moment. "If you want to run away, I'll do it with you. We can pack warm clothes and even saddle a couple of horses if you want. It will be okay."

"No. I think you're right. I don't think it would work. It was a dumb idea. When they found us, they'd both be really mad."

"What else can we do, then?"

"I don't know. You think about it and I'll think about it and maybe we can come up with something brilliant between now and Friday, when I'm staying over."

After she finally said goodbye and hung up the phone, Dylan lay on her horse-print quilt for a long time, staring out the window at the stars and worrying.

"Okay. Stand back and watch the master at work." With his greased fingers held up like a surgeon's sterile gloves on the way to the operating table, Matt approached the ball of pizza dough on the counter.

"This is so cool," Lucy said to Dylan. "He twirls it around just like you see guys do on TV." The two of them sat on the edge of the kitchen table, eyes wide with expectation.

"That's right." He lowered his voice dramatically. "You're about to witness a sight many have attempted but few have perfected."

"You're about to see a big show-off." Cassie rolled her eyes from across the kitchen, where she was chopping, slicing and shredding toppings for the annual Diamond Harte New Year's Eve Pizza Extravaganza.

"You're just jealous because this is one thing in the kitchen I can do better than you."

"The only thing," she muttered, and he grinned.

He picked up the dough and started tossing it back and forth between his hands, working the ball until it was round and flat. He finished off with a crowd-pleasing toss in the air that earned him two wide-eyed gasps, then caught it handily and transferred it to the pizza peel Cass had sprinkled with cornmeal.

He presented it to the girls with a flourish. "Here you go. Put whatever you want on it."

"That was awesome," Dylan said. "Do it again!"

"Sure thing, after we get that one in the oven."

The girls took the peel to the other counter where Cass had laid out a whole buffet of toppings from sausage to olives to the artichoke hearts he loved.

With them out of earshot, he finally had a chance to corner his sister. "So why didn't you go to the mayor's party?" he asked sternly. "I thought that was the plan."

She pressed her lips together. "I decided I wasn't in the mood for a big, noisy party after all. I'd much rather be here with the girls."

"I can handle the girls. It's not too late. You've still got time to get all dressed up and drive over to the Garretts'. A couple of the ranch hands are going, and they said there'd be a live band and champagne and crab cakes flown in all the way from Seattle."

"I'd rather stay here and have pizza and root beer and watch the ball drop in Times Square." She smiled, but there was that restless edge to it again that filled him with worry.

She was so distant lately. Distracted, somber. No matter how hard he tried to find out why, she kept assuring him everything was fine.

He sighed, knowing he had to try again.

"Cass—" he began, but she cut him off.

"Don't start with me, Matt. I didn't want to go, okay? I enjoy a good party as much as anyone, but I just wasn't in the mood tonight."

"That's just what my mom said. She didn't want to go anywhere, either." Dylan spoke from behind them.

He turned at the mention of the woman who was always at the edge of his brain. He hadn't seen Ellie since that morning in the barn three weeks earlier, but he hadn't stopped thinking about her, wondering about her. Brooding about her.

Questions raced through his mind. How was she? What had she been doing since he saw her last? Why wouldn't she answer his calls? Did she have a date for New Year's Eve? He almost asked, then clamped his teeth together so hard they clicked.

As much as he wanted to know, it wasn't right to interrogate her kid. To his vast relief, Cassie did it for him.

"What's your mom doing tonight?" his sister asked, and he wanted to kiss her.

"Nothing. She said she was just going to stay home and have a quiet night to herself."

Cass frowned. "That's too bad. I wish I'd known. We could have invited her to have pizza with us."

"I'm not sure if she would have come." Dylan paused, giving him a weird look under her lashes. "She's pretty sad lately."

He stiffened. No way would she have told her kid what went on between them in the barn. So why was Dylan looking at him like the news should mean something to him? Was Ellie upset because of him?

"Why is she sad?" he asked, trying to pretend he wasn't desperate to hear the answer.

Dylan cast another one of those weird looks to Lucy, who quickly looked at the pizza. "I think it's because we're moving back to California," she finally said.

"You're *what?*"

Dylan winced. "Don't tell my mom I told you. I don't think she wants anybody else to know."

He felt as if he'd been punched in the stomach. As if the whole damn world had suddenly gone crazy. "When?"

"I don't know. Nothing's definite yet. Anyway, I don't think she's in the mood for a party, either. That's why she told the mayor's wife she wouldn't be able to go to their house tonight."

It was none of his business, he reminded himself. She'd made that crystal clear the other week in the barn. If she wanted to pack up her kid and head for Timbuktu, he didn't have a damn thing to say about it.

Still, that didn't stop him from pounding his frustration on the second hapless ball of pizza dough. By the time he was done, anger had begun to replace the shock.

Finally he couldn't stand it anymore. He whipped off the apron Lucy gave him for Father's Day the year before and turned to Cassie.

"Can you handle the girls on your own for a while?"

"Sure." She looked at him curiously. "Where are you going?"

The last thing he wanted to do was tell his little sister he planned to go have a few hard words with Ellie Webster. He could just imagine the speculative look she'd give him. "I just need to, uh, run an errand."

She studied him for a moment, then smiled broadly. "Sure. No problem. And while you're there, why don't you ask Ellie if she wants to come out for pizza? I'm sure there'll be plenty left."

"Who said anything about Ellie?" he asked stiffly.

Cass grinned. "Nobody. Nobody at all. What was I thinking? Wherever you're going, drive carefully. You know what kind of idiots take to the road on New Year's Eve."

Still grumbling to himself about little sisters who thought they knew everything—and usually did—Matt bundled into his coat and cowboy hat and went out into the cold.

Well, this was a fine New Year's Eve, sitting alone and eating a frozen dinner. How pathetic could she get?

Quit complaining, Ellie chided herself. *You had offers.*

Several of them, in fact. SueAnn wanted her to go to Idaho Falls to dinner and a show with her and Jerry. Ginny Garrett, whose pet collie she'd fixed a few months ago, had invited her to what she deduced was the big social gala of the year in Salt River, the party she and her husband were throwing. And Lucy and Dylan had invited her out to the ranch to share homemade pizza and a video.

Of the three, the girls' party sounded like the most fun. Unfortunately, it was also the invitation she was least likely to accept. She couldn't imagine anything more grueling than spending the evening with Matt, trying to pretend they were only casual friends, that she hadn't come a heartbeat away from making love with him just a few weeks ago.

Despite putting plenty of energy into it, she hadn't been able to stop thinking about him since that morning. About the way his eyes had darkened with desire, the way his rough hands caressed her skin, the soft words that had completely demolished her defenses.

The way his lack of faith in her had broken her heart.

She'd been right to turn him down, to put this distance between them. She wasn't having much luck falling out of love with him, but at least she couldn't go down any deeper when she didn't have anything to do with him.

Anyway, spending New Year's Eve alone wasn't so bad. With the exception of the frozen dinner, the evening looked promising. She had already taken a nice long soak in the tub using the new strawberry-scented bath beads Dylan had given her for Christmas and put on the comfortable new thermal silk pajamas she'd treated herself to. She'd been lucky enough to find a station on the radio playing sultry jazz and big band music, she was going to pop a big batch of buttered popcorn later, and she had a good mystery to curl up with.

What else did a woman need?

She turned up the gas fireplace so that flames licked and danced cozily, then watched the fake logs for a moment with only a little regret for the real thing. Although she might have preferred a cheery little applewood blaze, with the crackle and hiss and heavenly aroma, she certainly didn't mind forgoing the mess and work of chopping, splitting and hauling wood.

After a moment, she settled onto the couch, tucking her feet under her. She'd just turned the page when the doorbell rang right in the middle of Glenn Miller's "Moonlight Serenade."

Marking her place, she went to the door, then felt her jaw sag at the man she found on the front porch.

"Matt! What are you doing here? Shouldn't you be digging in to a big slab of pizza right about now?"

"I came to talk some sense into you," he growled.

She stared at him, noting for the first time the firm set of his jaw and the steely glitter in his eyes. "Excuse me?"

"You heard me. Can we do this inside? It's freezing out here."

Without waiting for her answer—or for her to ask what it was, exactly, he wanted to *do* inside—he thrust past her into the house, where he loomed in the small living room like a tomcat trapped in a dollhouse, getting ready to pounce.

She closed the door carefully behind him, shutting out the icy blast of air, then turned to face him. He was obviously furious about something, but she couldn't for the life of her figure out what she might have done this time to set him off.

His glower deepened. "I can't believe you're just going to run away. I thought you had more grit than that."

She opened her mouth, but he didn't wait for her answer. "Isn't that just like a city girl?" he went on angrily. "At the first sign of trouble, you take off running and leave the mess behind for everybody else to clean up. Dammit, you can't leave. You've got obligations here. A life. Your kid deserves better than to be shuttled around like some kind of Gypsy just because you don't have the gumption to see things through."

She stiffened and returned his glare. "In the first place, don't you tell me what my daughter deserves. In the second, do you mind telling me what in blazes you're talking about?"

For the first time since he'd stomped into her house, he looked a little unsure. "About you leaving. Dylan said you're moving back to California."

"Dylan has a big mouth," she muttered.

"Are you?"

"I don't know. Maybe."

She was seriously considering it. Not that she wanted to—the very idea made her stomach hurt, her heart weep. But she couldn't keep her practice open without any patients. "I haven't made a firm decision yet and I probably won't for a few months yet. But even if I were leaving tomorrow, what business would it be of yours?"

He shifted his weight. "I just don't want you to make a big mistake. I know how much your practice means to you," he went on. "It wouldn't be right for you to give it up without a fight."

"Without a fight?" She hissed out a breath. "I feel as if I've been doing nothing *but* fighting for six months. Each time I treat an animal I wonder if it's the last one. Every time I pay a bill, I wonder if I'll be able to pay it the next month. At some point, I have to face the fact that I can't keep waging a losing battle."

"Things will get better. You've just had a few setbacks."

"Right. I believe that's what Custer said to his men halfway through the battle of Little Big Horn."

"Is this because of the outbreak?"

"Partly. Funny thing," she said pointedly, "but the rest of the ranchers around here don't seem as convinced as I am that I wasn't responsible."

He looked uncomfortable, and she regretted sounding so bitchy. "As I said," she went on before he could respond, "although I'm considering leaving, I haven't made any final decision yet. I don't know why Dylan would have told you otherwise."

"I think she's worried about you. She said you were sad."

A child shouldn't have to worry about anything more earthshaking than whether she'd finished her homework. She hated that Dylan had spent even a moment fretting about her mother, about the future.

For that reason, if nothing else, maybe she needed to give up this selfish desire for autonomy and take her daughter back to California, where she could make a safe and secure living, even if she found it suffocating.

She also hated that Dylan had blabbed to Matt about her melancholy. She didn't want to talk about any of it, so she turned the subject to him.

"I can't figure you out."

"What's to figure out?"

"Why would you pass up homemade pizza on New Year's Eve to come give me a lecture about perseverance? You don't even like me."

"That's not true. I like you plenty. Too much," he muttered under his breath.

Before she could figure out how to answer that growled admission, he went on. "I care about you.

When Dylan told me you were moving to California, I was furious."

His gaze locked with hers, his blue eyes burning with emotions she couldn't even begin to decipher, and he reached for her fingers. "All I could think about was how much I would miss you if you left."

She drew in a shaky breath. "Matt—"

"I know, it's crazy. I don't understand it myself. But I haven't been able to think about anything else except how right, how completely *perfect,* you felt in my arms. And how I want you there again."

She closed her eyes, helpless against the tumble of emotions cascading through her. Listening to this big, gruff man speak words of such sweetness, words she knew would not come easily for him, affected her more than a hundred love songs, a thousand poems.

How could she ever have been stupid enough to think she could lock her heart against him? She had no defenses against a man like Matt Harte. He might seem arrogant and authoritative most of the time, but he cared enough about her to drive out on a snowy night to try to prevent her from making what he considered a grave mistake.

Why was she still fighting against him when she ached to be with him more than she had ever wanted anything in her life?

She loved him.

The sweetness of it seeped through her like hard rain on thirsty earth, collecting in all the crevasses life had carved into her soul. She loved this man, with his rough hands and his slow smile and his soft heart.

When she opened her eyes, she found him watching

her warily, as if he expected her to kick him out of her house any minute.

"I've thought of it, too," she answered, barely above a whisper.

"So what are we going to do about it?"

"What else can we do?"

With a deep breath for courage, she stepped forward, wrapped her arms around his neck and lifted her mouth for his kiss.

For just a moment after she stepped forward and lifted her mouth to his, Matt couldn't move, frozen with shock and a fast, thorny spike of desire.

He never expected this. Never. She made it pretty damn clear the other day that she didn't want any kind of relationship with him. He hadn't liked it, but what could he do when she wouldn't give him much room for any kind of argument?

If he'd been thinking at all when he rushed over here after Dylan's little announcement—if he'd been able to focus on anything but his anger that she planned to leave Star Valley—he might have expected Ellie to throw him out the door after he finished giving her a piece of his mind.

Not this. He definitely wouldn't have predicted this soft, searching kiss that was curling through his insides like grapevines on a fence or her arms wrapping around his neck to hold him close.

Just when he was beginning to wonder if he'd ever be able to move again, he felt the whisper-soft touch of her tongue at the corner of his mouth. That's all it took, one tiny lick, and he was lost.

Need exploded through him like a shotgun blast. With a ragged groan, he yanked her against him and

devoured her mouth. She smelled like strawberry short-
cake and tasted like heaven, and he couldn't get enough.

He'd missed her these few weeks. Missed her laugh
and her sweet smile and her smart mouth. He'd wanted
to call her a hundred times and had even dialed the number a few times, but had always hung up before the call
could go through.

She told him she didn't want a relationship and had
obviously been going out of her way to avoid him. And
he had too much bitter experience with rejection to
push her.

He should have, though. Should have pushed them
both. If he'd known she would greet him like this, that
she would welcome him into her arms so eagerly, he
damn well would have been knocking down her door
to get here.

In the background, Miles Davis played some kind
of sexy muted trumpet solo. Matt's subconscious registered it with appreciation, but all he could focus on
was Ellie and her sweet mouth.

Her hands were busy pulling off his coat, which she
tossed on the floor. His hat went sailing after it, then
she raked her fingers through his hair, playing at the
sensitive spot at the nape of his neck.

He wanted to have her right now, to tangle his fingers in her silky clothes and rip them away, then thrust
himself inside her until neither one of them could move.

"I'm not stopping this time," he warned. He would
somehow find the strength to walk away if she asked it
of him, but he wasn't about to tell her that.

To his vast relief, she didn't argue. "Good," she
breathed against his mouth. "I don't want you to stop.
In fact, I'd be really disappointed if you did."

He had to close his eyes, awed at the gift she was offering him. On the heels of his amazement came niggling worry. He hadn't done this in a while, and his body wasn't in any kind of mood to take things slow. It throbbed and ached, eager for hot, steamy passion. Writhing bodies. Heated explorations. Feverish, sloppy kisses that lasted forever.

But Ellie deserved to be wooed, and woo her he would, even if it killed him.

"You smell divine," he murmured, trying fiercely to get a little control over himself.

"Strawberry bath beads." She sounded breathless, aroused. "I just got out of the tub right before you showed up."

He had a quick mental picture of her lithe little body slipping naked into hot, bubbly water—and then climbing back out—and groaned as his hard-fought control slipped another notch.

She would smell like strawberries everywhere, and he suddenly wanted to taste every single inch.

While she was busy working the buttons of his shirt, he trailed his mouth down the elegant line of her throat to whisper kisses just under the silky neckline of her shirt. Her hands stilled, and she arched her throat, unknowingly exposing a tiny amount of cleavage.

He took ruthless advantage of it and pressed his mouth to the sweetly scented hollow, licking and tasting while his hands worked their way under her shirt. She had nothing on under her thermal silk, he realized, and heat scorched him as his fingers encountered soft, unbound curves.

Her breath hissed in sharply when his thumb danced over a tight nipple, and she seemed to sag bonelessly against him. He lowered her to the soft, thick carpet in front of the fireplace, and she responded by tightening her arms around him, by pressing her soft curves against him.

She had somehow managed to unbutton his shirt, and her hands splayed across his abdomen, branding him with her heat. His stomach muscles contracted, and she smiled and shoved his shirt down over his shoulders.

While the music on the stereo shifted to a honey-voiced woman singing about old lovers and new chances, they undressed each other, stopping only for more of those slow, drugging kisses.

As he removed the last of their clothes, he leaned back on an elbow and stared at her, her skin burnished by flickering firelight. She looked like some kind of wild-haired goddess, and his heartbeat pulsed as equal parts desire and that terrifying tenderness surged over him.

He hadn't wanted this in his life, had done his best to push her away and pretend he wasn't coming to care for her. The scars Melanie had left him with still ached sometimes, made him leery to risk anything of himself.

But Ellie wasn't anything like his ex-wife. He knew it, had known it from the beginning. He just hadn't wanted to face the truth. It was much easier to focus on the few inconsequential things the two women had in common than the hundred of important things separating them. That way he could use the ugliness of his past as a shield against Ellie and her courage and her generous spirit.

Somehow this woman had sneaked into his heart. Now that she was firmly entrenched there, he wondered how he'd ever survived so long without her.

He wanted to take care of her. It sounded macho and stupid, and he knew his fiercely independent Ellie would probably smack him upside the head if he said it aloud, so he tucked the words into his heart along with her.

He wouldn't say them. He would just do everything he could to show her she needed him.

Why was he looking at her like that? Ellie squirmed, wishing his expression wasn't so hard to read sometimes. She felt vulnerable and exposed lying before him with her hair curling wildly around her. At the same time, she had to admit she found it oddly erotic having him watch her with those blue eyes blazing.

Finally she couldn't stand the conflicting emotions anymore. She reached out and pulled him to her, nearly shuddering apart as his hard, taut muscles met her softness.

This was right. Any lingering doubts she might have been harboring floated away into the night as his body covered hers, as his calloused hands skimmed over her, as his mouth devoured her.

She wanted to curl up against him, wanted to let his strength surround her.

"I've thought about this since that first time we kissed in the barn." His voice was low, throaty. "Why have we both been fighting this so hard?"

"Because we're crazy." She smiled a little and pressed a kiss to the throbbing pulse at the base of his throat.

"If I'm crazy, I know exactly who to blame. I haven't had a coherent thought in my head since a certain unnamed little red-haired vet moved into town."

He tugged gently on the hair in question so their

gazes could meet. His words and the undisguised hunger in his eyes made her feel fragile and powerful at the same time, beautiful and feminine and *wanted*.

Fresh desire pulsed through her, liquid heat, and she drew in a ragged breath and reached for him.

Their kisses became more urgent, their caresses more demanding. The jazz on the stereo shifted to something haunting, sultry, as he teased her breasts, as his fingers slid across her stomach to the aching heat centered between her thighs, and she shuddered, lost to his touch, to the music weaving sinuously around them.

He pushed one long finger inside her, readying her for him, and she gasped his name and arched against him eagerly.

"You're killing me, Ellie," he growled. "I can't handle much more of this."

"You're the one taking his dear sweet time."

His low laugh sounded raw, strained. "I was trying to go slow for you."

She shivered again as his finger touched on a particularly sensitive spot, and she thought she would die if he didn't come inside her. "Don't do me any favors, Harte," she gasped.

His low laugh slid over her like a caress. "Wouldn't dream of it, Doc."

He reached for something in his jeans—his wallet, she realized—then pulled out a foil-wrapped package. A moment later, he knelt between her thighs. His gaze met hers, and the fierce emotion there settled right into her heart, and then an instant later his mouth tangled with hers again as he entered her.

Love for this man—this strong, wonderful man—expanded in her heart then flowed out, seeping through every cell. She wrapped her arms tightly around him, wishing she had the words to tell him her feelings for him—or that she had the courage to give him the words, even if she managed to find them.

His movements started out slow, but she wasn't having any of it. She arched against him, begging for more, for fire and thunder and out-of-her-head passion.

He drew back, his breathing ragged. "Slow down. I don't want to hurt you," he growled.

"You won't. I'm not fragile, Matt."

With a harsh groan he drove into her, deep and powerful and demanding, and she shivered even as she met him thrust for thrust. He must have held himself under amazing control, she thought. Now that she'd given him permission to treat her like a woman instead of a china doll, he devoured her, kissing and stroking and inflaming her senses.

He reached for her hands and yanked their entwined fingers above her head so that only their bodies touched, skin to skin, heat to heat.

She never would have expected this wildness from him, the fierce desire that blazed out of him in wave after hot wave until she thought she would scorch away into cinders from it.

A wild, answering need spiraled up inside her, climbing higher and higher with each passing second. She had never known anything like this, this frantic ache. She gasped his name, suddenly frightened by how close she was to losing control, to losing herself.

He groaned in answer and kissed her deeply, tongue tangling with hers, demanding everything from her, then reached between their bodies to touch her intimately. Just that small caress, the heat of his fingers on the place where she already burned, and she shattered into a thousand quivering pieces.

"I can't get enough of you," he growled before she could come back together again.

He kissed her fiercely, branding her as his, then with one more powerful thrust, he found his own release.

Afterward, she trembled more from reaction than the cold, but Matt reached up to the couch behind them and pulled down the knit throw there. He spread it over them both and pulled her against him.

She snuggled close. "And here I thought I was in for another boring New Year's Eve."

His low laugh tickled the skin at the back of her neck. "Boring is not a word I would ever dare use in the same sentence as you, Doc."

She lifted her gaze to his. "Are you complaining?"

"Hell, no. Even if I had any strength left to complain, I wouldn't dare."

She smiled and settled against his hard chest. He held her tightly with one hand while the other stroked through her hair.

"I used to tell myself I was happy with boring," he said after a few moments. "That's what I thought I wanted. A nice, safe, uneventful life. Then you blew into my life, and I discovered I'd been fooling myself all these years. Safe and uneventful are just other words for lonely."

His low words slid over her, stirring up all kinds of terrifying emotions, and she tensed. Not knowing how to answer—and not at all comfortable with this yearning inside her to stay curled up against him forever—she chose to change the subject. "Cassie and the girls will be wondering where you ran off to."

He studied her, and she had the awful suspicion he knew exactly how uneasy his words made her, then he shrugged. "I doubt it. At least Cass won't. Apparently my little sister knows a lot more about me than I'd like to think she does. More than I know myself. She asked me to invite you out to the ranch for the rest of the pizza party, if the girls haven't eaten it all by now."

"Oh. That was very kind of her."

"You could stay over in the guest room."

She thought about spending the evening not being able to touch him and she sighed. "I'd better pass."

"Why?"

"We have to tread carefully here, Matt. Really carefully. Think about the girls."

"What about them?"

"They can't know about…about any of this. How would they react?"

She saw understanding dawn in his eyes, and he winced. "Right."

"This can't affect them. I don't want either of them hurt."

Dylan would build this into a happily-ever-after kind of thing, something Ellie knew was impossible. She knew perfectly well that her daughter pined for a father, and she'd be over the moon imagining Matt in that role. Ellie didn't want to see her heart get broken.

"What are you suggesting?" he asked quietly. "If you're going to tell me some bull about how you think this was a mistake that won't happen again, I might have to get mean."

If she were stronger, that's exactly what she *would* say. Letting this go any further would only end in heartache. For all she knew, she'd be moving back to California in the next few months. How much worse was it going to be to say goodbye now that she knew the wonder of being in his arms?

Still, she couldn't seem to find the words to push him away. "We just have to be careful," she said instead. "That's all I'm saying."

They stayed that way together on the floor for a long time, wrapped around each other while the soft music flowed around them. She couldn't touch him enough. His rough hands, his hard chest, the ridged muscles of his stomach. Eventually their caresses grew bold again, and she gasped when he picked her up as if she were no heavier than a runty calf and carried her to her bedroom.

There he made love to her again—slower this time, as if he planned to spend the whole new year touching her just so, kissing her exactly right, then he entered her and each slow, deep thrust seemed to steal a little more of her soul.

Afterward, she lay limp and boneless in his arms, content to listen to his heart and feel his arms around her. If the house caught fire just then, she wasn't sure she could summon the energy to crawl out of bed.

"I don't want you to leave," he said against her hair.

"This is my house." She was wonderfully, sinfully exhausted. "If anyone leaves, I'm guessing it will be you."

"You know what I mean. I'm talking about you going back to California." He was quiet for a moment, then he pressed another kiss to her hair. "You know, if your practice is really struggling that much, I could give you the money to keep it going."

In an instant, the world seemed to grind to a halt, like

an amusement park ride that had abruptly lost power. The sleepy, satisfied glow surrounding her popped, leaving her feeling chilled to the bone.

She wrenched away from him and sat up, clutching the quilt to her breasts. "You what?"

"I could give you the money. Just to tide you over until things start looking up."

The roaring in her ears sounded exactly like the sea during a violent storm. "Let me get this straight. You want to ride in like some kind of knight in shining armor and give me the money to save my practice."

He shrugged, looking faintly embarrassed. "Something like that."

Fury and hurt and shame vied for the upper hand as she jumped from the bed and yanked on her robe.

"What's the matter?"

She didn't even spare him a glance. "Your timing stinks, Harte."

"What?" He sounded genuinely befuddled.

He didn't have a clue. She drew in a deep breath. "Let me give you a little advice. Next time, don't offer a woman money when her body is still warm from having you inside her unless the two of you have agreed on a price beforehand."

She thought of her mother, of the faceless, nameless strangers who had skulked in and out of her bed after her father left. The squeak of the rusty screen door as another of Sheila's "friends" dropped by, the low, suggestive laughter in the kitchen, the heavy footsteps down the hall toward her mother's filthy bedroom.

Hiding in her room with a pillow over her head so she wouldn't have to hear what came after.

Even then, at seven years old, she'd known what they

were doing, had felt sick, dirty. And she'd known that in the morning, Sheila would have enough money for another bottle of oblivion.

That Matt would offer this, would put her in the same category as her mother, brought all those feelings rushing back.

"You know that's not what I meant." Anger roughened his voice. "I can't believe that kind of cheap thought would ever enter your head. It's demeaning to me and to you. Dammit, Ellie. I care about you. I want to help you. And why shouldn't I, when I have the means? What's wrong with that?"

"I don't want your help. I never asked for it."

"You'd rather have to give up the practice you love? The life you love? You'd rather go back to California and leave everything here behind?"

"If I have to, yes."

She stormed out of the bedroom, desperate to put space between them, but of course he stalked after her, fastening the buttons of his jeans and shrugging into his shirt as he followed.

"That's the stupidest thing I've ever heard you say. Why are you so upset about this? Just call it a loan. You can pay me back when business picks up."

"What if it doesn't? How will I pay you back then? By sleeping with you? Should I start keeping a little ledger by my bed? Mark a few dollars off every time you come over? Tell me, Matt, since I don't have any idea— what's the going hourly rate for prostitutes these days?"

He went still, and she knew her jab had struck home. "That's not fair," he said quietly.

It wasn't. She knew it even as the bitter words flowed

out of her like bile. He didn't deserve this, but she couldn't seem to stop, lost in the awful past.

All he did was offer his help. He couldn't be blamed because she found herself in the terrible position of needing it.

"I'm sorry," she said stiffly. "You're right. Thank you for your kind offer but I'm not quite desperate enough yet that I'd take money from you."

He glared at her. "Is that supposed to be an apology? Because it sure as hell didn't sound like one from here."

"It's whatever you want it to be."

He was quiet, his face a stony mask. "You don't want to take anything from anyone, do you?"

"Not if I can help it."

"And if you can't? What are you going to do then?"

She hated the coldness in his voice, the distance, even though she knew she'd put both things there. Regret was a heavy ache in her heart. A few moments ago they had shared amazing tenderness and intimacy, and now they were acting like angry strangers with each other. It was her fault, she knew it. This was a stupid argument, but it was also symptomatic of the greater barriers to any relationship between them.

She had been fooling herself to think they could ever have anything but this one magical night.

"I'll figure that out if that day ever comes," she finally said. "Go home, Matt. It's New Year's Eve, you should be with your family. If you hurry, you'll make it home before the clock strikes midnight."

He stood there glaring at her, looking big and gorgeous and furious, then without another word he yanked on his coat, grabbed his hat and slammed out the door.

Chapter 14

Three weeks into the new year, the temperature spiked in western Wyoming in what the locals called the annual January thaw.

Though the temperature barely hovered above forty degrees and genuinely warm weather was still months away, the mountain air smelled almost like spring. Snow melted from every building in steady drips, kids put away their sleds and took out their bikes instead, and a few overachieving range cows decided to drop their calves a few weeks early.

She was far from busy, but Ellie was grateful to at least have a few patients to occupy her time.

She'd spent most of the day trying to ease a new Guernsey calf into the world for one of her few remaining clients. She still had the warm glow of satisfaction from seeing that wobbly little calf tottering around the pasture.

In the excitement of watching new life, she had almost been able to forget the clouds hanging over her head, this terrible fear that her time here amid these mountains she had come to love so dearly was drawing to a close.

Her choices were becoming increasingly limited. Fight as she may against the truth, she knew she couldn't keep hanging on by her fingernails much longer.

She drew in a deep breath. Maybe she ought to just forget about trying to go it alone and join forces with Steve Nichols. At least then she could stay in Salt River.

He might not be willing anymore, though. He hadn't asked her about it for weeks, and lately he'd been cool and distracted every time they talked, making her wonder and worry what she had done. Maybe he, like everyone else in town, had lost all respect for her.

She could always take out a loan from Matt.

The thought, sinuous and seductive, whispered into her mind, but she pushed it away. Never. She couldn't do something that extreme, no matter what desperate straits she found herself in.

Despite her resolve, she knew she owed him an apology for her overreaction on New Year's Eve. Remorse burned in her stomach whenever she thought about how she had lashed out at him.

She hadn't seen him since the night he had come to her house. The previous evening, the committee for the Valentine's carnival had met for the last time before the big event, and she'd spent all day with her nerves in an uproar over seeing him again.

It had all been for nothing, though. He'd sent a message

with Sandy Nielson that a ranch emergency came up at the last minute and he wouldn't be able to make it.

She was relieved, she tried to tell herself. The last thing she needed to deal with right now was the inevitable awkwardness between them.

She sighed as she drove through town. Who was she kidding? She missed him. Missed his sexy drawl and the way his eyes crinkled at the edges and the way he could make her toes curl with just a look.

The sun was sliding behind the mountains in a brilliant display of pink and lavender that reflected in wide puddles of melting snow as she drove into the clinic's parking lot. She pulled the truck into the slot next to SueAnn's Suburban and climbed out, determined that she would do her best not to think about the blasted man for at least the next ten minutes.

SueAnn popped up from her desk like a prairie dog out of her hole when Ellie walked in.

"How did it go?" she asked.

Ellie forced a smile. "Not bad. Mama and calf are doing well. I was afraid for a while we'd lose them both but we finally managed to pull the calf and everything turned out okay."

"I'm sure that's a big relief to Darla. She loves that little milk cow."

Ellie nodded. "She says hello, by the way, and she'll see you tomorrow night at the library board meeting. Any messages?"

SueAnn handed her a small pink pile. "None of these were urgent. Mostly carnival committee members needing your input on last-minute details. Oh, but Jeb Thacker's having trouble with Cleo again. He wondered when he could bring her in tomorrow. I told him anytime. And here's the mail. Bills, mostly."

Ellie took it, wondering what she was going to do when she left Star Valley without SueAnn to screen her mail for her.

"Oh, I almost forgot. The lab finally sent the results for that tox screen you ordered."

Ellie froze in the process of thumbing through the messages. The culture results on the animals that had fallen ill before Christmas. "Where is it?"

"Here." SueAnn handed over a thin manila envelope, and Ellie immediately ripped it open and perused the contents.

"What does it say?"

"It looks like the samples all were infected with an unusual strain of bacteria, just like Steve suspected. That's why it took so long for the results. The lab had never seen it in horses before."

"Could it have been spread by your needles?"

"Maybe." It wasn't outside the realm of possibility that the needles had been contaminated, although she would never believe that had been the cause. Damn. She had hoped for answers, for something that could definitively absolve her of responsibility.

SueAnn touched her arm. "I'm sorry it wasn't better news."

She forced a smile as the weight of failure pressed down hard on her shoulders. "Thanks."

"You have anything left for me to do today?" SueAnn asked. "It's almost six, and Jerry's got a touch of the flu. Last time he stayed home sick from work, he maxed out three credit cards on the home shopping channel."

"You'd better hurry, then, or you'll get home and find he bought a dozen cans of spray-on hair replacement."

As SueAnn switched off her computer and turned on the answering machine, Ellie unfolded from the edge of the desk. "Where's Dylan? Is she in the back doing her homework?"

SueAnn froze in the process of pulling her purse out of her bottom desk drawer. "I haven't seen her. She never came in after school." Anxiousness crept into her voice. "I...I just assumed she went home with Lucy. You didn't mention it before you went out to Darla's, but I figured it must have slipped your mind."

Unease bloomed to life inside Ellie like a noxious weed. "I don't remember her telling me anything about riding the school bus to the ranch today."

"Maybe it was a spur of the moment thing."

"Maybe." If she went to the ranch without leaving a message, Dylan was in serious trouble. Ellie's one strict, inarguable rule was that Dylan had to leave her whereabouts with her mother or with SueAnn at all times.

A hundred terrible scenarios flashed through her mind in the space of a few seconds until she reined in her thoughts. No. This was Star Valley, Wyoming. Things like that didn't happen here.

"I'll just call the ranch. You're probably right. I'm sure that's where she is." She dialed the number then twisted the cord around her fingers while she waited for Matt or Cassie to answer. No one picked up after fifteen rings, and her stomach knotted with worry.

"I am so sorry, El." SueAnn looked sick. "I should have called you when she didn't show up just to make sure everything was cool."

"Let's not panic until we have reason. She and Lucy

are probably just playing outside in this warm weather, or maybe she went home with one of her other friends."

"Do you want me to run out to the ranch and see if she's there?"

"No. You go on home to Jerry. I'll just check at the house and buzz by the school. If I don't find her at either of those places, I'll drive out to the ranch."

She would find her daughter safe and sound. She *had* to. She absolutely refused to consider any alternative.

It had been one hell of a week.

The tractor bounced and growled as Matt drove through foot-deep muck on the way to the barn after delivering the evening feed to the winter pasture. Cows had been dropping calves like crazy with all this warm weather, the ranch was a muddy mess, and to make matters worse, two of his ranch hands quit on the same day.

He hadn't had a good night's sleep in longer than he could remember, every muscle in his body ached, and his shoulder hurt where he'd been kicked by an ornery horse that caught him off guard.

Days like this, he wondered if it was all worth it. All he wanted was dinner and his bed, and at this point he was even willing to forget about the dinner.

At the barn, he switched off the tractor, making a mental note that the engine seemed a little wompy and would need to be checked before planting season. He climbed out and shut the door behind him when he saw Ellie's battered pickup pull up to the house.

Of all the people he would have expected to show up at the ranch, she would just about come in last on the list. He hadn't been able to forget the bitter words she'd flung at him, the way she had thrown his offer of help back in his face.

He could see now that she'd been right, his timing could have been a whole lot better. But his intentions had been good.

A moment later, she swung open her truck door and hopped out. She was small and compact and, despite his lingering anger, heat rushed to his groin just remembering how that lithe little body had felt under him, around him.

She walked up the porch steps to ring the doorbell, and he made a face. Cassie wasn't home, and he was a little tempted to let her stand there ringing away in vain. He immediately felt spiteful for entertaining the idea even for an instant and headed toward the house.

As soon as he was close enough to catch a glimpse of the worry in her expression, he was heartily relieved he hadn't obeyed the petty impulse.

"What's the matter, Doc?"

She whirled, and relief spread over her face when she saw him. "Matt! I was afraid nobody was home. Did Dylan come home on the bus with Lucy today?"

He frowned. "Lucy didn't take the bus today. Cass picked her up after school so they could go shopping in Idaho Falls for something to wear to the Valentine's carnival. They're not back yet. She didn't come home?"

Ellie shook her head, her green eyes murky and troubled. "I don't know where she is. She usually walks to the clinic after school. When she didn't show up today, SueAnn thought she must have come home with Lucy."

"I suppose there's a chance she might have gone with them on the shopping trip, although I think she would have cleared it with you first. She's a good kid. Just taking off like that doesn't seem like something she'd do."

"No. You're right."

She looked helpless and frightened. As he saw her mouth tremble, his remaining anger slid away. He hurried up the steps and pulled her into his arms.

"We'll go in and call Cass on the cell phone. If she's not with them, maybe Lucy will know something. It'll be okay, Ellie."

She must be out of her mind with worry or she never would have let him lead her into the house and settle her into one of the kitchen chairs while he crossed to the phone hanging on the wall. He was just dialing the number when he heard another vehicle pull up outside.

"That's probably them now."

The words were barely out of his mouth when Ellie jumped up and headed toward the door. He followed close on her heels and saw her shoulders sag with disappointment when only Cassie and Lucy climbed out of his sister's Cherokee.

Cassie's eyes widened when she saw Ellie. "Everything okay?" she asked, instantly concerned.

In the circle of light on the porch, Ellie looked small and lost, her expression bordering on panic. A mother suddenly living her worst nightmare. Sensing she was on the verge of losing control, Matt grabbed her arm and guided her up the steps to the door and into the warmth of the house.

"Come on inside," he said over his shoulder to his sister. "I'll explain everything."

By the time they made it into the kitchen, Ellie had once more gained control of her emotions, although her eyes still looked haunted.

"Lucy," she began. "Dylan didn't go to the clinic after school today. Do you know anything about where she might have gone?"

For a moment, his daughter just stared, then color leached from her face and she looked like she was choking on something. She pressed her lips together and suddenly seemed extremely interested in the green-checkered tablecloth.

"Lucy?" he said sternly. "What do you know about this?"

"Nothing." She wouldn't look him in the eye and clamped both hands over her mouth, as if she were afraid something would slip out.

"Did she say anything to you after school about where she might be going? Can you think of any other friends she might have gone home with?" Ellie asked, her voice thin, pleading.

"No," Lucy said through her fingers in barely a whisper. Her chin wobbled, and she looked like she was going to cry any minute now. Once she started, they'd never get anything out of her, he realized.

Instead of obeying his first impulse to ride her hard about it until she told them what was going on, he knelt to her level and pulled her into his arms.

"Lucy, sweetheart, this is important. Her mom is really worried about her, just like I would be if you were missing. I know Dylan is your friend and you don't want to get her in trouble, but if you know anything about where she might be, you have to tell us."

She looked at the floor for a moment, and a tear slipped out of the corner of her eye and dripped down her nose. "She said she wasn't going to do it. She said it wouldn't *work*," she wailed.

"What? What did she say wouldn't work?" Ellie asked urgently.

Lucy clamped her lips together, then expelled the words in a rush of air. "We were gonna run away."

"Run away?" Ellie again looked lost and bewildered. "Why? What was so terrible that she thought she had to run away?"

"We weren't really gonna run away. Just pretend." Lucy sniffled. "Dylan thought if the two of you had to look for us together, you guys would finally see how much you liked each other and you would get married and we could be sisters for real."

Thunderstruck, Matt looked from his daughter to Ellie. At Lucy's admission, color flooded Ellie's face, and her horrified eyes flashed to his then focused on the same tablecloth Lucy had found so interesting.

Oblivious to their reaction, his rascal of a kid plodded on. "We decided it wouldn't work and that you'd be too mad when you found out what we did. We were trying to come up with a better plan but I guess maybe she decided to do it by herself anyway. I can't believe she didn't tell me what she was going to do," she finished in a betrayed-sounding voice.

"But where would she go?" Ellie exclaimed. "It's January. It's cold and dark out there."

"I don't know." Lucy started to sniffle again. "We were gonna hide out in one of the ranch buildings."

"She wouldn't have been able to walk all the way out here." Cassie frowned. "She must have gone somewhere in town."

Matt headed for the door. "I'll send the ranch hands out looking around for her just in case. Cassie, call Jess and let him know what's going on. Meanwhile,

Ellie, you and I can run back to town and see if she might have turned up at your house or at the clinic. Who knows, maybe her teacher has some clue where she might have gone."

Grateful to have a concrete plan instead of this mindless panic, she nodded and followed him out to his truck.

On the six-mile ride to town, she was silent and tense, her mind racing with terrible possibilities. While Matt drove, he compensated for her reticence by keeping up a running commentary about everything and nothing, more words than she'd ever heard from him.

He was doing it to keep her from dwelling too long on all those awful scenarios. She knew it and was touched by his effort but she still couldn't get past her worry to carry on a real conversation with him.

The trip from the ranch to town had never seemed so long. "Let's stop at your house first," Matt said when they finally passed the wooden city limit sign. "It's on the way and that seems the logical place for her to go."

When she didn't answer, he reached a hand across the seat to cover hers. "Hang in there, Doc. She's probably sitting at home waiting for you to get there and wondering if she'll still be grounded by the time she graduates from college."

She managed a shaky smile and turned her hand over to clasp his fingers. Reassured by the heat and strength there, she clung to his hand the rest of the way. When she saw her little brick bungalow was still dark and silent, her fingers tightened in his.

Matt pulled in to the driveway and turned off the pickup's rumbling engine. He gave her hand a comforting squeeze. "Okay, she's not here. But maybe she left a message for you."

Trying to keep the panic at bay, Ellie climbed from the truck and unlocked the side door leading to the kitchen. When she saw no blinking light on the answering machine, she almost sobbed. She probably would have if Matt hadn't followed her inside.

Instead, she flipped on every light in the kitchen, even the one over the stove. It seemed desperately important suddenly, as if she could fight the darkness inside her.

That done, she moved through the house urgently, only vaguely aware of Matt shadowing her while she turned on the lights in every single room until the house blazed like a Christmas tree.

The porch light. She should turn that on, too, so her little girl could find her way home.

She went to the front door and flipped the switch. Just as she turned away, something jarring, out of place, caught the edge of her vision through the small beveled window in the door.

She pushed aside the lace curtain for a better look, then felt the blood leave her face and a horrified scream well up in her throat. What came out was a pathetic little whimper like a distressed kitten's, but it was enough for Matt to grab her and shove her aside so he could look.

He bit out a string of oaths and yanked the door open. "What the hell is that?"

Her hands began to shake, and she was afraid she was going to be sick. "I…I think it's a calf fetus."

The yellow porch light sent a harsh glare on the poor little creature, still covered with the messy fluids of birth. She forced herself to walk toward it and saw at once that it was malformed and had probably been born dead.

Matt crouched beside the animal. "Dammit. Why can't Jesse find whoever is doing this to you?"

It had to be connected to the cat left in her truck. She could see that another note had been impaled to the side of the calf with an acupuncture needle.

She didn't want to look at it. She would rather shove the needle through her own tongue, would rather have a hundred needles jammed into every inch of her body than have to face the idea that there could be some link between this gory offering and her baby.

But there had to be. She knew it as sure as death.

"He's got her," she said raggedly.

Matt stared. "Who?"

"Whoever left this has Dylan. I know it."

She couldn't breathe suddenly, couldn't think. Could only watch numbly while he ripped the note away to read it, then uttered a long string of oaths.

"What does it say?"

Wordlessly, he handed her the note. Her stomach heaved after she read it, and she had to press a hand to her mouth as bile choked her throat.

"If you don't want your kid to end up like this," the note said in that same ominous black type that had been used for the note left in her truck, "you're going to have to prove it."

Chapter 15

Prove it? Prove it how?

Ellie stared at the note in her hand, afraid that if she looked away from those sinister words she would find the whole world had collapsed around her. This couldn't be happening. Salt River, Wyoming, was a slice of America. Soccer games, PTA meetings, decent, hardworking people. She would never suspect someone here could be capable of such hideous evil.

Her baby.

Someone had her little girl.

She thought of Dylan, helpless and scared and wondering where her mother was, and she felt herself sway as every drop of blood rushed from her head.

Instantly, Matt was there, folding her into his arms. "Hang on, sweetheart. Stay with me."

"I have to find her. He has her."

"Shh. I know. I'll call Jess. He'll know what to do."

The phone in the kitchen jangled suddenly, sounding obscenely loud in the quiet house. She stared at it, then her heart began to pound. It was him. She knew it without a shadow of a doubt.

She raced into the other room and grabbed the phone before it could ring again. "Where is she, you sick son of a bitch?" she snarled.

An electronically disguised voice laughed roughly in her ear. "You'll find out. If you do what you're told."

"What do you want?"

"You're still here. I thought I told you to leave. You obviously didn't learn your lesson."

"I'll go. I'll leave now, tonight. Please, just bring back my little girl." She hated the pleading in her voice but she would have groveled to the devil himself if it would have kept her baby safe.

A bitter laugh rang in her ear. "I won't make it that easy on you anymore. You had your chance. Now you have to cough up a hundred grand before you kiss Star Valley goodbye."

"I don't have that kind of money!" Sheer astonishment raised her voice at least an octave.

"You'd better find it by tomorrow noon. I'll let you know the drop-off site."

Before she could answer, could beg to at least talk to her daughter and make sure she was safe, the line went dead.

For several seconds, she stood in the harsh lights of her kitchen holding the phone while the dial tone buzzed in her ear. Then she carefully replaced it onto the base, collapsed into the nearest chair and buried her face in her hands.

* * *

Matt found her there when he returned to the kitchen after hanging up the extension in the bedroom. Everything in him screamed out to comfort her, but he knew he had to deal with necessities first. He called Jesse's emergency number, then quickly and succinctly laid out for his brother what had happened.

That done, he finally could turn his attention to Ellie. He knelt by her side and pulled her trembling form into his arms. "We'll get her back, Doc. Jesse's a good man to have on your side. He'll find her."

Her breathing was fast and uneven, and she seemed as fragile as a snowflake in his arms. "Where am I going to come up with a hundred thousand dollars in cash by noon tomorrow?"

"Me."

She stared at him, eyes dazed like a shell-shocked accident victim. "You?"

"I'll call the bank right now and get started on the paperwork." The ranch had a line of credit more than twice what the kidnapper was asking—plenty of credit and enough influence that he shouldn't have any problem rushing things through.

"It's almost seven-thirty," she said numbly. "The bank closed hours ago."

"The bank manager played football with me in high school. I'll call him at home. When Rick hears the story, I know he'll want to help, even if he has to work all night putting the ransom together."

He could almost see the objections gather like storm clouds in her eyes. Damn stubborn woman was going to put up a fuss even now. Sure enough, she shook her head. "No. I can't take your money. I'll…I'll figure something else out."

"Like what? Sell a kidney?"

That little chin of hers tilted toward the ceiling. "I don't know. But this is my problem, and I'll find a way."

It took everything in him not to reach out and shake her until her teeth rattled. This was for real. Didn't she realize that? He didn't have either the time or the patience to work at wearing down that brick wall of independence she insisted on building around herself.

"Look," he snapped, "I'm going to help you, whether you want me to or not, so just deal with it."

"This is serious money, Matt."

"Chances are the bastard won't get far enough away to spend even a few dollars of it before Jess finds him. I mean it, you don't have a choice, Ellie. For once, just accept my help gracefully."

She studied him, her green eyes murky with fear and frustration, then she crossed to the phone and ripped off a piece of paper from a pad next to it, scribbled on it for a moment, then handed it to him.

"These are my terms."

He read it quickly, then scowled. "What the hell is this?"

"I'll let you help with the ransom only if I can deed over the clinic and this house to you. It's probably not binding just handwritten like that, but I'll have official papers drawn up as soon as I can. You have my word on it."

"No way. Then what will you do without a clinic?"

"I'll be leaving anyway," she said tonelessly. "I won't be needing it."

He refused to think about how the idea of her leaving sliced into him like a jagged blade. "What am I supposed to do with an animal hospital? I'm a rancher, not a vet."

"Sell it and take the profits. It won't begin to cover what you're loaning me, but it will be a start. I'll have to figure out a way to pay back the rest as soon as I can."

He wanted to crumple it up and throw it in her face, but now wasn't the time for his temper to flare. If this was the only way she would take his help, he would let her think he was agreeing to her terms. Then he would shred the blasted thing into tiny little pieces and mail them to her.

As he pocketed the paper, a bleak resignation settled in his gut.

She was leaving, and there wasn't a damn thing he could do about it.

Her mom was gonna be so mad.

Dylan tried to keep from shivering, but it was really hard, not only because it was cool and damp on the straw-covered cement floor but also from the fear that was like a big mean dog chewing away inside her.

She didn't have a clue where she was or who had put her here. But she did know she was in serious trouble.

This was all her fault for disobeying. Her mom told her she was always supposed to walk right to the clinic after school, and she usually did. Today, though, she'd decided to take the long way.

Cheyenne Ostermiller said her dad was going to sell her pony since she got a new horse for her birthday and that if Dylan wanted to buy it, she could probably get a good deal.

She wanted that pony so bad.

It was all she had been able to think about since lunch, when Cheyenne told her about it. All afternoon, during math and music and writer's workshop, she hadn't been able to do anything but daydream about having her own horse. Taking care of it, feeding it, riding anytime she wanted.

Since it didn't look like her mom was going to marry Mr. Harte any time soon, she at least ought to be able to get a horse of her very own. It was only fair.

All she planned to do was walk by Cheyenne's house and take a look at the paint in the pasture. Maybe make friends with him, if he'd let her. It was pretty far out of the way on the edge of town, but she figured if she hurried she'd only be a little late to the clinic and SueAnn wouldn't even notice.

The pony had been perfect. Sweet and well-mannered and beautiful. She'd been standing there petting him and trying to figure out how she could convince her mom to buy him when she heard a truck pull up.

She hadn't paid much attention, thinking it was probably Cheyenne's mom or dad. Next thing she knew, somebody had grabbed her from behind and stuffed a rag that tasted like medicine into her mouth. It must have been something to put her to sleep because the next thing she knew, she woke up lying on the straw in this windowless cement room that reminded her of the quarantine room at the clinic.

She shivered again and pulled her parka closer around her. If only it were the clinic. Then she could bang on the door and bring SueAnn or her mom running.

This was newer than her mom's clinic, though. And instead of being clean and nice, this room had an icky smell, and the straw on the cement floor didn't seem very fresh.

Where could she be? And who would want to kidnap her?

If she weren't so scared, she might have been able to look on this whole thing as a big adventure, something to tell Lucy and the other kids at school about. But she couldn't help thinking about her mom and how worried she probably was and how mad she was gonna be when she found out Dylan hadn't gone straight home after school.

Tears started burning in her throat, and she sniffled a few times, but then she made herself stop. She couldn't be a crybaby. Not now. Crying didn't help anything, that's what her mom always said.

Her mom never cried. But she figured even her mom would have been a little scared a few moments later when there was a funny noise by the door then the knob started to turn.

She huddled as far into the corner as she could, her heart pounding a mile a minute, as a man walked through the door wearing a stupid-looking clown mask with scraggly yellow hair.

"You're awake." The voice from inside the mask sounded hollow and distorted, like when you talked into a paper cup, only a whole lot spookier.

She was afraid she was gonna pee in her pants and she was breathing as hard as she did when Mrs. Anderson made them run a mile in gym class, but she tried to stay calm, just like her mom would have done.

"Keep your hands off me. I know karate," she lied. "I'll kick you so hard in the you-know-where, you'll wish you were dead."

Through the round holes for eyes in the plastic clown mask, she could see pale blue eyes widen, and the alarm in them gave her confidence to sit up a little straighter.

"No. You've got this all wrong. That's disgusting! I'm not going to touch you. Look, I just brought you a couple of blankets and a pillow. It's cold in here. I'm sorry, but I didn't have any place else to put you."

She stuck her jaw in the air defiantly. "How about my house?"

The kidnapper made a sound that might have been a laugh. "Nice try. But I'm afraid that's not possible right now. You're stuck with me for a while, kid."

He handed the blankets and a small pillow to her but she refused to reach for them, just continued watching him warily.

"Nobody's going to hurt you," he said impatiently. "Just don't make any trouble and you'll be back with your mom by lunchtime tomorrow, I promise."

"Why should I believe you?"

"Believe what you want. Makes no difference to me. I have to go out for a while. Are you hungry? I can pick up some dinner for you on the way back, if you want. How about a nice hamburger and some French fries from the drive-up?"

Despite her fear, her mouth watered, since she'd been too busy talking about Cheyenne's pony to eat much of the cafeteria's chicken surprise at lunchtime. She wasn't about to tell him that, though, so she kept her lips stubbornly zipped.

The clown mask wobbled a little as the man sighed. "I'll take that as a yes. I'll be back in a little while. Maybe later, I can bring a TV in for you if that will help pass the time."

After he left, she wanted to throw a pillow at the door. What a jerk, if he really thought he could make everything all better by bringing her a hamburger and a TV.

She wanted to go home and hug her mom and tell her she was sorry. She wanted to sleep in her own bed, not in some stinky cement room with moldy straw on the floor.

There had to be some way to get out of here. But how?

She spread one blanket on the floor, then sat down and crossed her legs and wrapped the other one around her. She could figure this out. She just had to put her mind to it.

After a minute of thinking hard, a smile suddenly crept over her face, and she knew exactly what she was going to do.

See, she had this plan....

Matt stood in the doorway between Ellie's living room and kitchen feeling about as useful as a milk bucket under a bull.

His brother had taken over as soon as he arrived, and now Jess was on the couch holding both of Ellie's hands while he briefed her on what was happening. "The FBI handles kidnapping cases but they can't get agents here from Salt Lake City for at least an hour or two," Jess was saying.

"That long?" Her voice sounded small, tight, not at all like the confident, self-assured woman he'd come to care about so much.

"I'm sorry, Ellie. It takes time to mobilize a team and send them up here by chopper. In the meantime, I have every one of my officers and as many deputies as the sheriff could spare out interviewing anybody who might have seen her after school. They'll keep in constant contact and let us know if anything breaks."

She drew in a ragged-sounding breath, and Jesse squeezed her hands. "Dispatch is getting call after call from people wanting to help look for her. Your buddy Steve Nichols has offered to head up the volunteer search effort and he's getting plenty of support. Nobody in town wants to believe something like this could happen in Star Valley."

"Thank you so much for everything you're doing," she said softly.

Jess's mouth twisted into a reassuring smile. "We'll find her, El. I promise."

Given the circumstances, Matt was ashamed of himself for the powerful urge raging through him to yank his little brother off the couch and shove him out the door.

It really chapped his hide that she could sit there looking all grateful to Jess for what he was doing to help find Dylan and still go all prickly at Matt's offer to help.

She wouldn't grab Matt's hand if she were drowning, yet she seemed to think Jess hung the damn moon.

All this time, he thought she just had a hard time letting anyone help her. Now he realized it was only *him* whose help she didn't want. Why? Was it only his brother's badge that made the difference?

He cared about her a whole hell of a lot more than Jess did. They had a relationship, as stormy as it had been. So why did she continue to push him away?

"You've been so kind," she said to his brother, and Matt decided he'd taken just about all he could.

"I'm going to call Rick about getting started on the ransom," he said abruptly, daring either of them to argue with him. Her kid was a lot more important than his hurt feelings, and he needed to keep that uppermost in his mind. "I'll use my cell phone so I don't tie up your line here."

He stalked outside and noticed the temperature had dropped. A cold wind howled out of the south, promising an end to the January thaw. He barely felt it sneaking through his coat as he made his way to his truck, ashamed of himself for letting his temper get the better of him.

Inside the truck, he quickly dialed Rick Marquez's number. The bank manager answered on the second ring, and Matt quickly filled him in on Dylan's kidnapping.

"I just heard," Rick said, his voice tight with shock. "MaryBeth just got off the phone with Janie Montgomery, whose niece works over at the police station. Any leads on what kind of an SOB would do such a terrible thing?"

"Jess is working on it."

"How's Dr. Webster holding up?"

"Pretty shook up. Who wouldn't be?"

"It's a real shame. Nice woman like that. Anything I can do?"

"Matter of fact, Rick, there is. I need to borrow some money from my line of credit." He cleared his throat. "Um, a hundred thousand dollars. Think you could round up that much cash by tomorrow morning?"

There was a long, pregnant pause on the other end of the phone. Even though he was the meanest linebacker Star Valley High had ever seen and had fooled many an opponent into thinking he was just another dumb jock, Rick was as smart as a bunkhouse rat. "You're giving Ellie the money for the ransom?"

The speculation in his friend's voice made him bristle. Would everybody in town have the same prurient reaction? Probably, if word got out. He blew out a breath, suddenly realizing at least one of the reasons Ellie objected to his help. People were going to read far more into it than just one friend helping out another.

"Yeah," he said gruffly. "Yeah, I am. You got a problem with that?"

"You sure that's a good idea, Matt?"

He had no choice. Even though she would probably choke on her own tongue rather than admit it, she needed his help. And he was damn well going to give it.

"Can you get the money or not?" he asked, impatience sharpening his tone.

"It will take a lot of wrangling tonight, but I think I should be able to get my hands on that much."

"Good. Let me know as soon as the papers are ready and I'll come sign them."

After a moment, Rick ventured into risky waters again. "Is there something going on between you and Ellie Webster I should know about?"

Other than I'm crazy in love with her? The thought rocketed into his head, and he stared out the windshield as the wind rattled the skeletal branches of her sugar maple tree.

Love? No way. He didn't love her. He couldn't. He just didn't have that in him anymore. Not after Melanie.

On the other hand, what else could he call it when he suddenly couldn't imagine a life without her?

Yeah. He had it bad. He was only shocked it took him this long to figure it out.

"Matt?" Rick's voice yanked him back to the conversation.

"We're friends," he finally said.

"Pretty darn good friends if you're willing to cough up a hundred Gs for her."

"Look, I don't need a lecture. Her kid's been kidnapped, and I'm only trying to do what I can to make sure she comes back safely. Just get the money, okay?"

"I hope you know what you're doing."

He clamped his teeth together. It would have been easier to hold up a damn train. "I'll call you later to find out how it's going," he snapped.

He was getting ready to hang up when a thought occurred to him. "Wait a minute," he said to Rick. "You have your finger on the financial pulse of the whole valley, right? You probably have a pretty good idea who might be in need of a little cash, don't you?"

"Some." Rick drew the word out slowly, warily.

"So you could maybe point out a couple of people who might have a financial incentive to do something like this."

"I could. Of course, then I'd lose my job for handing out confidential bank information. I'm sorry, but I happen to like my job, Matt."

"A couple of names. That's all I'm looking for."

"No."

"What I can't figure out is why somebody would want her to leave town so badly they'd be desperate enough to risk fifteen to life on a federal offense like kidnapping. We're talking some major time here."

"Leave town?"

"Yeah. That's one of the conditions of him returning Dylan. Seems to me that was just as important to the kidnapper as the money. More, maybe. So who would benefit with Ellie out of the picture?"

"Even if I had any ideas, I couldn't tell you. You're not even a cop!"

"I can have Jess on the line in two seconds. Or better yet, why don't I call back and tell MaryBeth all about that little blond buckle bunny who followed you clear down from Bozeman after the college rodeo finals?"

"Hey, that was way before I got married." Despite it, Matt could hear the panic in his old friend's voice.

He pushed his advantage. "As I recall, you and Mary-Beth were almost engaged. Man, that blonde was one hot little number, wasn't she?"

There was a long, drawn-out pause, then Rick sighed heavily. "I don't know what you're looking for. But I can maybe give you one name of somebody who might have a motive."

"Go ahead. I'm listening."

As soon as Rick mentioned the name, his heart started to pound. This was it. He knew it in his bones.

Chapter 16

Ellie sat at the kitchen table drinking the glass of water Jess had forced on her.

This had to be a nightmare. But if it was, it was a pretty surreal one. Matt's brother sat beside her barking orders into the phone while the doorbell rang again with yet another concerned neighbor bearing food.

The Salt River grapevine worked fast. She'd received the ransom call less than forty-five minutes ago, and already she had at least four casseroles in the fridge and a half-dozen plates of cookie bars.

How did people whip these things up so fast? And did anyone really think tuna noodle bake with crushed potato chips on top was going to make everything okay?

Food seemed to be the panacea for every trouble in Star Valley. She wondered if there was some secret cookbook spelling out the best way to handle every situation. *Betty Crocker's Crisis Cuisine?*

Your neighbor's kid gets busted for growing pot? Take over banana nut bread. Your best friend's husband walks out on her for some secretary he met over the Internet? A nice beef pie ought to do the trick.

Your veterinarian's little girl is kidnapped walking home from school? Pick your poison. Anything was apparently appropriate, from soup to nuts.

Fortunately SueAnn had rushed right over to run interference at the door. There was nothing left for Ellie to do but sit here obsessing about what kind of monster would steal a nine-year-old girl.

She couldn't think about it. If she did, she would go crazy imagining Dylan's terror. Her mind prowled with terrible possibilities. Every time she started to think about it, she wanted to fall apart, to disintegrate into a mindless heap, but somehow she managed to hold herself together.

Still, when Matt burst into the kitchen a few moments later she had to fight with everything in her not to jump up and burrow against that strong chest.

She'd been so horrible to him, it was a wonder he would even stand to be in the same room with her. She had seen the hurt in his eyes when she pushed him away, when she rejected the comfort he wanted to give. She hated herself for it, but she couldn't seem to bend on this.

The need to lean on him, to let him take this terrible burden from her, was so powerful it terrified her. She couldn't, though. This was her burden and hers alone.

She had to be strong for her little girl.

Once she started down that slippery slope and let

herself need him, it would be so easy to tumble all the way to full dependence. She was afraid she would lose herself in the process. And then what good would she be for Dylan?

Matt spared her one quick glance, then turned to his brother. "I think I know where she is. Come on, let's go get her."

Jess stared at him like he'd just grown an extra couple of appendages. "Lou, I'm gonna have to call you back," he said into the phone. "Yeah. Let me know as soon as you hear from the Feds."

He hung up the phone and frowned at his brother. "Are you completely nuts?"

"I just got a lead I think you'll be interested in. Did you know Steve Nichols is delinquent on payments to the Salt River bank to the tune of about ninety-five thou? He's up to his eyeballs in debt and is just a few weeks away from foreclosure on that fancy new clinic he just built."

Ellie stared at him, trying to process the information. "Steve? You think *Steve* took Dylan?" She wouldn't have been more shocked if he'd accused Reverend Whitaker.

"It makes sense, doesn't it? Somebody's been trying real hard to run you out of town. Who would benefit more if you left Star Valley than your main competition?"

"I hardly have a practice anymore! I'm not much of a threat to him."

"If he's only breaking even by the skin of his teeth, maybe you're what stands between survival and failure."

"But…but we're friends. He even offered to head up the search effort for Dylan."

"Think about it, Doc. Whoever left those notes for you had access to two things—dead animals and needles. Doesn't it make sense that it might be another vet?"

She couldn't believe it. Not Steve. He had welcomed her into town, had treated her as a respected colleague and a friend.

"That's not enough for an interview, let alone a search warrant," Jess snapped.

Matt stared him down. "I'm not a cop, little brother. I don't need a warrant."

Jess glared for a moment, a muscle working in his jaw, then he picked up the phone again. "Lou, patch me through to Steve Nichols, will you?"

A minute later, he growled into the phone. "What do you mean, he's not there? I thought he was coordinating the civilian searchers."

After another pause, he hung up. "Lou says he had to take care of some business at his clinic. She said he told her he'd be back in an hour or so."

"Then that's probably where he took Dylan, to his clinic."

"You don't know that. It doesn't mean a damn thing."

Matt shoved on his Stetson. "I'm going, Jess. You can come along or you can sit here on your duff and forget we ever had this conversation. Your choice."

"I think you're crazier than a duck in a desert," Jess growled. "But I'm not about to let you head over there by yourself in this kind of mood."

"I'm going, too." Ellie jumped up from her chair.

Both of them looked at her with the exact same glower. "Forget it," Matt said. "It could be dangerous."

She glowered right back. "This is my child we're talking about. I'm going with you."

"You'll stay in the truck, then."

Not likely. She pressed her lips together, and Matt finally sighed. "Come on, then."

They took Jesse's big department Bronco so he could radio for backup if necessary, but he drove without sirens or lights.

Steve's clinic was a low-slung, modern facility on the other side of town. Ellie had always thought it looked more like some kind of fancy assisted living center than a country vet's office, with a porte cochere and that long row of high, gleaming windows.

The blinds were closed, but she could see the yellow glow of lights inside. If Dylan wasn't there—and Ellie wasn't nearly as convinced as Matt seemed to be that she was—Steve would be hurt and outraged when they barged in and accused him of kidnapping her.

She couldn't let it bother her, she decided. In the scheme of things, when it came to her daughter, the possibility of hurting Steve's feelings didn't matter at all.

"Let me do the talking," Jesse said after he drove under the porte cochere and turned off the Bronco.

"Sure, as long as you're getting answers."

Jess rolled his eyes at his brother, and Ellie felt like doing the same thing when Matt turned to her and ordered her to stay put.

She thought about obeying for all of ten seconds, then waited until they were at the front door of the clinic before she climbed out of the vehicle and followed them.

Matt scowled when he saw her but said nothing. As they walked inside, she thought she saw just the slightest movement behind the long, low wall separating the reception desk from the waiting area.

Before she could react, the men both tensed and

moved together, their shoulders touching so they created a solid, impenetrable protective barrier in front of her.

Jesse's hand went to his sidearm. "Nichols? Is that you?"

Time seemed to slow to a crawl, and the only sound in the room was their breathing. She couldn't see what was happening over their broad shoulders, so she stood on tiptoe for a better look as a small, frightened face peeked over the wall.

Ellie didn't know who moved first, her or Dylan, but an instant later she had shoved her way past the men and gathered her daughter into her arms.

Sobs of overwhelming relief welled in her throat as she held the small, warm weight. She forced them down, knowing she would have time later to give in to them. Right now her daughter needed her to be strong.

Dylan held tightly to her mother. "I'm so glad you're here! I was just calling nine-one-one when I heard a car outside. I thought maybe someone else was helping Dr. Nichols and I got really scared and tried to hide under the desk, then I heard Lucy's uncle. How did you know where I was?"

She couldn't seem to hold her daughter close enough. "It doesn't matter, honey. Are you okay? What happened? Where's Steve?"

A shudder racked her little frame. "In the back, in a quarantine room just like you have. That's where he kept me." She nibbled her bottom lip nervously. "Um, he might need an ambulance. He hit his head on the cement floor pretty hard."

Matt started to take a step toward the hallway, his face blazing with fury, but Jess reached a hand out to stop him. "No way am I letting you go back there right now. That's all I need is a murder investigation on my hands in addition to the kidnapping case. I'll handle this. You stay here with the ladies."

Despite everything, Ellie had to fight a smile when Dylan preened a little at being called a lady.

"Oh. The door's locked," she said suddenly. "I have the key."

She fished around in the pocket of her parka then pulled it out and held it out to the police chief. "Are... are you gonna shoot him?"

Jesse crouched and took her small hand, key and all, and folded it into his. "You want me to, sweetheart?"

"No," she said seriously. "He didn't hurt me. Just scared me a little."

"Sounds like you scared him right back."

Dylan gave a watery giggle then handed over the key, and Jesse disappeared down the hall.

After he was gone, Dylan's smile slid away and she looked nervously at her mother. "This is all my fault, Mom. I'm really sorry. I should have gone right to the clinic after school and I didn't. I just went to see Cheyenne's horse but I'll never do it again, I promise. Don't be mad. Please?"

"Oh, honey. I'm not mad. You're not to blame for this." She was, for not keeping her daughter safe. Just another thing she would have to deal with later. "What happened? How did you get away?"

"I tried to stay calm and use my brain, just like you always tell me to do. I didn't think he'd hurt me, but I still wanted to go home. The first time he came in, I saw he left the key in the lock and it gave me an idea. When he brought me dinner, I tripped him and he fell over and hit his head. I didn't know it was Dr. Nichols until he fell and his mask fell off but as soon as he did, I ran out and locked the door."

How on earth had she managed to raise such an amazing daughter? Ellie hugged her tightly again. "It sounds like you did exactly the right thing."

"You're about the bravest kid I've ever met." Matt's voice was rough, and he reached a hand out and squeezed Dylan's shoulders.

Dylan blushed at his approval and looked at him with an expression of such naked longing in her eyes that Ellie suddenly remembered Lucy's confession earlier in the evening, about how the two girls had connived and schemed to throw her and Matt together.

Dylan wanted a daddy, and she had obviously picked Matt for the role. *Oh, sweetheart.* Her heart ached knowing her daughter was destined for disappointment. She would give Dylan the world, but she could never give her this.

She pushed the thought away. She couldn't worry about how she would ever ease the pain of futile hopes and unrealized dreams. For now, all she could do was hold on to her daughter and whisper a prayer of gratitude that she had her back.

Hours later, Ellie sat in her darkened living room watching the gas logs and their endless flame.

Dylan was finally asleep, lulled only by the grudging promise that, yes, she could go to school the next day and tell everyone of her harrowing adventure and how she had single-handedly rescued herself.

Ellie had held her hand until she'd drifted off. Even long after her daughter was lost to dreamland, she hadn't been able to make herself move, had just sat on the edge of that narrow bed feeling each small breath and thanking Whoever looked over mothers for delivering her baby back safely.

Eventually she'd wandered here. Hard to believe that just a short time ago, the old house had been a frenzy of activity with people coming and going, the phone ringing, all the lights blazing. Now the air was still, with only the low whir of the artificial fire to keep her company.

She didn't mind. In truth, she was grateful for the chance to finally catch hold of her fluttering thoughts and sift through the amazing events of the day.

Every time she thought of Steve and what he had done, her stomach burned and she wanted to break something. He had tried to destroy her in every conceivable way. Financially, professionally, emotionally. She'd never before been the subject of such undiluted hostility, and it frightened her as much as it shocked her, especially because she had been so completely blind to it.

When Steve regained consciousness and found Jess and six other officers surrounding him, he had first tried to bluff his way out of the situation. Faced with the overwhelming evidence against him, though, he'd finally blurted out everything.

He had been desperate and had come to blame all his problems on her for scheming to take his uncle's clinic away from him. It should have come to him, Steve said. He'd spent years working there, even as a kid, cleaning cages and doing miserable grunt work, all with the expectation that someday the practice would be his and he could reap the benefits of his uncle's reputation in the community.

Then Ben had ruined everything by refusing to sell

the clinic to him, instead bringing in an outsider with wacky California ideas that didn't mesh at all with the conservative Star Valley mind-set.

Left with no other choice, Steve had been forced to build his own clinic and had ended up getting in over his head.

He told Jess he realized too late that the community wasn't big enough to support two veterinary clinics so he tried to persuade Ellie to go into business with him to cut down overhead. When she refused, he knew he had to find another way to make her leave, especially after she started to eat into his patient load.

He was the one who had left the warning in her truck. And, he confessed, he'd broken into her truck and read her planner. It hadn't been difficult to study her treatment log and inject specific horses with a virulent bacteria to make it look as if her shoddy care had spread disease.

When that didn't work, he knew he had to take drastic measures, so he'd come up with the twisted kidnapping plan.

She could forgive him the rest. Although it would take time and effort, she could rebuild her reputation, her practice.

But she would never be able to forgive him for terrorizing her little girl.

She'd been a fool not to see it before. No. She hadn't *wanted* to see it, the ugly bitterness he hid so well behind a veneer of friendship. It had been much easier to take Steve at face value, to see what she wanted to see.

SueAnn had seen it, had tried to warn her about him, but she hadn't listened. She had trusted him, and her daughter had ultimately paid the price for her mistake.

She wrapped her arms around her knees and gazed at the flickering flames. How had she forgotten the lessons she'd learned so early in life? Depend only on yourself and you won't ever have to know the cruel sting of disappointment.

A soft knock at the front door disturbed the silence of the house. She felt an instant's fear and then she remembered all was well. Her daughter was safe at home, where she belonged.

She pulled aside the lacy curtain at the door and felt only a small quiver of surprise to find Matt standing on the other side. He wore that shearling-lined ranch coat again, leather collar turned up against the cold night, and his chiseled features were solemn, unsmiling.

He looked strong and solid, and she wanted nothing more than to fall into his arms and weep after the emotional upheaval of the day.

She couldn't, though, and she knew it. Instead, she opened the door and ushered him inside. "Matt! What are you doing here? I thought you went back to the ranch hours ago."

"I did. But I couldn't stay away." He stood just inside the door watching her, a strange light in his blue eyes that suddenly made her as nervous as a mouse in the middle of a catfight.

She cleared her throat and seized on the only benign topic she could think of. Food. "Would you like something to eat? I've got enough here to feed most of the town. I haven't tried any of it, but SueAnn said Ginny Garrett's cinnamon sugar cookies were to die for."

To her intense relief, he shielded that strange light from her with his lashes. "Ginny does make one fine cookie," he said after a moment. "You sure you don't mind?"

"Eat as many as you want." She led the way to the kitchen, where the table practically bowed from the weight of all the plates of goodies covering it. "I've got enough stuff here to have a bake sale."

She peeled back the plastic wrap covering the plate the mayor's wife brought over, and Matt took one cookie and bit into it. "It's comfort food," he said after he'd swallowed. "Sometimes people don't know how else they can help."

"I know. Everyone has been so kind. I've just been trying to figure out how I'm going to find room in my freezer for everything. Maybe you should take some home to your ranch hands."

He leaned a hip against her counter. "Sure."

Grateful for something to do with her hands, she found some paper plates in the back of a cupboard and started loading them up with fudge and lemon bars and chocolate chip cookies.

"So how are you?" he asked solemnly while she worked.

She flashed him a quick look. "Okay. A little shaky still."

"Yeah. Me, too. I keep thinking, what if it had been Lucy? I wouldn't have handled it with nearly the guts you did."

A bitter laugh scored her throat. "I didn't handle anything. I completely fell apart."

He studied her solemnly out of those blue eyes, and for a terrible moment she feared he was going to cross the space between them and pull her into his arms. And then she really *would* fall apart, would give in to the tears of relief and hurt and remembered terror that choked her.

She turned to the table, ashamed that she couldn't control her emotions better, and after a moment of silence, he spoke again. "Almost forgot. One of the reasons I dropped by was to give you this."

Out of the corner of her gaze, she saw him hold out a wrinkled paper. It took her a few seconds to realize what it was, and then her face burned. It was the note deeding the practice over to him in exchange for the money to have her child returned.

She made no move to reach for it, mortified again that she had needed his help, that she had failed her daughter once more.

"Here. Take it. I don't want it," he growled.

As reluctantly as if it were covered in razor blades, she reached for it. A thousand unspoken words hovered between them. She would have preferred to leave them all that way—unspoken—but she knew she had to say something.

"I… Thank you for what you were going to do. I can't say I understand why you would be willing to do such a thing, but it meant a lot to me anyway."

"Did it?"

The hardness of his voice shocked her. "Yes! Of course!"

He didn't say anything, just continued to study her out of those blue eyes, and she flushed under his scrutiny.

"I said I appreciated it. I don't know what more you want from me."

"Why is it so hard for you?"

"What?"

"Accepting help from me. Admitting you're not some kind of superwoman and can't handle every rotten curve life throws at you by yourself."

She tensed. "I don't know what you're talking about." The lie burned her tongue, scorched her heart.

"No matter how hard I try, you keep pushing me away."

Better to hurt him by pushing him away than the alternative. He would leave her shattered if she let him. Would make her weak and needy and *vulnerable,* and she could never allow it, especially after tonight. She was all Dylan had, and she needed to remember that.

She said nothing, knowing there was nothing she *could* say. After a moment, he spoke again, his voice low and expressionless.

"It makes loving you pretty damn hard when you won't let anybody inside."

His words sucked the air from her lungs, every thought from her head. He didn't say he loved her. He *couldn't* have. It was a mistake. A terrible, cruel mistake.

Terror flapped through her on greasy bat wings. How could he say such a thing? Didn't he realize that she didn't want his love, that she couldn't handle it?

Her breath started coming in deep, heaving gulps. What was she going to do? She didn't want to hurt him, but she couldn't let him destroy her like her father had destroyed her mother.

"Aren't you going to say anything?" he finally asked.

I love you. Heaven help me, I love you. Even though I know you would leave me broken and bloody, I want to curl up against you, inside you, around you, and never, ever let go.

Instead, she made her voice tight, toneless, and hated herself for it. "What do you want me to say, Matt?"

He gazed at her, and she nearly sobbed at the hurt in his eyes, then those blue depths hardened. "How about the truth? That you love me, too. That you push me away because you're afraid."

He knew. Shame coursed through her. How could he say he loved her when he knew what a terrible coward she was?

"I'm sorry," she said, curling her hands into fists at her sides. "I can't tell you what you want to hear."

"You mean you won't."

"That, too." Her hands were trembling, and she didn't know if they would ever, ever stop.

"Dammit, Ellie. You don't think loving you, needing you, scares the ever-living hell out of me, too? It's the absolute last thing I ever wanted or expected."

She dared a look at him and found his eyes fierce with emotion.

"My wife walked out on me, Ellie. Before that, she screwed around with just about every guy in town. I told myself I didn't care, that I'd stopped loving her long before she took off, but Melanie still left me with deep scars covering every inch of my heart. I thought they'd be there forever, and I'd even learned to live with them."

He reached for her then, picked up one fisted hand and brought it to his lips. "But then you blew into town with your smart mouth and your compassion and your courage. And one day I realized I couldn't even feel those scars anymore. You healed them, Doc. I don't know how, but while you were treating my horses, you were working your magic on me, too."

This time a sob did escape her mouth, and she

yanked her hand back to press it against her mouth so the rest didn't follow.

"I love you, Ellie," he went on. "I want you in my life, forever if you'll have me. Up until now, you've shown more courage than any woman I've ever met. Don't let your fear win now."

For one wonderful, terrible moment, she let herself believe in fairy tales. In knights on white horses and orange blossoms and a happily ever after filled with laughter and love and joy.

And then the glowing picture faded.

In its place was a ramshackle trailer and a solemn-eyed little girl watching a woman who drank too much and sold her body and sobbed every night for a man who would never come back.

"I'm sorry," she whispered, and blood seeped from her heart.

"I won't ask again." His terse warning was edged with infinite sadness.

She hitched in a ragged breath. "I know. I... Goodbye, Matt."

With one last, searching look, he shoved on his Stetson and walked out into the night.

Only after he closed the door quietly behind him did her knees buckle, and she slid to the hard linoleum floor of her kitchen and wept.

Chapter 17

He never would have believed it.

Matt stood in the gymnasium of the elementary school on Valentine's Day, completely amazed at what creativity and a little elbow grease could achieve.

Instead of a dingy old room that smelled like a cross between canned peas and dirty socks, the gym had been completely transformed into a magical place.

Thousands of little twinkling white lights had been strung across the ceiling like stars in the night sky and wrapped around the branches of a couple dozen small trees temporarily commandeered from Jerry Clayton's greenhouse in town. A city skyline painted by the elementary school art classes graced the stage, covered by even more tiny white lights so it looked as if the windows of the buildings really glowed.

With the lights dimmed and the high school's jazz

band playing old dance numbers, this was the crowning jewel of the library fund-raiser—which by all accounts looked to be a smashing success.

It had been Ellie's idea to try to provide something for everyone at the fair. The little kids were still running from classroom to classroom using the tickets their parents had purchased for fishponds and beanbag tosses and cakewalks. Their older siblings were busy in the auditorium watching a PG-rated scary movie. And judging by the crowd already out on the dance floor, their parents and grandparents were obviously enjoying the romantic escape the committee had created.

He thought he would feel pretty weird about having his name listed on the program as one of the organizers, but as he watched couples dancing cheek-to-cheek under the starry lights, he had to admit to a fair amount of pride.

All evening, people had been telling him what a great job the committee had done. It seemed bitterly ironic that he'd been even a little instrumental in helping everyone else celebrate this holiday for romance, especially when things with Ellie had ended so badly.

She was here somewhere, but he hadn't caught more than a fleeting glimpse of her all night as she ran from crisis to crisis.

Even those brief, painful glimpses were better than what he had endured the last three weeks. Before today, he hadn't seen her since the terrible night he'd gone to her house, told her his feelings and had them thrown back in his face.

He wanted to be angry at her. He had been for a day or two, and the thunder and fury had been much easier to deal with than this constant, aching sadness that settled in his bones and weighed down his heart.

Why was she being so stubborn about this? He knew she loved him. She never would have given herself to him so sweetly, passionately, if she didn't. He couldn't make her admit it, though. Not when she so obviously wanted to deny her feelings, to him and to herself.

A couple of giggles sounded behind him, distracting him from the grimness of his thoughts, and he turned to find Lucy and Dylan being teased by Jess. The girls both wore dresses for a change and had put their hair up, and they looked entirely too grown up for his peace of mind.

"Hey, big brother." Jess grinned. "I think we need to escort these lovely ladies out on the dance floor. What do you say?"

The girls giggled again, and he summoned a smile for their benefit. "I think we'd be stupid not to grab the two prettiest girls here while we have the chance."

Jess had already snagged Lucy so Matt obligingly held his arm out to Dylan, who took it with a blush that reminded him painfully of her mother. Out on the dance floor, she stumbled around awkwardly for a moment then quickly lost her shyness and started jabbering away about her favorite subject, horses.

"My mom says maybe I can get a horse in the summer, when I'd have more time to take care of him and learn to ride him. That would be so cool. Then I could ride with Lucy around the ranch without anybody having to worry about us getting into trouble."

Like that day would ever come. The two of them invented the word. "I'll believe that when I see it," he teased.

Ellie's daughter giggled again. "Well, we wouldn't get into trouble because I don't know how to ride, anyway."

He smiled and twirled her around. Dylan was a great kid, despite her mischievous streak. Full of spunk and fire, just like her mother. He thought of the night she had spent frightened and alone in a concrete room because of that bastard Nichols and saw red again. Good thing the man was in the county jail awaiting sentencing after his guilty plea. Maybe by the time he was released, Matt might have cooled down enough to keep from beating the hell out of him.

"Oh, look," Dylan said suddenly. "There's my mom."

She pulled her hand from his arm and started waving vigorously to someone behind him, and he turned and found Ellie standing alone on the edge of the dance floor.

In the low, shimmering light, her green eyes looked huge. Haunted.

"Doesn't she look pretty?" Dylan asked innocently, and he dared another look. Like her daughter, Ellie wore a dress—a soft, sapphire-blue clingy thing that flared and bunched in all the right places.

He cleared his throat, but his voice still came out gruff. "Very," he said.

"I told her she'd be a lot prettier if she'd smile once in a while," Dylan said, sounding like a middle-aged, nagging mother instead of a nine-year-old, "but she hasn't been doing much of that lately."

"No?" He tried to sound casual and disinterested, even though the little scamp had his full attention, and she probably knew it.

"She's been really sad," Dylan said. "She even cries

at night sometimes after I'm in bed, so I know something must be really wrong. My mom never cries."

His heart stuttered in his chest at the thought of Ellie crying alone in her house.

Damn stubborn woman. If she was hurting, it was her own fault. Didn't she know how absolutely right they were for each other? He needed her to bring lightness and laughter into his life, to keep him from taking himself too seriously.

And she needed him to show her nobody expected her to bear the whole weight of the world by herself.

"Maybe you could talk to her, or ask her to dance, even. You're friends, aren't you? That might make her feel better."

Dylan's green eyes shone with hope, and he hated to douse it, but he was pretty sure he was the last person on earth Ellie wanted to talk to right about now.

On second thought, maybe that's just what he needed to do. He'd told her he wouldn't grovel. But just trying to talk some sense into her wasn't really the same, was it?

He had to try. Even if he looked like a lovesick fool, he had to try. Much more of this heartache was going to destroy both of them.

As soon as the dance was over, he would grab her, he decided, yank her into a dark corner and kiss her until she came to her senses.

But when the music ended and he walked Dylan back to Lucy and Jess, Ellie was nowhere to be found.

She couldn't do this.

Ellie stood outside the side door of the school breathing the February night air and praying the bitter cold would turn her heart to ice, would take away this pain.

She pressed a palm to her chest, breathing hard with the effort it took to regain control of her emotions. Seeing Matt tonight—looking so strong and gorgeous in his black dress jeans and Western-cut shirt—had been bad enough. Watching him spin around the dance floor while Dylan smiled at him like he'd just handed her the stars had been excruciating.

They looked like they belonged together—like they *all* belonged together—and she knew she had to escape.

What a fool she had been to think she could handle seeing him tonight without falling apart. She had spent three weeks trying to get through each day without thinking about him more than once every five minutes. Of course the shock of seeing him would be an assault to her senses, especially surrounded by all the trappings of the most romantic day of the year.

How was she going to get through this? They lived in a small, tight-knit community and were bound to bump into each other occasionally. Would it get easier in time or would her heart continue to pound out of her chest and her pulse rate skyrocket every time she saw him?

What could she do? She wasn't sure she had the strength to endure seeing him every week or even every month, not if it made her feel as if her heart were being sliced open again and again.

Yet she couldn't leave. She had a job here, a business that was booming now that people in town knew how Steve had tried to blacken her reputation. She and Dylan had a life now, and she couldn't walk away from that.

She blew out another breath. She could handle this. She was a strong and capable woman who could do anything she set her mind to.

Except stop loving Matthew Harte.

The door at her back was suddenly thrust out, and for one terrible moment she was afraid he had followed her outside. To her vast relief, Sarah McKenzie peeked her pretty blond head out the door.

"Ellie! I was wondering where you ran off to."

"I just needed a little air." A vast understatement. If she'd been any more breathless watching Matt dance with her little girl, she would have needed to yank old Bessie Johnson's portable oxygen tank right out from under her and steal a few puffs.

Concern darkened the schoolteacher's brown eyes. "Everything okay?"

"Sure." Ellie managed a smile. "I've been running all night and I just needed a breather."

"That's why I came to find you. I had to tell you what a fantastic job you and Matt did organizing this evening. I've had so many comments from people telling me it's the best carnival they've ever attended, and they can't remember having such a good time."

"I'm glad people are enjoying themselves."

"And the bottom line is that we've already raised twice what we were expecting for tonight! The school library will have more books than shelf space now."

Ellie smiled. "Maybe next year you can raise enough money to build a whole new library."

"I hope you'll help us again next year. You and Matt both."

Sure. When monkeys fly out of my ears. "Let's get through tonight before we worry about next year."

"Well, I just wanted you to know how good you have been for Salt River. This town needed shaking up. I'm so glad you're staying—we would all miss you very much if you left."

After Sarah slipped inside the school, Ellie stood looking at the rugged mountains glowing in the pale moonlight and thinking about what she had said. If she had given anything to the town, she had received it all back and then some.

She thought of all the people she had come to care about in the months since she had come to Wyoming. Sarah. SueAnn. The rest of the friends she had made on the carnival committee, and the people—some perfect strangers—who had rallied around her after Dylan's kidnapping, bringing food and offers of help and comfort beyond measure.

Her life would have been so much poorer without all of them.

She stared at the mountains as the truth she had refused to see finally slammed into her.

She needed them. All of them.

How stupid she had been. She thought she was so damned independent, so self-sufficient. But she would have crumbled into nothing after Dylan was taken if not for the people of Salt River she had come to love.

She had been trying so hard to stand on her own two feet that she never realized she would have fallen over long ago if it hadn't been for the people around her providing quiet, unquestioning support.

The door pushed open behind her once more, and she thought it would be Sarah again or one of the other committee members. She turned with a teary smile that fell away instantly at the sight of Matt standing in the open doorway, looking strong and solid and wonderful.

Her heart began a painful fluttering in her chest when she thought of how she had wounded him by rejecting the incredible gift of his love.

He had been right. She had pushed him away because she was afraid of needing, of trusting. It had all been for nothing, though. She had needed him from the very beginning, his slow smile, his strength, his love. Especially his love.

She had just been too stubborn to admit it.

Tears choked her again and she suddenly knew, without a shadow of a doubt, that he would never hurt her. He would protect her heart like he had tried to protect her body that day in Steve's office, by placing himself in front of anything that threatened her.

"Hi," she whispered.

He continued to study her, his beautiful, hard face as still as the mountains, and for one terrible moment she was afraid that her epiphany had come too late. That she had lost any chance she might have had.

Then she saw his eyes.

They looked at her with hurt and hunger and a vast, aching tenderness, and she forgot to breathe.

"It's frigid out here," he finally said. "Come inside. Are you crazy?"

A tear slid down her nose, and she quickly swiped at it before it could freeze there. "Yeah. Yeah, I am. Completely crazy. I must be or I wouldn't be so miserable right now."

He said nothing, just continued watching her, and she gathered up that courage he seemed to think she had in spades and took a step forward. "I'm sorry, Matt. I'm so sorry."

He stared at her for several seconds, blue eyes wide with disbelief, then she was in his arms. Her heart exploded with joy as he kissed her, his mouth fierce and demanding.

"I have to say this," she said, when she could think straight again. She pulled away and wrapped her cold hands around the warmth of his fingers. "You were right the other night. I didn't want to let you help me, to let you inside. I think I knew even from the beginning that you would have the power to destroy me if I let you."

"I never would," he murmured.

"I know. I should have realized it then, but I'm afraid I don't have much experience with this whole love thing."

His eyes turned wary suddenly, and she realized she had never given him the words. "I love you, Matt," she said softly. "I love the way you smile at your daughter and the way you take care of your horses and the way you hold me like you never want to let me go. I love you fiercely and I hate so much that I hurt you."

Emotions blazed out of his blue eyes. "I'm tough. I'll survive. Just don't do it again, okay?"

Another tear slipped down her cheek. "I won't. I swear it."

His thumb traced the pathway of that lone tear. "Dylan says you never cry."

She sniffed. "See all the bad habits you're making me develop?"

A soft laugh rumbled out of him, then his face grew serious. "I want everything, Ellie," he warned. "Marriage, kids, the whole thing. I won't settle for less. Are you ready for that?"

She thought of a future with him, of making a home together among these mountains she loved, of raising their daughters together—and maybe adding a few sons along the way with their father's eyes and his strength and his smile.

She couldn't imagine anything more wonderful. In answer, she lifted her mouth to his and wrapped her arms tightly around him.

His exultant laugh rang out through the cold February night. "Come on. Let's go inside where it's warm and tell the girls. Hell, let's tell the whole world."

She went still in his arms, suddenly horrified. "Oh, no. The girls."

He shrugged. "What's the problem? This is what they wanted all along. They figured out we belonged together months before we did."

"That's what I mean." She groaned again. "They are going to be completely insufferable when they find out how well their devious little plan worked."

He winced. "Good point. So what do we do about it?"

"I don't think there's anything we *can* do, just accept the fact that our nine-year-old daughters are smarter than either of us."

"That's a terrifying thought."

"Get used to it, Harte. I have a feeling the two of them are going to make our life extremely interesting."

His smile soaked through her, filling every empty corner of her heart with sweet, healing peace. "I can't wait," he murmured.

She smiled and took the hand he offered. "Neither can I, Matt. Neither can I."

* * * * *

THE COLOR OF COURAGE

Patricia Davids

To Joshua.
You're the best grandson in the world, honey.
Now get those grades up! And to all the
men and women serving in the
United States military. Please accept my thanks
and my humble gratitude.

Prologue

"Lindsey…I need you…to do this."

Standing beside her brother's hospital bed, Sergeant Lindsey Mandel fought back tears. She held his hand though she knew he couldn't feel it. "Danny, what if it doesn't work out?"

"You'll make it work… I know you will." He spoke quickly because he could only talk when the ventilator keeping him alive breathed out.

She brushed her hand over his close-shaven head. He was six years older than she was, thirty-one to her twenty-five. Today, he looked decades older than when she had seen him three months ago. "Don't give up, Danny. You can still get better."

A wry smile twisted his lips. "Who are you…kidding?" What might have been a chuckle turned into a cough and an alarm sounded from the monitor above his bed.

Frightened, Lindsey glanced to Danny's wife, Abigail, sitting on the other side of the bed. Behind her, the door to the room opened and a nurse in green scrubs looked in. The beeping stopped and Abigail waved the woman away. "It's all right. He just needs to stop talking for a while."

Admiring her sister-in-law's calm, Lindsey willed herself to relax. Abigail rose, moved to Lindsey's side and asked, "Why don't we go grab a cup of coffee?"

"Good idea.... Get her...out of here...for a while."

Abigail leaned down and kissed his forehead. "You just want us to leave so you can flirt with the cute nurses."

"Rats...you found...me out." He closed his eyes.

Lindsey leaned down to kiss him, too. "I'll be back," she promised.

He nodded, but his eyes remained closed. He looked so weary. When she turned to go, she heard him say, "I'm proud of you...First Sergeant...Mandel."

A heavy band of emotion squeezed her heart. "I'm proud of you, too, Master Sergeant Mandel."

"Don't spend...your whole leave...in this hospital."

"I'll spend my leave anywhere I choose," she retorted.

A fleeting smile crossed his face. "Headstrong... as ever."

"Because you raised me that way. Stop talking and rest."

Outside of his room, Lindsey paused as several men in uniform walked past, pushing others in wheelchairs. Everywhere she looked, the halls of Walter Reed hospital bustled with activity. Walking silently beside Abigail to a small waiting room, Lindsey waited until her sister-in-law filled two cups from the vending machine. Dressed in a pair of rumpled beige slacks and a wrinkled mauve shirt with her dark hair pulled back haphazardly into a silver clip, Abigail looked worn to the bone.

"The coffee isn't good, but I've had worse." She handed one to Lindsey.

Lindsey stirred a packet of creamer into the piping brew. "I can't believe Danny wants me to take Dakota away. He loves that horse. He's given up, hasn't he?"

Initially, her brother's will to live in spite of his injuries had helped Lindsey cope, but the unfairness of it all weighed on her.

Abigail gestured toward the red vinyl chairs lining the wall. "Why don't we sit down. I don't think he has given up. He's just coming to terms with the reality of the situation. The shrapnel severed his spine. He's a quadriplegic. After three months of therapy, he knows he isn't going to get much better."

"But there's still hope."

"The doctors think, with work, he'll be able to breathe on his own, but he'll never ride again. Yes, he loves that horse. That's why he wants you to take Dakota back to Fort Riley with you."

"Danny has lost so much already. It doesn't seem right to take Dakota away, too."

"Look around you, Lindsey. Most of the men and women who are patients here were wounded in action. Do you know what the majority of them say they want? To stay in the service. To get back to their units. Danny knows he can never go back, but he needs to do something positive. He feels he can do that by donating Dakota to your unit. You have no idea how excited he was when he heard about your transfer into the mounted color guard last year."

"Danny tried to transfer into the Third Infantry a number of times. The Old Guard has a mounted unit. Why not donate Dakota to them? That way Dakota would still be in Washington, D.C., and Danny could go and see him when he's better."

"I thought about that, but the Old Guard only takes black, gray or white horses. Your unit takes bays."

Brown horses with black manes and tails and minimal white markings were the traditional mounts of the Seventh Cavalry, the regiment Lindsey's unit portrayed at Fort Riley, Kansas. Dakota wouldn't be excluded for that reason, but less than half of the horses brought to the fort passed the intensive training requirements.

"What if he isn't suitable for us? Then what?"

"He's just got to be, Lindsey. Please, make this work. It would mean so much to Danny. He desperately needs something to look forward to, or else—or else I'm afraid to think about what could happen."

Chapter 1

Leaning forward in the saddle, Lindsey patted Dakota's neck and tried to quell her nervousness. "This is it, boy. This is your final test. You have to get this right."

The dark brown gelding responded by tossing his head and pulling at the reins as if to show her that he was eager to get down to business. She couldn't help but smile.

Running a hand down her mount's sleek, muscular neck, she found the calmness she needed. She drew a deep, cleansing breath. The cool breeze carried the smell of dust, fallen leaves and the earthy scent of horses. Looking over the fence to the hills rising just beyond the road, she saw the golden-hued stone buildings of old Fort Riley where they stood nestled between oaks, elms and sycamores bearing the first touches of fall colors. Dakota pulled impatiently at the reins again.

"Okay, I'm the one stalling," she admitted. "I just

want this so badly—for you and me, but mostly for Danny."

Each week her brother called for updates about Dakota's training, offering advice and pointers that she didn't really need but accepted anyway. Today, he would be waiting impatiently for her call. She intended to give him good news.

Reaching down, she checked that her saber and rifle would slide easily out of their scabbard and boot. The reproduction models of the 1860s U.S. Cavalry equipment were spotless after her careful preparations that morning. Even the brass buttons of her blue wool cavalry jacket gleamed brightly in the late-morning sun. She was as ready as she could get.

Be with us today, Lord, for Danny's sake.

At the touch of her heels, Dakota bounded forward. Together, they sailed over a series of low jumps, then slid to a halt and whirled back at the end of the field. On the return run, Lindsey drew her saber and headed into a series of poles topped with red and white balloons. As Dakota wove in and out, she slashed left and right, breaking as many as she could. He didn't even flinch at the loud pops or the swish of the sword cutting close beside him.

Four men on horseback waited for her at the end of the course. She slowed to a trot. Each man drew his saber and held it over his head with the tip pointing backward. One by one she struck their swords with her own as she passed close behind them, making the steel weapons ring with bell-like tones.

Sheathing her saber, she drew her pistols. Digging her heels into her mount's sides, she headed into the jumps again, this time blasting the balloons with her revolvers. Dakota raced on without faltering until they cleared the last hurdle. Only one maneuver remained.

Holstering her guns, she pulled the horse to a sliding stop and dismounted. Drawing her carbine rifle from its boot, she gave a low command, lifted Dakota's foreleg and pulled his head around. "Throwing the Horse" was the hardest movement for the young gelding to perform. Many horses refused the command.

To her relief, Dakota knelt, then lay down and rolled onto his side without hesitation.

"Stay down," she ordered. Stretching out behind his back, Lindsey rested her rifle on his shoulder and fired off three rounds. They were only blanks, but the sharp reports were as loud as if they had been real bullets. Dakota jerked slightly at the sound of the first discharge, but remained quietly on his side, providing lifesaving cover for his rider as cavalry horses have been trained to do through the ages.

As the echoes of the last shot died away, Lindsey rose to her feet and gave the command to stand. After scrambling to his feet, Dakota shook himself and waited patiently for her to remount. She wanted to throw her arms around his neck and hug him, but not now, not yet.

"Good boy, you were perfect. Just perfect," she murmured as she swung up into the saddle. She knew she was grinning like a fool, but she couldn't help it. After only three months of training, Dakota had proved himself worthy of a place in the elite Commanding General's Mounted Color Guard at Fort Riley. Danny would be so proud.

She returned to the end of the field, where other members of her unit sat on their horses. Beside the men, Captain Jeffery Watson, her unit commander, stood with his arms crossed and a faint frown on his face. Stopping in front of him, Lindsey saluted smartly.

"Well done, Sergeant Mandel."

"Thank you, sir."

The other men in her unit gathered around. "You looked fine out there." Private Avery Barnes was the next to offer his opinion. The dark-haired Boston native pushed his cap back to smile at her with a roguish grin.

"She always looks good. It was Dakota who looked great," drawled Corporal Shane Ross as he leaned over and patted the horse's neck. It was no secret the tall blond Texan was fond of all the four-legged members of the unit. He took as much pride in their skill as he did in the abilities of the horses' human partners.

"So, does this mean Dakota is in?" the third soldier queried. Private Lee Gillis, the newest enlisted member of the mounted color guard, was watching their captain closely.

Captain Watson reached out to rub Dakota's cheek. "I will admit that I was worried when I learned that Dakota belonged to your brother, Sergeant."

Lindsey gave him a puzzled look. "May I ask why?"

"The last thing I wanted to do was to tell a wounded veteran that his horse wasn't suitable for our unit. Thanks to your hard work, I won't have to do that. I think Dakota makes a fine addition to our stable."

She nearly melted with relief as the men around her grinned and offered their congratulations. "Thank you, sir. I know I speak for my brother when I say that it is an honor to have Dakota accepted."

Crossing his arms again, the captain allowed a smile to soften his stern features. "As the icing on this cake, I wanted you all to know that I just received word from the Joint Task Force-Armed Forces Inaugural Committee that the Commanding General's Mounted Color

Guard has been invited to participate in the upcoming Presidential Inauguration parade."

A cheer of excitement went up from the men. Lindsey grinned at their enthusiasm, "That's wonderful news, sir. Will Dakota be going, too?"

"Dakota has earned his place. And, of course, as the highest ranking non-commissioned officer, you will be the U.S. flag bearer for our unit. I'm sure you'll want to ride Dakota for that, but if you prefer another mount, I'll understand."

"Oh, no, I'll be riding Dakota." Wait until she told Danny. He would burst his buttons with pride.

"I've decided to include Dakota in Saturday's performance. Can he handle the crowd at a Kansas State football game?"

"I know he can, sir."

"Good. That will be all, Sergeant. Dismiss the detail." Captain Watson stepped back from the horses.

Lindsey saluted, dismissed the men and then let the overwhelming happiness sink in. Being asked to participate in the Inaugural parade was an incredible honor. She might be the one bearing the flag, but she would be carrying it for her brother. Giddy with delight, she headed for the stables. This was one phone call she couldn't wait to make.

Early Saturday afternoon, Brian Cutter walked along the edge of the Kansas State University football field in Manhattan, Kansas, leaning heavily on his cane. Half-time activities for the first home game of the year were well underway. The energetic shouts of cheerleaders dressed in purple and white, the noise from thousands of fans and the blare of the band was almost deafening.

But Brian had his eye on a group of halftime performers who seemed unfazed by the clamor.

Beneath the goalposts at the north end of the field, six horses stood quietly waiting for their riders. The matching bays all sported dark blue blankets and Mc-Clellan Cavalry saddles.

He had watched them being unloaded behind the stadium and something in the third horse's gait had caught his attention. The gelding's walk wasn't quite right. Maybe it was nothing more than a bruise from the trailer ride, but he wanted to make sure the horse's rider was aware of what he'd seen. Until the horse was examined, it shouldn't be ridden.

The riders were out now and preparing to mount. Brian tried to hurry, but his bad leg was aching again. He didn't need a weatherman to tell him a cold front was moving in. Sharp pain shot through his hip and forced him to rely more heavily on his cane, making him feel much older than his thirty-two years. He arrived at the temporary picket line just as a young woman dressed in Civil War military garb was checking her saddle and girth.

"Excuse me, miss. I need a word with you." Brian knew he sounded curt and short of breath. She turned her attention on him and whatever he had intended to say flew out of his mind the way a yearling bolts out the barn door and into a summertime pasture.

She was a stunning woman. Even dressed in men's clothing did little to hide her feminine figure. The round, flat-topped soldier's cap with its short bill sat atop a mass of thick, auburn curls, but it was her eyes that captured his attention. An unusual color of silver green, they reminded him of the springtime quaking aspen near his Montana childhood home. A sprinkling of freckles dusted her cheeks and nose. Her lips were full and parted in a sweet smile.

"Yes?" she prompted. Something in her wide smile reminded him of Emily.

He pushed the ridiculous idea aside. His deceased wife and this woman didn't look alike at all.

The female soldier glanced to where the other members of the group were forming up. "You said you needed a word with me? I'm about to go on. Can you make it quick?" Her tone was polite but dismissive. He found himself irritated with her attitude.

"Your horse is lame. You shouldn't be riding him until someone looks at his right front leg."

She frowned, as if deciding whether or not to take him seriously. "Dakota seems fine to me."

To her credit, she walked around the animal and ran her hand down the horse's leg, then led him a few steps to observe him before giving Brian a frosty smile. "I don't see a problem."

"I saw it when he got off the trailer."

She swung up into the saddle with ease. Looking down at him, she managed a smile that wasn't quite polite. "We just finished a fifteen-minute warm-up. He's fine, honest. I'm sorry, but my men are waiting on me."

"You're doing the animal a disservice. You should pull him out of this exhibition until he can be examined."

"Thank you for your concern, but I know this horse better than anyone. If he were having trouble, I'd be the first to notice."

He stepped forward and laid a hand on the horse's bridle. "I'm a vet. I get paid to notice when an animal isn't moving right."

From the corner of her eye, Lindsey saw that several

of the support men from her unit who weren't riding had begun to move toward her. If this guy didn't back off, he might find himself in a lot of trouble. A scene was the last thing she wanted. A big part of the CGMCG's mission was public relations.

"That may be true, but you aren't our vet. Thank you for your concern. Excuse me, I have to go."

"Suit yourself, but you'll only make him more lame. When he's limping tomorrow, remember that I told you so." He stepped aside to let her ride out and join her group.

Lindsey cast a look back at the rude man who seemed to think he had some say in what she did. He was a little above medium height and slender, but not skinny. His gray eyes were piercing and a perfect match to the leaden sky overhead. Nicely dressed in a gray tweed sport coat over a blue button-down oxford shirt and gray slacks, he wasn't a bad-looking guy. She might even have said he was kind of cute except for his personality. *Arrogant* wasn't a strong enough word to describe him.

Dismissing the man's brusque words, Lindsey forced herself to concentrate as the unit lined up for their first maneuver. Today they would begin the exhibition by riding two by two and taking four low hurdles as a column while their bugler blew "To the Gallop." It was a sure crowd-pleaser.

Lindsey patted Dakota's neck while they waited. They were the first horse and rider in a line of three. During his warm-up, he hadn't seemed as eager as usual, but they had been training hard the past few days and they were both tired. Still, he certainly hadn't been favoring either front leg.

"We'll take a few days' rest after today, fella. How does that sound?"

Actually, it sounded like a really good idea. She hadn't realized how tired she was until her conversation with the grumpy guy.

She glanced back once more. He was watching her from the picket line. The wind blew his shaggy blond hair this way and that. The frown on his face made him look intimidating. He was rubbing his right thigh until he saw her looking. He stopped and straightened. Still scowling, he walked down the sidelines in front of the stands. She couldn't help wondering why he needed the cane. Was it a recent injury?

Perhaps the last woman he had tried to bully had kicked him in the shin. The image made Lindsey smile until she realized how unkind it was. The man had only been trying to help.

Beside them, the bugle sounded and Lindsey leaned forward as they began at a walk, then advanced to a trot and then into a gallop down the football field. Making a turn in tight formation, the horses thundered toward a row of jumps set up on the fifty yard line. As they approached the first obstacle, she felt Dakota hesitate then jump off stride. With another horse close behind them, there was no room for error.

Something was wrong. Before she could pull out of line they were on the second jump. Dakota launched forward, and she relaxed. This jump was good. He was fine.

Only he wasn't. His knees buckled when his front feet hit the ground. He fell, catapulting her forward. Lindsey threw out her arms and tried to kick free of the stirrups. She had an instant to breathe a prayer for help before she felt the impact of her body hitting the ground, followed by Dakota's weight rolling over her.

Chapter 2

Brian watched in horror as the woman and her horse went down directly in front of him. The next rider was so close behind that he couldn't turn aside and his horse fell on top of the downed pair. In a split second the precision-riding exhibition had turned into a melee.

Brian hurried toward the pileup even as the other members of the team leaped from their horses to race toward their fallen comrades. One horse scrambled to his feet and limped a few feet away. His rider sat on the ground looking dazed, with blood oozing from a cut on his forehead. The first horse that had gone down was struggling to rise but couldn't gain his feet because the rails and the pillar of the jump were tangled with his legs.

Brian didn't see the woman until he reached the horse's head, but he heard her bloodcurdling scream. She was lying facedown with her right arm pinned beneath her mount. He grabbed the horse's bridle and spoke softly. "Easy boy. Miss, lie still."

She dug the fingers of her free hand into the thick turf. "Get…him…off!"

Each word sounded as if it was being torn from her throat by unbearable pain.

Brian sank to one knee, his stiff leg stretched awkwardly out in front of him and pulled the frightened horse's head into his lap. He knew the animal's struggles could inflict more injury on the trapped rider. He stroked the gelding's cheek until he quieted. "I can't move him yet. Help is coming."

"Is he hurt?" Her voice was muffled, but her concern was unmistakable.

"I can't tell."

She raised her head to look at him. Her hat had come off. Bright auburn curls framed her oval face in stark contrast to her frightening pallor. One cheek was smeared with dirt and scratches. When she met his gaze, her eyes gleamed with anguish and unshed tears.

"Why…isn't he…getting up?" She moaned, then bit her lip.

"His legs are caught in the jump pillar. Don't try to move. We'll get you both free in a minute."

Brian saw with relief that medical personnel were swarming onto the field. A soldier from her unit dropped to his knees beside her. "Lie still, Lindsey. How badly are you hurt?"

Lindsey dropped her head back onto the turf and sucked in a series of quick breaths. The scent of trampled grass and loamy dirt filled her nostrils. Dakota's weight was crushing her arm. Trying not to scream, she gritted her teeth and dug her fingers into the thick grass again. Screaming would only frighten the horse and make him struggle.

"I think my arm is broken."

"We'll get you free in a minute."

Please, God, let them hurry.

She felt Shane take her hand and she gripped it tightly. Don't scream, she thought, be brave. Act like a soldier. She squeezed her eyes shut and tried to stay calm. Only it was so hard. It hurt so much.

Through clenched teeth, she managed to say, "We tripped Avery…and Socks. Are they okay?"

Shane said, "Socks is up. Avery looks a little shaken, but I think he's okay. Hold on, kid."

"Dakota is all right, isn't he, Shane?" She panted, trying to block out the merciless agony. "Please, tell me he's all right."

"I'll check him over once we get you free." She recognized the voice as the grouchy vet who had suggested Dakota wasn't sound. If only she had heeded him instead of resenting his interference.

Pride goeth before a fall. Dear Lord, why did I have to find that out the hard way?

She raised her head once more to look at him. "This is my fault. I should have listened to you."

Two men in EMS uniforms reached her, saving Brian from having to reply. For that, he was thankful. As they attended to Lindsey, soldiers from the unit quickly dismantled the jump and pillar, making room to move the stricken horse. With their help, Brian coaxed Dakota to roll off his side and onto his stomach, but kept the horse from rising. The move freed Lindsey's arm, but tore a scream from her that ripped into his heart.

While the medics worked on her, she kept asking about her horse. Others offered her reassurances, but Brian remained silent and avoided her pleading eyes. When she was finally placed on a stretcher and taken off the field, he breathed a sigh of relief. She obviously cared a great deal for the animal. The last thing he wanted was to have her see the brave fellow put down.

For the horse was being brave. Brian's admiration of the bay gelding grew as the big fellow remained still in spite of the activity going on around him. Even though his eyes were wide, with the whites showing all around indicating pain and fear, he didn't struggle or thrash the way most horses would have.

When the area had been cleared, Brian gave up his position to a color guard member and rose awkwardly to his feet. He leaned heavily on his cane until he was sure he could take a step without falling on his face. He then moved to check out the horse's leg. There was already serious swelling below the delicate ankle joint. It didn't look good.

Several of the football officials in black-and-white striped shirts approached the group. One of them asked, "How soon can you get him off the field? We have a game to play."

"Your game will have to wait." Brian didn't bother to hide his ire.

The man Lindsey had called Shane remained crouched beside Dakota, keeping him still with a hand on the horse's neck. He ignored the officials completely. "Should we let him try to get up?"

Brian shook his head. "Not with the way that leg is

swelling. We don't want him to do more damage. Let me get a splint on it first. My truck is parked outside the gate next to your trailers. It's white with College of Veterinary Medicine in purple lettering on the side. I've got first-aid equipment in there."

"Private Gillis will get what you need if you'll give him your keys."

One of the soldiers stepped forward and held out his hand. After giving him a detailed list of what he wanted and where it was located, Brian waited impatiently for the private's return. It seemed to take forever, but in reality only a few minutes had passed when the breathless soldier raced back and handed Brian his kit and the supplies he had requested.

With the help of the other color guard members, Brian soon had the leg encased in a cotton wool wrap. He applied a lightweight but sturdy aluminum splint and secured it with Velcro straps.

"All right, let him try and get up, but if he doesn't make it on the first attempt, we'll need to get a lift in here."

"We'll get one, but I sure hope we don't need it. Do you think he has a fracture?"

"I do, but I can't say for sure until we get him to the clinic and X-ray the leg."

With a gentle tug on the reins and some quiet words of encouragement, Shane urged Dakota to stand. After a brief hesitation, the horse lurched awkwardly to his feet. The crowd in the stands broke into loud cheering and applause. Brian looked up in surprise. He had forgotten he had several thousand onlookers watching his every move. No doubt some of his students were in attendance. Perhaps he'd present a pop quiz on splint application on Monday to check if they had been paying attention.

"If you can get your trailer in here, I think he can be loaded. The ride to the clinic isn't far. You'll need to wedge him in securely. I don't want him moving around at all."

"Thanks, Doc. It is *doctor,* isn't it? I'm Corporal Shane Ross." He held out his hand.

Brian took it in a firm grip. "Yes, I'm Dr. Brian Cutter, Professor of Equine Surgery for the College of Veterinary Medicine here at K-State."

"Then it sounds like Dakota will be in good hands. I sure hope this isn't a serious injury. The horse belonged to Lindsey's brother. She'll never forgive herself if he has to be put down."

Lindsey endured her examination at the fort hospital in stoic silence, answering between clenched lips only the questions posed to her. The pain she could deal with, but the fact that her arm hung useless against her side had her truly frightened. She couldn't even move her fingers—they had no feeling at all. Thoughts of Danny's paralysis crowded in her head. She fought down her rising panic as she addressed the physician attending her. "Sir, why can't I move my hand?"

The gray-haired doctor sat on a stool beside her narrow bed. "Your humerus is fractured, that's the bone in your upper arm. I'm going to splint it for now and send you to see an orthopedist. This is a nasty break."

Like she needed anyone to tell her that. "I still don't understand why I can't move my fingers."

"The nerve that controls hand movement runs in a groove along the bone of the upper arm. When a break occurs the nerve is often damaged. You should recover full use of your hand in a few months."

"Months?" She couldn't believe what she was hearing.

"You'll be on restricted duty until then. I'm giving you some pain medication. Take it regularly, don't try to tough it out. I'll write some instructions on icing the arm and have the nurse make an appointment with the specialist. Do you have any questions?"

"How soon can I ride?"

"Not for at least eight weeks, maybe longer depending on the nerve damage."

She turned her face away, not wanting him to see the distress she knew was written there. The Inauguration was only ten weeks away. Did this mean there wouldn't be a trip to Washington, D.C., for her?

No, she wouldn't accept that. She wouldn't let her chance to honor Danny and all he had stood for pass by without a fight. Besides, even if she couldn't ride, Dakota could make the trip. Danny could still watch him striding down Pennsylvania Avenue. Every recent phone conversation with her sister-in-law had been filled with stories of Danny's determination to attend the parade in person.

"You won't be able to drive," the doctor said gently. "Do you have someone who can get you home?"

She nodded. Captain Watson was waiting for her. Exactly how she was going to get back and forth from her off-post apartment to her duty station until she *could* drive was a worry she'd put aside until later.

After they applied the splint and sling and gave her some pain medication, she managed to walk out of the room under her own somewhat shaky power. She found

Captain Watson perched on the edge of a chair in the waiting area. He looked nervous and ill at ease. Her heart sank.

Bracing herself to hear the worst, she asked, "How's Dakota?"

Captain Watson sprang to his feet at the sound of her voice. "I haven't heard. How are you?"

She gave a rueful glance at her big blue sling. "My arm is broken. The doctor said I'll be on restricted duty for at least eight weeks, but it may be longer than that before I regain the use of my hand."

"If you're released, I'll drive you home."

"I need to find out how Dakota is."

"Shane and Lee are with him. As soon as they know something, they'll call. You are going straight home and that's an order."

"With all due respect, sir, I need to be with him. Please?" For a moment, she thought he was going to refuse, then his shoulders slumped in defeat.

"All right. They took him to the veterinary clinic at K-State. I'll take you, but only because I want to see how he is doing myself."

"Thanks. I just need to get these prescriptions filled and then I'm ready."

Half an hour later, they pulled up to the large, white stone buildings on the outskirts of the college campus that comprised the veterinary teaching hospital. Signs at the entrance to the driveway directed them to the Large Animal Clinic at the back of the building. Lindsey's pain pills were making her woozy, but she tried to hide it. She suspected that the captain would drive her straight home if she showed any sign of weakness. Inside the building, they found the waiting area. The long, narrow room had panels of fluorescent lights across the ceiling that seemed to glare back painfully into her eyes from the shiny, beige linoleum floor.

The far end of the room was taken up by a wide reception desk where a pretty, young blond woman was talking on the phone. An American flag stood proudly displayed near the front of the desk. Lee and Shane were seated on the one of several mauve utilitarian chairs with bare wooden arms that lined the walls. They both rose and saluted when they caught sight of their captain. They were all still dressed in their exhibition uniforms and they were gathering odd looks from the staff and clients waiting with them.

Captain Watson returned the salute. "Any word yet?"

"No, sir. The doc hasn't been out to talk to us."

"That doesn't sound good." Lindsey settled gingerly on a chair but still took a quick, indrawn hiss as pain shot through her arm and shoulder. For a second, the room spun wildly and she grabbed hold of Shane's arm.

"Easy, kid. Are you sure you're okay?"

"The pain medicine they gave me is making me light-headed, that's all."

When the room stopped spinning, she looked up to see the vet from the stadium crossing the room toward them. His thick blond hair was still mussed, but he had traded his sport jacket for a white lab coat.

He stopped in front of the group, but his gaze rested on her. Frowning, he said, "I'm surprised to see you here. How's your arm?"

The unrelenting, throbbing pain was almost unbearable. "It's broken," she snapped. "I want to hear about my horse."

Shane laid a hand on her good shoulder. "Lindsey,

this is Dr. Brian Cutter. He's been looking after Dakota. Doctor, this is Sergeant Lindsey Mandel. I don't think you two managed introductions with all that happened earlier."

Lindsey realized that she must have sounded rude. The fiery agony in her arm wasn't helping her disposition. She rose to her feet and was pleased when she stayed upright. "I'm sorry, Doctor. I'm just really worried about Dakota. How is he?"

"He has a fracture of the plantar proximal eminences of the second phalanx."

Lee glanced around the group, then said, "Do you want to try that again in English for those of us who are new to all this horsey stuff?"

Dr. Cutter looked confused by Lee's statement. "I assumed you are all expert horsemen."

Captain Watson smiled in amusement. "My soldiers come from the ranks of ordinary units assigned to Fort Riley either as volunteers or as transfers. No previous riding skill is required. The men receive instruction from manuals used by Civil War cavalrymen. Private Gillis has only been with us a few weeks."

Lee grinned. "I'd never ridden a horse before then, so I still have a lot to learn."

Dr. Cutter managed a thin smile. "I see. All right, the animal has a fracture in one of the bones in the pastern joint between his ankle and his hoof."

If Lindsey hadn't been so upset herself, the look of horror on Lee's face might have been comical when he said, "They shoot horses for that, don't they?"

Dr. Cutter frowned sharply. "We are long past the days of shooting horses here. If an animal does have to be euthanized, we use humane methods."

Lindsey sank onto the chair's edge before her legs gave out and tried to gather her scattered thoughts. "What can be done for him?"

"You have several options but the best one is surgical arthrodesis. That means we fuse the joint using special pins and a bone graft from his hip. His recovery should take about four months."

Lindsey bit her lower lip. Dakota wasn't going to Washington, D.C. It was so unfair. Why had God given her a chance to do something special for her brother only to snatch it away?

Dr. Cutter raked a hand through his hair, giving Lindsey a clue as to why it looked unkempt. "Actually, I am hoping to begin trials of a new procedure using an experimental gene therapy that will speed healing, and this type of fracture is exactly the type I'm look-ing to study. Unfortunately, I haven't received grant approval yet."

The captain asked, "Will Dakota be able to return to duty?"

"A horse can lead a normal life after a fusion. Some horses have even returned to being successful athletes. There are, of course, risks involved, as with any sur-gery."

Lindsey studied his face, hoping to see some en-couragement, but there wasn't any. "What are our other options?"

"We can try and cast the injury. You will need to keep him confined to a stall to rest the leg and hope for the best. He's a calm fellow, so he may do well, but the re-covery time will be much longer. The only other choice is to have him put down."

Captain Watson crossed his arms over his chest. "What will the surgery cost?"

Dr. Cutter's scowl turned into a look of sorrow. He said gently, "Around fifteen thousand dollars, depending on how well he does. Complications can raise the cost considerably. The clinic typically asks for half of the payment up front."

"That much?"

"Or more."

Lindsey's heart sank at the expression on her captain's face. She knew even before he spoke what he was going to say.

"I'm afraid the unit doesn't have a budget to cover a medical bill like that. We are just scraping by as it is."

"The costs for the cast and follow-up will be much less than the surgery. Is that the treatment you want us to use?"

Quickly, she said, "Couldn't we at least try to requisition the money?"

"Of course I will, but with the budget cuts we've had, I doubt command is going to give up that kind of money for a horse. I'm sorry, Sergeant, I know how much he means to you. Can he be transported back to the fort, Doctor?"

"I'll need to keep him here for several weeks to make sure the cast doesn't need any adjustments and monitor his condition. After that, I'm sure the fort vet can manage his care. We'll need follow-up X-rays to make sure the leg is healing, but those can be done at your stable."

Captain Watson held out his hand. "Thank you, Dr. Cutter. We'll leave Dakota here until you think it's safe to move him."

Brian shook the offered hand. "Our equine services

here at the Veterinarian Medical Teaching Hospital are among the finest in the world."

It was his standard line when clients were worried about leaving their animals, but this time he was the one who was worried. The young woman was so pale he thought she might pass out at any moment. The horse must mean a great deal to her if she came straight from the hospital in her condition to check on him. Brian knew how much pain a broken bone caused.

She looked up. "Can I see him?"

"I'm not sure. You look like you need to lie down."

Rising, she faced him with determination blazing in her eyes. "I'm not leaving until I see him."

He looked to her captain, but all the man did was shrug and try to hold back a grin. Brian could tell he wasn't going to get any help from that direction. He shoved one hand into his lab coat pocket and nodded toward the door. "All right, but if you pass out, you'll just lie on the floor. I don't do humans."

"What a blessing for us," she shot back.

He turned away without voicing the comment on the tip of his tongue and led the way to the door beside the reception desk. She was stubborn, irritating and yet pathetic at the same time. So, why did he find her so attractive?

It made no sense. The sooner she saw her horse, the sooner she would leave. Then maybe he could forget those beautiful eyes and the effect they seemed to have on his common sense.

He held open the door, but she stopped so close beside him that he could smell a subtle scent like peaches in her hair. He was tempted to lean closer to make sure.

He didn't, when he realized how unprofessional it would appear.

"What do you think his chances are without surgery?" she asked in a low voice as she stared at him intently.

Such beautiful, sad, green eyes. How could he add to her sorrow? This was the part of his job he dreaded most. He glanced back at the other unit members. They were watching him intently. The words he needed to say stuck in his throat. He sought to give her some hope. "Every patient is different. Only time will tell."

"If he were your horse, what would you do?"

"If he were my horse and surgery wasn't an option?"

"Yes."

"I wouldn't let him suffer. I'd spend as much time as I needed saying goodbye, then I'd have him put down."

"No! I couldn't stand that." The last bit of color leached from her face. She turned away, and the sudden movement caused her to lose her balance. His cane clattered to the floor as he caught hold of her.

Chapter 3

"Easy, I've got you." Brian held the slender form of the woman against his chest and struggled to keep upright for both their sakes.

Her hair did smell like peaches. Funny, he hadn't pictured her as the type of woman to use a scented shampoo. She struck him as a soldier through and through. It was intriguing to know she had a feminine side. He steadied himself by leaning back against the wall.

"I'm fine. It's just a dizzy spell," she said quickly.

The tight grip of her hand on his lab coat lapel told him more than words how much distress she was in. If there was one thing he knew well, it was the signs of pain—in animals and in humans.

A second later her fellow soldiers reached them. Shane swept Lindsey up into his arms without a moment's hesitation and Brian had no choice but to let him.

Seeing how easily and gently the man lifted her made Brian acutely aware of his own physical shortcomings. Years ago he had carried Emily just as effortlessly. He thought he had come to terms with his disability a long time ago, but obviously he hadn't.

His limp was only a small reminder of the tragedy his carelessness had brought about. In one night he had lost both his wife and their unborn child. His mistake had cost him everything he held dear and he had only himself to blame.

Lee quickly retrieved Brian's cane and handed it to him. Taking the polished wooden staff, Brian nodded his thanks and ignored his feelings of inadequacy. He extended one hand indicating a door a few steps down the hall. "My office has a sofa in it. You can lay her down in there. Do you want me to call nine-one-one?"

"No." The weak murmur came from Lindsey.

"Are you sure?" Shane asked, looking uncertain.

She nodded as if more words were beyond her.

"This way," Brian said, and moved to open his door. Inside his office, he swept up a few papers and books from the brown leather sofa to make room for her.

Shane lowered her gingerly, then stood back. None of the men seemed to know what to do next. Brian cleared his throat. "Would you like a drink of water?"

"Yes, please," she whispered. She still hadn't opened her eyes.

Brian grabbed a paper cup from the dispenser on the wall and filled it from the bottled container beside it. Moving back to her side, he settled himself on the edge of the couch. He lifted her head and held the cup to her lips. She took a sip then sighed. He lowered her head back to the cushion.

She opened one eye. "I thought you didn't do humans."

"I make exceptions for women dressed in Civil War uniforms."

For an instant a smile tugged at the edge of her lips before she winced in pain again. "How fortunate can a girl get?"

"Are you sure you don't want me to call nine-one-one?"

"Two rides in an ambulance in one day would be more than my ego can take. I don't suppose you have some really good pain medicine handy. The pills they gave me at the hospital don't seem to be doing much."

"I've got a ton of good stuff here."

She opened both eyes. "Really?"

He nodded. "I've got drugs that will knock out a horse."

"Ha-ha. What does a girl have to do to get some?"

He was pleased to see her smile return, along with a bit more color in her cheeks. "She would need to grow two more legs and a tail."

"Are you telling me I don't measure up as one of your patients?"

"I never said anything of the kind. It's actually nice to be able to ask a patient where it hurts and get an answer."

"It hurts exactly where my horse landed on me."

"From my vantage point that looked like almost all of you."

"You are so right. If you aren't going to supply me with drugs, can you help me sit up?"

Brian didn't have a chance to help her. Her comrades were more than happy to oblige. He moved out of their way. When she was sitting upright she waved them aside. "I'm okay now. Don't hover."

The men backed up, but they didn't look ready to leave her to her own devices.

Brian filled the cup again with more water and handed it to her. To his relief, he saw that her color was almost back to normal. "If you won't go to the hospital, at least go home and lie on your own sofa so I can have mine back."

Taking the offered drink, she sipped it and nodded. "Once I see Dakota, I'll do just that."

All of the men began to protest together, but she ignored their scolding and stood. Cradling her arm, she winced but remained steady on her feet. "Show me the way, Dr. Cutter."

"He's down the hall, through the doors at the very end and in the first stall on the left."

He felt slightly cheated as he watched her fellow unit members guide her out the door, one on each side with her captain close behind. It wasn't that he wanted her to fall into his arms again. Of course not. He simply wanted to make sure she was all right. But that was what her friends wanted, too, he reminded himself. And they certainly had more of a right to care for her than he did. He was nothing but a stranger.

The thought brought back his frown. He was more than that. He was the man who might have to put her beloved horse to sleep.

Early Monday morning, Lindsey begged a ride to the Large Animal Clinic with Shane. When they arrived, they saw Lee and Avery just going in. It seemed that all of them wanted to check on Dakota before they started their duties for the day.

As she approached Dakota's stall, Lindsey was surprised to see Captain Watson had arrived before them. He was deep in conversation with Dr. Cutter.

When her captain caught sight of them, he smiled. "I've been talking to the doctor and he has a way to do surgery on Dakota at a reduced cost to our unit."

Lindsey's heart jumped as happiness surged through her. "How is that possible?"

Dr. Cutter cleared his throat. "Using a new surgical procedure that I've developed—I told you about it the other day. Dakota's break is exactly the sort I'm hoping to trial this repair on."

"But you said it wasn't an option." Shane frowned at the doctor.

"I received notice of my grant acceptance this morning. It is an experimental procedure. If Dakota is entered in the study, it will mean I will have total control of his care. My fees and much of his care will be covered, but that will still leave the bill for his boarding and supplies that the army will have to pay. Unfortunately, the grant isn't a large one."

"We can raise the money if we have to," Captain Watson said.

"Absolutely," Avery chimed in. "He's one of our own. We won't let him down."

"Of course not," Lindsey added. She had a little in savings. She would gladly give the money to help pay for Dakota's care. "When you say experimental, Dr. Cutter, do you mean there is a chance that this won't help him?"

"There is that chance, but I have every confidence that he will do well. If my procedure works, he could be out of his cast in as little as six weeks."

Six weeks. That meant Dakota would be able to

travel to Washington, D.C., in time for the Inaugural parade. Lindsey's joy danced like a soap bubble in the wind.

Thank You, God, for giving Dakota into the care of this man.

Captain Watson turned to Brian. "You have my permission to enroll Dakota in your study."

"Excellent. There are some forms you'll need to sign. If you'll follow me to my office, we can take care of that now."

When the two men walked away, Lindsey opened the gate and stepped into the stall where Dakota stood quietly. He rested with his head lowered and his eyes half-closed. His dazed look worried her until she realized that they would be giving him pain medication and sedation to keep him quiet.

"Hey, Dakota. How's it going, fella?"

His head came up at the sound of her voice and he whinnied softly. Delighted at his responsiveness, she stepped closer and began to rub the side of his face. "Don't worry about a thing. Dr. Cutter is going to fix you up in no time."

Behind her, Avery said, "Do you think an experimental surgery using gene therapy is the best way to go?"

Shane moved up to stand beside Lindsey. Reaching out, he patted Dakota's neck. "It sounds a bit like science fiction to me."

"I have faith that it will work. I think the Lord brought us here at exactly the right time for Dakota to get this care."

Lee shoved his hands into his front pockets. "It

would have been better if He had kept Dakota from breaking a leg in the first place."

Lindsey didn't answer. This, too, had to be part of God's plan, but like Danny's injury, it was a bitter pill to swallow.

She ran her hand over Dakota's soft nose. Her faith was being tested. The words of Psalm 9:9 echoed in her mind.

The Lord is a refuge for the oppressed, a stronghold in times of trouble.

In her time of trouble, had she turned to the Lord as she should have? Perhaps that was what she was being shown. Little by little, she let go of the anger she had been holding on to.

I will try to listen with my heart for Your wisdom, Lord. Show me the path and I will do my best to travel it.

Three days later, Lindsey was struggling to use the can opener with her left hand when the doorbell rang. She stared at the container of corn that refused to fit in the opener. "We're not done. I won't be defeated by an inanimate object."

She noticed the faint smell of burning mozzarella, but the oven timer said her frozen pizza still had five minutes to go. The doorbell chimed again. Leaving the tiny kitchenette of her apartment, she crossed the living room to the front door. She opened it and stared in stunned silence.

"Surprise!" Her sister stood on the stoop with a suitcase resting beside her. Speechless, Lindsey could only stare.

Looking uncertain, Karen said, "Say something."

Shaking herself out of her stupor, Lindsey enfolded

Karen in a one-armed hug. "Hello. This certainly is a surprise. What are you doing here?"

Karen returned the embrace. "I'm just visiting."

Taking a step back, Lindsey studied Karen's face. Her sister had always been the rebel in the family. Her shaggy, cropped blond hair haloed a heart-shaped face. Danny often said Karen's big brown eyes and ready smile could make men weak in the knees, but her quirky wit was her greatest gift. Karen had a smile on her face now, but it didn't erase the sadness that lurked in the depths of her gaze.

"From the look on your face I'd say this is more than just visiting. What brings you all the way from Washington, D.C. to Kansas?"

"Invite me in and I'll tell you about it. Oh, you poor woman, look at you. You're covered in bruises."

"Having a horse roll over you will do that. Honestly, Karen, why are you here? Did Dad send you to take care of me?"

"No, although I'm sure he would have thought of it in a day or two," Karen added quickly.

"You should be helping Abigail and Danny. I can take care of myself."

Karen cleared her throat. "I just needed to get away for a while. I'm sorry I didn't call. Showing up and surprising you seemed like a good idea at the time, but it wasn't, was it?"

Lindsey reached out and took her hand. "It's a wonderful idea. You know I'm always happy to see you. Come in and tell me why you're here."

Karen's face brightened. "Later. You don't happen to have some tea, do you?"

"I'll tell you what. If you can wrestle open a can of corn for me, I'll make you a whole pot."

Inside the apartment, Karen followed Lindsey into the kitchen. At the entrance to the small room decorated with rooster wallpaper and rooster border above the few white cabinets, Karen paused and stared up at the large rooster-shaped clock on the wall. The avocado-green refrigerator began its noisy rumbling and Lindsey gave it a sharp shove to silence the sound. After a moment, Karen said in a tentative murmur, "You have a…nice place."

"Don't even try to be kind. It's a rental and it's cheap. I don't care what the wallpaper looks like as long as the roosters don't crow."

"What a marvelous attitude."

"I'm easy, what can I say?"

Karen wrinkled her nose. "I think something's burning."

"Oh, that's just my lunch. Can you help me with this? I damaged a nerve when I broke my arm and my hand is completely useless. I can't feel a thing." Handing her sister the offending can, Lindsey indicated the opener with a tilt of her head.

Karen's eyes widened in alarm. "Dad never mentioned that you had no feeling in your arm. Is it permanent?"

Lindsey rushed to reassure her, knowing she was thinking about Danny's condition. "No, the specialist said in two or three months I'll be as good as new. Dad didn't say anything because I haven't told him."

"Does this mean you won't be riding in the Inaugural parade?"

"I haven't given up hope. I've got two months and then some to recover."

"Lindsey, you should let the family know you might not be there. Everyone is making plans to attend."

"By everyone, I assume you mean Danny, too?"

"It's all he talks about to the nurses and therapists who come to the house. He is so proud of you. He insists he'll be there to watch you and Dakota in person."

"Now you know why I don't have the heart to say anything yet."

"Yes, I guess I do," Karen said softly.

Lindsey hesitated. "There's more."

"What?"

"Dakota broke a bone in his front leg when we fell."

"Oh, no!"

"He's had surgery and we think he is going to be fine."

Karen pressed a hand to her forehead. "No wonder Abigail thought there was something you weren't telling us the last time you called."

"I didn't want to keep secrets, but I wanted to be sure of things one way or the other before I gave Danny that news."

"Are you sure of things now?"

"Not really."

"Lindsey, you have to tell him. Danny is stronger than you think. If you could only see the way he tackles his therapy sessions. He's able to raise his right shoulder now and he's up to almost two hours off his ventilator each day."

"He's working hard because he has a goal to reach. That is exactly why I'm not going to tell him yet. I can't risk taking away his motivation. I have faith that Dakota and I will both be in Washington, D.C., and Danny will be strong enough to be there to see it."

"I don't agree with you, but I won't say anything for now."

"That's all I'm asking. Thank you. So, are you going to open that can for me or not?"

Smiling, her sister tossed the can in the air and caught it again. "I'll give it my best shot."

Karen successfully extracted the yellow kernels from their stubborn metal prison while Lindsey put the kettle on to boil. A minute later the oven timer rang. Karen snatched up the pot holder before Lindsey could reach it and opened the oven. She pulled out a cookie sheet with a small pizza on it.

"This is your lunch?"

"That and the corn."

"Pizza and corn?"

"It's not as weird as it sounds."

"Yes, it is. You need something healthy." Karen set the cookie sheet on top of the stove.

"This is healthy."

"At least drink some milk with it." Karen pulled open the refrigerator door.

Lindsey winced. She knew there wasn't any milk. In fact, there wasn't much of anything in her fridge except a half-empty bottle of ketchup and one lonely dill pickle in a jar. "I haven't had a chance to get to the commissary."

Karen shut the door and frowned at Lindsey. "Since when?"

"Since before the accident."

"Obviously, it's a good thing I stopped by. Eat while

I have a cup of tea and then I'll drive you to wherever you need to go."

Lindsey used a spatula to transfer her overly crisp pizza to a plate and then set the plate on the table. "You don't have to run errands for me."

"I can see that no one else is. Where are the tea bags?"

The kettle began to whistle. After finding a cup and filling it with hot water, Karen joined Lindsey at the table. Waiting until after her sister had fixed the tea, Lindsey asked, "Are you going to tell me why you're here?"

Karen raised her cup to her lips and blew on the steaming brew. She took a sip and set the cup down. "This is very good tea. What kind did you say it was?"

"Earl Grey, and don't change the subject."

Taking a deep breath, Karen closed her eyes and said, "It's Dad."

"I don't understand."

Karen leaned her elbows on the table. "He won't stop fixing me up. I'm only twenty-one but all of a sudden he acts like I'm the only chance he'll ever have for grandchildren. There has been a steady parade of guys who just *happen* to stop by our apartment. He's driving me crazy."

"I'm sure Dad—like the rest of us—is having a hard time adjusting to Danny's condition. Do you want me to talk to him?" Lindsey took one bite of her pizza, then pushed the unappetizing concoction to the side.

"Thanks for the offer," Karen said gently. "But I'm hoping a little separation will be good for both of us. That's why I'm at your door begging to stay and nurse you through this injury. And before you say no, I did discuss this with Abigail. She can do without me for a few weeks. Please, can I stay?"

Lindsey patted the orthopedic brace and sling the specialist had fitted her with. "I don't need a nurse, but a roommate who can grocery shop and run the can opener will be a welcome addition until I'm out of this contraption."

"Honey, that sounds great." Karen's relief was evident.

"Don't be too sure. This is a one-bedroom apartment and that means *you* get the sofa."

Karen's tinkling laughter was music to Lindsey's ears. During their frequent and lengthy phone conversations, the sound of happiness had been sadly lacking in her sister's voice. Danny's injury had affected everyone. They were all trying to find a new "normal" for the family.

Picking up her teacup, Karen said, "Roommates pay rent. What's space on a lumpy couch going to cost me?"

"The use of two good arms and your skill as a chauffeur. If you really don't mind driving me, I'm dying to get over to the university to see how Dakota is doing. But what about school? Can you afford to take the time off?"

Setting the white cup down, Karen picked up her spoon and began to stir. "I had already decided to take a semester off. I couldn't concentrate in class. There was no use flunking out on top of everything else."

Seeing Karen's grief made Lindsey acutely aware that her baby sister was dealing with a lot more than their father's matchmaking. "I wish I was closer so that I could help, too."

Rising, she carried her plate to the counter. After

dumping the remains of her uneaten lunch in the trash, she laid the dish in the sink and turned on the water. It was then that she felt Karen's hands on her shoulders turning her around.

Tears blurred Lindsey's vision and she loathed the fact. She had tried so hard not to cry. "I hate that this has happened to him."

"I know." Karen's voice was low and brimming with emotion. "But Danny believed that protecting his country was more than a job. It was something that he knew in his heart he had to do."

Lindsey squeezed her eyes shut against the pain that swallowed her heart and made it hard to breathe. "But the price...was too high. He is the best...and the brightest...and this seems so cruel." The words, when she finally managed them, were ragged and broken between her sobs.

"I know you love him. He knows it, too."

"I haven't told him that often enough."

"You don't have to. He sees it. I wish I could hug you, but I'm afraid I'll hurt you."

"My left side is fine," she hiccuped. To prove it, she embraced Karen with one arm and the two of them clung together as they wept.

From the corner of his eye, Brian caught the fugitive movement. Without looking up from the grant application on his desk, he said, "Isabella, don't chew on that pencil."

The culprit ignored him.

He tried injecting more menace into his tone. "Isabella, I said, no!"

The oversize brown lop-eared rabbit perched on the

corner of his large desk chose to disregard his warning. She pulled her prize from the purple Wildcat mug he used to hold his writing utensils. Settling the yellow number two under one paw, she began to nibble it to bits.

"You little minx." He rose from his chair and scooped her up, tucking her firmly under one arm. He stuck the pencil back in the mug with numerous other scarred victims.

He drew a hand down her soft, furry body, then scratched her favorite spot behind her left ear. "Why do you always zero in on the new ones?"

Lifting his cane from the back of his chair, he crossed the office and pulled open the door. Seated at the reception desk was one of the young students who doubled as a part-time secretary for him.

"Jennifer, will you put Isabella in her outside cage, please?"

"Of course. What did you do to get banished from Dr. Cutter's desk this time?" she asked the rabbit as she took her from Brian.

"The usual," he answered.

"Ah, pencil nibbling, were we?" She, too, scratched the bunny behind the ears.

"I can't break her of the habit."

"You could try switching to pens."

"I like pencils. They let me change my mind as often as I need to."

"So does the delete key on your computer."

"It isn't the same."

Rolling her eyes, Jennifer headed for the outside door and said, "Therein lies your problem, Doctor. You have to learn to say what you mean the first time."

Brian turned back to his office. He knew how to say

what he meant, but he was often accused of being too gruff. Whenever he needed to draft a letter or a grant application, he worked and reworked the words until they seemed soft and polite enough. Pencils worked best for the task. After he had the tone he wanted, he typed his work into his computer. Some might say he was making twice the work for himself, but he still preferred his tried-and-true method.

Certainly, his upcoming lecture on pastern arthrodesis for the Equine Surgical Conference in January was no exception. It was an honor to be asked to speak and he wanted his address to be perfect. He intended to rework it until he was completely satisfied. Fortunately, the college bookstore had an excellent supply of the large yellow legal pads he liked best.

Back at his desk, he put aside his work on his presentation for the moment and opened the file on Dakota. The gelding wasn't doing as well as he had hoped. The surgery itself had gone well, but the big horse seemed to be having more pain instead of less. That wasn't encouraging. A knock at his door caused him to look up. Jennifer stood in the doorway minus the rabbit.

She motioned toward the folder he held. "Is that the file on the army horse? I was wondering how he was getting along."

"I'm not happy with his progress. Even with the medication he's getting, his respiratory rate and pulse rate are higher than they should be. The staff has been reporting that he's restless and he isn't eating well."

"None of those are good signs."

A smile twitched at the corners of his mouth, but he held it back. "So you *have* been paying attention in class. Will wonders never cease?"

She blushed and looked chagrined. "Is there anything else you need, Doctor? If not, I'm going to take off."

He hadn't meant to offend her, but before he could form the right words to apologize, she was out the door.

Of all the females he had known in his life, only Isabella never seemed to care what tone he chose or how gruff his words sounded. If only more women had her tolerance, his life would be a lot easier.

Before he had a chance to dwell on the current poor state of his interpersonal skills, Jennifer opened the door again. "Doctor, Sergeant Mandel is here to see you."

The sudden rush of pleasure he felt at hearing her name unnerved him. He tried unsuccessfully to stifle his excitement.

"Show her in."

"Yes, Doctor."

She nodded but before she could close the door, he said, "Jennifer, I was teasing earlier when I made that remark about you paying attention in class."

"You were?"

"Of course. I think you have an excellent future in the surgical field."

She looked doubtful. "You do?"

"I do."

She flipped her long blond hair back over one shoulder. "Wow! Okay, but next time you're kidding someone, Doc, you should smile."

"I'll certainly try to do so."

Chapter 4

Jennifer held open the door so that Lindsey and another young woman could enter Brian's office. Lindsey appeared much more rested today, he noticed when she walked in. To his surprise, she looked even prettier than he remembered. She radiated an energy that seemed to warm a place inside him that he had almost forgotten existed. Like the dancing flames of a campfire on a cold night in the mountains, she left him longing to draw closer to the warmth.

Wearing a camouflage shirt and matching pants with black boots, she looked every inch the soldier—except for the blue sling on her arm. She certainly wasn't the type of woman that normally would have interested him. Since his wife's death he couldn't think of a single woman he had been this attracted to, but there was something about this woman that intrigued him. He didn't care for the sensation. When he realized he was staring, he shook off the fanciful notion and rose to his feet. "Please come in, Sergeant Mandel. Have a seat."

Her smile flashed briefly and was gone. She appeared hesitant as she sat on the sofa. "Thank you for seeing us. This is my sister, Karen Mandel."

He nodded to the woman dressed in jeans and a tailored navy shirt. "I'm pleased to meet you."

Addressing the two of them, he said, "As you may know, Dakota's surgery went very well. He's tolerating his cast, which is always a good thing. In two to three weeks he'll go back to surgery to have the pins removed and a new cast applied."

"Yes, Captain Watson has been keeping us informed," Karen said softly.

"Captain Watson is the reason we're here," Lindsey began. "Because of this arm, I've been reassigned to light duty. My orders are to oversee Dakota's care."

"I don't understand."

"I'll be doing what I can to help here. Karen has asked to be involved, as well, and Captain Watson has agreed. Providing we're not in the way, of course."

"Are you sure you're fit to work?"

"I can do whatever is needed, within reason."

"Working around sick and injured horses can be dangerous."

She leaned toward him, her smile changing from hesitant to forced. "I know that, Doctor."

Of course she did. She was the one with the broken arm. Retreating into his most professional demeanor, he said tersely, "That is something you can't forget when you are here. Given your injury, I'm not sure what you will be able to do."

Her smile disappeared. Did he only imagine the room grew a few degrees cooler?

"I've been taking care of the unit's animals for over a year, Doctor. All sixteen horses plus the two mules. I'm sure I can manage to be of some help to you and your staff, even if all I do is muck out the stall. I know how to follow orders."

He sat back in his chair, registering her annoyed tone. She was upset, but he didn't know why. "Very well. I'll let the staff know that you'll be…assisting here until the horse is fit to return to the army's stables."

"Thank you," she snapped back.

"May I see Dakota now?" Karen asked, glancing between Lindsey and himself with an odd gleam in her eyes.

"Certainly. He is through the double doors at the end of the hallway. His stall is the first one on the left down the first aisle. I need to speak with my secretary and then I'll join you at his stall in case you have any questions."

Brian tucked the file under his arm and escaped from his office. Fortunately, Jennifer had already left for the evening. He laid the file down and raked his fingers through his hair as he tried to gather his scattered thoughts.

The idea of having Lindsey in the clinic every day was a disturbing one. Without understanding exactly why, he knew she would interfere with his work. She would be a distraction he didn't need, but he couldn't see how to prevent her from coming.

Her request wasn't all that unusual. Animal owners occasionally spent long hours with their pets and he'd rarely had to forbid access. Besides, she had her orders. There wasn't much he could do about it except try to avoid her.

Even as the thought occurred to him, he knew that avoiding Lindsey wasn't what he really wanted.

"Take a deep breath, Lindsey," Karen said after Dr. Cutter had left the room.

Lindsey tried to swallow her irritation with the man. "I'm a soldier in the United States Army. I've been trained to do my duty no matter what the circumstances. A broken arm is no treat, but I've been assigned to Dakota's care and I'll follow my orders. It doesn't matter if he thinks I can or not."

"He's only trying to be kind."

"I didn't hear a lick of kindness in his tone."

"Maybe not in his tone, but I certainly saw it in the way he was looking at you."

Lindsey turned to Karen in stunned surprise. "You've got to be kidding."

"I don't blame you for being interested in him. He's attractive and he loves animals—what's not to like?"

"I certainly don't see the same thing you do. Come on, I'll show you where they're keeping Dakota."

Leaving his office, Lindsey glanced toward the reception area. Dr. Cutter was standing at the desk, but his cute young secretary was nowhere to be seen. Not that it mattered what his hired help looked like. It certainly didn't matter. Not to her, Lindsey decided.

Leading Karen toward the recovery stalls, Lindsey waited until they were through the door before she spoke her mind.

"The man is rude and he's arrogant and I am certainly not interested in him."

"I'll admit he needs a little fine-tuning, but he has potential."

"Potential for what? No, don't tell me or you'll sound like Danny. He never lets up with the 'When are you going to settle down?' speech. Once he got married, all he could think about was how I needed to find someone, too."

Being in love had made him forget the painful scenes from their childhood, but Lindsey never forgot them. She knew better than to believe she could make an army career and a marriage work. Her own parents had been perfect examples of how wrong it could get. The endless fights, the recriminations, the tears and the broken promises she had witnessed as a child were things she couldn't forget. As far as she was concerned, it was better not to have children than to subject them to the kind of childhood she'd had.

Marriage was hard enough without adding frequent reassignment, long separations and dangerous duty to the mix. Danny had been willing to take the chance that he could make it work with Abigail, and maybe they would be one of the blessed ones, but Lindsey wasn't willing to open her heart up to that kind of pain.

At Dakota's stall, Karen leaned through the rails and ran a hand down the big bay's nose. "Whatever made you think I was talking about settling down?" she quipped. The sly smile she cast Lindsey over her shoulder made Lindsey want to shake her.

Leaning on the gate beside her sister, Lindsey decided to set her straight. "For your information, I have no intention of starting a relationship. The army is my life. I love moving to new posts, seeing new places, meeting new people."

"Why? I hated it as a kid."

"I guess the good Lord gave me the wanderlust gene. Our father had it and the next generation of Mandels will probably have it, too."

"Except that there won't be a next generation of Mandels." Karen's soft words brought the extent of their loss into sharp focus.

Lindsey slipped her good arm over Karen's shoulders. "I'm sorry. That was a thoughtless comment on my part. We can pray that Danny and Abigail may still be blessed with a child."

"I guess we can't spend our lives trying not to say or do something that will remind us of Danny's condition. I think it has been hardest on Dad. He really wanted to see the traditions of the family carried on."

"I know. That's my duty now. I'm going to carry on and serve with distinction."

"Why? Hasn't our family given this country enough?"

"You don't mean that."

"I've often wondered if you aren't trying to live the life you think Dad wanted without finding out what kind of life you wanted for yourself."

"This *is* the life I want," Lindsey insisted.

Karen sighed in defeat. "As long as that's true then I'm going to be happy for you, but you don't have to do it alone. Sharing life's burdens is part of the reason God made it so that two could become one."

Reaching out, Lindsey tweaked her sister's nose. "When did you get so wise?"

"I think it was in Philosophy 101 my freshman year."

Lindsey smiled at her joke. The door to the hallway opened and Brian walked over to join them. "Do you have any questions, ladies?"

Lindsey turned to study Dakota. The cast extended from above his knee to below his hoof. It was wrapped in bright blue cloth.

"As you can see," Brian began, "he is wearing special shoes on his other feet to accommodate the height of the cast and keep him standing level."

"Why is that important?" Karen stepped over to make room for Brian to stand between herself and Lindsey.

"It will help prevent undue stress on his other legs. Horses carry most of their weight on their front legs. Unlike dogs or cats, they can't stand three legged for long. We want him standing evenly, but not moving around much."

"I expected to see him hanging from a sling."

"We do use slings if we have to, but usually that is for bone breaks in the upper legs."

Lindsey drew her hand down Dakota's neck. "He doesn't look as if he feels well. Is he in pain?"

Brian flipped through the chart that was wired to the front of the stall. "I've ordered pain medication. He's been receiving regular doses. His X-rays show the pins are in excellent position. He should recover full use of the leg."

Lindsey finally voiced the question she had been afraid to ask until now. "Do you believe Dakota could be healed enough to walk three miles with a rider by late January?"

"It might be possible, but I can't give you a guarantee."

"He has to be fit by then. If it's possible, then that's good enough for me. If you do your best for him, prayer will take us the rest of the way."

"I'm sorry, but why does he have to be fit by late January?"

She turned to face him. "Because the Commanding General's Mounted Color Guard will be participating in the Inaugural parade in Washington, D.C., on January twentieth and Dakota has to be there."

Brian shook his head. "That's only ten weeks away."

"But is it possible?"

"If this new treatment works as well as I hope, perhaps, but you certainly can't count on it."

"He'll make it. I know he will. I have faith."

"Unrealistic expectations will only lead to disappointment, Sergeant Mandel."

"Aren't you a man of faith?" Karen asked.

"I'm a man of science, especially when I'm in this building. Dakota's progress will be carefully documented and analyzed to help gauge the success or failure of this therapy. I believe in what can be documented. I believe in results that I can quantify."

Lindsey studied his face and noticed again the stormy gray color of his eyes. Was he always so serious, she wondered? What did he do for fun? Was he married? She glanced at his hand. He didn't wear a ring.

The direction her speculations were heading surprised her. She forced herself to stick to the important topic at hand. "Has this therapy been tried before?"

"In small animals like rabbits and dogs, but surgical repairs on horses are very different. Their weight is the biggest issue. The stress load on the healing break can be very high. That can lead to repair failures, especially if the horse is high-strung and doesn't remain quiet."

"Dakota isn't high-strung, but he loves to work. I'm not sure how he'll take being confined."

"He has been quiet for us."

Lindsey ran a hand down Dakota's back. "I still think he is in pain. Isn't there something else you can do for him?"

"I don't want to add additional medications unless I have to. If he is having pain, I'm sure it will decrease soon."

Lindsey noticed that Brian seemed ill at ease. He didn't make eye contact with her. He kept a tight grip on the chart as if it was some type of shield. His superior manner began to irritate her. Either he wasn't really concerned about the horse or he didn't think she knew what she was talking about. Why did everything this man said rub her the wrong way?

"It isn't fair that Dakota has to suffer because you don't want to mess up your study."

"I assure you we don't let our patients suffer needlessly."

"How can I be sure of that?"

His eyebrows shot up in surprise. "Are you questioning my judgment?"

"Of course not, Dr. Cutter," Karen interjected calmly. "I'm sure Dakota is getting the best of care."

"He is. If you intend to make yourself useful, Sergeant, I suggest you see my secretary first thing in the morning. She will supply you with a list of duties and the times we have set up for Dakota's treatments. I'm sure she'll be able to find something you can manage with one arm."

With that, he left the two women and exited through an outside door.

Lindsey cast a sideways glance at Karen. "You're right, he has potential. He has the potential to annoy me to no end. He isn't the only one who knows about horses. There's more than one way to treat pain in an animal."

"You aren't giving him a chance, Lindsey."

Maybe Karen was right. "I know, but something about him gets to me."

"Why?"

"Maybe it's because he never smiles. When he's talking to me, I get the feeling that he'd rather be somewhere else. Maybe I just don't like that he was right and I was wrong the day Dakota fell."

Karen studied Lindsey for a long moment. "I think there is more to your feeling than dislike. You know, I think I'm going to enjoy watching the two of you butt heads."

As he pulled into the driveway of his home, Brian decided he had wasted enough time thinking about Lindsey Mandel. Why should he care if she didn't trust his judgment? Except that he did care.

Stepping out of his pickup, he opened the small carrier on the front seat that Isabella rode in and lifted her out. "Come on, girl, we're home. Let's see what the mailman left for us."

With Isabella tucked under one arm, he made his way up the walk to a small white cottage with dark blue shutters. The house stood on a tall hilltop overlooking the Kansas River as it wound its way eastward out of the plains and through the rolling hills of eastern Kansas before it emptied into the wider Missouri River near Kansas City.

The view was one of the reasons he'd purchased the place. It reminded him a little of the view from his parents' home in Montana. Although the Kansas hills didn't compare to the foothills of the Bighorn Range, the view and the smell of the tall cedars and pine trees beside the front door always took him back to the mountains—back to where he and Emily had been so happy together. He let the grief pour out now that he was alone. The ache in his heart had become a part of him. It never left.

From the brass mailbox, he extracted a handful of envelopes and flyers. "Looks like you're in luck, Isabella. There's lots of junk mail."

He tucked his mail under his chin as he struggled to unlock the door without dropping the rabbit, the correspondences or his cane. Once inside, he closed the door, then set his pet on the floor. She scampered to a box beside his chair and hopped in.

Brian crossed the hardwood floor and sank with a sigh of relief into his recliner. He rubbed his thigh for a minute before leaning back and raising the leg cushion. From the table beside him, he picked up a silver-framed photo. In it his wife, Emily, smiled sweetly back at him. He had taken the picture of her when they were on their honeymoon. It had been her favorite.

"You wouldn't believe the day I've had," he began. "My newest patient has the most irritating owner."

He often told Emily about the challenges of his job, but tonight he found he didn't want to tell her about Lindsey. It didn't seem right.

The silence of the house closed in, filling him with an aching sense of loss that never faded. He didn't deserve to have it fade. He had killed the woman he loved and nothing would ever change that fact.

He set the picture aside and picked up his mail. Sorting through it with Isabella was also a nightly ritual. The flyers from the local grocery stores he tossed into the box with the rabbit. She instantly began to shred them into pieces. Next to nibbling pencils, paper shredding was her favorite pastime and one he allowed her to indulge in only in her special plastic bin.

It hadn't taken him long to learn that a bored rabbit could be very destructive. He'd had to replace the wooden handle on his recliner twice during the first year Isabella lived with him. Fortunately, he had discovered the cure before any other items of furniture had to be replaced. If he gave her something fun to do, she was as good as gold.

He turned over the first envelope. "Hey, we might have won ten million dollars. It says all we have to do is enter to win. Like that will happen."

He crumpled the envelope and contents and tossed it into the box. Isabella attacked the new paper with glee. The next two envelopes were bills. He considered tossing them in with the rabbit, but decided against it. Telling the electric company that his rabbit had ripped up the bill wasn't likely to keep the lights on if he missed a payment. The third envelope bore the logo of the United Jockey Club Research Foundation. Knowing the UJC Research Foundation had donated nearly one million dollars in grants the previous year, he quickly tore open the letter.

"Listen to this, Isabella. They are interested in my new study. They're calling it groundbreaking work and their grant committee is interested in learning more. They plan on sending a representative to hear my presentation and review my data at the Equine Surgical Conference in January."

Brian glanced at his pet, but she was only interested

in her game. Picking up Emily's picture, he studied the face he knew so well.

"Do you know what this means, honey? If they back my project, I won't have to beg money and cut corners to make ends meet at the clinic for years."

Things were falling into place for his work. The conference would bring the best and brightest equine surgeons in North America to hear him, along with a dozen other speakers. If he could persuade Equine Equipment to have one of their ambulances on display he might be able to convince the college advisory board to actively pursue purchasing one for the clinic. Just the thought of the horses who could be saved by being safely transported to the clinic brought a lump to his throat.

He held Emily's picture close to his heart. "I wish you were here to share this with me."

After a while, the unshed tears stopped stinging the back of his eyes. Little by little, the silence of the house lulled him into sleep. As he did almost every night, he fell asleep in the chair with Emily's face pressed to his chest and her presence filling his dreams.

Sometime later, Brian awoke with a start. He had been dreaming, but not about his wife. The woman he saw riding toward him on a bay horse had had red hair and green eyes. Disgusted with himself for letting Lindsey intrude into his personal life, he got up and put Isabella in her cage before making his way to his bedroom.

Sleep was a long time in coming. When it did arrive, he dreamed about his childhood—about lying on his back and looking up through the green aspen leaves and feeling the whole world was full of promise. Green leaves that were the same color as Lindsey's beguiling eyes.

* * *

Early the next morning, Brian walked into the entrance of the Large Animal Clinic with a half-formed plan for the day. Isabella lay firmly tucked in the crook of his arm. He hadn't slept well and he was sure it showed. Thoughts of Lindsey had kept him up until long into the night.

Why on earth he couldn't stop thinking about her was something he couldn't understand. And she was going to be here again today. The plan he had come up with for dealing with her was to make rounds as early as possible and then barricade himself in his office. It wasn't much of a plan, but it was all he could come up with at three-thirty in the morning. Looking up, he was surprised to see Jennifer crossing the room quickly to meet him.

"Good morning, Dr. Cutter. Let me take Isabella outside for you."

"Thank you, but I'd like to have her with me in the office today." He had a feeling he was going to need her comforting presence to help keep him on track and not think about Lindsey. Sergeant Mandel, he corrected himself.

Jennifer gave him a tight smile and took Isabella out of his arms. "I'm just going to take her anyway. You know how loud voices upset her."

"Not that I've ever noticed." Puzzled, he tried to make sense of Jennifer's tense demeanor. "Are you planning on yelling at me? Whatever I did, I apologize."

Gathering the oversize rabbit into her arms, Jennifer said, "It's not something *you* did."

"I'm glad to hear that. Oh, before I forget, Sergeant Mandel is going to be in today. Give her a list of her horse's treatments and let her do what she can to help."

Jennifer's look held a trace of pity. "She's already here. I'm just going to be outside with Isabella for a while."

With the rabbit in her arms, Jennifer hurried out the door.

Shrugging off her peculiar behavior, Brian limped toward his office. So Lindsey was here already. That shot down the first stage of his plan. He would certainly encounter her when he made rounds. As he was unlocking his door, two of the fourth-year students came down the hall from the holding area. They stopped short at the sight of him, then hurried past with their heads down. He glanced after them with a puzzled frown. What was going on? Whatever it was, he wasn't ready to face it until he had at least one cup of coffee.

Inside his office, he set out the carpet-covered boxes Isabella used as steps to reach the top of his desk and her favorite spot—an old towel in a shallow tray at the far corner. After starting the coffee, he held his cup under the brewer until it was full, then slipped in the pot. The first sip of the scalding hot, dark brew was exactly what he needed. Taking a second sip, he set the cup on his desk, put on his lab coat and headed down the hall to check on his patients.

The first thing he noticed when he entered the stall area was the large group of students clustered outside Dakota's stall. He hurried forward. If something had gone wrong and he hadn't been called, heads were going to roll.

Chapter 5

"What's going on here?" Brian's irate bellow caused the students hovering outside Dakota's stall to part like the waters of the Red Sea.

Lindsey winked at the elderly woman inserting hair-fine acupuncture needles along the horse's neck and turned to face the oncoming battle. She even managed to put on her sweetest smile. "Good morning, Dr. Cutter."

"What is the meaning of this?"

"Allow me to introduce Mia Chang. She is a horse acupuncturist."

"I can see that. What is she doing with my patient?"

"I am relieving his pain and the great stress he is suffering from," Mia said with a slight bow in Brian's direction before turning her attention back to Dakota.

"It's quite remarkable, actually," one of the students

ventured. "His pulse and respirations are back to normal and he has a brighter look in his eyes after only twenty minutes of therapy."

"Yes, he is feeling much better. This will help strengthen the healing bones." Mia pulled a handful of pellets from her pocket and held them under Dakota's nose. He nibbled them up with relish.

"What is that?" another student asked.

"My special blend of healing herbs with a little honey to sweeten the taste. I can give you the recipe if you like."

Lindsey didn't think Brian's scowl could get any deeper, but it did. He leaned forward on his cane. "Ms. Mandel, may I speak to you privately in my office?"

His cold, clipped words told Lindsey not to expect a thank-you. He turned and left without waiting for her answer. She followed him down the hall, fully prepared to fight for Dakota's well-being. It was obvious that the horse was feeling better and she wasn't about to let Dr. Grumpy change that.

Inside his office, he indicated she should take a seat. She preferred to stand, but the thought that he might be uncomfortable or in pain standing made her hasten to sit on the sofa. She wondered what the carpeted boxes stacked up beside his desk were for but decided not to ask.

Brian sat with a tiny sigh of relief that made her glad she hadn't insisted on confronting him while he was on his feet. Knowing that the best defense was a good offense, she launched into her prepared speech. "I'm sure you're happy Dakota is obviously in less pain. I'm certainly glad Miss Chang was able to come on such short notice."

"Sergeant Mandel—"

"Her techniques have worked wonders with some of our other horses. My father was stationed in South Korea when I was ten and I saw firsthand the value of their nontraditional medicine."

"I appreciate your desire to help your horse, but—"

"I knew you would. That's why I asked her to come. She is also a trained veterinary assistant."

"Miss Mandel—"

"Her fee will be covered by me personally, so you don't need to worry about that."

"Lindsey, please."

The husky way he said her first name sent an unexpected shiver along her nerve endings and blotted all other comments from her mind. She waited in silence for his next words. For a heartbeat he simply stared into her eyes and she wondered what he was thinking.

He looked down and took a deep breath. When he looked up again he didn't appear angry, just tired. She had the craziest urge to take his hand and offer him comfort or at least a cup of hot tea.

"Lindsey, do you know how many horses are put down each year in this country for a simple fracture of the leg? I don't mean just the expensive racehorses or show horses, but horses that belong to ordinary people who love them?"

"No."

"Hundreds. Maybe even thousands. I've euthanized far too many of them myself. Do you know why I put most of them down?"

"Because the breaks can't be healed?"

He shook his head. "No. It would be easier to take if that were true. Money is the single biggest reason a horse gets put to sleep. The average person simply can't afford to spend fifteen thousand dollars on an animal's medical care. But what if that cost could be cut in half?"

"More horses could be saved?" she ventured, feeling less in the right with each passing minute.

"Maybe hundreds more each year. That is what I'm trying to do with the study Dakota is in. I'm trying to prove this therapy will cut healing time and therefore the cost of a break significantly. But to do that I have to have absolute hard facts. Facts that can be reproduced in other horses time after time. Facts that can be published in a reputable journal."

She listened to him with a sinking sensation. "You're trying to tell me I've altered the study."

"I'm trying to make you understand how important this work is. I don't want to see your horse in pain any more than you do. But I have to know that what I give him to help won't interfere with what I'm trying to accomplish."

"I don't see how simple acupuncture can interfere with your gene therapy."

"In all likelihood it won't. But what if he begins to run a fever? What if the herbs he ate today react with the antibiotics I have to give him? Just because a substance is a natural remedy doesn't mean it can't have side effects. The fewer variables I have to deal with, the better."

"I understand what you're saying. I wasn't thinking about how important Dakota's recovery will be for others. I was only thinking of how important it is for me. I'm sorry if I've interfered with your work."

She looked so contrite that Brian was tempted to smile. "I want your help and input. All I'm asking is that you discuss your ideas with me first. Can I have your promise on that?"

Nodding, she said, "Of course."

"Good. This is a teaching hospital and acupuncture is gaining ground as a legitimate treatment for pain and lameness in horses. The students seemed quite interested in Miss Chang's techniques. I may see about including her in our guest lecture series next semester."

"She would like that."

The sudden silence between them seemed weighted with tension and expectation.

"Will you be staying long today?" he asked, not wanting to see her leave in spite of his earlier plan.

"I have to get back to the post. Karen and I are helping organize a fund-raiser for the cost of Dakota's care that isn't going to be covered by your grant. The men and women at the fort have been overwhelming in their offers of support. We've already raised nearly a thousand dollars just with donations from the troops and their families."

"That's amazing."

"Dakota is an army horse. He's no different than any other injured soldier. We take care of our own."

"I'll see you tomorrow then."

"Tomorrow our unit is traveling to Medicine Falls for their centennial celebration. I'm on restricted duty so I won't be riding, but I'm going along to help the ground crew and do the PR part of the job."

"PR?"

"People are always curious about the unit. We are ambassadors for the army, as well as a living history exhibition. We put on a really good show if you ever get the chance to see it."

She rose to her feet. Brian headed for the door and held it open for her. "If you need any help with the fund-raising, please don't hesitate to call me."

Brian could hardly believe what he heard himself saying. The words were out of his mouth before he even had a chance to consider the ramifications. He didn't get involved in the lives of the people who brought their animals to him. He certainly had no intention of getting involved with someone as impulsive and outspoken as this woman. His life was quiet and orderly. It was exactly the way he wanted it. At least it had been until he arrived at work this morning.

Lindsey cocked her head to the side and grinned at him. "Thank you. I may take you up on that offer."

As she walked out the door, he realized with a sinking sensation that she might do just that.

Ten minutes later he looked up from his work at the sound of a timid knock. The door opened and Jennifer peeked in. "Is it safe to bring Isabella in?"

"For her, but maybe not for you."

She pushed the door open and stepped in with his pet draped over her arm. "Why? What did I do?"

"You took off faster than the proverbial rabbit at the first sign of trouble. I'd like to remind you that you work for me. The next time there's trouble brewing in this office, I expect you to be the first one to inform me of it."

"Was there trouble this morning?" she asked, giving him a wide-eyed innocent stare.

He glared back at her, but she simply put Isabella on the floor. The rabbit made a beeline for the steps he'd set out and quickly climbed to his desk. She paused in front of him long enough to have her head stroked, then she hopped to the far corner and settled herself in her favorite spot.

"I like Sergeant Mandel, don't you?" Jennifer asked, still lounging in the doorway.

He felt the heat of a blush creeping up his neck. "I haven't given it much thought."

"You spent a long time with her in here this morning."

"We were discussing Dakota's plan of care."

"I just noticed that the two of you seem to be getting along rather well when she left."

"Because we weren't shouting at each other?"

"That was my first clue, but I think it was your offer to help with fund-raising that clinched the deal. Is she married?"

"That is none of our business. She is a client."

"She's a cute client, even if she does wear combat boots. Don't you think so?"

Exasperated with her prying, he said, "Is there something you wanted, Jennifer?"

"Oh, right. The people who make that horse ambulance are on line one. I knew you'd been waiting for their call."

He picked up his phone, but hesitated before pressing the blinking button. It was his hope that he could convince Equine Enterprises to allow the school the use of one of their new ambulances for an extended period of time. The need to transport injured horses safely was no different than the need to transport people. He wanted to raise awareness of the issue and hopefully convince the school's board to purchase one. His first challenge would be to persuade Equine Enterprises to loan him the vehicle, only *his* PR skills weren't the best.

The image of Lindsey pressing his case popped into

his mind. *She* was a persuasive person. She would be hard to stop when she had her mind set on something.

"Do you need anything else, Doctor?" Jennifer asked.

"No, thank you. Oh, wait. How far away is Medicine Falls?"

"It's about an hour northwest of here."

"Can you pull up a map on your computer?"

"Yes," she drawled. "But why would you want to go to Medicine Falls?"

That was a very good question, and one he wasn't sure he knew the answer to, except that Lindsey would be there.

"I have Saturday off. I heard they were having their centennial celebration. I thought I might take a drive up that way."

As answers went it was pretty weak, but it was the best he could do on the spur of the moment.

The look she gave him said louder than words that she wasn't fooled. "If you don't want to give me a straight answer, I can take a hint."

"Fine." He waved his hand in dismissal before she could probe deeper into his motives—motives he didn't understand himself. He picked up the phone and, with renewed determination, launched into his plea for the loan of an ambulance.

When he finished his call, he had the satisfaction of knowing the company was at least considering his proposal. He had begun putting away his papers and shutting down his computer when Jennifer came in and held out a thick manila folder.

He scowled at her. "What's this?"

"The map you asked for and the file on the Shetland pony you did hip surgery on last spring. Remember fat

338   *The Color of Courage*

Dolly? The family was from Medicine Falls. I thought since you were going out that way, you could do a follow-up visit to see how they're getting along. Besides, it's a better excuse than saying you thought you'd take a drive. The whole, 'I just happened to be in the neighborhood' line is kind of lame, but this way you can back up your story with a straight face."

"I don't need an excuse to go for a drive. This is a free country."

"I believe Sergeant Mandel will agree with you when you see her in Medicine Falls. Did you know they're putting on a performance tomorrow?"

"And how do you know that?" Had she been eavesdropping on his conversation with Lindsey?

"Avery told me. He drove Lindsey out here this morning. Isn't his accent the cutest thing?"

"I hadn't noticed."

She smiled. "Don't lose that map."

Brian opened his mouth to tell her he had changed his mind about going, but instead found himself saying, "Jennifer, I'm beginning to see you in a whole new light."

"Finally. I've worked here, what, two years? And this is the first time you've noticed that I'm a genius?"

"I was going to say I've begun to notice that you're rather devious."

"Oh. Well—only when I know it will help."

"Will help what?"

With a long-suffering sigh, she said, "Never mind. You'll figure it out."

Lindsey watched from the running board of the unit's candy-apple-red pickup as eight other members of her unit led their horses out of the matching red trailer emblazoned with the unit's name. The CGMCG was preparing for their last event of the season. The busy schedule of travel and performances over a five-state area would begin again in late spring. Usually by this time all the horses and riders were looking forward to a much-needed rest, but this year rest wouldn't be on the duty roster until after the trip to Washington, D.C., in late January.

All the men were looking forward to participating in the Inaugural parade with excitement and pride. The talk of late had been about little else.

Looking up, Lindsey noticed that the flawless blue sky overhead promised beautiful weather for the little town's special day. Even the relentless Kansas wind seemed to be taking a break. The flag jutting out from the ornately carved limestone post office hung quietly with barely a whisper of a breeze to ripple the Stars and Stripes. The stark branches of the trees that lined the streets radiating out from the town square were the only sign that fall had descended. The sun on Lindsey's shoulders was hot enough to make her glad she was wearing the unit's red T-shirt and not one of the dark wool uniforms.

"Lindsey!" Avery called from the rear of the truck where he was throwing a saddle on a gray gelding named Tiger. "My saber is in the back of the trailer. Can you get it for me?"

"Sure thing." She stood and moved toward the trailer, taking the time to speak softly so that all the horses knew she was passing behind them. In the trailer, she opened the door of the storage compartment and pulled out Avery's sword.

"Is that real?" a small voice asked behind her.

She turned to smile at two young boys who were obviously brothers. They boasted the exact same shade of ash-blond hair and identical pairs of bright blue eyes. The oldest boy looked to be about ten years old. She pegged the younger one at six or seven.

"Yes, this is a real saber. It's a replica of the type used by the U.S. Cavalry back in the Civil War. If your parents take you over to the rodeo arena after the parade, you can see how they are used."

"Wow," said the littlest, wide-eyed youngster.

"Told you it was real," his brother said smugly.

"But soldiers don't ride horses anymore. They drive jeeps and tanks," the younger one stated with a glare at his older sibling.

Lindsey vividly remembered arguing with Danny over silly things when they were kids. Her memories of him were good ones, she realized. For the first time since his injury, those memories didn't bring pain, but rather a quiet joy.

"You're right," she said. "Modern soldiers do drive jeeps and tanks, but there are special units like mine that are keeping the traditions of the Old West cavalry alive. We are real soldiers and this is our job."

"Cool."

"Way cool. Can I hold the sword?"

She shook her head. "I'm afraid not."

Clearly disappointed, the young pair took off back into the crowd forming along one side of the town's main street.

Lindsey carried the saber to Avery. He tipped his head in the direction of the boys. "New recruits?"

"Maybe. The little one would have been more impressed if you had a tank instead of a horse."

"Boys and their toys."

"You know that's true," Lee Gillis said as he led his horse over to stand beside them. "How's the arm, Lindsey?"

"Not painful as long as I don't bump it, but I still can't feel my fingers or use my hand. I won't be riding for a while. Who gets to stay behind with me?" Lindsey asked, looking over the line of saddled horses.

"Captain said to leave Socks with you. He's been a little nervous since the fall and we don't want him acting up in the parade. The captain is riding Tiger."

"That's fine. Tiger will be happy he doesn't have to wait here while the rest of the boys run off and have fun."

Having one of the horses waiting beside the trailer was a good way to get people to stop and visit. Tiger, as the oldest and most calm four-legged member of the unit, usually had that honor.

Lee frowned as he looked toward the gray gelding standing alert at the end of the picket line. "I heard Captain Watson telling someone that it was time to retire Tiger."

If that was true, Lindsey was happy Tiger would be able to participate today. "He's been with the unit for more than fifteen years. That's a long time."

"What will happen to him?" Lee asked.

Shane patted his shoulder. "Don't worry. We'll find a good home for him."

Once the unit was mounted and ready to proceed, the grand marshal, who was also the mayor and the local grocery-store owner, fired a starter pistol into the air and the small-town parade began. The floats might have been put together on hay wagons, but they had been decorated with as much care and pride as any Rose Bowl entry.

All along the street people rose from lawn chairs and curbsides to stand as the unit rode past with the flag unfurled and the horses' hooves clattering in unison. Farmers, mill workers and townsfolk alike took off their hats. Most placed a hand over their heart and, beside them, their children did the same. Here and there in the crowd, a few men saluted and Lindsey knew with certainty that those proud few knew exactly what price freedom asked.

As the parade moved away, Lindsey waited beside the pickup prepared to answer questions from people who were interested in military history, who were horse lovers, or who were simply curious about the unit. It was a part of her job that she truly enjoyed. Once the last float left the staging area, she didn't have to wait long before a few people began to gather around and venture close enough to pose inquiries.

It always touched and humbled her when people came up just to say they were proud of America's military or to say thank you for serving their country.

Lindsey had just finished telling several high-school-aged girls about what it was like to serve in the army when she spied a familiar figure walking toward her. Her heart gave a funny little leap. "Dr. Cutter, what a surprise. What are you doing here?"

"I was in the neighborhood…what I mean is…"

Lindsey thought she detected a blush on his tanned cheeks.

He cleared his throat and began again. "I was doing

a follow-up visit on one of my patients and I remembered that you mentioned your unit would be here today. I thought I would see firsthand what type of work your horses do. It will help me better evaluate when Dakota will be fit to return to duty. I had a glimpse of what you do the day you fell, but I'd like to see the whole thing minus the pileup."

"I'd be delighted to have you attend our exhibition. When the men return from the parade route, we'll travel over to the rodeo arena and set up there."

"Great, I'll see you later."

"I'll look for you."

Brian found the rodeo arena without difficulty. It wasn't long before the parade ended and those planning on attending the Little Britches rodeo began filling the seats. Sitting on the wooden planks of the grandstands, he watched for Lindsey. He spotted her along with the other unit members when they rode into the arena on the back of a flatbed truck loaded with rails and jump pillars. Dressed in red shirts and matching red ball caps, they went into action with military precision.

Lindsey was in charge of carefully measuring the distance between jumps and directing their setup down the middle of the course. As she was doing that, other men marked off and placed a series of upright poles along one side. Yet another soldier walked onto the field carrying a huge bunch of red, white and blue balloons. Soon they were divided up and secured to the jump pillars.

Once they were finished, the truck pulled out of the gates and Lindsey, breathless and bright eyed, joined Brian in the stands.

"Are you ready to be amazed and awed by fabulous feats of skill and daring?"

"I'm ready." The words were barely out of his mouth before rock music began blaring from the loudspeaker. The gates opened and eight horses and riders thundered in and circled the enclosure at a gallop. By the time they had made their second pass around the area, Brian was entranced.

Dressed in blue period uniforms and with banners waving, the detachment looked exactly like a piece of Western history come to life.

At a shouted command that he couldn't quite understand, the group came to a halt, head to tail. A second shout of orders had the horses wheeling into a single line. Like the sweep hand of his watch, they all turned in tight formation. The inside horse was actually prancing backward as they kept a straight line until a full circle had been made.

"Pretty good, huh?" Lindsey leaned forward and grinned at him.

"Very impressive."

"You ain't seen nothing yet."

She was right. The line broke apart and reformed into a column of twos, then charged down the course flying over each balloon-decorated jump. At the end, they split apart and galloped back to the start where they formed into twos again.

A unit member on foot walked into the arena. He carried a red-painted milk jug in one hand. Stopping near the center, he turned to face the mounted men and held up the jug in his hand.

Lindsey leaned toward Brian. "In the old days they used melons to practice this."

All the soldiers drew their sabers. Suddenly, the first horse exploded off the line and charged toward the man on foot. With precision that Brian couldn't believe, the rider impaled the jug off the man's hand and bore it aloft like a trophy until he reached the far end of the arena. Wheeling his horse around he held his saber and the jug out to his side and raced back. A second horse and rider charged down the field and speared the jug from the extended saber as they flew past each other. All eight riders repeated the maneuver, transferring the jug from sword to sword at a full gallop without a single miss.

Brian looked at the small woman seated beside him. "Can you do that?"

"Sure. Piece of cake."

"Now *that* is amazing."

"There are about seven historical mounted color guards in the United States military, but we are one of the few that train in combat techniques. Here, there is no distinction between women and men and the jobs we perform."

"Did you know that the equestrian sports are the only Olympic event in which men and women compete as equals?"

"I did. Do you know that we have our own cavalry competitions?"

He shook his head. "No, but after watching this, I'd like to see one."

"You'll have to wait until next September. I forgot to ask, how is your other patient doing?"

He looked momentarily perplexed. "My other patient?"

"The one you came here to see?"

"Oh, right, that patient. Dolly is getting along very well. Her owners say she is doing everything she was doing prior to surgery and more. That consists mainly of eating a lot and giving rides to their grandchildren when they visit on the weekends. I've advised them on a better diet for her and stressed the need for more exercise."

"Like having the grandkids over twice a week?"

"Three times a week would be better."

She laughed. "It was never hard to convince me to ride a pony when I was a kid. Hopefully, Dolly's family is the same way. Do you have any children?"

The smile that had been lurking in his eyes vanished. His face turned stone cold so quickly that Lindsey was taken aback.

"My wife and our unborn child died in a car accident several years ago."

His voice held the hard edge she had noticed the first time she had spoken to him. Back then, she had wondered if his leg was giving him pain. Now, she knew his suffering went much deeper than that.

She laid a hand on his arm. "I'm sorry for your loss."

He stood up. "Thank you. If you'll forgive me, I just remembered that I have to get back to the clinic."

Surprised, she said, "Aren't you going to stay for the rest of our performance?"

"Another time, perhaps. Good day, Sergeant Mandel." He made his way out of the grandstands, leaning heavily on his cane.

Lindsey watched him walk away and couldn't help but think that he looked like a very lonely man, even with the festive crowd milling around him.

Chapter 6

"Do we have everything?" Karen pushed a cardboard box in on top of a stack already filling the front passenger's seat of the Jeep nearly to the roof. The backseat was equally loaded.

"If you don't, that's too bad," Shane said, holding open the door for her. "Nothing else will fit in here."

"There's still room for a few more things," Karen insisted. Dressed in faded jeans and a pink cable-knit sweater with her blond hair pulled back in a ponytail, she looked much younger than twenty-one.

"Only because I'm not sitting in the driver's seat yet. Once I'm in, we won't have room for a toothpick. I may have to eat a box or two of cookies just to reach the gearshift."

She thrust her hands on her hips. "Don't you dare eat anything unless you pay for it, soldier."

"Yes, ma'am," he replied with a good-natured grin.

Lindsey listened to the exchange with a little smile playing on the edge of her lips. It didn't require mind-reading skills to see that Shane had taken a liking to her little sister. She wasn't sure how Karen felt about him, but she hoped nothing serious was forming.

She knew she was getting ahead of herself. A few smiles and jokes didn't make a relationship. They'd only known each other for a few weeks.

Almost exactly the same amount of time that she had known Brian.

Giving herself a mental shake, she dismissed the idea that Karen was interested in Shane. Knowing Karen's dislike of the military, and after seeing what had happened to Danny, Lindsey was sure her sister wouldn't want to become involved with a serviceman. Perhaps she should mention as much to Shane. He was a friend and she didn't want his feelings hurt.

"Are you sure you know where to take this stuff?" Karen asked as she moved aside and let Shane shut the door.

He didn't exactly roll his eyes, but he came close. "The east entrance of the K-State football field."

"Good. We'll meet you there. Lindsey, are you ready to go?"

"I am. Thanks for doing this, Shane."

"Anything to help, Lindsey. You know the whole unit is rooting for Dakota. The captain said his second surgery went well yesterday."

"According to Dr. Cutter, he removed the pins and replaced the cast without any problems."

The curt postoperative report yesterday had been the longest amount of time Brian had spent in her company since that day at Medicine Falls. He was obviously a busy man with a heavy surgery schedule, lectures to prepare and students to teach. Each time Lindsey saw him he seemed to be heading somewhere else. All week she had wondered if he was deliberately avoiding her.

Shrugging off the hurt that idea caused, she glanced into the packed vehicle. "You'd better get going. We'll meet you there."

Once Shane pulled away from the curb, Karen's liveliness visibly deflated, causing Lindsey to take a closer look. Karen seemed pale and there were dark circles under her eyes that she had tried to disguise with makeup. Without a word, Karen climbed into her blue sedan. It was then that Lindsey remembered her cell phone was still sitting in the charger in the living room. "I'll be with you in one second, Karen."

She dashed into the apartment, snatched up the phone and raced back down the steps. As she hurried around the front of the car to the passenger's side, she saw that Karen was resting her forehead on her hands at the top of the steering wheel. Opening the door, Lindsey slid into the seat. "Are you okay?"

Looking up, she gave Lindsey a wan smile. "I have a headache, that's all. I guess I stayed up too late baking last night."

"You've been baking for three days nonstop. I told you we would have enough. Just look at how much food the people on post donated. You didn't have to try and do it all by yourself."

"I wanted to do my part."

"You've done more than your part. You've been my driver, my cook, my nurse and my constant companion for the past two weeks. Why don't you stay here and lie down? I can catch a ride with someone else."

"Don't be silly, I'll be fine."

Lindsey wanted to believe her, but an hour later she could see that Karen truly wasn't feeling well. Once the tables and home-baked goodies had been set up outside the stadium, Shane returned to post, leaving the two women to hopefully sell all of their baked goods to hungry college football fans.

The day couldn't have been much better for a football game or for a bake sale, Lindsey decided. The temperature wasn't bad as long as she stayed in the sunshine. The bright rays kept the breeze from feeling cold until one of the white clouds with a flat gray bottom blocked the sun as it drifted past. Then, it wasn't hard to imagine that Thanksgiving was less than a week away.

Before long, they were doing a brisk business, but Lindsey kept one eye on her little sister. When they had a break in customers, she insisted Karen sit down and put a cool cloth on her forehead.

"That feels good. I'm sorry to be a drag, Lindsey. I don't get these headaches often, but when I do, they really take it out of me."

"You should go home and rest."

"I can't leave you to sell all this by yourself. Besides, how would you get home?"

"I could drive her."

Lindsey looked up in surprise to see Brian standing with a loaf of homemade bread in his hand. He wore a long-sleeved, pale yellow shirt tucked into khaki chino pants. The perpetual frown was missing from his face as he smiled at her.

After the way he had been avoiding her, she hadn't expected to see him today.

"How much for this bread?" he asked, holding out a loaf.

"Two dollars," Lindsey answered, willing her suddenly erratic pulse to calm down and her voice to sound casual. He shouldn't have this effect on her, but every time she laid eyes on him, it was the same.

"Are you sure you don't mind driving Lindsey home, Dr. Cutter?"

"Please call me Brian. Of course I don't mind giving her a lift." He handed over the bills.

"But it's out of your way," Lindsey protested as she took his money. She wasn't prepared to deal with the emotions his sudden appearance evoked. She needed more distance between them, not less.

"I don't mind."

"Good, it's settled then," Karen cut in quickly. "You're an answer to my prayers."

If Lindsey didn't know better, she might have suspected that Karen was doing a little matchmaking. But because she knew her sister really wasn't feeling well, she swallowed any further protests.

"Go home and lie down, Karen. I can handle the sales by myself."

"You won't be by yourself. I can stay and help."

Brian's offer caught her off guard. "That's all right, I can manage."

"I'm sure you can, but I'm going to help anyway." He came around to her side of the table. With him close beside her, she noticed the crisp, spicy scent of his aftershave. All her senses suddenly seemed heightened. He began rolling up his sleeves and she took note of the tanned muscles on his forearms. His fingers were long and well manicured. He had the gentle but strong hands of a surgeon.

She looked up to find him watching her in return. Sunlight glinted off his blond hair. He didn't look the least bit grumpy. *Handsome* was the word that came to mind. Her breath caught in her throat. He definitely was good-looking when he wasn't scowling. So why did he want to spend time with her?

The flattering notion that he might enjoy her company as much as she enjoyed his was quickly discarded. She wasn't looking for a man in her life, handsome or otherwise.

Once Karen had gathered up her belongings and left for her car, Lindsey turned to Brian. "You don't have to stay or give me a ride. I can call one of my friends on post and have them come get me."

"I don't mind helping. Besides, you're going to be overrun with customers in a few minutes."

"Why do you say that?"

"My secretary saw your flyer about this sale and suggested I have an announcement made during the game. A lot of these kids saw your fall and I'm sure they'll want to help."

"That was very kind of you."

"Don't give me too much credit. It was Jennifer's idea."

"I'll have to remember to thank her tomorrow."

"You can, but don't overdo it. The woman already has a high opinion of herself."

Before Lindsey could think of something else to talk about, his prediction came true. The football game ended and they were swamped with fans eager to buy cookies, cakes and brownies for a good cause. A few people even made donations without buying anything.

Brian sat at the cash box making change while Lindsey stayed busy answering questions about Dakota and visiting with the customers. Whenever he had a free moment, he spent it studying her. Having one arm in a sling didn't appear to hamper her as she boxed up the requested items. She was a true people person with a ready smile and an easy laugh that everyone around her responded to. It was no wonder he found her attractive.

For the first time he admitted the truth of those feelings, but that didn't change the fact that she wasn't for him. She deserved someone with a whole heart to give her. He wasn't a whole man in body or in soul.

Thrusting aside his somber thoughts, he resolved to keep a tight rein on his feelings. He would be foolish to allow something other than a professional relationship to start between them.

Before long, the last bag of chocolate fudge was bought and paid for and Lindsey dropped into a folding chair beside him.

"I can't believe we sold everything."

"Everything except these cookies." He pushed the plastic bag with a dozen dark brown oatmeal cookies toward her.

Lindsey opened the Ziploc top and offered him one. "Please accept this humble payment in return for your help today."

He took the cookie and bit into it. "I see why they didn't sell. They're kind of burnt."

"I know." She zipped the bag shut and tossed it into a box at her feet.

He indicated the bare tables. "What do we do with these?"

"They belong to the college. We just rented them for the afternoon. They can stay here."

"Are you ready to leave then?"

"I guess I am. Hey, didn't you have a loaf of bread in your hand earlier?"

He checked around. "It must have been sold out from under me."

"I'm sorry."

"Don't worry about it."

"I'll have Sergeant Link's wife bake you another one."

"You didn't bake it yourself?"

A bark of laughter escaped from her before she pressed her hand to her lips. "I made those oatmeal cookies. Baking is not one of my strengths as you can plainly taste."

He grinned. She didn't seem the least bit embarrassed to confess her shortcomings. He admired that. "What is one of your strengths?"

Wrinkling her brow, she considered his question. "Adaptability. That's my strength. I lived in five states and four countries before I turned twenty. I'm not even sure how many schools I attended as a kid."

"That must have been hard."

"It might have been worse if I hadn't had Danny and Karen. Having Danny looking out for us made it easier to always be the new kids. That and the riding schools. No matter where Dad was stationed he always enrolled us in riding classes."

"Where is your brother now?"

A deep sadness settled over her features. "He lives

in Washington, D.C., but I wish he lived closer. Danny was wounded in action last summer. He's a quadriplegic, now. He's finally at home, but he still requires around-the-clock nursing care."

"I'm sorry."

"Thank you."

"So, do you ever get tired of moving around?"

She tilted her head to the side. "No. Karen hated it when she was little, but Danny and I did okay. Maybe someday I'll find a place that will make me want to settle down, but for now the army is my home."

He rose and grasped his cane. "That must be my cue to return you to your post."

She rose, too, and finished stuffing several empty boxes in a nearby trash barrel. "Are you sure you don't mind?"

"Not at all. I'm parked over there." He pointed across the emptying parking lot to his white truck.

Lindsey fell into step beside him, adjusting to his slower pace without any sign of impatience. The silence lengthened between them, but he didn't find it uncomfortable. At his truck, he unlocked the vehicle with his remote key. She moved without hesitation to the passenger side, not waiting for him. He tried to hurry and open the door for her. She realized what he was doing when their hands closed over the handle at the same time.

The softness of her skin caught him by surprise. The bones of her hand felt delicate and dainty beneath his palm. A warmth stole over him that had nothing to do with the sunshine beating down on them.

She gave him a chiding look. "Oh, puleeze. I can get my own door."

At least she seemed unaware of the effect she had on

him. He strove to keep his voice neutral. "Perhaps, but my mother raised me to be a gentleman."

"And my father raised me to be a grunt."

"A what?"

"That's slang for a foot soldier."

"It's not a very nice term."

"It's not always a nice job."

"In a test of wills, I'll match my mother against your father any day of the week. They don't make them any tougher than she is. Please allow me." He nodded toward the door.

Slowly, she pulled her hand out from beneath his. "You win. This time."

"Duly noted." He pulled open the door and waited while she climbed in.

Lindsey watched Brian move around to the driver's side and took a few quick breaths to calm her racing heart. Never had the touch of a man's hand unnerved her the way Brian's touch did. The idea that she might be attracted to him was something she didn't want to contemplate. Falling for him was a sure road to heartbreak.

"Please, Lord. More heartache is the last thing I need," she whispered under her breath before Brian opened his door.

He stowed his cane on a rack in the rear window and started the ignition without a word. The silence that had seemed so comfortable only a few minutes before now seemed tense. They were only a few blocks from the stadium when his cell phone rang. He pulled it from his shirt pocket. Lindsey listened to the terse conversation with interest. After a few questions, he gave brisk instructions to the person on the other end of the line and then snapped his phone closed.

"I'm sorry, Lindsey, but I have to get back to the clinic. I have an emergency coming."

"Don't worry, I totally understand. I'll call a cab or get a friend to pick me up at the hospital."

"Are you sure?"

"Absolutely. It will give me a chance to spend a little time with Dakota."

He pulled onto a side street to turn around and in a few minutes they were heading back the way they had come. At the clinic, he hurried inside and met with several young men and one young woman. Lindsey knew they were the senior students on call for that day. As they walked toward the surgical suites, Lindsey found herself standing in the reception area where a young girl in a colorful Western costume sat with an older man dressed in jeans and boots. His cowboy hat rested on the chair beside him. The young girl was sniffling into a tissue. The man put his arm around her shaking shoulders and spoke to her softly. Lindsey couldn't hear what they were saying, but it was obvious that these were the people with the injured horse.

Pulling her cell phone from her back pocket, Lindsey punched in Shane's number. If he wasn't free to give her a ride, she'd try Avery next. Shane answered on the third ring. She could hear the sounds of laughter and cheering in the background. "It sounds like you're having a party."

"I'm watching a football game with some of the guys. What's up?"

"I'm looking for someone to give me a ride back to post."

"I thought Karen was driving you."

"She had a nasty headache so I sent her home early. I thought I had a ride, but it fell through."

"Bummer." He groaned loudly. A chorus of groans from his friends was followed by one lone cheer.

"What was that about?" she asked.

"Lee's team just made the tying touchdown. If they make this extra point, they'll move ahead at the half."

"Are Avery and Lee both there?"

"Yup."

"All right, never mind. I'll find another way back."

"Are you sure? Wow! Did you see that block? That's the way we Texas boys play ball!"

"Thanks, Shane. Enjoy your game." She hung up without waiting for his reply. It was obvious she was going to have to take a cab.

She walked up to the reception desk and asked the young man seated there for the use of a phone book. He had just handed it to her when Brian came back into the room. His face looked grimmer than she had ever seen it.

He walked up to the tearful young girl and sat down beside her. Lindsey tried not to listen in, but she couldn't help overhearing his words.

"I'm sorry. There isn't anything we can do for Storm. He is suffering a lot of pain. The kindest thing we can do is to put him to sleep."

The young girl's heartfelt cry tore at Lindsey's heart. Tears of sympathy pricked her eyes.

Brian awkwardly patted the weeping girl's shoulder, then rose to his feet. "You can come and say goodbye first, if you like."

As the pair went down the hallway, Brian stopped beside Lindsey. "Is someone coming to pick you up?"

"I was just about to call a cab."

"If you don't mind waiting a few more minutes, I can take you. I won't be needed here, after all."

"I'm so sorry."

"Thanks. Why don't you wait in my office?"

"I think I'd rather visit with Dakota. Whenever you're ready. Don't hurry on my account."

"This is the one part of my job I hate." He turned away and followed Storm's grieving family.

Lindsey walked down the hall and out into the large room that housed Dakota's stall along with eight others. Opening the gate, she slipped in and circled his neck with her good arm. He swung his head around and nuzzled her side briefly before lowering his head and closing his eyes. Leaning against his warm coat, she breathed deeply, drawing solace from his familiar scent.

"Dear Lord, offer Your comfort to those people and to Brian at this sad time. Let them know that You will wash away every tear and heal every heart."

She wasn't sure how long she stood there before she heard Brian's voice behind her. "There's something about the smell of a horse that makes you think of hot summer days and shady rests under the spreading branches of a tall cottonwood tree."

"I love the feel of them," she said softly, not looking up. "They feel like living silk over powerful muscles."

With each breath Dakota took, she listened to air rushing and rattling in and out of his lungs. His heartbeat was like a muffled drum, steady and strong, and yet so vulnerable.

Brian stepped closer. As if he were reading her mind, he said, "They are so powerful. It's always a shock when we see one get hurt."

She turned her face to look at him without letting go of Dakota. "Is it over?"

Brian nodded. "He was a four-year-old quarter horse and according to his young owner, he had the makings of a barrel-racing champion. It was such a shame."

"What happened to him?"

Brian moved up beside her and began to stroke Dakota's face. "He suffered a fracture of the pastern much like this fellow's. We see a lot of breaks like that in horses who make quick turns and sliding stops."

"Why couldn't you do surgery on him?"

"He started out with a simple break, but by the time the family got him here, he had done so much damage to the leg trying to stand in the trailer that we couldn't do anything for him."

"I don't understand."

"There was irreparable damage done to the soft tissue and blood supply by the broken bone fragments. If he could have been brought to us in an equine ambulance, we might have been able to save him."

"Do you have one?"

"Not at present, but I haven't given up hope. For the most part, you'll only see them at big racetracks like Belmont Park or Santa Anita. However, I'm trying to persuade the company that makes them to loan us one to have on display during our conference here on January twenty-first."

"I remember seeing one on television when that Kentucky Derby winner broke his leg."

"They're quite expensive. It seems that the board forgot to add the money for one to my budget," he joked.

"We could hold another bake sale. I would contribute more cookies."

"Another burnt offering?"

Delighted to see the ghost of a smile on his face, she grinned. "I don't always singe them. The oven in my apartment is fickle. Some days it gets hotter than others."

"I'm sure that is totally true."

"Speaking of hot things, Dakota feels warm to me."

"Now that you mention it, he does. I see that he hasn't eaten much today. There's still feed in his bucket."

"That's not like him. He's always ready to eat. Do you think he's sick?"

Dakota coughed deeply. Alarm raced through Lindsey's body and her gaze shot to Brian's face. He pulled his stethoscope from the pocket of his lab coat and moved to examine the animal. After listening to the horse's chest, he stepped back. The frown she hated seeing was etched between his brows.

"What is it? What's wrong?"

"I'll need an X-ray to confirm, but I'm afraid he's developed pneumonia."

"That's bad, isn't it?" She knew it was a stupid question the second the words were out of her mouth. Of course it was bad. Brian's look of deep concern only confirmed it.

Chapter 7

Over the next days Dakota's life hung in a delicate balance. With his head held low he wheezed and coughed until Brian thought he couldn't possibly draw another ragged breath. It hurt just to watch him try. Brian knew minimizing the animal's distress was just as important as keeping him warm and well hydrated. Lindsey rarely left his side. Her presence seemed to bring the horse comfort. Somehow, her presence was a comfort to Brian, as well.

On the second night, a traffic accident with an overturned horse trailer brought in three more injured horses and the hospital's staff was stretched to the limit. With Brian's permission, Shane and Avery brought in a cot and placed it in an empty adjacent stall. All the unit members, Karen and numerous students took turns staying to help care for the animal. Their dedicated presence seemed to be all that was keeping the tired horse from slipping away.

Brian gave up going home and slept fitfully on the sofa in his office at night. During the daylight hours, the clinic operated normally and his surgery and teaching schedule kept him busy. At night, he rose every two hours to take vital signs and temperature readings looking for the least sign of improvement in Dakota. He could have left the horse's care to the senior students on duty, but he didn't. Dakota had become a special patient. Every four hours he gave the horse pain medication and every six hours he gave the massive doses of antibiotics needed to help stem the infection. In spite of all they were doing for him, Brian knew that it was Dakota's will to live that would ultimately be the deciding factor.

By the middle of the third night, he had given up urging Lindsey to rest. Instead, they worked side by side. While he administered the intravenous drugs, Lindsey held an inhaler over Dakota's nose to make sure he breathed in all the medicine designed to ease his labored respirations.

A few hours before dawn on the fourth night, Brian stifled a yawn as he leaned on the gate to Dakota's stall.

"You should go and rest," Lindsey suggested as she came to stand beside him.

"I'm all right, but I think your sister is out for the count." He nodded toward the cot in the next stall.

Lindsey looked over to see Karen had fallen asleep. "I can't say that I blame her. I feel like taking a nap myself."

"You're welcome to use the couch in my office."

"I may when I'm sure Dakota is doing better. What is his temperature now?"

Brian entered the stall and took a quick reading. "A hundred and five down from one hundred and six point five. His fever looks like it's breaking."

"Still, it isn't normal."

"No, it's not a hundred and one, but it's a definite improvement."

"Thanks to you." She entered the stall and held out a slice of apple. She was happy to see Dakota nibble it up.

"You're the one who has managed to coax him to eat. Nutrition is really important when a horse runs a fever." He gave a weary sigh as he sank onto a bale of straw in the corner.

"He's just used to me, that's all. Besides, apples are his favorite treat."

"I've noticed you slipping in horse chow and vitamins along with those slices."

"Do you think he is out of the woods?" She came over and sat on the bale beside him.

"In my professional opinion, I think he is."

"Are you ever wrong?" she asked.

"Frequently when it comes to people, but rarely about horses."

She managed a tired smile. "Are you saying you lack people skills?"

He called up a smile to match hers. "Why do you think I'm a vet?"

"You have been a blessing for us, that's for sure. I hate to think of Danny facing Dakota's loss on top of everything else he has been through."

Brian heard the catch in her voice and saw such pain on her face that he hesitated to ask any more questions.

As if sensing his scrutiny, she glanced up and gave him a sad, sweet smile.

He reached out and covered her hand with his own. "Do you want to talk about it?"

"Danny was wounded while serving in Afghanistan. He singled-handedly saved the lives of two men in his unit when they were ambushed in a roadside attack. He risked heavy fire to pull those men to safety. Then, when a mortar exploded nearby, a piece of shrapnel hit him in the back of the neck and severed his spine."

"He sounds like a very brave man."

She looked toward the ceiling. "He is very brave. He's facing his disability with a determination that's amazing."

"It's all about having the will to live."

She studied him for a moment and then asked, "What happened to your wife?"

The question caught him off guard. He had never told anyone the details of the accident. For years he had kept those terrible hours and days locked away in his mind. He met Lindsey's gaze and saw only compassion looking back at him.

Sitting beside her in the dim building, he discovered a need to share his pain and his loss. "I had been working a lot of long hours that winter. I had only been out of school a year and I was intent on building up my practice. The Sunday before Valentine's Day, Emily planned to go visit her family. She wanted to share the news about the baby in person. I should have let her go alone. I was dead tired. If only I had let her drive…" His voice trailed off into silence.

"What happened?"

"While we were visiting her parents, the weather

started to turn bad. She wanted to spend the night, but I wanted to get back. I thought my practice couldn't do without me for another day. I insisted we leave." He grew silent as the memory of the terrible night fanned the guilt he always carried.

"You don't have to tell me about it if you don't want to."

"I don't remember much about the accident itself. I do remember how hard it was to keep my eyes open looking into the snow. I must have fallen asleep at the wheel."

He patted his leg. "When I woke up rescue workers were cutting me out of what was left of our car. I reached for Emily. I found her hand in the darkness and then I felt her leave me. I felt her spirit touch mine and then she was gone."

"I'm so sorry."

Instead of answering, Brian rose and took another temperature reading on his patient. He had exposed enough of his soul for one night. "The fever is definitely going down."

"Thank the Lord for answering our prayers."

"I would say it is thanks to modern medicine."

"Perhaps the Lord's plan called for both medicine and prayers."

"I doubt it. I'm sorry. It's just that I gave up praying a long time ago."

"Because of Emily?"

He wanted to say yes, but he wasn't sure the words would make it past the lump in his throat.

She laid a hand on his arm. "It's okay. God will be there when you are ready to pray again."

"I don't think much of a God who allows terrible things to happen to good people."

"The Lord never promised that we wouldn't suffer. He did promise that He will always be with us."

"You surprise me."

"Why?"

"Religion and a military life don't seem to go together."

She smiled slightly. "Maybe not to you, but to most of us serving our country, it makes perfect sense. If I'm called to put my life on the line, I know that God has my back."

"Didn't your brother's injury leave you with doubts about that?"

"My brother's injury left me with the same anger and grief that everyone feels at a time like that. What God gives me is comfort, and the sure and certain knowledge that He is with me. My strength comes from Him."

Deciding it was time to change the subject, he asked, "Whatever possessed a woman like you to enlist in the army in the first place?"

She looked at him askew. "Why shouldn't a woman join the army?"

"I not saying a woman can't do the job. I'm just wondering why a woman would want to. You could be sent into a combat zone."

"You mean people might shoot at me?"

"Well, yes."

"Here's a news flash. I've been trained to shoot back. I even have a gun."

"Would you? Shoot back, I mean?"

"Yes. Does that make me a bad person in your eyes?"

"Of course not. Do you plan to make it a career?"

Leaning against the wall, she stretched her legs out and stared at her feet. "You have to understand that I come from a military family. The Mandels have served with distinction since the Civil War. Growing up, I always knew that I would enlist when I was old enough. I don't think my father would have approved of any other choice. He certainly wasn't happy when Karen started talking about becoming a teacher instead of a soldier."

"Teaching is an admirable profession."

"Not for a Mandel."

"So will Karen enlist, too?"

"Not for all the tea in China. She has stated categorically that she has no interest in wearing fatigues or taking orders from strangers."

"What does your mother think about your career choice?"

It was the first time Brian had seen uncertainty and regret in her eyes. She looked down and plucked a piece of straw from the bale. "My mother doesn't care one way or the other."

Brian sat down beside her. "What makes you say that?"

Fighting back ugly memories, Lindsey wrapped the piece of straw around her finger like a wedding ring. When she realized what she was doing, she pulled it off and threw it aside. "My mother left my father when I was ten. Two days before my birthday, actually. We never heard from her again."

"That must have been rough," he said gently.

"We managed." Only because she, Danny and Karen had had each other. Their father had retreated into his work, the work their mother had hated. He spent long hours away from home, and it wasn't long before he was transferred to a new post. After that, Lindsey gave up watching for her mother to come back.

It was at the new post that they met a wonderful man by the name of Chaplain Carson. A kind and generous man, he always made time for the lonely kids who lived next door. In more ways than one, he helped all of them through that terrible time as he taught them about God's love.

"Does your father still feel the same way about the service after your brother was wounded?"

Brian's question jerked Lindsey out of the past. "I'm sure my father suffers as any man must suffer to see his son injured and hurting. But Dad is as proud as I am of what Danny did."

"Of course. I just thought that he might want you out of harm's way."

"He worries, but he knows I'll do my duty. It's up to me to carry on the family tradition. My father doesn't have to tell me that. It's understood."

"What would you do if there wasn't an army?"

She scowled at him. "What kind of question is that? There will always be an army. 'The price of freedom is eternal vigilance.' Thomas Jefferson said that and he was right."

"But what if you couldn't stay in the service for some reason? What would you do?"

The question was so foreign that Lindsey wasn't sure how to answer it. It had always been the army or nothing.

"Come on," he coaxed. "Think outside the box."

"I honestly don't know."

"What did your father do after he retired?"

"Drove us nuts."

Brian chuckled and Lindsey found to her surprise that she adored the sound. Still, she wanted to change the subject, so she asked, "What do your parents do?"

"They're ranchers. My family owns a spread outside of Missoula, Montana. They both still work as hard as they ever did, according to my older brother. He ranches with them."

"Why didn't you stay in the family business?"

"That's a long story."

She glanced at her watch. "Looks like I have time to listen."

"Okay. Long story short. As a kid, I was reckless. I thought more about impressing my friends than my own safety. One day, on a dare, I tried to ride my horse down the side of a steep embankment the way they do in the movies. We fell. How I wasn't killed outright I'll never know, but my mare broke both her front legs. When my friends brought my father to the scene, Dad gave me the rifle and told me to put her down because it was obvious her life didn't mean anything to me."

"What a cruel thing to say."

"Maybe it was, but he was right."

"Did you do it?"

"I couldn't, so my father did. But that day I vowed I'd never be the cause of another horse's suffering. I knew then that I'd be a vet."

"And you never wanted to be anything else?"

"Occasionally, I have this recurring desire to work in a movie theater and make popcorn."

"You're kidding, right?" She stared at him in amazement.

"Think about it. The smell of buttery popcorn all day long. Can't you just imagine it?"

Lindsey closed her eyes. "The sound of the popper and the sight of fluffy white kernels pouring out from under a silver lid."

"Can you think of a better job?"

"Driving a tank," she stated without hesitation. "You'd never be caught in another traffic jam. You could roll over anything in your way."

"Parking on campus might be a problem, though."

"Not a bit. Find the space you want and park on top of the car that's there." She glanced at him trying to control the laughter building inside. "After all, who is going to argue with a woman in a tank?"

"Good point. Can I rent one from you?"

She giggled and he began to laugh outright. His laugh had a wonderful, deep timbre. One she wanted to hear over and over again.

His smile slowly faded. "Since it looks like Dakota is through the worst of it, I'd better get home for a few hours and make up with Isabella."

The name was like a douse of cold water on Lindsey's joy. Did he have another woman in his life? The thought was a sobering one. Then the realization hit her. It mattered. It mattered more than she cared to admit. She swallowed hard. "Who is Isabella?"

"My bunny."

She wasn't quite sure she'd heard him correctly. "Your bunny. As in rabbit?"

He looked at her sharply. "Yes. Why is that so odd?"

She grinned, almost giddy with relief. "I'm not sure. I guess I pictured you as the kind of guy who kept a bulldog or maybe a python."

"Sorry to disappoint you. All I have is a domineering French Lop."

"I sense a story."

He glanced at his watch. "One that will have to wait for another day. I'll be back in a few hours. I have a surgery scheduled for eight o'clock this morning. You have my beeper number if you need me. I only live about ten minutes away."

"Dakota seems much better. I'm sure we'll be fine on our own for a few hours."

"There is always a student on duty if you need anything. I'll see you later."

"Good night, Brian."

He stood and she rose to face him. The air between them suddenly seemed charged with electricity. She longed to reach out and smooth his rumpled shirt. She wanted to comb her fingers through his tousled hair and coax it into some kind of order. Instead, she stuffed her hand into the hip pocket of her jeans and took a step back.

For a long moment, he simply stared into her eyes, then with a nod, he walked away. It wasn't until then that she remembered to breathe.

A few hours later, Dakota's temperature had fallen to a normal level. His appetite returned with a vengeance and he made short work of any apple slices that came within range. When Lindsey turned away to pull another piece of fruit from the brown paper bag by the cot, he whinnied loudly, waking Karen.

She sat up rubbing her eyes. "That sounds like he's feeling better."

"Much better."

"What time is it? Or maybe I should ask what day is it?"

Lindsey glanced at her watch. "It's the day before Thanksgiving and it's after nine."

"Why did you let me sleep so long?"

"You looked so peaceful that I didn't have the heart to wake you."

Tipping her head first to the right and then to the left, Karen winced. "My neck would have been happier if you had. Where is Brian?"

"He had a surgery this morning."

"You two seemed to be getting along rather well last night."

"I thought you were asleep?"

"I was—most of the time. What did you and he find to talk about until the wee hours of the morning?"

"This and that. You know how it is. Small talk mostly."

"Small talk?" Something in Karen's expression told Lindsey that she wasn't buying that line.

"All right, if you want me to admit that I'm beginning to like the guy, I will."

"I thought so." She folded her arms over her chest and looked smug.

Lindsey turned away and began to toss flakes of hay into Dakota's stall. "Just because I like him doesn't mean anything except that it will be easier to keep working with him."

"I wouldn't be too sure about that. I sense more than a casual interest."

"I'm not looking for love, Karen, if that's where this is going. I have plans to make the army my career. Marriage and the military don't mix. Not for me, anyway."

"You're thinking about Mother. Just because our parents couldn't make their marriage work isn't any reason to believe you can't make a relationship work. I don't remember much about Mom because I was only six when she left, but from all that Danny has told me, I can see you are a much stronger woman than she was. You have a good heart and a strong faith. Why not trust that God will bring the right man into your life?"

She glanced at Karen. "What makes you think Brian is the right man?"

Karen stepped up and took her by the shoulders. Giving her a gentle shake, she said, "Girlfriend, what makes you so sure he isn't?"

Chapter 8

The Monday after the holiday weekend, Brian sat in his office trying to concentrate on drafting a letter of appeal for funds to buy an ambulance when he noticed Isabella creeping toward his Wildcat mug. He knew that look in her eye. Picking her up before she could snatch one of his freshly sharpened pencils and chew it into splinters, he scolded softly, "I see what you're trying to do. I've got to get this letter done, so that means you have to go outside."

Outside was one of her favorite words. She loved racing up and down the long fenced area he'd had built beside the building and nibbling on the fresh grass.

He needed a break anyway. The words on his yellow legal pad weren't anywhere near the tone he wanted to convey. Instead of fine-tuning his letter, all he had done that morning was think about Lindsey.

Rising, he picked up his cane from where it leaned against his desk and made his way toward the door. As he pulled it open, Isabella suddenly leaped out of his arms and took off toward the stall area. He hurried after her, knowing she could easily be hurt if she ran into one of the occupied pens. Fortunately, he saw the double doors at the end of the hall were closed.

He was only a step away from his pet when one of the doors opened and two students came through. It was all the opportunity Isabella needed.

"Catch her," he called out.

By the time the befuddled students realized what he was talking about, the rabbit had darted between them and through the doorway.

"Isabella, come back here!" His shout did nothing to stem her headlong flight.

Running past the students, Brian entered the stall area and scanned the large enclosure for any sign of his fleeing pet. Checking each pen as he hurried past, he didn't see Private Barnes until he almost ran into him.

"Whoa, there, Doc. What's the rush?"

"Did you see a rabbit come this way?"

"A what?"

"Isabella is loose?" The familiar female voice made Brian look past the young soldier. Jennifer was sitting on a folding chair beside the army cot, but she jumped to her feet, a look of alarm on her face.

Happy to have an ally who understood what was needed, Brian nodded. "Make sure all the outside doors are closed."

She grabbed the soldier's arm. "Of course. Avery, you go that way and I'll make sure everything on this end is shut. Give a shout if you see her."

"What sort of rabbit am I looking for?"

She rolled her eyes and gave him a shove. "The fuzzy kind that hops. Now hurry, but don't scare the horses."

Brian retraced his steps and began searching more slowly. There were numerous bales of hay and bags of feed stacked along the center of the wide aisles. She could be behind any of them or under the wooden pallets they rested on.

He'd only finished checking a small area when Jennifer returned. "None of the outside doors are open. I've left Avery in charge of seeing that no one goes in or out."

Brian stared around the large building. "Why would she suddenly decide she wanted to come in here? She loves going outside. I distinctly told her she was going outside."

"That may be my fault," Jennifer admitted with a pained look. "I brought her out here with me yesterday."

"And why were you out here instead of at the desk?"

"Avery…that is…Private Barnes asked for some help with the thermal thermometer."

His scowl prompted her to add quickly, "I held on to Isabella the whole time. I didn't let her run loose. She wasn't even frightened by the horse when he came over to check her out."

Brian sighed, trying to hide his vexation. "All right, we'll talk about this after we find her. You take that aisle and I'll take this one. Check everywhere."

"We don't have to. There she is."

He turned to see Jennifer pointing toward Dakota's stall. The big horse was lying down with his legs tucked under him. His neck was arched as he sniffed the bunny cuddled up against his chest. Brian approached the stall slowly. He didn't want to startle Dakota into lunging to his feet. One misstep and the little rabbit could be seriously injured, or worse.

"Come here, Isabella," he called softly. Dakota looked up at the sound of his voice, but the rabbit didn't move. Brian didn't see any choice. He would have to go in and get her.

"All right, big fella, you just stay relaxed." Brian opened the gate slowly and stepped inside the stall. Dakota threw his head up as if he was about to rise.

"Stay down, Dakota." The command came from behind Brian. He shot a quick look over his shoulder. Lindsey stood at the gate.

"He'll stay still now. It's okay," she assured him.

"How can you be so certain?"

"It's what he's been trained to do. He has to follow orders just like the rest of us."

Trusting her word, Brian walked to the pair and scooped up Isabella. She squirmed and tried to get down again, but he held on tightly.

Lindsey arrived beside them and squatted to pat Dakota's neck. "They look so cute together. Why don't you leave her here. She certainly seems to make him happy."

"It would be too risky." Brian ran his hand down Isabella's long, soft ears. "Lindsey, allow me to introduce you to Isabella the Terrible."

Rising, Lindsey stroked the rabbit's small round head. "You don't look very terrible to me."

"Reserve judgment until you know her better," Jennifer suggested. "Shall I take her outside?"

Brian shook his head. "No, I'll take her and then you and I are going to have a talk in my office."

"Yes, Doctor." She turned away meekly and left the building.

"I can't believe it," he said in astonishment.

"What?"

"She always has some sort of snappy comeback."

"Maybe she's saving it until you're alone."

"That's a scary thought." He made a mental note to be gentle with his secretary when he took her to task for neglecting her duties.

He glanced at the woman beside him.

Thoughts of Lindsey kept him from sleeping, kept him from working, and, worst of all, they kept him from thinking about Emily. It certainly wasn't Lindsey's fault, but he had decided it would be best if he didn't see as much of her in the future. During the past two days, he had accomplished his goal with difficulty. Like today, she always seemed to turn up when he least expected her.

Determined to put some distance between them now, he said curtly, "I have to put Isabella away. Excuse me."

Lindsey watched his abrupt retreat and wondered why he always seemed to be rushing out the door as she came in. After their exchange of confidences during Dakota's illness, she felt she had gained a better understanding of the man, perhaps even made a friend. Obviously, she had been mistaken. Brian couldn't have made it plainer that he didn't need or want her friendship.

"Not a very sociable chap, is he?" Avery said, coming to stand beside her.

She felt compelled to defend Brian in spite of his recent attitude. "He can be."

"I'll take your word for it."

"Where have you been?"

"Jenny had me guarding the doors to keep the rabbit from getting away. She stopped by to tell me the rodent has been recovered. Where was she?"

"Making nice with Dakota."

"No joke? I didn't know horses and rabbits got along."

"I've seen horses that weren't happy unless they had a stall mate. Usually it's a pony, but I've seen them adopt goats or dogs, so why not a rabbit?" Lindsey said.

"If it helps Dakota get better, I'll buy him a whole herd of rabbits."

"I'll second that. Speaking of Dakota, how is he today?"

"Relaxed, eating and drinking well. I'd say he's much improved. And how are you? You saw the doctor again today, didn't you?"

"The bone is mending, but I still don't have feeling in my fingers or my hand."

"How much longer does he think that will last?"

"You know doctors. It could be a week, it could be a month. Time will tell."

"Bummer."

"No kidding. It sure would be nice to be able to drive myself again and not have to depend on everyone to get me places. Karen is a doll, but I think even she is tired of being my chauffeur."

"Is your car a stick?"

"No, why?"

"Because if it isn't a stick, then you only need one arm to drive. Get a spinner for your steering wheel."

"What's that?"

"A kind of doorknob that attaches to the wheel and allows you to steer with one hand."

"Isn't that only for handicapped people?"

"Have you looked in the mirror? You *are* handicapped even if it's temporary. But no, they aren't only for people with disabilities. I've got one on my sports car."

"Don't tell me, let me guess. So you can keep one arm around a girl while you're driving your Jag?"

"Exactly."

"How did a guy like you end up in the army?"

"You mean how did one of Boston's most eligible bachelors find himself enlisted as a private?"

"Yes. I've been wondering about that."

"So have I. My grandfather has some explaining to do when I get home. And for the record, the evils of alcohol cannot be overstated."

"You got drunk and ended up enlisted?"

"I'm ashamed to admit that I was so plastered I don't remember, but even my grandfather's lawyer couldn't get me out of Uncle Sam's contract. If he actually tried."

"Why wouldn't he?"

"I've done a lot of dumb things in my life. I was careless and selfish because I thought money fixed everything. My grandfather was at his wit's end with me. Maybe he thought the army could straighten me out."

"I think he was right."

A half smile pulled at one corner of his mouth. "It's nice of you to say so. At least I've given up drinking anything stronger than soda."

Lindsey patted his shoulder. "The Lord moves in mysterious ways."

"So does my grandfather," he grumbled.

"The spinner is a good idea. Would you be able to put one on my car if I gave you the money to buy one?"

"It would be my pleasure. But before you get behind the wheel, I insist you let me take you to an empty parking lot for some practice before you try it alone."

"You've got a deal. Thanks, Avery. Now, you're relieved. Is there anything I need to know about Dakota?"

"The Doc wants us to keep checking the cast for hot spots with the thermal thermometer at least once every four hours."

"Any signs of pressure sores?"

"No, his leg is as cool as a cucumber, but he is getting up and down more and that could cause problems. Are you taking leave for Christmas?"

"I hadn't planned on it. I don't want to desert Dakota after his close call." Voicing her excuse out loud didn't lessen the nagging guilt she had been saddled with since her conversation with Karen that morning.

"What about your family?"

"Karen has decided to spend the holidays with my brother since I won't be going home."

She dreaded the coming holidays. It was hard to think about celebrating Christmas with Danny's injury looming like a dark cloud over everyone's mood. "What about you?"

"I'll be here. Maybe we should have our own Christmas party."

"That's a good idea. I'll talk to the captain about it."

After Avery left, Lindsey walked into the stall and sat down beside Dakota. He nuzzled her shoulder briefly, then began nipping at her pocket.

"Okay, I do have a few alfalfa treats in there, but don't get greedy. You're not the only horse in this place.

See that little pinto across the way?" She pointed to a pony across the aisle. Dakota ignored her extended arm.

"He likes alfalfa, too, so you'll have to share." She pulled a handful of green pellets from her pocket and held them out for him. He lipped them up quickly.

After visiting with the horse for half an hour, Lindsey rose and began walking between the pens, stopping to visit with several other inmates. At the end of the building she glanced out the window and saw Isabella racing back and forth in a wire run.

Slipping out the door, Lindsey stopped beside the rabbit's kennel and knelt down to put her fingers through the chain links. Isabella stopped running long enough to investigate the potential new playmate. "Have you been banished from his office?"

She glanced toward the front of the building. "Care to share any secrets about your owner? Do you know why he's treating me like a plague victim?"

Isabella sniffed at Lindsey's fingers then dashed away. "I can see you aren't going to be any help."

From inside the barn, Lindsey heard Dakota's whinny. Rising, she headed back into the building. With only horses and rabbits to talk to, it promised to be a long day. Mainly because the one creature she really wished to spend time with had retreated to his office and she couldn't think of a good reason to follow him.

It was late afternoon and Lindsey had just closed the book she was reading when the sound of raised voices reached her.

Brian stormed through the doorway. A deep frown etched a groove between his eyebrows.

Jennifer was hard on his heels. "I didn't take her out of her pen, honest."

"Is she in here?" he demanded, stopping in front of Lindsey.

Not a word all day and now he had the nerve to behave like this? He wasn't the only one capable of pretending indifference. "More rabbit troubles, Doctor?" she drawled.

"Isabella has never run away before. You want me to believe she's done it twice in one day?"

"Dakota and I haven't seen hide nor hair of her, have we, boy? How much trouble is it to keep track of one bunny?" She rose from the cot where she was sitting and looked toward her horse. He stood in the corner of his pen with his head down. She assumed he had been sleeping. It was then she noticed the small bundle of fur beneath his nose.

Brian spotted his pet at the same time. "She *is* here."

Taken aback, Lindsey turned to him. "I'm sorry. I never saw her come in. I was outside by her pen for a little while, but I didn't take her out. She was inside her run when I left."

"I seriously doubt a six-pound rabbit could open a kennel door and then a barn door all by herself."

"I wouldn't put it past her," Jennifer muttered.

Brian glared at her but didn't allow himself to be diverted. "It isn't safe to let her in with Dakota no matter how cute you think it is."

Lindsey opened her mouth and closed it again. Anger at his accusation momentarily robbed her of speech. She took a step toward him.

"Are you saying you think I took your precious rabbit out of her cage and put her in with my lame horse just because I thought they looked cute together?" Resentment lent a steely edge to her words.

"You go, girl." Jennifer crossed her arms and looked smug.

Brian took a step back. Lindsey could see the indecision wavering in his eyes. "If this is another one of your harebrained ideas for stress reduction…"

"I have no idea how your rodent found her way out of her pen and into here, but I had nothing to do with it."

"Rabbits aren't rodents, they're lagomorphs," Jennifer supplied with a bright smile.

"My horse doesn't need a lop-eared fur ball to reduce his stress and keep him company. He has me. Perhaps if you paid more attention to *your* pet, she wouldn't be looking for love in all the wrong places."

"Lagomorphs have four upper incisors. The second pair is peglike and posterior to the first. Rodents only have two upper incisors."

Both Lindsey and Brian turned to stare at Jennifer.

"Well, it's true. A rabbit *isn't* a rodent. I can't believe the pair of you. There's absolutely nothing wrong with a hare's brain and don't ever say *rodent* like it's a bad word."

Brushing between Brian and Lindsey, Jennifer slipped through the gate into the stall and picked up Isabella. Slipping out again, she paused and looked from Brian to Lindsey and back. "Any more name-calling and someone is going to find their mouth washed out with soap. Apologies are in order, and I mean now."

Lindsey watched Brian's secretary exit through the main doors with the squirming rabbit under her arm. Dakota whinnied frantically as his new friend was carried away.

Without taking her eyes off the doorway, Lindsey asked, "Did she mean it?"

He stood beside her looking in the same direction. "I'm not sure, but I'm not taking any chances. I'm sorry I suggested you were harebrained."

"I've been told there's nothing wrong with a hare's brain, so apology accepted. I'm sorry I called Isabella a rodent."

"You're forgiven."

"She's kind of a weird woman," Lindsey ventured.

"I had no idea until recently just how strange she is," he acknowledged.

Glancing at Brian from the corner of her eye, Lindsey suddenly found herself overcome with giggles. Brian shot her a dour look but couldn't keep the smile off his face. A second later he was chuckling, too.

By the middle of the following week, Dakota's condition had improved enough to allow him to be transferred back to the fort stables. With the unit members providing around-the-clock care, Brian knew there wasn't any reason to keep the horse at the clinic. Except that it meant he wouldn't be seeing Lindsey anymore.

The day after the big bay left it suddenly became a much quieter building. At least twice before noon Brian found himself standing beside the empty stall and staring into the space. He should be wondering how Dakota was getting along, but he had confidence that Lindsey and the men would follow his instructions to the letter. What he found himself wondering was how Lindsey was getting along. What was she doing? Was she resting her arm the way she should, or would she be trying to do too much?

Jennifer came up beside Brian and propped her chin on the rail. "I miss him already."

"He'll get the best care possible and he'll be happier in his own stall with the other horses he knows."

She sighed. "I know the horse will be happier, but I'm not sure the rest of us will be."

Puzzled at her depressed tone, he looked at her closely. "You're not taking about missing the horse, are you?"

"Duh? I'm talking about that gorgeous hunk."

"Forgive me if I seem a little slow, but which hunk would that be?"

"Private Avery Barnes. That Boston accent of his was to die for. Can't you think of some reason to send me out to the fort?"

"Jennifer, if Private Barnes is interested in seeing you again, he'll call."

"Oh, like you're going to call Lindsey?"

"That's neither here nor there."

"Which means, no." She shook her head as she walked away muttering, "Men are *so* not bright."

At the doorway, she stopped and looked back. "How is it that so many of you are in charge of stuff?"

Brian watched her walk out without replying. He had no intention of seeing Lindsey unless it was in an official capacity. He liked her, but it would never be more than that. The love of his life was dead and he knew there would never be another.

Yet, he did miss Lindsey.

He rested his arms atop the cool metal bar of the gate. The hay bale where they had shared bits and pieces of their lives still sat in the corner of the stall. In those hectic hours when Dakota had been so ill, Brian had learned a lot about Lindsey Mandel.

She was dedicated and tireless when it came to doing

her duty. She was witty and funny, often when he least expected it. The mental image of her parking a tank outside the clinic made him smile even now. She was sure of her place in the world and that place was in the army. Yet she didn't believe in mixing marriage with her career.

It was a shame, really. She had so much to offer. She was more than a pretty face. She was a woman with a heart and a soul. Her faith in God seemed unshakable in spite of being abandoned by her mother as a child and her brother's devastating injury. She would make some man a fine wife if he didn't mind her going off to war.

Like most Americans, he listened to news and saw almost daily the way brave young men and women sacrificed everything for the freedom he took so much for granted. He was ashamed to admit that he had thought of them as foolishly brave. But there was nothing foolish about Lindsey or about her love of country.

Emily would have liked her.

Pushing away from the gate, he made his way back to his office. He had a mound of paperwork waiting for him. The extra work would be good. It would help keep his mind off the void that had formed in his life. Lindsey and her horse were gone. Now his life could finally get back to normal.

But was that what he really wanted?

Chapter 9

Lindsey ran the flat brush from Dakota's withers to his rump and worked down his side until his coat held a high shine. Inside the cavernous limestone stable that had been built in 1889, she listened to the sounds of other horses being led out for their morning exercise. Their shod feet clattered noisily on the uneven cobblestone floor. The cool interior smelled of old wood, horses, hay and oiled leather. It was a scent she had come to love in the sixteen months that she had been assigned to the unit.

The repetitive motion of brushing Dakota didn't require much thought, leaving her mind free to wander. The place it chose to go was back to the Large Animal Clinic.

Had Isabella managed another escape only to find Dakota gone? What was Brian doing today, Lindsey wondered? Was he thinking about her?

"A penny for your thoughts?"

She turned to see Shane leaning on the lower half of the wooden stall door and looking bored now that their season was over.

"They aren't worth that much," she replied, picking up a mane and tail comb.

"Need some help?" he offered.

"Sure. Trying to comb a tail one-handed is harder than it looks."

"How's the arm doing?"

"It hurts, it itches, and the fact that I can't use my hand is driving me nuts—other than that, it's fine."

"At least you don't have to stand on it." He motioned to the cast on Dakota's leg.

"I know. Poor boy, I can't imagine being uncomfortable and not being able to tell anyone."

"He'll tell us, just not with words."

"He has been nipping at the wrap today."

"See what I mean?"

Lindsey ducked under Dakota's neck and began grooming his other side. Shane spoke softly and patted the big bay's rump before pulling his tail to one side to comb it.

Lindsey glanced at him and her hand stilled.

"What?" he asked when he noticed her staring.

"Danny and I were doing this very thing the last time I saw him before he was wounded. It was only a few days before he shipped out. Neither one of us wanted to say goodbye, so we worked side by side grooming Dakota without saying a word. Danny loves this horse. I thought he was crazy to pay boarding fees and buy feed on an enlisted man's salary, but he vowed he would trailer Dakota to any post in the U.S., including Alaska, rather than sell him. I think he would have taken him overseas if he thought it was safe."

"Karen said the same thing."

It was just the opening she had been looking for to ask Shane about his feelings for Karen, yet was it really any of her business? Because she cared for both of them, she took the plunge. "Shane, about Karen—"

"Rest easy." He cut her off before she got any further. "Karen is a wonderful person and as sweet as they come, but there isn't anything between us."

"I only wanted to say that I wouldn't object if there were. I think you're a great guy."

"I think I am, too," he agreed loudly. "Feel free to fix me up with any of your friends. This down-home Texas boy will show 'em a good time."

"I beg to differ," Avery said from the doorway. "If any of your friends want to be treated like a lady, they need to go out with a gentleman like myself, not a hayseed cowboy."

Lindsey chuckled at their good-natured teasing. "I want to keep my friends, so I won't let them go out with either of you."

Avery wrinkled his brow. "Ouch."

Shane looked at him. "Did she just insult us?"

"Yes, but she did it with a smile. It makes me wonder if I should show her our new toy?"

Glancing between the two of them, she pressed her lips together, then said, "Okay, I'll bite. What toy?"

Avery held up a small gray case the size of a camcorder. "Our new thermal-imaging recorder. This way we can keep an infrared eye on Dakota's leg and report any hot spots or inflammation in his other legs before they get serious."

She ducked under Dakota's neck and came over to examine the camera. "This is great. Did Brian send it over?"

Shane shook his head. "No, your boyfriend didn't splurge on this. This is army issue."

"He isn't my boyfriend. How does it work?"

"I'll show you." Avery flipped up the screen, pointed the camera at Dakota and a multicolored image of a horse appeared.

"What do the colors mean?" Lindsey pointed to the screen.

"Blue is cool. The warmer an object is, the closer to red it appears on the screen. See how the floor and walls show up as blue. Dakota is warmer than the floor. He shows up as greens and yellows."

"Except for that spot on his cast," she pointed out.

Avery moved closer. "Yes, he has quite a bit of heat coming from the lower portion of his leg."

"Does that mean there's a problem?"

"It means I'm going to give your boyfriend a call and have him check it out."

"Stop it. I told you he isn't my boyfriend."

Avery closed the camera and winked at Shane. "Methinks the lady doth protest too much."

Brian finished rewrapping Dakota's new cast with a bright blue elastic webbing designed to help prevent the horse from chewing on it.

"That was a good call, Captain. If the rub had gotten much worse we could have had a real problem with a pressure sore."

"Private Barnes is the one who found it."

"Your men have done a good job of looking after

this fella." Rising from the short three-legged stool he used when he was out in the field, Brian patted Dakota's shoulder.

"We want to see him well and back on active duty."

"I hope that happens, Captain." Putting his supplies back into his case, Brian tried to sound casual. "Where is Sergeant Mandel today? When Dakota was at the clinic she stuck to him like a burr."

"She had to report for physical therapy up at the hospital."

"Her arm isn't worse, is it?"

"No, but there is some concern about the damage to the nerve. It's too bad, really. She and Dakota were to carry the U.S. flag in the upcoming Inaugural parade."

"She mentioned that Dakota needed to be healed enough to walk three miles with a rider by January twentieth."

"Do you think he'll be able to do it?"

"Six weeks in a cast would leave four weeks for rehabilitation and strengthening. He might be ready by then, but it's a big if."

"This ride is very important to Lindsey."

"Keep doing what you're doing and he may improve enough to go. I'll have some of our students check back in a couple of days to see how he's doing."

The two men shook hands and Captain Watson walked back to his office. Brian began repacking his bag and supplies into the special compartments built into the bed of his truck. He had just closed and locked the tool chest when a dark blue sedan pulled up beside him. The door opened and Lindsey got out. It was as if the sun had come out from behind the clouds.

"Hi," she said as she walked up to him.

"Hi." He couldn't think of anything else to say. Oddly enough, she seemed at a loss for words, as well.

He gestured toward her car. "I didn't think you could drive."

"Avery suggested I get a spinner for my steering wheel. It works great, but I still overcorrect a little. How's Dakota?"

"Fitted with a new cast and doing fine." The silence lengthened again. He closed the truck door.

"So, how is Isabella getting along?" Lindsey asked quickly.

"She's good."

"Not making any more escapes?"

"Not a one."

"Glad to hear it."

"I guess I'd better be going."

"Oh, sure. I didn't mean to keep you." She took a step back, uncertainty clouding her eyes.

"I'll be back the day after tomorrow to check on Dakota. Maybe I'll see you then?" He knew he should send some of his fourth-year students, but he found he wanted the excuse to come back and spend time with Lindsey.

"Great. I'll look for you." Her bright smile tugged at his heartstrings.

He climbed into his truck and drove away. Glancing in his side mirror, he saw her watching him from the edge of the roadway. Resisting the urge to turn around and go back was the hardest thing he had done in a long time.

A week later, Lindsey was leaning against Dakota's stall door when she heard halting footsteps on the cobblestones behind her. She knew who it was without turning around and her heart gave a happy leap. Brian had been out to check on Dakota twice during the past week, but at the last visit, he had pronounced Dakota well on the way to recovery. Since there wasn't any problem with the horse, had he come to see her?

"Good morning, Lindsey." The sound of Brian's voice sent a sparkle of happiness shooting through her veins. She turned to face him, hoping her delight didn't show. "Good morning, Brian."

"How's my patient doing?"

"Getting better every day."

"I'm glad to hear it."

He stopped close beside her, his arm just brushing hers. She didn't pull away as she realized how much she had missed his company and how right it felt to be with him. "What are you doing here?"

"I want to take a few X-rays to document the bone's healing progress."

Of course he hadn't come just to see her. Lindsey pushed aside the tiny disappointment she felt and resolved to be content with his company no matter why he had chosen to come. "Do you need any help?"

"I will if you aren't busy."

"I'm afraid I have a tour due any minute. I'll get one of the other men to help."

"I'm not in any rush. What sort of tour?"

"It's a group of schoolchildren from Topeka."

"Is that why you're dressed in your itchy-looking blues?"

She brushed at the shoulder of her short cavalry jacket with one hand, then tugged the hem down as she stood up straight. "How do I look? Notice anything different about me?"

"Is this a trick question?"

"No, I got my cast off yesterday."

"I see that now. Good for you, but you still have the sling."

"I don't have much feeling in my hand or arm yet. This way it isn't dangling against my side."

"Nerves heal slowly. Give it some time. Even with the sling, I think you look very nineteenth century."

"That's the idea." She dusted the top of her knee-high black riding boots by rubbing them on the back of each pant leg.

At the sound of a vehicle, she looked toward the parking lot and saw a small yellow school bus pulling up. She settled her cap snugly on her head. "Pardon me while I see to our visitors."

Lindsey was proud of the CGMCG and she especially enjoyed giving tours to the dozens of Scout troops, grade-school classes and veterans' groups that visited the post each year.

Brian asked, "Is there any reason I can't join the tour? I'd like to know more about your unit."

"I'd be delighted to have you, provided you help keep the kids in line. I've found that the boys especially tend to get rowdy when no one is looking."

She put on her best welcoming smile and walked outside. In the courtyard, she noticed a wheelchair lift being lowered to the ground at the back of the bus. A middle-aged man waved to her and instructed the group of ten-year-old boys next to the van to stop horsing around. The girls, standing off to one side, were giggling and whispering to one another.

"Good afternoon, and welcome to the Commanding General's Mounted Color Guard stables."

"Hey, you're a girl." The biggest boy in the group smirked. "Girls can't be in the army."

"Actually, women serve in many units in today's military. But during the period when this stable was built, women were not allowed to enlist."

"Didn't a few women serve in the Union Army during the Civil War?" Brian asked.

She shot him a grateful look. "That's correct. Both the Union and Confederate Armies had women who fought disguised as men. It goes to show that women can be good soldiers and as brave as men in battle. If you'll come this way, we'll start our tour with the barn."

She paused inside the large double doors where a life-size model horse stood before a wall displaying photographs of cavalry horses in action.

"Please watch your step. These old cobblestones can be treacherous." She gestured toward the uneven floor.

"Wouldn't it be better for the horses to have these torn up or paved over," Brian suggested.

She wrinkled her nose. "Don't think we haven't asked. Unfortunately, this is a historical building and can't be altered. This is the last remaining original stable building. It was constructed of native limestone and timber in 1889. It originally housed sixty mounts. At one time it was converted into a pistol range before being returned to its original function when our unit was formed. Before we get started, I'd like to have each one of you sign our guest book."

One by one, the children signed their names in a ledger on a podium until only the boy in the wheelchair was left. Brian took the book and handed it down to the youngster. The boy shyly smiled his thanks.

"As you can see," Lindsey continued, "our model horse, Stick and Stone, carries everything a cavalry horse would have been equipped with in the 1880s. The saddle is called a McClellen and has the unique feature of an open split down the center and a rawhide seat. Would anyone like to guess why?"

The boy in the wheelchair raised his hand. Lindsey pointed to him. "Yes?"

"It allowed air to circulate and help keep the horse's back from getting sore?"

"That's right."

"Brainiac," one of the group muttered.

"The only thing he knows about riding a horse is what he reads in a book," the big boy scoffed.

As Lindsey led the group down farther into the barn, Brian replaced the visitors' log and waited while the boy in the wheelchair struggled to maneuver his chair down the wide aisle.

"Do you need a hand?" Brian offered when it was obvious that the boy's wheels weren't rolling well over the uneven stones. He put his hands on the handles of the chair.

"No, I can manage," the kid said defensively, pushing harder.

"I'm sure you can. I only offered because…please don't tell anyone…but walking on a rough surface like this makes me afraid of falling."

The child looked back at him. "It does?"

"Would you mind if I just held on to the back of your chair to steady myself?"

Sitting up straighter, the boy shrugged. "I guess that would be okay."

"We'd better catch up with the group or we'll miss the tour."

"I'm not really interested in it anyway."

"You don't like horses?"

"They're okay."

"Their big size can make them scary." Brian tipped the wheelchair backward slightly freeing the front wheels.

"I'm not scared of them."

"You're not? That's good. My name is Brian. What's your name?"

"Mark."

"It's nice to meet you, Mark."

"How'd you hurt your leg?"

Taken aback, Brian hesitated before answering. He'd forgotten how forthright children could be. "I hurt it in a car accident."

Mark's eyes widened. "Me, too. Was it a drunk driver?"

"No, it was my own fault."

"Will you get better?"

"I'm afraid this is as good as I'm going to get. I'll always need a cane."

"I got hit by a drunk driver when I was riding my bike home from school. Do you like horses?"

"I like them very much." Brian followed the abrupt change of subject easily.

"Does anyone make fun of you because you can't ride?" Mark's dejected tone told Brian how much the earlier gibe had hurt.

Brian let the group move farther ahead. "I don't pay

any attention to them if they do. Besides, being handicapped doesn't mean you can't ride a horse."

Catching Lindsey's eye, he motioned for her to continue with her tour. She nodded and began walking.

"All our tack repairs are done here in the leather shop. This is Corporal Shane Ross. He's going to explain the different types of leather we use and show you how we repair our harnesses," Lindsey said.

Lindsey stepped aside as the group crowded into the small room where Shane sat behind a large sewing machine. She walked back to where Brian had stopped pushing Mark.

Looking up with a mixture of disbelief and interest, Mark asked, "How can someone like me ride a horse?"

"I have a friend who runs a riding stable just for kids with disabilities. She has special saddles that will hold you strapped in place. Her horses are very gentle. All kinds of kids learn to ride there."

"Is it far away?" Mark's tone was wistful.

"It's only a half-hour drive from here. Why don't I give you my card. Have your parents call me and I'll tell them all about it."

"I don't know. Mom is funny about me doing stuff."

"Tell her that it's a very safe place and they have trained therapists there."

"Okay."

Lindsey dropped to one knee beside the boy. "How would you like to meet one of our horses up close and personal?"

He nodded eagerly. "That would be totally sweet."

"Good." She sent a questioning look at Brian. He nodded his approval.

"Right this way." Standing, she led them to Dakota's stall and opened the door.

Brian maneuvered the chair into the stall and Lindsey closed the door, shutting him and the boy inside. Dakota limped a few steps forward to investigate his visitors.

Mark held out one hand. "Come here, fella."

Lowering his head, Dakota sniffed at the boy's hand and then took another step closer so that Mark could pet the side of his face.

"What's wrong with him?" Mark gestured toward the cast.

"He broke his ankle and Dr. Brian fixed it for him," Lindsey said from the doorway.

Mark looked up with interest. "You're a horse doctor?"

Brian nodded. "I'm a veterinary surgeon and I specialize in horses."

"That's tight, dude."

Brian glanced back at Lindsey. She grinned. "That means he thinks you have a cool job."

"Oh."

"We should get on with the tour," she said, holding open the door.

"Aw, do we have to?"

"I think we should." Brian waited until the boy said goodbye to Dakota and then pushed his chair out of the stall.

Outside the leather shop, he waited until the rest of the children came out and then followed the group and listened intently as Lindsey talked about the unit's job, their performances and the history of Fort Riley. It was obvious by the way she answered the children's questions that she enjoyed sharing her knowledge.

It wasn't until the last child was herded onto the bus and the vehicle pulled away that he saw her sag with relief and rub her arm.

"Are you hurting?"

"A little. Tell me more about the riding stable for disabled children." They began walking back into the barn.

"It isn't just for children. Hearts and Horses is run by a woman I met when I treated one of her horses for colic. What she does is called hippotherapy."

"What is that exactly?"

"Hippotherapy uses the movement of the horse as a treatment in physical, occupational and speech therapy for people living with disabilities. It has been shown to improve their muscle tone, balance, coordination and motor development, as well as emotional well-being."

"That sounds like you have some firsthand experience."

"I volunteer at Hearts and Horses on the last Saturday of each month. It's a great way to spend an afternoon."

"I've heard of places like that, but I didn't know there were any near here."

"Actually, there are a half dozen such stables in the eastern part of Kansas. Some are members of the American Hippotherapy Association. Others belong to NARHA, the North American Riding for the Handicapped Association."

"I wonder if something like that would help my brother?"

"Every case is different, but didn't you say he lived

in Washington, D.C.? I know they have a center that works with veterans."

"I'll tell my sister-in-law to look into it. I think it would do Danny a world of good to be around horses again.

"Places like that would need very calm horses. We have a horse named Tiger who is getting ready to re-tire. I'll mention your friend's place to the captain. Tiger might be a good fit for that kind of work."

"They also need trained volunteers to work with the children. Unfortunately, both good horses and volun-teers are in short supply."

"That's a shame. I could see how eager Mark was to ride and yet how guarded he was about expressing his desire. I know it was because he was afraid of being disappointed."

"You should have children of your own," Brian said.

The second the words were out of his mouth he knew it was the wrong thing to say. It was a very personal comment. He glanced at her to see her reaction. Other than looking bemused, she didn't seem upset by his odd statement.

"I'm afraid children aren't on my agenda for quite a few more years."

Not exactly sure why he felt compelled to press the issue, he said, "Agendas can change."

"Yes, they can, but I don't have a reason to change mine."

"I forgot. The army is your life. Is that enough?"

She cast a sideways glance at him. "I've always thought it would be."

He decided to change the subject. "I haven't seen Karen for a while. How is she?"

"Karen's fine. She's gone home for the holidays, but she is actually thinking of moving here and attending college next semester. She wants to become a grief counselor."

Brian looked down and used the tip of his cane to draw circles in the dirt. His family in Montana had tried to get him to see a grief counselor after Emily's death, but he had refused. He deserved the pain his grief brought. "What do you think of the idea?"

"Karen has a good heart and a great faith in God. I think she is taking my brother's tragedy and turning it into something positive. I really respect her for that."

He considered the idea that he hadn't allowed anything positive to come from Emily's death. He had wanted to stay wrapped up in his grief, but was he doing an injustice to Emily's memory?

He cocked his head to one side as he studied the woman who seemed so in control of her life.

"You did a good job with those kids today. Keeping a bunch of ten-year-olds interested in history for an hour is no easy feat."

She patted the holster at her side. "I wouldn't attempt it if I wasn't armed."

"I don't believe that for a minute."

She held up her free hand in a gesture of surrender. "Okay, you've found me out. I like kids. Arrest me."

Her smile was so adorable that he leaned in and kissed her.

Chapter 10

Lindsey was so startled by Brian's kiss that she froze for an instant. Her next thought was how right it felt.

Abruptly, he took a step back. He looked as surprised as she was. She smiled shyly and touched her fingers to her lips.

Without a word, he began walking again. Not understanding exactly what was going on, she followed, perplexed by his silence.

"Brian, wait. Would you like to talk about what just happened?"

He stopped and faced her. "I'm sorry, I don't know what came over me."

Disappointment followed close on the heels of his words. "That is not exactly what a woman likes to hear after a man kisses her."

"You're a very attractive woman, but that isn't any excuse. I was way out of line. It won't happen again."

"So I guess we're clear on that?" About as clear as mud, she decided.

"Absolutely clear. I value your friendship and I admire you as a person. I hope my lapse won't affect how we work together."

"Of course not." She had no idea what else to say.

"Good. That's good," he muttered.

At the barn door, Shane stood waiting for them. "I heard you needed some help with your X-ray equipment."

Brian nodded. "If you'll come with me, I'll show you what I need." The two of them walked to Brian's truck.

Lindsey entered the barn and walked into Dakota's stall. She began rubbing his cheek. Glancing around to make sure she was alone, she leaned forward and whispered in the horse's ear. "Brian just kissed me."

A happy glow swelled from within and she couldn't keep her smile contained any longer.

"As kisses go, it was pretty nice until he opened his mouth and began apologizing."

Her glow dimmed by several watts. He had certainly backpedaled quickly enough. Obviously she shouldn't read more into it, but she wouldn't mind if it happened again. She had begun to care a lot for Brian, but it was foolhardy to think that anything could come of those feelings. No, the best thing would be to put the episode firmly out of her mind.

If only it hadn't been such a nice kiss.

In a few minutes, Shane came in carrying several black cases. He and Brian were laughing about something and her heart quivered at the sound. Putting his kiss out of her mind wouldn't be easy.

Brian produced a tall block of wood from one case. "Lindsey, can you put this under his hoof, please?"

He was all business again. She did as he asked and tried to be as professional as possible. "Yes, sir."

"Now that Dakota is doing so well, you'll be seeing less of me. Once a week should be often enough for follow-up visits. My students can handle those."

"We've gotten kinda used to your company, Doc," Shane drawled from the stable door.

Lindsey realized with sudden clarity that Brian might simply fade out of her life the way numerous other friends had done over the years. Dakota was the reason they had spent so many hours together. When the horse was healed, their paths might never cross again. The happy glow she had been basking in went out like the flip of a switch.

Brian soon had his portable X-ray machine set up. By positioning Dakota's hoof on a block of wood to raise it off the ground, they were able to get the views Brian wanted while Lindsey kept the horse still by talking to him and scratching him behind his ear.

Shane watched from outside the stall. "Do you have big plans for Christmas, Doc?"

"No. I usually take call so that the other staff with families can have the day off."

"You're welcome to join us for dinner," Lindsey offered, and then thought of slapping her forehead with her hand. Would he think she was desperately trying to hold on to the relationship?

"Sure," Shane chimed in. "We're on duty, too. We

usually get together in the ready room and bring in all the fixings."

Brian slanted a look at Lindsey. "Will you be doing the cooking?"

Her heart lightened at the sight of the humor glinting in his eyes. He was thinking about her burnt cookies. She grinned back. "No, my contribution will be two pumpkins pies from the commissary—already baked."

"I don't know. I hate to intrude on your party."

"You won't be intruding, Doc," Shane assured him. "After all you've done for Dakota, you're practically a member of the unit yourself."

"Thanks, I'll think about it."

"You could bring Isabella along," Lindsey suggested with a cheeky grin. "Dakota has been missing her."

Now that was desperate, but if it enticed him to come to dinner, she didn't care.

"I think she's been missing him, too. At least, she has been pouting about something."

"Who's Isabella?" Shane asked.

Lindsey winked at Brian. "She's Dakota's new friend, and she's as cute as a bunny."

Shane looked interested. "Is she that pretty blond secretary at the clinic?"

Brian shook his head. "She's much cuter than Jennifer."

Sending him a chiding look, Lindsey said, "Oh, I'm going to tell Jennifer you said that."

His eyes widened in mock alarm. "Please don't. I shudder to think what she might do to me."

"All right, I won't squeal on you if you promise to join us for dinner on Christmas Day."

"Barring the need for my services at the clinic, I promise to try."

"We plan on eating about six, and don't feel that you have to bring something. We'll have more than enough."

"I'll keep that in mind."

Lindsey grinned as she rubbed Dakota's neck. Suddenly, this holiday had become something special to look forward to, and Brian was the reason.

Christmas morning dawned bright and clear with just enough bite to the cold air to remind Brian that winter had arrived. As he scraped the frost from his truck's windshield, he still hadn't decided whether to accept Lindsey's invitation to dinner.

He tried telling himself that she had only offered out of kindness. It certainly couldn't be construed as a date even if it was a dinner invitation. After all, a half dozen other men would be there, too. He would go, and he would give her the present he had found for her. The trinket had caught his eye in the window of a gift shop downtown. The moment he saw it, he knew Lindsey would love it.

On the drive to the clinic with Isabella beside him, he passed one of the local churches. The tall white spire silhouetted against the clear blue sky looked Christmas-card perfect. The parking lot was already filling with early worshippers.

Lindsey would be at the fort chapel this morning.

He envied her certainty, her belief in God's love above all else. Brian knew his heart was made of weaker clay. He had turned his back on God after Emily's death. He didn't expect his feelings would change anytime soon. He drove past the church without stopping, but the image of Lindsey bowing her head to pray stayed with him. That and the memory of their kiss.

Suddenly, he began to think of all the reasons he shouldn't go to Christmas dinner. One by one they crowded into his mind. He didn't belong to their group. He was an outsider invited out of charity. His presence would put a damper on their camaraderie and fun. His gift would seem too personal. The more he thought about it, the more certain he became—he wouldn't go.

Although the clinic was officially closed and he could have taken call from home, he decided to go in to catch up on some work. No holiday was complete without someone needing a vet in a hurry. If he was at the clinic already, it would speed up his response time. Throughout the day he glanced frequently at the clock. By noon he hadn't seen a single patient or taken a single call. His conference presentation had been worked and reworked until he couldn't stand looking at the numbers and slides another minute.

Around two o'clock he decided there wasn't any reason his holiday should turn into a total waste. He could enjoy a meal that wasn't takeout or warmed up in a microwave for a change. He didn't have to stay long and make small talk. He would go.

As the afternoon dragged on, he finished reviewing a stack of odds and ends of paperwork, checked the clock, and then his watch a half dozen times. Isabella did nothing but nap in her box so he didn't even have her antics to help pass the time. After sharpening all his pencils and straightening his desk, he checked the clock again. It was four-fifteen and he finally made up his mind.

He wasn't going.

At five-thirty he closed the clinic doors and carried Isabella to his truck. Setting her in her carrier, he climbed in and shut the door. With his hands on the steering wheel, he sat in his parking space without starting the engine. It had turned colder outside. Gray clouds had moved in and occasional snowflakes drifted earthward to vanish as soon as they touched anything. It might be snowing, but the forecast was only calling for a trace of the white stuff.

"We should get going," he told Isabella. But he didn't move. The thought of heading home to an empty house tonight left him feeling forlorn.

I don't have to be alone tonight.

He had spent so much time avoiding people that he wasn't sure he knew how to interact in a purely social situation. Especially with a woman as lovely and lively as Lindsey. The last thing he wanted to do was to stir up feelings that were better left buried.

Who was he kidding? Those feelings had been coming to life since the first day he met Lindsey Mandel—and it scared him half to death.

Lindsey's anticipation slowly seeped away as six o'clock, then six-thirty slipped past. She tried to enjoy the feast brought together by the men, but disappointment made even the cranberry salad taste bland.

Why hadn't Brian come?

Maybe he'd had an emergency surgery. If she knew that for certain she might be able to enjoy what was left of the day, but something told her he wasn't tied up at work. Some small part of her knew that Brian didn't want to see her. He had kissed her, but it had meant nothing to him. If only it had meant nothing to her, too.

"How about some dessert, Lindsey?" Lee held out a

paper plate loaded with a huge slice of pie and mounds of whipped cream.

She held up her hand. "No, thanks. I'm full."

"Full? You hardly touched a bite of the captain's smoked turkey."

"I ate my share. Just because I can't put away as much chow as you do is no reason to imply that I'm finicky."

"Leave her alone," Shane said as he snagged the plate from Lee's hand. "She has to watch her girlish figure."

He forked a piece into his mouth as he whirled away from Lee's attempt to grab the plate back. "Hey, fix your own!"

Lindsey smiled at their foolishness but didn't feel like joining in as they returned to the folding chairs positioned in front of the small portable TV Avery had provided for the evening. Instead, she began to gather up the dirty paper plates and toss them in the trash.

"Is something wrong, Lindsey?" Captain Watson moved to help her clean up.

"No, sir."

"I thought maybe your arm was hurting."

"It aches, especially with the weather turning colder."

"Are you getting any feeling back in your hand?"

"A little, but I still don't have any kind of grip."

"Dakota looks like he's doing well."

"I think so, too. How are you doing, sir?" She had heard through the grapevine that he and his wife had separated.

He looked at her sharply. "You mean on my first major holiday as a divorced man?"

"Something like that. Not that I want to pry."

"It's okay. No, it's been rough."

"Do you have kids?"

"Two. My son is fifteen and my daughter just turned thirteen. I've been gone for so many holidays during my career that I doubt they even miss me tonight."

"I'm sure that isn't true."

"Maybe not, but I wasn't there much for my kids when they were little. I can't blame them if they ignore me now."

"Don't let them. Nothing is more important than your family. Pick up the phone and give them a call. Let them know you care."

Indecision crossed his face, followed by a growing look of determination. "Thanks, I think I will."

As he walked away to his office, Lindsey thought back to all the times her father had been gone when she was little. He had missed more than his share of Christmas days even after their mother left. That had left Lindsey, Danny and Karen to fend for themselves. They had worked hard at making presents for each other and even harder at sneaking around to fill stockings when no one was looking. They had made the holidays something special for one another.

Did her father regret those missed opportunities the way Captain Watson did? She wanted to believe that was true. There was really only one way to find out. Talking to her father wouldn't change the past, but it might make the future brighter for both of them.

Pulling out her cell phone, she walked into the hall away from the noise and laughter and dialed her father's number. The least she could do was follow the advice she gave out so freely.

He answered on the second ring. "Hello?"

"Dad, it's Lindsey."

"Lindsey, honey, it's so good to hear your voice."

She relaxed at the sound of his genuine happiness. "It's good to hear you, too. I wanted to wish you a Merry Christmas, only…it doesn't feel right to be celebrating."

"I know." His voice became choked with emotion. "But life goes on."

"Yes, it does." She wanted to cry away the pain she had been holding inside. She wanted to feel the comfort of her father's arms around her.

After a long pause, he asked, "How's your arm?" His voice sounded more in control.

"I got my cast off last week, but my arm is still pretty weak and I can't use my hand much. Will you be coming to the parade?" she asked quickly.

"Of course. You'll still be riding, won't you?"

"Yes, Dakota and I will be there."

"So the horse is doing better?"

"Karen told you?"

"She did. I agree with you. As long as things look like they're going to work out, I don't think we should tell Danny. The last thing he needs is to start fretting about the animal. Are things looking good? Because if they aren't, I can't keep that from him."

"Dr. Cutter says Dakota may get his cast off in a few days."

"That's good, but you won't be carrying the flag if you can't use your hand."

"I haven't given up. I still have time to get better. I do my exercises, and I'm as determined as Danny to get in shape for the big day."

"That's my girl. Make your old man proud and show the world what we Mandels are made of. I know Danny is looking forward to seeing the pair of you."

"I won't disappoint him or you."

"Have you talked to him lately?"

"I called them last night, why?"

"Did he tell you that with his tracheotomy capped off, he can stay off his ventilator for eight hours?"

"Yes, Abigail mentioned it."

"He's getting stronger every day and we have you to thank for that."

"Danny is doing the work, Dad."

"Yes, but Abigail and I both think you and that horse are the reason he's found the focus he needs. We both thank God that you have done this for him."

"He's my brother. I'd do anything for him."

"I know you would, honey."

She finished talking to her father and talked briefly with Karen, then ended the call. Stuffing her phone back in her pocket, she stared at the ceiling.

Please, Lord, let Dakota be healed enough to travel and let me be strong enough to hold the flag. I couldn't bear it if I had to let Danny down.

She had started to rejoin the men in front of the TV when a knock sounded at the front door. Hope sprang up in her heart. She pulled open the door and saw Brian standing in front of her. The darkness behind him was filled with soft, feathery snowflakes drifting down. It was a perfect Christmas evening.

Thank You, Lord, for bringing him here tonight.

"Merry Christmas," she said, knowing she had to be grinning from ear to ear.

"Merry Christmas." He held out a small red box with a silver bow. "This is for you."

She took the gift and clutched it close to her chest. She had a present for him, too, but it could wait until later. "Thank you. Come in. The guys are watching TV in the other room."

"Did I miss dinner?"

"I saved you a plate."

"Good, because I'm starved."

She looked behind him toward his truck. "Where is Isabella?"

He motioned with his head toward the stables. "I put her in with Dakota in his stall. I couldn't believe how excited she was to see him."

"The horse and the holiday hare. There's a children's story in that somewhere." Lindsey stepped back and allowed him to come inside.

Brian shook the snow from his black overcoat and hung it on an empty peg behind the door. He couldn't get over the way Lindsey stood watching him with that adorable, kissable smile on her face.

He smiled back. "Aren't you going to open your present?"

"Not yet. After you've had your dinner."

"All right, lead the way." He followed her into the crowded room where other members of the unit were gathered around the television set.

Shane noticed him first. "Hey, look who decided to join us. Have a seat, Doc. The game's tied and Baltimore has the ball on the six-yard line."

Lindsey pulled him by the arm toward a table set up in the opposite corner of the room. "After he gets a plate. Turkey or ham, Brian?"

"Both."

"Help yourself, we have plenty left."

After loading his plate, Brian took the seat Shane offered. Lindsey sat crossed-legged on the floor in front of him and it wasn't long until they were all engrossed in the football game.

The rapid-fire banter and good-natured teasing going on around him reminded Brian of his own family gatherings when he was a kid. Oddly enough, he didn't feel like an outsider among these people. They were all far from their families and homes. They were strangers joined together by the special bond of military service. He relaxed and joined in the chatter, adding his own armchair-coaching comments and rooting for the team opposite the one Lindsey urged on.

In the end, his team lost, but he didn't care. Watching Lindsey's brief victory jig was enough of a reward.

As the evening grew late, one by one the men left until only Shane, Avery and Lindsey remained. Brian wished them all good-night and was headed toward the door and his coat when Lindsey rushed up beside him.

"I'll go with you to fetch Isabella."

"It may take two of us to pry her away from Dakota. Let me help you with your coat."

"Thanks." She turned around and slipped one arm into the heavy military-issue jacket he held. The other sleeve hung empty as he covered her sling.

"You need to button up. You'll catch cold running around like that." He pulled her jacket closed and began doing up the snaps.

"I can manage," she protested.

"So can I," he countered, and continued until he had the last one snapped beneath her chin. In the sudden stillness, he gazed down at her in wonder. His heart had been bound by grief for so long that he wasn't certain what he was feeling. He was only certain that this woman had somehow managed to work her way past that barrier and plant seeds of kindness and friendship. What, if anything, might grow from those seeds he had no way of knowing, but he was willing to wait and see.

He stepped back and opened the door. "It's getting late. I don't want to keep you up past your bedtime."

She wrinkled her nose. "Duty call does come early. Oh, wait a minute, I forgot something."

Hurrying down the hall, she vanished around the corner and reappeared a few seconds later with a bulge in one pocket. "Okay. Let's go round up the rabbit."

Outside, the air had turned colder and the snow had begun to accumulate on the cars. A light dusting covered the ground, as well. Brian leaned on his cane heavily as they crossed the asphalt parking lot made slippery by the still-falling snow. Lindsey hurried on ahead. Brian was thankful she didn't seem to notice his difficult progress. He really disliked walking on slick surfaces. He hated knowing one slip might leave him unable to rise unaided.

Once inside the barn, he breathed a sigh of relief. Lindsey, a few yards down the aisle, was turning on the lights at Dakota's end of the stable. The commotion woke the other horses, who moved to hang their heads out the stall doors and check out their nighttime visitors.

Brian stopped to pet the onlookers as he made his way slowly over the rough cobblestones. "Merry Christmas, Trooper. Merry Christmas, Socks. Merry Christmas, Tiger."

"They all wish you a Merry Christmas, too," Lindsey said when he reached her side.

She nodded toward Dakota's stall. "You won't believe where your rabbit has decided to take a nap."

"Where?" He leaned over the half door to look inside.

Dakota lay at the back of the stall with his legs folded under him. Isabella lay perched on his broad back sound asleep with her head pillowed on her front paws and her long ears draped on either side of them.

Brian glanced at Lindsey and they both began to laugh. "You are right," he said. "This really has the makings of a great children's story."

"Before you go, I want you to have this." She pulled a black box from her pocket. "It's actually from all of us, including Dakota, but I picked it out."

"Thank you, but you didn't have to get me anything. The turkey and dressing was more than enough." He took the box from her and opened it. Inside lay a gold pocket watch engraved with a U.S. flag.

She leaned forward eagerly. "Turn it over and read the inscription."

He did as she suggested. "'To Dr. Cutter with endless gratitude. The CGMCG.'"

"I hope you don't mind the initials. Writing out the Commanding General's Mounted Color Guard would take up most of a large wall clock."

"This is beautiful. Thank you."

"I'm glad you like it."

"I do. This makes two terrific presents this year."

"What was your other one?"

"The equine ambulance company called the day before yesterday. They're loaning us their newest model for our conference."

"Brian, that's great. I know how much it means to you."

"True, but I'm still a little disappointed."

She cocked her head to one side. "Why?"

"I didn't get to see you open your gift."

With a saucy smile, she pulled his box from the depth of her pocket. "I didn't want to open it in front of the guys."

"Open it now," he suggested quietly.

"I can't get the ribbon off one-handed, and I'm sure you don't want to watch me try to do it with my teeth."

"Let me help." He hung his cane over the stall door and took the gift from her. Carefully, he worked off the silver satin ribbon and bow without breaking it, then held out the box.

She lifted the top and gasped with delight. "Brian, it's beautiful."

With the utmost care, she lifted out a small delicate snow globe. Inside the glass dome a bay horse pranced between snow-laden pine trees. She shook it and sent the glittering snowflakes whirling about him. "It looks just like Dakota!"

"There are fifteen bays in the stable. How can you tell that it looks like Dakota?"

"Because it's my present and I say it's Dakota." She shook it again and the snow whirled faster.

"I'm glad you like it."

"It will always remind me that your presence with us tonight was a special Christmas blessing."

More than anything, he wanted to kiss her again, but something held him back. Some part of him didn't trust the new emotions churning inside him the way her miniature blizzard swirled inside the glass bubble.

He said, "It's getting late. I should get going."

"Of course." Did she look disappointed? She turned away before he could read her face.

He opened the stall door and stepped inside. Lindsey followed him and spoke softly to Dakota. She squatted by his head while Brian plucked his pet from her perch and cradled her in his arm.

"I'll be back the day after tomorrow without the rabbit. If Dakota's X-rays look good, we'll get his cast off."

She stood and shoved her free hand in her coat pocket. "Once that's done, will you still need to see him?"

"I'll need monthly follow-ups for at least six months to document his recovery."

"And after that?"

"You won't see me ever again." He tried to make it sound like a joke, but his words fell flat.

She stepped close and he didn't move away. She pulled her hand from her pocket and laid it on his chest as she gazed into his eyes. "I hope that isn't true, because I would miss you."

Raising on tiptoe, she brushed her lips softly against his.

Chapter 11

For the next day and a half, Brian couldn't put Lindsey's kiss out of his head. The scene played over and over in his mind and left him wondering constantly what he should have done or said differently. Anything might have been better than standing like a mute statue while every trace of common sense and logic evaporated from his brain, leaving nothing but the yearning to gather her close in his arms.

At least he hadn't done that. Instead, she left him without a word, but her shy smile and knowing glance made it pretty obvious that the next move would be up to him.

So exactly what would he say to her today?

Packing his equipment into his truck, he prepared to go and take another set of X-rays of Dakota. In spite of the setbacks, the horse's recovery had progressed much better than he had hoped. His combination of arthrodesis and bone-growth-gene therapy certainly looked like a success. The first draft of his report on the procedure sat on his desk. Having serial X-rays and a sound horse to back up his hypothesis would certainly make for a more interesting presentation at the conference.

He should be happy that the horse's recovery was almost complete, but he wasn't. Once Dakota's cast was off, Brian knew he wouldn't be seeing Lindsey unless he decided to become involved in a relationship with her.

Shoving an awkward piece of equipment into place, he tried not to think about her—about the softness of her lips or about the way she made him feel. He didn't have time for a relationship. The more he tried to convince himself that was true, the more often thoughts of Lindsey intruded into his working day. When he was alone, it was even worse.

He stowed the last X-ray cassette in the truck and closed the door. He knew by the tenderness of her kiss that Lindsey had grown very fond of him. He wanted to be fair to her. She needed to understand that he couldn't give her more than friendship. Not even if he found himself wondering exactly where *more* would take them.

He moved to the driver's side and yanked open the door. It was with mixed emotions that he headed toward the Fort Riley stables.

Lindsey coasted through her morning duties on the same cushion of air that had held her up since Christmas night. Everything seemed right with the world and she couldn't stop smiling. She was in love with Brian Cutter.

She hadn't planned it. She still didn't know how they could make their different situations work, but she knew that he was the man of her heart.

It was a secret she hadn't told anyone. Karen had returned from Washington the night before, but the feeling was just too new and special to share.

Humming her favorite Christmas tune, she carried a bucket of grain to each of the horses and the mules in the barn and made sure that they all had water. The sprinkling of snow that had helped to make Christmas night so special had quickly melted. Today's bright sunshine would soon dry the lingering mud. On one hand, Lindsey would have liked the Christmas white to last a little longer, but the horses were eager to get out into the open pastures and she didn't relish the idea of brushing down a muddy herd when they came back in.

As she worked, she kept glancing out the stable doors toward the parking lot. Brian should be here soon.

Dakota whinnied loudly and she turned to him with a chuckle. "Are you anxious to see Brian, too?"

Shane came down the aisle pushing a wheelbarrow loaded with straw. He set down his load and rubbed Dakota's forehead. "I think he's anxious to get his cast off."

"I know exactly how he feels. I couldn't wait to get mine off, but I hope he does better than I did."

"You're getting better."

She massaged her hand in the sling. "I can move my fingers a little, but my arm is still weak. I have a doctor's appointment at four o'clock. I'm hoping he'll let me out of this thing."

"Hey, your boyfriend just pulled up."

She spun around to peer out into the bright sunshine. "Brian's here? Where?"

Shane lifted the handles of the wheelbarrow and pushed it past her. "No denials today? Do I hear wedding bells, Sergeant?"

Grinning back at him, she shook her head. "Don't be silly. We haven't even had a first date."

"If he doesn't snap you up, he's a fool."

"What a nice thing to say. Thank you, Shane."

"I mean it. Morning, Doc," he called out.

"Good morning, Corporal." Lindsey watched Brian make his way toward them and she drank in the sight of him. He was dressed in a dark maroon sweater over faded jeans and his hair looked as unruly as ever. She resisted the urge to comb it out with her fingers. He stopped a few feet away from her. She wondered if he was as delighted to see her as she was to see him.

Shane glanced at the two of them, then chuckled as he pushed his burden outside. "I'll be back to give you a hand with Dakota in five minutes."

Brian looked down at the cobblestone floor. "How are you?"

"I'm good. How are you?"

"Fine. Lindsey, I'd like to speak to you in private."

"I'd like that, too." Avery and Lee walked by a second later. She tried to look nonchalant as she smiled and nodded at them.

Once they were out of earshot, Lindsey said, "It seems privacy is hard to come by around here, today."

Brian seemed ill at ease, too, and she found that adorable. Love left her feeling shy but happy to be in his company.

Just then two soldiers came in with their saddles headed for the leather shop. Any hopes she had of finding time alone with Brian vanished. Knowing that they could be overheard, she said, "I mentioned your friend's place, Hearts and Horses, to Captain Watson as a possible retirement place for Tiger."

"What did he think?"

"He's interested. He wants to talk to you about it and perhaps have us visit the facility. I know you said you volunteered there on the last Saturday of each month, but will you be going out there this Saturday?"

"They'll be closed because of the holidays, but I did promise my friend that I would be there next Saturday. I should stay home and work on my lecture, but I really hate to disappoint any of the kids. Do you remember Mark, the boy in the wheelchair from your tour group?"

"Of course."

"My friend told me his mother enrolled him as a Christmas present."

"That's great. I know he's going to love it."

Shane came back into the barn followed by a dozen unit members. "I brought the cheering section, Doc."

"Then let's get started."

With the help of Shane and another soldier, Brian soon had his X-ray machine in place. That left Lindsey free to watch him work. He didn't allow his stiff leg to hamper his job. Instead, he seemed to accomplish things with a minimum of motion, as if he had learned to make every move count.

"It will take a few minutes to print these," he said as he exited the stall and headed for his truck. More of the men from the unit had gathered in the barn.

When Brian walked back in, Captain Watson was with him. As they stopped in front of the group, Brian held the black-and-white film aloft. "The cast can come off."

A cheer went up and everyone began pounding each other on the back, shaking hands with Brian and giving Lindsey heartfelt hugs.

The captain was the one who asked the question they all were wondering about. "Does this mean Dakota can travel to Washington, D.C.?"

"No, it means he can begin his rehabilitation. He'll need to be hand walked for short periods only. I'll give you a schedule of times to start with and then we'll see how he progresses. I want to be notified at the first sign of any lameness."

Lindsey clasped her hands together in front of her. "But there's still hope that he'll be able to make the trip, isn't there?"

"A slim hope, I'm afraid."

"That's good enough for us, isn't it?" Lindsey asked the men around her. They responded with resounding affirmatives.

"We have faith in you and in Dakota, Dr. Cutter," Lindsey said. "He's going."

Brian studied the determined and hopeful faces around him and decided not to press the issue. No one here would endanger the horse by insisting he make the long trip if he wasn't ready when the time came.

"Before I remove his cast, he'll need new shoes put on. The ones he has on now will be too tall and I don't want him to experience an uneven gait."

"We have our farrier standing by, Doctor," Captain Watson assured him. "It shouldn't take long to change them."

Once the new shoes were in place, Dakota stood quiet and calm as his cast was removed. Brian stepped back and asked Lindsey to lead him around the stall. At first, Dakota balked, but with some easy coaxing, he finally took his first steps. Without the weight of the cast, he raised his newly freed leg higher than the others several times but soon seemed to realize he didn't need to.

"He has a slight limp, but I think he's going to do fine," Brian said to Captain Watson as both men watched the horse closely.

"You've done great work and the army is grateful."

"I'm the one who is grateful, Captain. You allowed me to enroll him as my first patient in my clinical trials. His success will certainly add weight to my upcoming conference presentation. He may even make more funding available for the study. I can't tell you how important that is to me."

"We wish you all the best."

"Thank you, sir."

The captain crossed his arms over his chest. "I wonder if we might ask one more favor of you?"

"Certainly, if I can."

"Sergeant Mandel mentioned you know of a riding stable for handicapped children that might be interested in Tiger. He's extremely well trained, as are all our horses, but I'd like your opinion on his suitability before I officially ask for his release from service."

"I'll be happy to look him over and make sure he's sound, but the only way to tell how he'll do is to expose him to the new environment. We'll need to see how he reacts to wheelchairs, noisy children, unsteady riders, any number of unexpected occurrences. Hearts and Horses has an evaluation program and I know they would welcome the opportunity to see if Tiger would be right for them."

"We can do that. Sergeant Mandel, assign a detail to arrange transport for Tiger to the Hearts and Horses facility. At the facility's convenience, of course. We'll go ahead with his evaluation, but make sure they know that he won't be available until our return from Washington, D.C. I don't want our senior member to miss this Inaugural parade. Fifteen years of service has earned him the right to participate."

"Yes, sir."

Brian felt the sensation of his beeper vibrating on his belt. He pulled it from his clip and read the message. He was wanted back at the hospital, but he still hadn't had a chance to speak to Lindsey in private. He looked around and saw she was talking to Shane and Avery. It seemed that he wasn't going to get a chance today.

Maybe it was for the best. Now that they wouldn't be seeing each other so often they could simply allow the relationship to fade. Besides, what if he had read more into her kiss than she meant?

No, he decided, not speaking to her was taking the coward's way out. He walked up beside her. "Lindsey, I've got to go."

"Now?" She couldn't have looked more disappointed if she had tried.

"I'm needed back at the clinic. Is there any way I could see you later this afternoon? I need to talk to you."

"Sure. I have to go into Manhattan tonight. Why don't I stop by the clinic later."

"That would be fine. If I'm not in surgery, we can get a cup of coffee or something." He wasn't happy with the way that sounded. It was too much like asking her for a date, but he had no way to change his words. Why couldn't a guy buy a verbal eraser?

"I'd like that. I'll drop by about five-thirty. Is that too late?"

"Five-thirty will be fine. See you then."

His emergency turned out to be a horse with a severe cut to its left hind leg. It took less than an hour to supervise while his fourth-year student stitched up the patient and another twenty minutes to update the owners and outline a plan of care. He had just finished his paperwork and was handing it to Jennifer to be filed at the front desk when he saw Lindsey coming in the front doors. His breath froze in his chest.

She paused inside the doorway and slipped off her tan coat, then draped it over her arm. It was then that he noticed she wasn't wearing her sling. Smiling, she waved when she saw him.

She wore a dark green blouse with tiny flowers embroidered around the gathered neckline and on the short puff sleeves. A full black-and-green print skirt flared about her slim legs as she walked toward him. Dainty, high-heeled black shoes made those legs look even longer.

Jennifer pulled the file folder from his slack hand. "Wow. That is a big improvement over combat boots."

He couldn't have agreed more.

Lindsey stopped in front of him. Her bright smile turned his insides to pudding.

She said, "Hi. Am I too early? I can wait if you aren't finished with your work."

He found his voice and tried for a professional tone. "Ah, no, your timing is good. Why don't we just step into my office?"

"Okay."

He turned to his secretary. "Jennifer, hold my calls please."

"With pleasure." She winked.

He wanted to strangle her. Instead, he said, "Sergeant Mandel and I won't be long."

He allowed Lindsey to precede him down the hall. As he opened the door for her, he spied his rabbit in the middle of his desk engaged in her forbidden activity.

"Isabella, put down that pencil!" Brian strode to the desk and pulled the prize from between her paws. He picked her up and sent Lindsey a defeated look.

"I've tried everything and I can't break her of getting into these."

He raised Isabella to eye level and scowled at her. "You are a bad bunny. Do not chew on my pencils."

Then, as if regretting his harsh words, he tucked her under his arm and stroked her head. Walking to the door, he opened it and called for Jennifer. She arrived and took one look at Isabella and the yellow paint flakes on her face and feet.

"Pencils again?"

"Will you put her in her outside kennel for me, please?"

"Of course. Come here, you naughty little girl," she cooed as she took the bunny from him. Ruffling the rabbit's fur, Jennifer continued to talk baby talk as she carried the offender away.

Lindsey watched the whole exchange, then raised one eyebrow. "Do you treat her that harshly each time she chews up a pencil?"

"I didn't think I was too harsh."

"You picked her up, petted her, gave her to Jennifer so that she could pet her and then sent her to the place she most likes to go—outside. In spite of all that she won't stop chewing your pencils. Will wonders never cease?"

Walking to the desk, she picked up his pencil cup,

opened the deep drawer on the right-hand side of his desk and set the cup in it.

"Have you tried this?" She stared at him as she closed the drawer.

Brian pursed his lips searching for a good reply. None came to him. Feeling sheepish, he stepped closer. "Is your advice to simply remove the temptation?"

Oh, what a temptation this woman presented. Her bright eyes were brimming with mirth. The subtle scent of her perfume filled him with a desire to hold her close and breathe in the freshness she brought to his life just by being near.

"You're the animal specialist." Her sassy tone was almost too much. Calling on every ounce of self-control that he possessed, he resisted the urge to take her in his arms and kiss her. He didn't deserve to love another woman, but somehow Lindsey had a way of making him forget that fact.

Could that be the reason their paths had crossed? Was it time for him to move past the grief that had controlled his life until now?

He pulled open the drawer and set his cup back in its place in the center of his desk. "I like my pencils where they're easy to reach."

She grabbed a new one out of his cup and tapped it gently against her cheek. "I see."

He knew he was in trouble the moment he saw the mischievous glint in her eyes.

"So, is this what a girl has to do to get some attention from you?" She grinned and placed the pencil between her teeth.

Her playfulness melted the last of the icy barrier that enclosed his heart. Reaching up, he took the pencil from her and dropped it onto his desk, then he took her by the shoulders and drew her into his arms. She stepped into his embrace and lifted her face. Lowering his mouth to hers, he tasted again the poignant sweetness that was so uniquely her.

After a long second, he pulled away. Tucking her head under his chin, he drew a ragged breath. "I've been thinking about doing that all day."

"If I had known, I would have come sooner. Just don't start apologizing again."

"I won't."

"Good. You could give a girl a complex that way."

"Somehow, I don't see that happening to you. You're much too sure of yourself and your place in the world."

Resting in the comfort of his arms, Lindsey knew Brian was mistaken about that. She might sound sure of her plans, but more and more she had begun to question what she really wanted out of life. She had dismissed the idea of having a husband and children because she had seen how badly her parents had mismanaged their marriage. She never wanted to subject a child to that kind of pain. Only now, being held by Brian, she wondered if she had been wrong.

She drew back, determined to regroup her scattered wits. "I believe you asked me here for a reason. We seemed to have gotten sidetracked."

"It wasn't anything important, but I do owe you a cup of coffee."

"Yes, you do." She reluctantly stepped out of his embrace.

"We can make some here or we can go out to one of those trendy coffee shops that have sprung up all over town."

"Yours will be fine. It can't be worse than what Shane makes for us at the office."

"Don't be too sure about that. But you're all dressed up. Are you certain you don't want to go out?"

"I'm dressed up because I have a Bible-study class in about half an hour."

"Is it on post?" He busied himself with filling the coffeemaker and adding heaping scoops of grounds to the filter.

"No, it's at Grayson Community Christian Church." She sat down on the sofa, remembering the gentle way he had cared for her the first time she had been in his office. So much about Brian Cutter was a contradiction. He often sounded gruff and uncaring, but the more she came to know him, the more certain she was that he was a man with a tender heart.

"I know that church. It's on the road that leads to my house."

"Is that where you worship?"

He paused in the act of pouring water into the coffeemaker. "I haven't been to church since my wife died."

"Did the two of you attend before that?"

"Emily was really involved with our church back home. She sang in the choir and helped out in the nursery. She even edited the newsletter for the pastor. She had such boundless energy. I attended when I could, but animals get sick and injured as much on Sunday as any other day. At least, that was the excuse I used."

"Why haven't you been back?"

"I blamed God for her death. I blamed myself. I can't get past the anger."

"Forgiveness is such a large part of our faith, Brian. You can't truly love someone else unless you first love yourself. And you can't truly forgive someone else unless you first forgive yourself."

He didn't answer her. He finished pouring in the water and pressed the on switch. She rose from the sofa and crossed to his side. Linking her arm through his, she laid her head on his shoulder. "Come with me tonight."

"To Bible-study class?"

"Yes."

"I don't know."

"Brian, we all struggle to find where we fit into God's plan, but if you aren't looking, you'll never find the answer."

"How can you be so sure that God *is* the answer?"

She straightened and cupped his cheek with her hand. "We use our head to make a lot of decisions in life, but some decisions have to be made with the heart. This is one of them. Do what your heart tells you is right."

He covered her hand with his own. "My heart is telling me that kissing you again is the right thing to do."

"See, your heart knows best," she whispered as she leaned toward him. Their lips met and the kiss was everything she had dreamed it would be. After a long moment, she pulled away and placed her palm over his lips.

"Okay, my head is telling me that I'm going to be late for class."

He kissed her palm, then drew her hand away from his mouth. "Smart, as well as beautiful. I never thought I could feel this way about someone again. I'm not sure this is real."

"It's real enough for me. I care for you deeply, Brian."

"And I care for you, so where exactly does this leave us?"

"I'm not sure." There were so many things to consider, but with happiness zinging through her veins, she couldn't think of anything but how wonderful it felt to be in his arms.

"Lindsey, I want to keep seeing you."

Smiling softly, she said, "That sounds like an excellent start."

"I want to know everything there is to know about you."

"Everything?"

He pulled her close and kissed the tip of her nose. "Everything," he whispered.

"I'm just an ordinary girl."

"Who happens to be a sergeant in the U.S. Army."

"Is that a problem?" She held her breath, hoping he didn't see her career as a roadblock to this budding relationship.

"I don't know. Have you thought about leaving the service?"

She frowned and leaned back to study his face. "Are you asking me to do that?"

"I'm asking if you have considered it."

"I will admit that I've been toying with the idea, but it's something I would have to give a lot of thought."

"Of course. I don't want to rush you or pressure you into making a decision you'll regret."

"Thank you."

"I know that I want to see more of you. I want to be a part of your life."

"My life includes church, Brian. Can you accept that?"

"I'll try. I can't promise anything more than that."

A small voice in the back of her mind pointed out that he hadn't mentioned the word *love*. She ignored it by telling herself that things were happening too fast, for both of them.

Chapter 12

Lindsey let herself into her apartment a little after ten-thirty that night. She tried to be quiet, but Karen was a light sleeper.

"Lindsey, is that you?" she asked from the sofa.

"Yes, I'm home. Go back to sleep."

"I will, but I'm supposed to give you a message. Dad wants you to call him."

"Tonight?"

Karen sat up and stretched. "He said whenever you got home. You know how he likes to watch the late shows. He'll be up."

"Did he say what he wanted? Is something wrong?"

"I don't think so. I got the feeling he wanted to discuss your next duty station."

"Great. After years of ignoring me, he suddenly wants to pick my career moves." She tossed her purse on the overstuffed chair in the corner and hung her coat in the closet.

"He's trying to be a better father, Lindsey. Danny's injury was a wake-up call for Dad. He knows he hasn't always been there for you. Give him a chance."

"You're right, I'm sorry. It's just that he was always so eager to hear about what Danny was doing, but I got the feeling that he thought my duties weren't important."

"You've been invited to participate in the Inaugural parade. How many people ever get the chance to do something like that?"

"I know. I'm thankful for the opportunity, but it's not because of anything I've done. Don't get me wrong. I'm delighted to be able to honor Danny and all the other men and women who have given so much for us, but it isn't like I've done anything special."

"It's because of you that Danny is working so hard in rehab. It's only because of you that the army accepted Dakota. Don't sell yourself short. What you do counts for a lot."

"Thanks."

"You're home late—did your class run over?"

Lindsey settled on the sofa beside Karen. She needed to share her happiness with someone. "Brian went with me to Bible study tonight. Afterward, we stopped and had a cup of coffee together."

"That's wonderful! Did he like it? What did he say?"

"He said, 'Double-chocolate latte, no foam.' Or something like that, and he really seemed to enjoy it."

Karen growled as she punched Lindsey's shoulder. "I don't mean what did he say about the coffee. I meant, what did he say about the class?"

Lindsey rubbed the tender spot. "Careful. That's my only good arm."

"It won't be good for long unless you tell me ev—everything."

"He said it gave him a lot to think about."

"That's great. I'll pray that he finds his way back to God."

"I'm praying for that, too."

"And I'll add a special request that he ask you out on another date."

"It wasn't exactly a date."

"Close enough. Oh, I can't wait until Danny meets Brian. I think they'll like each other."

Lindsey took her sister's hand and squeezed it. "They will, won't they? I'm so in love. Does it show?"

"Yes. Oh, girl, I'm so happy for you." She enveloped Lindsey in a quick, hard hug.

Lindsey returned the hug. "Thanks, sis."

Karen drew back. "Now go call Dad and let me get back to sleep."

Lindsey wanted to talk about Brian all night long, but she kept the rest of her happiness in check. "All right. Good night, kid."

Alone in her bedroom, Lindsey sat on the side of her bed and dialed her father's number. He picked up on the first ring.

"Hi, Dad. It's me. Did I wake you?"

"No, I was up."

"What did you need?"

"Nothing really. I just wanted you to know that we plan to be in front of the Hoover Building so you'll know where to look for us."

"I'm glad you're going to be there."

"I wouldn't miss it. My daughter in the Inaugural parade. Makes me mighty proud just to think about it."

She had longed to hear those words from him for so many years that she could barely speak. "Thanks, Dad. How is Danny?"

"He's making good progress. How's the arm?"

"I'm out of my sling. I can make a fist now, but my grip is still weak. I don't know if I'll be able to hold a flag."

"You'll be ready. I know you will. Say, your enlistment will be up soon, won't it?"

"I've got two months left."

"How long are you reenlisting for?"

It was the question she least wanted to hear. "I'm not sure."

"If you give them eight years you can just about pick any billet you want. I've got friends here in Washington. A Pentagon job isn't out of the question. That way you'd be close to Danny."

Eight years—it sounded like an eternity. For the first time she gave voice to the thought that had been roaming around in the back of her mind. "There isn't anything that says I have to reenlist."

"What? Mandels have always been soldiers. It's in our blood." He sounded appalled that she would even suggest not reenlisting.

"It was just a thought."

"I know you've taken Danny's injury hard, but think how he would feel if you quit because of him. You're not going to leave the service. Not my daughter. I raised you better than that."

"Karen isn't in the service." Lindsey felt a fleeting

touch of envy for the way Karen had always stood her ground on the issue.

"No, that one takes after her mother's side of the family for sure, but I haven't given up on her. You, on the other hand, take after me. You'd be lost in civilian life."

Maybe he was right. She had wanted to be a soldier all her life. Just as she had wanted to earn her father's respect all her life, she thought with sudden clarity. The two issues were so closely intertwined she wasn't sure she could tell which was which, not that it mattered. But he was right about one thing—she couldn't have Danny thinking she left the service because of him.

"It was just a thought, Dad. I'm sorry I said anything."

"That's more like it. You had me worried."

"If you had left the army, would it have made a difference with you and Mom?"

He was silent for a few seconds, then he said, "There were a lot of things wrong with our marriage, Lindsey. Being in the service was only part of it. Your mother was miserable in our situation, and I knew I would be miserable if I got out of the army. In the end, we did what made us both less miserable. I'm sorry you kids were caught in the middle."

"You did your best, Dad."

"And it must have been good enough. Two of my children joined up and followed in my footsteps. A man couldn't ask for more than that." His obvious pride came shining through in his words.

"I'll give some thought to working in Washington, D.C."

"You do that. Wherever you decide to go, I know you'll make me proud."

Tears pricked her eyelids. "Thanks, Dad."

"The army will take you places, kid. It's a great life."

The army had already taken her to the far-flung corners of the earth. Would it be so bad to stay in one place?

Not if it was the right place.

As she hung up the phone, she realized that the right place for her had nothing to do with a physical location. The right place would be where she could make a home and a life with Brian.

Were his feelings as strong? She simply wasn't sure. He liked her, she could tell that, but his guilt over his wife's death had a strong hold on his heart. She prayed she could help him find the forgiveness he needed.

Over the next week, Brian managed to make time to see Lindsey almost every day. One night they enjoyed quiet conversation over a delectable dinner at a small romantic café. On New Year's Eve, he joined both Lindsey and Karen for dinner at their apartment. Lindsey freely gave Karen credit for the hearty cooking he sampled. While the sisters laughed together over stories of previous cooking failures, he was free to admire how beautiful Lindsey's face looked when she was happy and carefree.

The following Friday night he took her to see the latest blockbuster action movie. The place was nearly empty with most of the students gone for the holiday break. Holding Lindsey's hand in a dark theater, he paid little attention to the story unfolding on the screen. What he saw was a new chapter unfolding in his own life and he liked what he saw. He knew it was too soon to talk about marriage, but the idea took hold in the back of his mind and wouldn't leave.

When he took her home that evening, they stood for a short while on her front porch and shared another sweet kiss full of promise and hope. Unbidden, the words, "I love you," rose from his heart and crossed his lips.

Her luminous eyes widened and filled with joy. "Oh, Brian, I love you, too."

"I could stand to hear those words every day of my life."

"It would be easy to say them every day," she said with quiet sincerity.

He wanted to say more, but found he didn't yet have the courage. For now, it was enough to know that she loved him. In time, they would talk about what the future might hold for them together.

On Saturday morning, Brian was determined to enjoy a few quiet hours at home after his evening with Lindsey. The trouble was, he couldn't stop thinking about her. In the light of day, it all seemed unreal. Had she really said that she loved him? Could they have a future together? The new year seemed to hold so much promise. Just thinking about it scared him witless.

All he wanted to do was to be with Lindsey. He wanted to see her eyes light up when they met his. He wanted to hold her in his arms and kiss her soft lips. He wanted to feel this happy every day of his life.

Their evening at the Bible-study class had given him a lot of food for thought. He wasn't certain that he was willing to accept Lindsey's version of a loving and caring God, but he was willing to listen and learn more from the energetic young pastor he had met.

Deciding it was better to work than to moon over a

woman, he took out his seminar speech and began practicing it aloud. An hour later, Isabella went scampering through the living room past his chair toward the front entrance. She slid into the door panel then began to hop up and down.

He listened carefully and heard the faint clank of the mailbox closing. Limping to the door, he scooped up the excited rabbit and held on to her as he opened the door and fetched his mail. The grocery store flyers were exactly the kind of paper Isabella delighted in shredding. Back inside the house, he closed the door firmly before putting her down. Her recent escapes at work had made him much more cautious about keeping an eye on her.

Once she was on the floor, she darted to her special box, hopped in and then stood on her hind legs to peer at him over the rim. Her anticipation was obvious.

Sitting in his recliner, he quickly tossed the discount ads in with her. As the crackle and ripping of paper replaced the quiet of the house, he grinned and began to look through the rest of his mail. A small, pale blue envelope caught his attention. A painful spasm clenched his stomach when he read the return address. He glanced at his wife's face in the photo on the table beside him.

"It's from your mother."

His in-laws had spoken to him only once after Emily's death. Three days after the accident, his father-in-law had come to Brian's hospital room to tell him they had arranged to have the funeral in their hometown sixty miles away the following day. Groggy from pain medication and still in traction for his shattered hip, Brian had begged him to wait until he could attend, but Emily's father had walked out of the room without saying anything else.

No words could have conveyed more strongly the blame they placed on Brian for their beloved daughter's death. He tried phoning, but they never took his calls. The few letters he wrote came back unopened. Now, after all this time, the note in his hand was the first contact he'd had from them.

Irritation battled with his curiosity. He had loved Emily and she had loved him. If her parents had offered even the slightest sign of forgiveness, perhaps he could have found a way to forgive himself, too.

He held the unopened letter over Isabella's box, but he didn't drop it. Instead, he tore open the envelope and pulled out a single sheet of pale blue stationery.

Brian,
This coming February will mark the fifth anniversary of Emily's death, as I'm sure you are aware. Her father and I have planned a memorial service for the occasion. As the passing years have dulled our grief, we have come to regret the way we excluded you from our lives. You were Emily's one true love and we know that you never meant to hurt her. Our excuse is that our lives ended with the death of our only child. Our grief and anger needed an outlet and it was easy to blame you.

I hope you will accept our invitation to attend her memorial service. Perhaps in this way we can begin to make amends for the way we treated you. Please join us as our family and friends come together to celebrate Emily's life.
Grace and Emit Todd

Tears blurred his vision as he glanced to his wife's face smiling at him from the silver frame. She would be happy to know her parents were making an attempt to repair their relationship with him. Noticing a thin coat of dust on the glass, he realized that he hadn't held her picture close in weeks. Guilt cut deep in his heart.

He picked up the photo and wiped the front with his sleeve then pressed it to his chest. "I've been forgetting you. How could I do that? I'm sorry, sweetheart. I'm sorry about everything."

It was because of Lindsey. Lindsey had turned his life upside down and made him dream about happiness again. How could he be happy when he had ruined the lives of so many people? Her life, their child's life. Her parents were suffering still. What right did he have to any happiness in the face of so much sorrow?

The clock on the wall chimed twelve times. Today was his day to volunteer at Hearts and Horses. He was scheduled to be there at two o'clock. For a second, he considered calling to say he couldn't make it, but that would only place more of a burden on his friend. He would go, but first he would answer the letter from Emily's parents and tell them he would join them in February.

Later in the afternoon, Brian stepped out of his truck in front of the Hearts and Horses stable. He turned up the collar of his black overcoat against the chilling wind, then pulled his cane out from behind the front seat. As he made his way across the gravel driveway to the office door beside the barn, he glanced around at the well-groomed farm.

White rail fences bordered the road and enclosed several corrals. The old two-story house was also painted white, but bright blue shutters kept it from looking austere. An American flag fluttered in the breeze from its holder on one of the porch's tall square columns. In the spring and summer, Brian knew the green lawns were bordered with colorful flower beds, but winter had put an end to their bright displays weeks ago.

He stopped at the office door, but Patience Duncan opened it before he had a chance to knock. Patience's erect bearing and boundless energy belied her sixty-odd years. Her salt-and-pepper gray hair was cut in a simple bob. Her worn jeans were tucked into tall black rubber boots and her green hooded parka had a hole in one elbow where an occasional down feather found its way to freedom.

"Brian, thank you for coming." She threw her arms around him in a hearty hug.

"I'm always happy to help." He was glad now that he had come. He needed to get away from his somber thoughts.

Patience stepped back. "Come in out of the wind. It sure turned cold fast. Makes me doubly glad our indoor arena is finished."

Brian followed her inside the office. A second door connected the cluttered room to the larger pole barn. "Are my pupils here yet?"

"I'm only expecting one child today. The boy you referred to us."

"Mark? Is this his first time?"

"It is. He was disappointed when I told him he wouldn't actually be riding today, just getting to know Sprite and learning to take care of her. His mother seemed very relieved. I think she needs this therapy more than her son does."

"You may be right."

"I'm happy for the light schedule because the army is sending out one of their horses for evaluation today."

His heart sank. The last thing he wanted to do was face Lindsey today. Perhaps she wouldn't be one of the people who brought Tiger. He could only hope. "I've seen the horse in action. I think he'll be great for you."

"I hope so. Speaking of the army, I think that must be them." Patience stepped to the office window and drew the blue-and-white-checked curtain aside.

Brian moved to stand beside her. The red pickup and matching red trailer rumbling into the circle driveway were unmistakable. His heart jumped into overdrive when he noticed Lindsey in the front seat between Avery and Shane.

Patience let the curtain fall back into place. "Why don't you show them where to take their horse."

"Mark and his mother are waiting. I should get started with them."

"All right. I've set up the arena so that you can have the back third. I'll go meet the troops." Patience gave him an odd look as she walked past.

Lindsey had noticed Brian's truck in the driveway as soon as they pulled in. Excitement and delight raced through her, leaving her giddy with joy.

Resisting the urge to run and find him and fling herself into his arms took a fair measure of her resolve. There would be time for that later. Today, she was under orders to assess this facility as a possible home for a valued member of their unit. She didn't take her assignment lightly.

A middle-aged woman came out of the office and

walked toward them. "Hello, and welcome to Hearts and Horses. Call me Patience. You'll never meet anyone so misnamed." The woman flashed a broad friendly smile that put Lindsey instantly at ease.

"Good afternoon, ma'am. I'm Sergeant Mandel and this is Corporal Ross and Private Barnes."

"It's a pleasure to meet you. Well, let's get a look at your horse, shall we?" Patience strode to the rear of the trailer without waiting for anyone. "How old did you say he was?" she called over her shoulder.

"Eighteen," Shane answered as he hurried to keep up with her.

"A good age for horses and for men. How old are you, sonny?"

Lindsey smiled at Avery. "I like her already."

A clang signaled the rear gate of the trailer opening. Lindsey and Avery followed as Shane and Patience led Tiger into the barn. Across the arena, Lindsey saw Brian introducing Mark to a small black mare with two white stockings and a star on her forehead. Mark's grin told Lindsey exactly what he thought of his new friend. When Brian looked their way, Lindsey smiled and waved. He nodded in acknowledgment, but continued to give his attention to the boy. Puzzled by his less-than-enthusiastic greeting, she worried that she had done something to upset him. The idea was ridiculous. He had seemed fine when they parted company last night, but she couldn't shake the feeling that something was wrong.

Patience quickly began a series of tests for Tiger. First, she rode him bareback around a small section of the barn to get the animal used to her and his surroundings. Next, she asked Shane to walk him on a loose lead and guide him beside a long ramp. Once alongside the platform, Patience turned around backward and had Shane continue to lead the horse while she shifted her weight numerous times. It was obvious that Tiger was surprised by the activity, but he remained calm and composed. Patience dismounted and pushed a wheelchair up to Tiger. He sniffed it over, then proceeded to ignore it as she pushed it close beside him, even bumping into him slightly.

While Tiger and the men got a workout with Patience, Lindsey had time to watch Brian's interaction with Mark and the horse. His quiet confidence and gentle encouragement soon had the boy and his mother brushing the mare's coat and feeding her treats. A few minutes later, Brian took them over to show them the special saddle Mark would be using. It was fastened to a stand with handrails around it and Brian had Mark practice transferring on and off until he seemed satisfied the boy could do it without difficulty.

After a half hour, Mark and his mother left. Brian began walking toward the door just as Patience declared an end to her test. She told Shane to tie up Tiger and follow her. Dusting off her hands, she came to stand beside Lindsey. "I think he's a keeper. He's cool, calm and collected and he seems readily adaptable. That's exactly the kind of horse we need. My thanks to the army for thinking of us."

"It was Brian's idea." Lindsey was happy to give him credit.

"Then my thanks to you, Brian," Patience called out. He stopped as the group led by Patience closed the distance between them.

"I have tea and coffee in the office and a dozen oatmeal cookies that I don't want going to my waist—so you are instructed to go in and enjoy them. Let me put Sprite up and then I'll give you the grand tour afterward so you can see if my stable meets your requirements. No arguments. Brian, show them the way."

"I really should be going."

"Nonsense. I've never known you to pass up one of my cookies. What's wrong with you?"

"Nothing's wrong with me," he said defensively.

"Well, then, go show my guests a little hospitality until I get back," she muttered as she tromped off.

Lindsey studied Brian, but he wouldn't look at her. Something was definitely wrong.

Avery settled his cap more tightly on his head. "Nobody has to tell me twice to eat oatmeal cookies."

They all began walking toward the office. "She would have done well in the military," Shane said as he held open the door for the others.

"She certainly enjoys giving orders," Avery agreed.

Shane patted Brian on the shoulder. "I've found most women do, especially women sergeants. Have you sent in your reenlistment papers yet, Lindsey?"

"They're filled out, but I haven't turned them in."

"You're still planning to reenlist?" Brian asked, a scowl on his face as he looked at her for the first time.

The disapproval in his tone cut her to the quick. "Brian, the army is my career."

He glared at her. "I thought things had changed."

"Have they? I don't recall being asked anything except to consider it."

Shane cleared his throat. "I'm going to go load Tiger. Avery, come help me." He grabbed two cookies and pushed Avery toward the door back into the barn.

Lindsey crossed her arms over her chest. "I thought you understood my feelings."

"Yes, you always made them clear."

"I hope I have." She couldn't help the defensive tone in her voice. "I plan to ask for an assignment at Fort Riley."

"But you can't guarantee they'll give you that assignment, can you?"

"Of course not."

"For you it's the army, your country, your family, your horse and then Lindsey somewhere way at the back of the line."

"Brian, what's wrong? Why are you so angry?"

"I thought we had something good between us."

"I thought so, too."

"Then where do I fit in your list, Lindsey? After the army but before the horse?"

"That's not fair." The hurt his tone caused went deeper than she had ever imagined.

"Life isn't fair and you didn't answer my question."

"How can I give you an answer when we've never talked about it?"

Shaking his head, he walked to the door and pulled it open. "The same way you made your decision to re-enlist without talking to me about it."

He slammed the door behind him, leaving her staring after him with no idea what had just happened.

Chapter 13

Lindsey tried to pretend that everything was okay. She went to work and to her physical therapy sessions, but her arm seemed to be getting weaker instead of stronger. She spent long hours walking Dakota, first around the small pen beside the stable and later longer trips through the pastures and along the less traveled roads of the fort. When it was only the big horse walking beside her, she didn't have to pretend, and the tears that she tried to hold in check would slip out.

Shane, Avery and Lee offered a few times to go with her, but she politely refused. After a few days they seemed to realize that solitude was exactly what she wanted and needed. Captain Watson made sure that the unit ran smoothly as preparations got underway for their trip to Washington, D.C. All the horses were outfitted with the special shoes that were required, uniforms were pressed and boots were buffed to a high gloss. Lindsey went through the motions without thinking about them.

When the first heavy snowfall blanketed the fort, she tried not to remember how happy she had been with Brian in the snow on Christmas night. Her heart might be broken, but it would heal in time the way her arm and Dakota's leg had healed. Breaks were excruciatingly painful in the beginning, but with time the pain would fade to a dull ache. If she could just find a way to get through it until then.

When anyone asked about Brian, she would smile and say he was too busy to come out to the fort. She thought she had convinced the rest of the unit that she was fine. It was her sister she couldn't fool.

A week after the trip to Hearts and Horses, Karen confronted Lindsey in the kitchen of their apartment.

"All right. What is going on?" Karen demanded, standing in the doorway with her hands propped on her hips.

"I'm not sure I know what you mean. I'm setting the table for dinner."

"You know exactly what I mean. What happened between you and Brian?"

"Nothing happened." She lined up the spoons beside the knives.

"One night you float in here telling me how in love you are and the next night I hear you crying yourself to sleep. Okay, call me crazy, but I think something is going on."

"It didn't work out. What do you want me to say?"

"A little more than that."

Stepping up to her sister, Lindsey laid her hand on

Karen's shoulder. "It didn't work out. That's all there is to it. Now can we please talk about something else?"

"Do I need to have Shane go punch his lights out?"

Lindsey managed a weak smile. "As satisfying as that may sound, it won't help."

"I didn't think so. Oh, honey, I'm so sorry."

"Thanks, but it's better to find out now than after we've spent seventeen years together the way Mom and Dad did."

"I think it's better to fall in love and stay in love."

"That isn't the path God has chosen for me."

"You shouldn't give up so easily. You love the guy. Take my advice and go talk to him. Isn't he worth fighting for?"

He was, but she didn't know how or who to fight. Brian had made the choice to end their relationship before it truly began. She strongly suspected his motives had more to do with his guilt over his wife's death than her career choice, but she didn't know how to make him see that. Tonight, she was too tired to search for answers.

"I've got a more important battle to win. I have to get Dakota fit to go to the Inauguration. I'm not going to disappoint Danny when he has worked so hard. After Washington, D.C., maybe I'll go and see Brian. Until then, can we please not talk about him anymore?"

Karen reluctantly agreed and Lindsey was almost sorry she did.

Lindsey threw a saddle up on Dakota for the first time since their fall. It proved to be difficult with her weak arm, but she managed. It had been three weeks since his cast had come off. He was up to walking five miles a day without problems. To her eye, he looked as sound as a dollar, but the real test would be to see if he could carry her weight.

The company horses were due to depart for Washington, D.C., in two days. The decision whether or not to take Dakota had to be made within the next forty-eight hours.

In the small enclosed riding pen beside the stable, she spoke softly to him and stepped into the stirrup. He stood motionless as she swung up onto his back.

"Good boy. Let's try a walk, okay?" She nudged him with her heels and he began walking with a smooth stride that gladdened her heart.

After ten circuits of the area without any sign of lameness, she pulled him to a halt.

"How does he feel, Sergeant?" Captain Watson asked from the stable doorway.

"As good as he looks, sir." She patted Dakota's neck.

"Excellent. All we need now is Dr. Cutter's okay and Dakota is on his way with the rest of the herd."

Just the mention of Brian's name was enough to make her want to cry, but she didn't give in to the urge. Once more she'd had it pounded into her head that a military life and romance didn't mix. This time she had learned her lesson for good.

"I don't see any reason Dr. Cutter won't release him. His walk is sound."

Captain Watson stepped out of the stable and came to stand beside her. Under one arm he carried the unit's banner.

Lindsey's heart sank. Her grip wasn't strong in spite of the physical therapy that she had been doing religiously.

"Are you ready to try this?" he asked, nodding toward the staff in his hand.

"Yes, sir." Lindsey was happy her voice sounded calm even if she was quaking inside.

Please, dear Lord. I need Your help now. Lend me the strength I need to do this for my brother.

Captain Watson handed up the banner. As soon as her fingers closed around the staff, she knew she couldn't hold it. The flag slipped out of her grasp. He caught it before it hit the ground.

He didn't say anything. He didn't have to. She dismounted and spent a long moment staring at her boots before she looked up and met his sympathetic gaze. The choking pain in her chest made it almost impossible to speak, but she did. "I respectfully request that you appoint another soldier to carry the flag, sir."

"Lindsey, I'm sorry."

"Don't be sorry. It never was about me. It's about honoring men and women like Danny—people who have given everything, including their lives, to protect and defend our flag. The last thing I want to do is disrespect their sacrifice by dropping the colors."

"Do you feel that you can hold a saber in salute?"

Oh, how she wanted to say she could, but the truth came out instead. "I doubt it."

"I see."

"Does this mean that I'll stay behind as part of the rear detachment?"

"No. Your family will be there and so should you. As you know, normally flag bearing goes by rank."

"Yes, sir. Highest-ranking soldier carries the U.S. flag, next highest rank carries the army flag and so on."

"That means Corporal Ross will carry the American flag in your place."

"Sir, my concern is that Shane's weight will be too much for Dakota."

"I agree. I'll leave it to you to decide who will ride Dakota in your place. At least he will be in the parade to represent your family if Dr. Cutter okays the trip."

"Yes, sir. I know Danny will be honored to have any one of our unit members ride Dakota."

"Thank you, Sergeant. You're dismissed for the day. Let me know who your choice is tomorrow morning."

Trying hard to maintain control, Lindsey saluted smartly, then watched the captain walk away. When he was out of sight, she buried her face in Dakota's mane and gave in to her tears.

Brian pulled up the most recent digital X-rays of Dakota's leg on the computer in his office. They weren't the best-quality films. The fourth-year students he had sent to the post to take the X-rays that morning hadn't done as good a job as he would have liked. He should have gone himself, but he hadn't wanted to risk running into Lindsey.

He leaned forward to examine the pictures more closely. He couldn't be sure if the faint line extending into the second phalanx bone was artifact or new trouble brewing for Dakota.

He looked up at the sound of a knock on his door. Jennifer opened it and said, "Doctor, Captain Watson and Sergeant Mandel are here to see you."

His heart sank. So much for avoiding Lindsey. He steeled his heart against the pain he knew was coming. "Send them in."

He rose and extended his hand as Captain Watson entered. The captain took it in a firm grip. Lindsey came in and stood quietly behind her commander.

"We've come to get a travel release for Dakota."

"I'm afraid I have some concerns about that."

Captain Watson frowned. "What type of concerns?"

"His last X-ray shows a small area that has me worried. I'd like to repeat the films tomorrow."

"I'm sorry, Doctor, but the horses are due to ship out tomorrow morning and my men will be flying out the following afternoon. The custom hauler the army has hired will be at the stable at ten sharp. If you need more films you'll have to get them today."

"You're using a custom hauler? I thought your men would be taking the horses."

"Army regulations make that difficult. If we haul the horses ourselves, we would have to stop every eight hours and rest the animals. The trip would take days. By hiring an outside firm, the horses can be transported straight through to Washington, D.C."

Brian frowned. "You're talking about almost twenty-four hours without a break."

"That's correct."

"I'm afraid I can't release Dakota to travel under such conditions."

"Why not?" Lindsey demanded, looking at him for the first time.

"Standing in a moving trailer and being jostled in among other animals for so many hours would place entirely too much stress on his leg. I'm sorry, but I won't grant his release under such circumstances."

Captain Watson glanced at Lindsey. "I'm certainly disappointed to hear that. This is a very important event for my men. They've worked hard to get Dakota fit and ready to go."

"I understand that, but the risk to the animal's welfare is simply too great."

"I can't take the horse without a release." He looked back and forth between Brian and Lindsey as if waiting for more to be said. When neither of them spoke, he drew a deep breath. "That's it then. Thank you for your time, Dr. Cutter."

Lindsey waited until Captain Watson left the room. When he closed the door behind him, she swung around to face Brian. "How can you do this to me? You know how important this is!"

"I'm not doing anything *to* you. I'm doing this *for* Dakota."

Lindsey stared at Brian in growing disbelief. "He's healed."

"And I intend to see that he stays that way."

"Brian, you know how important it is that he be in the parade, how important it is to my brother."

"I know you want Dakota there to honor your brother, but what good will it do if Dakota's leg fails on the trailer ride and he has to be destroyed? I know you don't want that."

"He can make the trip. He's strong enough."

"Maybe he is and maybe he isn't. As his vet, this is my call. I can't let you risk his life for a few minutes of fame."

"You mean you won't risk letting the world see that your wonderful new procedure doesn't work." Disappointment gave her words a bitter edge.

"It did work. Dakota was out of his cast in record time."

"But his leg isn't strong enough to stand the trip to Washington, D.C.? How is that a success? Why not let us at least try using a sling or some way to support him?"

"I might agree to that if I knew the trip could be made in easy stages, but you heard Captain Watson. The horses are going nonstop by commercial hauler. That means hours of being shaken and jarred and crowded in with fifteen other animals. The risk is too much. Especially after all it took to save him in the first place."

"But to not even try?"

"You're upset. I don't think this discussion needs to go any further."

"I thought you understood what was at stake. My brother is going to be at that parade. How am I going to tell him Dakota won't be?"

"Lindsey, I'm sorry."

"I wanted to carry the flag for him, but I can't. My arm isn't strong enough. So, I want Dakota there because he was an important part of Danny's life. When my brother gave Dakota to the army, it was his last piece of freedom, his last ounce of pride. He had nothing left to give his country and now you're going to say that sacrifice means nothing."

"Do you honestly think your brother would want you to risk Dakota's life?"

At his question, the fight went out of Lindsey. "No."

He stepped close. If only he would take her in his arms the way he had before. How could the feelings between them have changed so quickly?

"Go to Washington, D.C., Lindsey. Ride beside the flag with your unit. Honor your brother's sacrifice, even if it isn't in the fashion you had hoped."

She pulled away from his touch. "I want to thank you for all you have done for Dakota, Dr. Cutter. You have the gratitude of the U.S. Army. I can see myself out."

As she walked out the door of his office, Brian knew with a sinking heart that she was walking out of his life.

He started to go after her, but stopped with his hand on the doorknob. It was for the best. He didn't have a heart to give her. He had buried it with his wife and child.

If I don't have a heart, then what is breaking inside me?

Chapter 14

Work had always been Brian's answer to keeping his innermost pain locked away. Today should have been no different, except nothing helped erase the memory of the disappointment on Lindsey's face when she had walked out of his office two days ago.

He glanced at the clock above his desk. It was only a few minutes after nine. The unit's horses would be almost to Washington, D.C., by now. Except for Dakota. Lindsey and the other soldiers would be flying out in a few hours. The Inaugural parade would take place tomorrow at noon.

"And my conference is less than forty-eight hours away," he muttered.

What he needed now was to concentrate on his presentation, to make sure he had enough hard facts to impress the United Jockey Club representatives and ensure substantial grant monies for his research. He needed to focus. Reaching for a pencil, he paused with it in his hand. The memory of Lindsey grinning at him with one between her teeth made him smile. Remembering the kiss he had shared with her in this office erased all thoughts of work from his mind.

"You're a fool, Brian Cutter," he stated forcefully. "What right did you have to fall in love again?"

It was a question to which he already knew the answer. He had no right to love another woman. His carelessness had cost Emily her life. She had loved him with all her heart and trusted him to care for her always. He never should have survived the crash. He should have died with her and the baby.

Passing through what was left of his days without love had seemed a fitting punishment for living. Until Lindsey.

Lindsey had made him think about a future and not about the past.

He heard a timid knock at the door. An irrational hope rose that it might be her, but it was quickly dashed when Jennifer peeked in.

"I thought I made it plain that I didn't want to be disturbed." He turned away before she could read the disappointment he knew must be written on his face.

"Someone is in a sour mood today."

"What do you want?"

"Wow, the list is so long. A new car, a diamond tennis bracelet, a trip to Jamaica…"

"If you think you can get all of those things with your first unemployment check, keep making jokes."

The sudden silence told him he had made his point. After a moment, she cleared her throat and said meekly,

"I wanted to inform you that your ambulance has arrived."

"Thank you, I've been informed. Is that all?" When she didn't reply, he turned around. She was standing in the doorway tapping her cheek with one finger as she stared at the ceiling. She sighed as if she had come to an important decision.

"The unemployment check might make a down payment on the tennis bracelet, so I'm going to go ahead and tell you that you are an abject idiot."

The last thing he needed was one of her scoldings. "Jen, please. Not today."

"You let your friend down. Even if there was nothing romantic between you and Lindsey, and I don't believe that for a minute, but even if there wasn't, she was your friend."

"I had no way of proving that Dakota's leg would be strong enough for the journey."

"You mean you don't have enough data to make that assumption."

He threw his hands up. "Exactly. Finally, someone understands."

"But you believe in your work, don't you?"

"Of course I do. Dakota will be as sound as ever."

She crossed her arms and asked, "How much proof would you need?"

"I don't understand."

"How much proof of his soundness would you need to let him go to Washington?"

"Perhaps another month without any signs of lameness."

"Was he sound before?"

"Before the accident? I assume so."

"He was sound and he broke his pastern anyway."

"Jennifer, what are you getting at?"

She stepped forward and laid a hand on his arm. "What I'm getting at is that we never get a guarantee in life. All we get are opportunities. In life and in love there are no guarantees. We get hurt, we lose, we cry and then we get up and keep going because God made us this way. The only guarantee of failure is in not trying."

Why did what she was saying suddenly make so much sense?

She crossed her arms over her chest again and stared at him. Arching one eyebrow, she asked, "So, am I fired?"

Her cheeky question pulled a wry smile from him. "I'll let you know by the end of the day."

"I'd like to know now. Stylish Gems jewelry shop is having a sale. My bracelet is twenty percent off if I put it on layaway by noon."

"You aren't fired."

She sighed. "It's just as well. I never learned to play tennis. Okay, come outside and show me your new toy."

It beat trying to work surrounded by memories he couldn't forget. The horses had already left. Even if he did change his decision it wouldn't change the outcome for Dakota. Grabbing his cane, he accompanied Jennifer out the main doors.

In the parking lot beside the clinic, the equine ambulance sat looking like a white, overly tall and extrawide horse trailer.

"This is it? This is what you've been begging for?" Jennifer didn't look impressed.

"Don't let its unassuming exterior fool you. This is

the best they make." Brian had spent long hours poring over the features of this particular model. He pressed a switch on the front. A muffled hiss filled the air as the hydraulic system allowed the entire trailer to sink to ground level.

A second switch lowered one whole wall of the vehicle and turned it into a gentle ramp. "This will keep an injured horse from having to step up."

"Cool." Apparently intrigued, she ventured closer. "What's that?" She pointed inside.

"Those are hydraulic padded sides that move in and hold the animal still so he doesn't have to shift his weight. There is a sling, too, if one is needed, and a winch to pull the horse in if it can't stand."

"So a horse could ride in this thing and never put a hoof on the floor?"

"I guess that's true."

"If the army had something like this, then Dakota could travel to Washington, D.C., and not risk injuring his leg."

"The Army doesn't have anything like this, believe me."

"No, because we have it. For how long?"

"Two weeks."

She patted his shoulder. "I knew you'd think of something."

He followed her sudden shift in logic way too easily. "No. No! I'm not giving this vehicle to the army."

"Loan, not give. Loan for a few days. Calm down."

He rubbed his chin as he considered what she was suggesting. It was crazy. Unthinkable. "The unit is leaving today. There isn't time to get over there."

"Avery said they aren't leaving until noon. It's only ten-thirty. You've got plenty of time."

"This is insane. They wouldn't even know how to operate it."

"You know how."

"Me? I can't go to Washington, D.C. I've got to present a lecture at the conference the day after tomorrow."

"What will you lose by missing one lecture?"

"Funding, respect, a chance to prove my work is making a difference."

"Fair enough. What will you gain by missing it?"

What would he gain? A chance to make things right with Lindsey? A chance to make amends for his cruel behavior? A chance to let a brave man see that his sacrifice meant something to this nation?

He turned to walk away. "No. I'll get fired."

She raced to stand in front of him, blocking his retreat. "You have tenure. They won't fire you."

He stepped to the side, but she moved to match him. "I'll end up teaching the first year's bone lab."

"So what? You'll be great at it."

He shook his head. "No, I can't do it."

"Dr. Cutter, look at me." When he did, she said quietly. "Tell me that you don't love her."

The words couldn't come out of his mouth, because he knew they weren't true. He did love Lindsey. He would always love her. God had blessed him and he had turned his back on that blessing. He had been too scared of coming alive again, of risking more heartache, and because of that he had pushed Lindsey away. Would this wild scheme give him another chance? Or was it already too late?

Like a gentle whisper in his ear, he heard Lindsey's

voice saying, "We use our head to make a lot of decisions in life, but some decisions have to be made with the heart. This is one of them. Do what your heart tells you is right."

Lord, I know it's been a long time since You've heard a prayer from me, but please let this be the right decision.

Lindsey stood apart from the rest of the unit as they waited beside the barn for the bus that would take them to the airport. She didn't want to dampen the excitement of the others. Attired in their sharply pressed dress uniforms, the men were laughing and joking and bursting with pride. This was the most prestigious event many of them would ever attend in their entire lives. Tomorrow, families from across the nation would be glued to their televisions hoping for a glimpse of their sons, grandsons or fathers as this unit rode proudly down Pennsylvania Avenue—without her.

Lindsey blew on her hands and wished she hadn't packed her gloves away. The air was cold and crisp enough to frost the windows of the office with lacy patterns. Karen sat beside her on an overstuffed suitcase bundled up to her ears with a thick red-white-and-blue scarf over her heavy quilted blue parka. The captain had managed to secure a seat for her on the military flight and for that Lindsey was grateful. When the bus rolled into sight at last, Lindsey said, "I'm just going to run in and say goodbye to Dakota. I know he wonders why he was left behind."

Karen pulled down her scarf enough to say, "I won't let them leave without you."

"I almost wish they would."

"No, you don't. Danny, Abigail and Dad all want to see you."

"I let them down. I let Danny down."

"Did he take it badly when you called last night?"

"It almost broke my heart to tell him that Dakota and I were going to have to sit this one out." Her heart was already in so many pieces that Lindsey wondered if it would ever be whole again.

"I'm sure he understands that it wasn't your fault."

"He tried to be cheerful and upbeat, but I could tell he was so disappointed."

"Our brother is a strong guy."

"He is. He tried to make me feel better by telling me he was glad he didn't have to get out in the cold tomorrow. I let him down. I don't know how I'm going to face him."

"You did your best. You can feel sorry for yourself all you want, but your family still loves you, so get over it." She covered her nose again.

Lindsey couldn't help but smile. "When we were little I used to ask God over and over again why He gave me such a pain in the neck for a sister. Little did I know what a favor He did me and how much I would come to cherish you."

"What a sweet thing to say. But for the record, I thought you were a pain in the neck, too," came her muffled reply.

Lindsey's giggles mingled with her sister's. It felt good to laugh again.

The bus pulled into the parking lot, but a second vehicle pulled in behind it. Lindsey looked on in amazement as Brian got out of his truck and started toward her. The laughter and voices of the men grew silent as they watched him approach. Shane, Lee and Avery stepped in front of her, blocking Brian's way.

Facing the men with their arms crossed over their chests and scowls on their faces, Brian knew it wouldn't be easy to persuade Lindsey's friends to let him speak to her.

Captain Watson stepped out in front of the group. "Dr. Cutter, what brings you here today?"

Brian decided his best chance would be to make this offer seem professional instead of personal. "I've come to put a proposal to you, Captain."

"What type of proposal?"

"I'd like to transport Dakota to Washington for you."

He saw Lindsey's eyes widen in surprise. A murmur ran through the group until the captain held up his hand for silence. "I don't think I understand. You said it wouldn't be safe for him to make such a long trailer ride."

"I now have a special ambulance that can transport Dakota in complete safety without placing any undue stress on his leg. I'm willing to take him if I can have another man go with me to share the driving."

Lindsey spoke at last. "I thought the ambulance was going to be on display for the conference. How did you get permission to take it across the country?"

Since he didn't exactly have permission, he chose his words carefully. "The vehicle is on loan to the clinic for two weeks. There is no stipulation that it stays in our parking lot. In fact, we especially asked that we be allowed to use it for patient transports." He shrugged. "No mention was made about how far those transports might be."

He watched as the possibility of seeing her dream come true brightened her eyes, replacing the coolness she had regarded him with. He hoped she could read the regret on his face as easily as he read her growing excitement.

The captain looked at his watch. "You would be cutting it close to make D.C. by assembly time tomorrow."

"I know that."

"I wouldn't feel right sending one of my men with you knowing they might miss riding in the parade."

Lindsey stepped between her friends and addressed Captain Watson. "Sir, I respectfully request that I be allowed to accompany Dakota since I won't be riding."

"Me, too," Karen added, wiggling between Shane and Lee.

Captain Watson rubbed a hand over his jaw. "This is highly irregular, but I do have orders for *all* our horses to travel to Washington, D.C., by independent contractor."

Karen looked around. "Does that mean he can go?"

"Corporal Ross," the captain barked.

"Sir." Shane stepped forward.

"Get the forge fired up and get those special shoes on Dakota."

"Yes, sir," he replied with a bright grin.

Karen's shriek of joy was echoed in Brian's heart. Now he would have twenty-four hours to try to set things right with Lindsey.

With the help of all the unit members, they soon had Dakota shod and secured in the trailer along with enough feed and water to last the trip. Lindsey and Karen stowed their suitcases behind the seat of the truck and then came to stand beside Brian.

He said, "There's a jump seat in the trailer. One of us should ride back here and keep an eye on him. There's a walkie-talkie by the seat and one in the truck cab so we can keep in touch."

"I'll ride with him," Lindsey said and moved to climb in.

Karen caught her by the arm. "Oh, no you don't. I'm taking the first turn with Dakota." She pushed past her sister to stand in the open doorway at the rear of the trailer.

Brian could have kissed her. He walked to the front of the truck and waited beside the passenger door.

"Karen, you're riding in the truck and that's an order." Lindsey's low tone brooked no argument.

"I'm not in the military. I don't take orders. Stop being a coward and go get in the truck or we'll never get there."

Lindsey considered jerking her sister out of the trailer, but decided she didn't want to look that undignified in front of her men. Instead, she slammed the rear door shut, walked up beside Brian and climbed into the cab.

Moments later, he got in behind the wheel, started the engine and pulled out onto the road. Long minutes passed as they drove through the fort on the winding, narrow road. She didn't say anything and neither did he.

It wasn't until he pulled out onto Interstate 70 fifteen minutes later that she gave in and spoke first.

"I thought your big conference was the day after tomorrow?"

"It is."

"You'll never make it back from D.C. unless you plan to fly."

"I can't fly. I have to drive this trailer back."

She looked at him in surprise. "What about your presentation? What about the bigwigs with money who will fund your research if you wow them?"

"They won't be wowed by me. Hopefully, my research will speak for itself when I publish the study later on."

Lindsey couldn't quite get her mind around the idea that he had given up a chance for peer recognition and substantial additional funding...for her. A slim thread of hope began to bind up the shattered pieces of her heart. "Why are you doing this?"

He looked over at her. "Because my head said this was a crazy idea, but my heart said it was the right thing to do."

His eyes, so intense and full of sincerity, begged her to believe him. A whirlwind of emotions swirled through her mind. "I don't know what to say."

"Then let me start by saying I'm sorry that I treated you so badly that day at Hearts and Horses. I know I have some explaining to do."

She settled back in the seat and crossed her arms over her chest. "Yes, you do."

"Until I met you, I had kept the pain of my wife's death very much alive. The accident was my fault and I wanted—no, I needed—some kind of punishment for being the one to live."

"Survivor's guilt."

"Is that what they call it?"

"Yes. That still doesn't explain why you were so angry about my reenlistment."

"I wasn't angry about that. I was angry because I had allowed myself to fall in love with you. Your reenlistment was just an excuse to push you away. I would have found some other reason to stop seeing you. I didn't believe that I deserved to be loved."

She wasn't sure she was ready to accept what he had to say at face value.

"You really hurt me."

"What can I do to make you forgive me?"

"Groveling might be good," she suggested.

He managed a small smile. "I'll do that the first chance I get."

"Telling the truth is always a winner, too."

"All right, the truth. I have been afraid since the first moment I saw you."

"Afraid of what?"

"Of living and loving and perhaps losing that love. I couldn't face those risks, but I couldn't forget about you, either, and that scared me witless."

"All of life is a risk, Brian. Only God knows what lies in store for us."

"I'm trying to accept that, but it's hard to have faith in something I can't see or touch."

She reached across and laid her hand on his arm. "You can't see or touch love, yet you still believe in it, don't you?"

"Yes, I do believe love exists."

"Then so does God. God *is* love."

"Is it really that simple?"

"It really is."

"Have I told you how beautiful and wise you are?"

"No, but I may allow you to do so for the next thousand miles."

He chuckled, but quickly sobered. He took one hand

off the wheel to clasp hers tightly. "Lindsey, I need to know that I haven't ruined what we had between us."

Her hand felt so small and snug in his grip. When she was eighty years old, would she still want to hold this man's hand? "My feelings for you haven't changed, Brian. I don't expect that they ever will."

"If I wasn't driving seventy miles an hour I would kiss you, darling. I love you so much it hurts."

"I love you, too, and we're going to have to stop for gas sometime."

He laughed out loud and squeezed her hand. "I promise to make up for lost time at our first pit stop. Sergeant Lindsey Mandel, will you marry me?"

In the sudden and telling silence, Brian glanced at Lindsey in concern. A second later his newfound bubble of happiness nose-dived toward the floor. "What? What's wrong?"

"Oh, talk about being scared. Brian, my family have always been good soldiers, but we make lousy spouses."

He sought for the words to reassure her. "You make your own decisions, Lindsey. What your parents or grandparents did doesn't automatically determine what you will do. I don't need an answer now. Think about it—that's all I'm asking."

"I will."

He managed a smile and tried to recapture their easy banter. "Do I still get a kiss when we stop for gas?"

A grin pulled at the corner of her lips. "I'll think about that, too."

Brian settled back in his seat. There were a lot of miles to go and nothing to do but look at the passing winter scenery and think. Her decision was much too important to risk pressing her for an answer. Instead, he said, "Why don't you call your brother and tell him that Dakota is on his way to the parade."

The walkie-talkie crackled on the dash as Karen's voice came over it. "I've already called him. He's as excited as a five-year-old on Christmas morning."

Brian chuckled as Lindsey grabbed the radio and demanded. "Karen, have you been listening this whole time?"

"I heard someone mention stopping for gas and that was all. I just turned this talkie thing on to report that Dakota seems happy as a clam in his snug, padded… holder thing."

Lindsey looked as if she wasn't certain she believed her sibling. "All right. I'll trade places with you when we make our first stop."

"How long will that be?"

Brian checked the gas gauge. "About three hours."

"That long?"

"Yes, little miss busybody. Try taking a nap," Lindsey suggested.

"Back here with a smelly horse? I don't think so."

Brian listened to their chatter and drew a deep breath. He had three hours to wait until he could collect his kiss. Three hours alone with the woman he loved. He looked down the long four-lane highway and smiled. He was determined to make the most of every minute God had given him.

For the next few hours, he talked about Emily, about Isabella and about his early years on the ranch. He listened to Lindsey's stories of her childhood as an army brat and her worries about her brother and about Karen. When they finally stopped, he was rewarded with a kiss that was pleasant but far too brief.

After Lindsey took her turn in the trailer, he received a very different version of their youthful experiences from Karen. It was obvious that Lindsey found the military lifestyle to her liking while Karen didn't. He tolerated some not too gentle grilling by Karen about his intentions and listened to some hopefully useful advice about Lindsey, as well. Every four hours they took a short break to let Dakota stretch his legs and let the women change places.

East of St. Louis, Brian finally gave up the wheel to Lindsey, and just outside of Cincinnati, Karen took over for a few hours while Brian rode with Dakota. It wasn't until they were heading into Wheeling, West Virginia, that the weather began to turn bad. Brian didn't know about the growing storm until they stopped to switch drivers at a roadside rest stop. As Karen walked the horse for a few minutes, Brian took Lindsey aside.

"This could slow us down."

She looked up through the flakes that filled the night sky. "How much farther do we have to go?"

"A little over three hundred miles. Five, maybe six hours."

She tilted her watch to see it better in the vehicle's headlights. "We need to be at the staging area by ten at the latest. That's six and a half hours from now."

"We'll make this Dakota's last exercise stop. We go straight through from here. I'll drive next. Dakota has been as quiet as a lamb so far. I think both you girls can ride in the truck from here on out."

For the next hour, he drove into the swirling whiteness as Lindsey and Karen leaned against each other and tried to sleep. The excitement of the trip had worn off hours ago, and Brian struggled to stay awake. He couldn't stop. He had promised Lindsey that Dakota would reach Washington, D.C., in time. He glanced at the clock on the dash and saw it was nearly five-thirty in the morning. They were falling behind schedule. From the radio forecast bulletins he figured they should be driving out of the worst of it soon. If the weathermen were right for a change.

Forcing himself to concentrate, he peered into the snow. After a few more minutes, he found himself blinking repeatedly. The thick flakes flying into his headlights were mesmerizing. He rubbed his face with one hand. The glare reflecting back from the snow was making it hard to focus. If only he wasn't so tired. He closed his heavy eyes for just a second....

Chapter 15

The sickening lurch of the truck woke Lindsey from her doze. She sat up abruptly, instinctively throwing her arm across Karen.

"Ouch! What was that for?" Karen said, pushing her sister's arm aside and sitting upright.

"I'm sorry." Brian's voice sounded weary and defeated. "I hit a drift pulling over. We have to stop. The storm is making it too dangerous. I'm not risking your lives in this weather."

He leaned forward and turned on the emergency flashers then leaned back with a deep sigh. Thinking of what he had told her about his wife's death, Lindsey leaned toward him and took his hand between her own. "It's okay. We tried. No one is faulting you."

He looked at Lindsey and reached out to cup her

cheek with his free hand. "I wish I could have gotten you there."

"I know you do and I love you for that."

She raised her face and met his kiss with only gladness in her heart.

Karen cleared her throat. "At least you two won't freeze to death. The temperature on your side of the truck is rising fast."

Brian slipped his arm behind Lindsey's shoulders and jerked Karen closer by the sleeve of her jacket. "I'll do my best to keep both of you warm."

Tightly sandwiched between them, Lindsey enjoyed a feeling of rightness. She was disappointed they wouldn't make it to Washington, D.C., but she was so very glad they had taken this trip.

She said, "Don't worry about freezing, Karen. I've had survival training."

"Can you make fire with two sticks?" Brian asked, his amusement clear.

"Doing it with two sticks is hard. I'd rather wait until the sun comes up and use a soda can and a chocolate bar."

"What?" the other two said in unison.

"It can be done. I'll show you someday. For now, I think we could all use a little sleep."

"I know I could," Brian said, leaning his head back.

Lindsey settled herself against his shoulder and drew Karen into the same position against her. This was where she truly wanted to be, held safe in Brian's arms while the storm outside raged on. This was the one place that was the right place for her. She knew it in her soul.

Thank You, Lord, for bringing this man into my life.

Sometime later, she opened her eyes at the sound of a large truck rumbling past them. She looked at the clock. It was a quarter till seven. Brian sat up and pulled his arm from behind her. Flexing it, he grimaced.

"What was that?" Karen mumbled, sitting up and rubbing her eyes.

Brian turned on the windshield wipers and the white blanket enclosing them was swept aside. The first faint light of dawn tinged the sky to the east of them.

"Hey, it stopped snowing," Karen said in delight.

Brian reached down and started the engine. "Yes, it has, and that was a pair of snowplows." He looked at Lindsey. "What do you think?"

"I think we are closer to Washington, D.C., than to Kansas. Let's finish the trip."

He leaned forward. "Karen?"

"Finish what we started. Maybe we'll get to see the tail end of the parade."

"All right. I'm going to check on Dakota and then we'll get back on the road."

He stepped out of the truck and used his cane to find firm footing. When he closed the door, Karen jerked on Lindsey's arm. "Well, what is your answer going to be?"

"I said let's go to D.C."

"Not that. Your answer to his marriage proposal."

"You were listening in!"

"I promise you I wasn't listening on purpose. I was trying to find a way to turn the silly thing off."

"Right. Like the dial on the side that says Off is so very hard to find."

"It was dark in the trailer, but never mind that. What's your answer?"

"You'll be the second—no, the fourth—person I'll tell after I make my decision."

"Fourth? I'm your only sister."

"You're a pain in the neck."

Karen sat back with a huff. "I think you should say yes."

"I'll take that under advisement."

Karen opened her mouth to say something else, but by that time Brian had returned. Thankfully, she kept what she wanted to say to herself.

Once they were back on the road, their spirits revived. Within an hour they had driven out of the snow-covered area and onto dry roads. Brian pushed the speed limit trying to make up some of their lost time.

It was eleven o'clock when they reached downtown D.C. and passed through the first of the security stops. It was then they got their first bit of good news.

The marine handing back their papers said, "The start of the parade has been delayed. It's set to go for one o'clock."

"Do you know why?" Brian asked as he took the forms.

"No, sir."

Rolling up his window, Brian said, "Lindsey, call your Captain and tell him we're almost there."

"They aren't going to wait for us."

"Just call them and let them know we're close."

She dialed the number with hands that shook. "Lord, please don't let him have turned off his cell phone yet."

He answered on the third ring. "It's about time you called, Sergeant."

"Sorry, sir. I knew you would be busy."

"Where are you?"

"We just passed the first checkpoint."

"Okay. All I can say is hurry. We aren't going to be able to wait if we get the order to go."

"I understand, sir."

At the next checkpoint, they waited as a police officer with a bomb-sniffing dog made a circuit through the trailer. Dakota lowered his head to check out the four-legged visitor, but the German shepherd gave him only a cursory glance before moving on.

Karen shifted from one foot to the other as she stood beside Lindsey. "Why won't they hurry up?"

"They are doing their job."

"They could do it a little faster."

Lindsey turned from watching the search to face her sister. She put both hands on Karen's shoulders. "It doesn't matter if we don't make it. Danny will still get a chance to see Dakota after the parade and he'll get to meet Brian. That's reward enough for me."

"Oh, you're just happy because you're in love. Are you guys done yet?" She called over Lindsey's shoulder. "The President is waiting on us."

"Karen!"

"He might be," she said defensively. "You don't know why the start was delayed."

"You're all clear," the officer said.

"Thank you," Karen called sweetly, then hurried to climb in the cab.

Fifteen minutes later they pulled into the staging area and located Lindsey's unit. They were all mounted except for the captain. A drill team from a high school in Iowa was just stepping out, while their marching band was hurrying to form up behind them. The Commanding General's Mounted Color Guard was next in line. Shane and Avery dismounted and hurried toward the trailer.

Captain Watson motioned for them to hurry and then turned to speak to a parade official. Brian had already opened the door and was backing Dakota out of the trailer. He handed the horse's lead rope to Shane. Avery grabbed the tack and began to saddle the big bay.

Brian moved to speak with Captain Watson then accompanied him back to Lindsey. She stood gazing at Dakota with tears of joy in her eyes. "Wait until Danny sees you. You behave yourself out there and make him proud."

"Sergeant Mandel, you're out of uniform." Captain Watson stood scowling at her.

She looked down at her rumpled dress uniform in confusion.

"You heard me, change into the unit's performance gear ASAP."

"But I'm not riding."

"Oh, yes you are." Brian pushed her toward the trailer. "Is your uniform in your suitcase?"

"I've got it," Karen cried as she hefted it into the back of the trailer. "Come on, I'll help you."

Captain Watson grinned. "Sergeant, you didn't think you came all this way just to stand on the sidelines, did you?"

"Sort of."

"No. Get dressed. That's an order, soldier."

Brian watched as Lindsey snapped to attention. She saluted smartly and climbed into the trailer with her sister.

A few minutes later she emerged in period uniform

as she pulled on a pair of white gloves. She walked up to Captain Watson.

"Sergeant Mandel reporting as ordered."

"Give the order to mount up, Sergeant."

"Sir, yes, sir."

She barked out the command, mounted Dakota and rode out into the street. At the order to unfurl the colors, three flags were taken from their covers. Captain Watson took the American flag and handed it to Brian. "As a way to say thank-you for all you have done for this unit, would you please present this flag to First Sergeant Mandel."

"It would be my honor, sir."

Brian looked to where Lindsey sat and read the fear in her eyes.

Lindsey called on every ounce of inner strength that she possessed when Brian handed her the symbol of her country—the country her brother and so many other brave young men and women had given so much to defend.

She closed her hand around the staff, but her grip failed and the wind pulled it from her grasp. Brian caught it before it hit the ground.

"I can't do it." Tears sprang up in her eyes, blurring her vision.

"You can do it, honey. God didn't bring you and Dakota this far to fail you now. Have faith, Lindsey. I have faith in you. Give me your hand."

He placed the end of the rod into the metal cup on her stirrup and folded her fingers around the staff. "Which color in our flag stands for courage?"

"The colors have no official meaning, but to me, all of them stand for courage."

"Show me that courage now."

She closed her eyes and willed her grip to strengthen. An instant later, she heard the sound of tearing cloth and looked down. With the flag braced against his shoulder, Brian ripped a piece of tape from a wide, white roll and made a quick loop around her wrist.

"Open your fingers."

She did and he made two quick passes around the staff and then back around her wrist. The tape blended with her white gloves. When she closed her fingers, it didn't show on the pole.

"Now you don't have to be afraid. You couldn't drop it if you tried."

"Brian, you're a genius."

"Be sure and tell Jennifer that when we get back."

"I haven't turned in my reenlistment papers," she said quickly.

"Why not? I hope it wasn't because of anything I said."

"I love the service, but maybe it's time for *me* to make a change in my life."

"Whatever you decide to do, I'm behind you 100 percent. If you want to remain in the army, we'll find a way to make it work for both of us."

"What about your research? You love your work."

"I do, but I love you more. If we are meant to be together, the Lord will show us the path."

"Proverbs 16:9, A man's heart plans his way, But the Lord directs his steps."

Grinning, he patted Dakota's neck. "He certainly directed my steps to you."

Looking into his love-filled eyes, Lindsey smiled. "Yes, he did. And the answer to your question is yes."

"Yes, what?"

"Yes, I'll marry you."

"You will? But I can't kiss you up on that horse. Lean down here."

"Meet me after the parade," she suggested with a wink. "I love you, Brian Cutter."

"I love you, too. Now, go make me proud."

Nodding, she touched her spurs to Dakota's sides and rode to the head of the column.

"This is for you, Danny," Lindsey whispered.

Suddenly she knew she wasn't alone. The wind died away to a gentle breeze and a deep warmth surrounded her. An inner strength filled her and her grip on the flag's staff tightened. This had all been a part of His plan.

Thank You, Lord, for giving me this day.

Captain Watson gave the command to move out. The Commanding General's Mounted Color Guard left the staging area and rode out to take their place on Pennsylvania Avenue.

As Brian watched her ride away, his heart was filled with more happiness than he had ever expected to know again. A second later, Karen was pulling at his sleeve.

"Come on. If we hurry, we can find Dad and Danny before Lindsey passes by. They're going to be in front of the Hoover Building. It's only a couple of blocks."

Following her, he tried to hurry, but she soon disappeared into the crowd. Looking up at the tall, imposing structures lining the street, he wondered if he would recognize the Hoover Building when he saw it.

Just when he had decided to rest and watch the presidential detail passing by, Karen appeared at his side. "They're right over here. Come on."

"Right over here" turned out to be another block. He

was gritting his teeth against the pain in his hip by the time Karen announced, "There they are."

He slowed down to catch his breath. Karen hurried toward a man in a wheelchair stationed at the curbside and threw her arms around him. When the man didn't hug her in return, Brian realized what a high price Danny Mandel had paid for the idea of freedom in a country half a world away. Karen knelt beside him and motioned to Brian.

Stepping closer, Brian nodded to the man about his own age held strapped upright in a specially designed chair. Karen quickly made the introductions to Danny, his wife and to Lindsey's father.

Danny grinned. "So you're the rabbit guy Lindsey is always talking about."

"I've been called worse."

Abigail extended her hand. "Dr. Cutter, I want to thank you for the information you sent about hippotherapy. We found out that the Old Guard has a program here. We're looking into it."

"That's great." Brian shook her hand then turned to the senior Mandel. Lindsey's father was an imposing man. Brian could only hope he wouldn't object to a civilian marrying his daughter. With his gray hair still short in a military buzz, he looked quite capable of holding his own in any kind of a fight.

"Thanks for getting my daughter and my boy's horse here. It means a lot to us."

"I'm glad I could help."

"Oh, look, here they come." Karen pushed Danny's chair closer to the curb. Marching in a straight line, Lindsey's unit passed by, pride evident in everyone's ramrod-straight bearing. Lindsey was looking straight ahead, but Dakota swung his head toward them and whinnied loudly.

Karen dropped to her brother's side. "He remembers you."

"He did, didn't he? But he never broke stride. He's a trouper. I'm glad he made it into Lindsey's unit. I'm so proud of both of them."

"Not half as proud as Lindsey is of you," Brian said, laying a hand on Danny's shoulder.

On the other side of them, a young man with a press badge stepped closer. "Excuse me, do you have family in the parade?"

Karen rose, smiling at the young man. "My sister."

"Would you mind if I asked you a few questions about her? The magazine I work for is looking for a common-man angle to the Inauguration."

"There's nothing common about my family," Mr. Mandel declared, turning back to the parade.

Karen wrinkled her nose and stepped closer to the reporter. "Don't mind my dad. But he is right. This is no common family. My sister is a sergeant in the army, my brother here, Danny, was also in the army until he was wounded in action. After that, he selflessly donated his beloved horse to my sister's unit at Fort Riley. Then what happened? The horse fell and broke his leg."

She paused to catch her breath. The reporter was quickly making notes.

She looked at Brian and winked. "That's when Dr. Brian *Cutter,* that's *Cutter* with a *C,* came to our rescue. He used a new gene therapy to heal Dakota's leg in record time."

Looking around at her family, a mischievous glint brightened her eyes. "Did I mention to everyone that he's going to marry Lindsey?"

* * *

Hours later, when the parade was finished and the crowds had dispersed, Brian waited beside the equine ambulance while Lindsey visited with her family. Still dressed in her turn-of-the-century uniform, the woman Brian loved with his whole heart finally made her way to his side. He slipped his arm across her shoulders as she slid her arm around his waist and leaned against him. Standing together, they drew comfort and happiness from each other. He looked down at her but she was watching Danny and Dakota.

It was obvious that Danny was tired but just as obvious that he wasn't ready to go home. Joy radiated from his expression. Dakota stood beside his wheelchair nuzzling his former master's face and searching his pockets in hopes of hidden treats. The smile that Abigail flashed at Brian made every minute of the long trip worthwhile.

"Thank you," Lindsey whispered.

"It was nothing," he answered softly.

"Oh, it was certainly something, Dr. Brian Cutter. How can I ever repay you?"

He looked down at her and smiled. "I'm sure I can think of something, darling."

Her soft laughter in response was all he needed to make this day and every day of his life—complete.

* * * * *

We hope you enjoyed reading
THE VALENTINE TWO-STEP
by *New York Times* bestselling author
RAEANNE THAYNE
and
THE COLOR OF COURAGE
by *USA TODAY* bestselling author
PATRICIA DAVIDS

Both were originally **Harlequin® Special Edition**
and **Love Inspired** stories!

Uplifting romances of faith, forgiveness and hope.

From passionate, suspenseful and dramatic
love stories to inspirational or historical,
Harlequin offers different lines to
satisfy every romance reader.
Up to eight new books in each line
are available every month.

H HARLEQUIN®

NYTHRS0218R